AFTER SHE'S GONE

Books by Lisa Jackson

Stand-Alones
SEE HOW SHE DIES
FINAL SCREAM
RUNNING SCARED
WHISPERS
TWICE KISSED
UNSPOKEN
MOST LIKELY TO DIE
WICKED GAME
WICKED LIES
SOMETHING WICKED
WICKED WAYS
SINISTER
WITHOUT MERCY
YOU DON'T WANT TO KNOW
CLOSE TO HOME
AFTER SHE'S GONE
REVENGE

Anthony Paterno/Cahill Family Novels
IF SHE ONLY KNEW
ALMOST DEAD

Rick Bentz/Reuben Montoya Novels
HOT BLOODED
COLD BLOODED
SHIVER
ABSOLUTE FEAR
LOST SOULS
MALICE
DEVIOUS
NEVER DIE ALONE

Pierce Reed/Nikki Gillette Novels
THE NIGHT BEFORE
THE MORNING AFTER
TELL ME

Selena Alvarez/Regan Pescoli Novels
LEFT TO DIE
CHOSEN TO DIE
BORN TO DIE
AFRAID TO DIE
READY TO DIE
DESERVES TO DIE

Oregon Novels
DEEP FREEZE
FATAL BURN

Published by Kensington Publishing Corporation

LISA JACKSON

AFTER SHE'S GONE

KENSINGTON BOOKS

www.kensingtonbooks.com

KENSINGTON BOOKS are published by

Kensington Publishing Corp.
119 West 40th Street
New York, NY 10018

All Kensington titles, imprints, and distributed lines are available at special quantity discounts for bulk purchases for sales promotion, premiums, fund-raising, educational, or institutional use.

Special book excerpts or customized printings can also be created to fit specific needs. For details, write or phone the office of the Kensington Special Sales Manager: Attn. Special Sales Department. Kensington Publishing Corp., 119 West 40th Street, New York, NY 10018. Phone: 1-800-221-2647.

Kensington and the K logo Reg. U.S. Pat. & TM Off.

Library of Congress Card Catalogue Number: 2015951103

ISBN-13: 978-1-61773-465-6
ISBN-10: 1-61773-465-9
First Kensington Hardcover Edition: January 2016

eISBN-13: 978-1-61773-468-7
eISBN-10: 1-61773-468-3
First Kensington Electronic Edition: January 2016

10 9 8 7 6 5 4 3 2 1

Printed in the United States of America

AFTER
SHE'S GONE

Prologue

Portland, Oregon
January

He watched.

Carefully.

Paying attention to every detail as the rain sheeted from the night-dark sky and streetlights reflected on the wet pavement.

Two women were running, faster and faster, and he smiled as the first passed into the lamp's pool of illumination. Her face was twisted in terror, her beautiful features distorted by fear.

Just as they should be.

Good. Very good.

The slower woman was a few steps behind and constantly looking over her shoulder, as if she were expecting something or someone with murderous intent to be hunting her down.

Just as he'd planned.

Come on, come on, keep running.

As if they heard him, the women raced forward.

Perfect.

His throat tightened and his fists balled in nervous anticipation.

Just a few more steps!

Gasping, the slower woman paused, one hand splayed over her chest as she leaned over to catch her breath beneath the streetlamp. Rain poured down from the heavens. Her hair was wet, falling in dripping ringlets around her face, her white jacket soaked through. Again she glanced furtively behind her, past the empty sidewalks and storefronts of this forgotten part of the city. God, she was beautiful, as was the first one, each a fine female specimen that he'd picked precisely for this moment.

His heart was pumping wildly, anticipation and adrenaline firing his blood as an anticipatory grin twisted his lips.

Good. This is so good.

Silently he watched as from the corner of his eye, the first woman raced past him just as he'd hoped. Eyes focused ahead, she was seemingly oblivious to his presence, but in his heart he knew she realized he was there, observing her every movement, catching each little nuance of fear. He saw determination and horror in the tense lines of her face, heard it in her quick, shallow breaths and the frenzied pounding of her footsteps as she flew past.

And then she was gone.

Safely down the street.

He forced his full attention to the second woman, the target. She twisted her neck, turned to look his way, as if she felt him near, as if she divined him lurking in the deep umbra surrounding the street.

His heart missed a beat.

Don't see me. Do not! Do not look at me!

Her expression, at this distance, was a little blurry, but he sensed that she was scared to death. Terrified. Exactly what he wanted.

Feel it. Experience the sheer terror of knowing you're being stalked, that you are about to die.

Her lower lip trembled.

Yes! Finally.

Satisfaction warmed his blood.

As if she heard a sound, she stiffened, her head snapping to stare down the darkened alley.

That's it. Come on. Come on!

Her eyes widened and suddenly she started running again, this time in a sheer panic. She slipped, lost a high heel, and she kicked off the other, never missing a step, her bare feet still slapping the wet pavement frantically.

Now!

He shifted slightly, giving himself a better view, making sure that he didn't miss a thing.

Perfect.

She was running right on target.

At that moment a dark figure stepped from a shadowed doorway to stand right in front of the woman.

Screaming, she veered a bit, slipped, and nearly lost her balance, only to keep on running, angling away from the man.

Too late!

The assassin raised his gun.

Blam! Blam! Blam!

Three shots rang out, echoing along the empty street, fire spitting from the gun's muzzle.

She stumbled and reeled, her face a mask of fear as she twisted and fell onto the pavement. Her eyes rolled upward, blood trickling from the corner of her mouth. Another spreading red stain bloomed darkly through her white jacket.

Perfect, he thought, satisfied at last as he viewed her unmoving body.

Finally, after years of planning, he'd pulled it off.

Shondie Kent looked dead.

As she lay in the street he waited, focusing on the body, noticing how it neither twitched nor moved in any way.

Exquisite.

From years of experience he counted silently. *Five, four, three, two, one.* Still no movement, the "corpse" in place, the street empty, rain and a bit of fog visible. The camera had zoomed in on the open mouth, glazed eyes, and dark blood on the white blouse.

Satisfied that the shot was flawless, he yelled, "Cut!" and punched the air from his director's chair. He felt ridiculously triumphant that the death scene had finally worked. Man, what a relief! They'd shot the scene over and over the day before, never getting the action and ambience to meld to his satisfaction. Something had always been missing. But today after several failed attempts, finally everything had worked like clockwork, the actors and crew were spot-on, the energy on the set was right for this, the climax to the end of the scene. "That's it!" he yelled, then added under his breath, "Thank God," because truth to tell, the scene had been a bitch.

As he climbed out of his chair, the lights came up and the darkened Portland street was suddenly illuminated, its asphalt still shining from the mist provided by the sprinklers used to simulate the gloomy Northwest rain. The quiet that had been the set was replaced by a cacophony of voices and sounds. Crew members were spurred into action, hustling to break down the facades and get them moving so that the street could be reopened. In the bright lights, the sidewalks and storefronts appeared less ominous than they had.

Sig Masters, the actor who played the assassin, tore off his ski mask and headed off set for a smoke. The fake rain pouring from hidden, overhead sprinklers was turned off, only a bit of drizzle remaining as the lines emptied. Everyone was going about their business, already breaking down the pieces of the set that had been added to the cordoned-off street, everyone but Lucinda Rinaldi, the body double who still lay unmoving on the pavement.

Dean Arnette, the director of *Dead Heat*, a movie he already believed would become a blockbuster once it was released, smiled to himself. The script was cutting-edge, moody, the dialogue razor-sharp, the emotions raw, and his star, Allie Kramer, was rapidly becoming a household name. Her on-screen portrayals were mesmerizing and her offscreen life the stuff of tabloid fodder. She had a famous mother, a tragic, complicated past, an intense love life, and a hint of the bad-girl image she didn't try to erase. It all kept her fans guessing and her public interested. Allie Kramer had no trouble trending on the Internet.

More perfection.

A sense of relief ran through him as he absently reached into the empty pocket of his shirt for a nonexistent pack of cigarettes. God, he still missed smoking every damned day, especially after sex, a meal, or like now, a satisfying final take on a particularly difficult movie.

"Something's wrong," his assistant whispered as Arnette climbed down from his director's chair.

"The scene was perfect."

"I know . . . but . . ."

"But what?" He didn't bother hiding his irritation. Beatrice Little was always finding something wrong. Barely five-two, she couldn't weigh a hundred pounds soaking wet and wasn't quite thirty. Still, she took "anal-retentive" to a new level. She was shaking her head, a dark ponytail fanning the back of her T-shirt with the movement.

"It's Lucinda."

Arnette figured if he was satisfied, the whole damned film crew should be, including Little Bea as she was often called. "What about her?" Arnette glanced at the still unmoving actress. "She was great."

"I know, but—"

"Hey!" a sharp female voice cut in. "That's it. Let's go," Sybil Jones, one of the associate producers, yelled in Lucinda's direction. She clapped twice. When Sybil didn't get a response, she rolled her expressive eyes beneath the brim of her cap as she turned to Arnette. "Maybe you should talk to her, Dean. She's not paying attention to me. Big surprise."

Lucinda, B-list on a good day, was always working to be noticed, hoping to overachieve her way up the stardom ladder, even though in this film she was used only as a body double. No matter how small the role, though, Lucinda was known for staying in character long after a scene had wrapped. "Come on," he said, walking briskly in her direction. "That's it, Lucy!"

Still she didn't so much as turn her head toward him. His skin crawled a bit. There was something off about her and it bothered him, a niggling worry that burrowed deep in his brain. This production had been a bitch from the get-go. The stars were always at each other, there was that sibling rivalry crap on the set between the Kramer girls and now they were here, reshooting this scene at the very last minute. "Hey! Time to get a move on," he said, and then a little more loudly, "Come on, Lucinda, that was great. It's a wrap!"

Still she didn't flinch, her eyes staring upward, even when one of the booms was moved, swinging only a foot from her face.

His stomach knotted.

As he reached her side he noticed that the bloodstain on her coat was far more than the bag of red dye would release. *Oh, crap!* "Lucinda?" he said, bending down on a knee, his heart beginning to drum. "Hey." Anxiety mounting, he stared into eyes fixed on the middle distance. What the hell?

"Lucinda, come on, it's over," he said, and leaned closer, hoping to feel her breath against his face or see her blink, silently wishing this was her ploy.

No movement. None.

Shit!

He touched her neck, felt no pulse, and his fears escalated.

Sybil and Beatrice had followed him across the street. He looked up, over his shoulder, to meet Sybil's eyes, which were still guarded by her baseball cap. "Get the medic," he ordered, "and get him now."

She nodded sharply, didn't wait for another command, then turned and started yelling for help. "We need a medic," she yelled, turning back. "ASAP! Where the hell's Jimmy?"

"Oh, Jesus," Bea whispered as Dean turned back to the woman lying on the street. His fingertips pressed a little harder, hoping to find even the faintest tremor of a pulse.

"Oh, God," another female voice choked out. He looked up to spy Holly Dennison, a set designer, for Christ's sake. Hand clapped over her mouth, she was backing up. Her huge eyes were round with sheer horror. "Oh, God, oh, God, oh, God."

He ignored her; turned back to the actress lying on the wet street. What the hell had happened? No one was supposed to get hurt on the set of *Dead Heat.* Other movie-set tragedies slid through his mind as he heard the sound of footsteps and conversation buzzing around him. "For fuck's sake, someone call nine-one-one!"

"On their way," the producer said as the medic, talking rapidly into a cell phone and carrying a bag, finally hurried to Lucinda's side.

"Back off," the man, all of twenty-two, nearly shouted.

Gratefully Arnette gave up his post, climbing to his feet and stepping backward, knowing in his heart that it was too late. The harsh klieg lights illuminated her beautiful, motionless face. And just like Shondie Kent, the character she'd been so feverishly portraying, it appeared Lucinda Rinaldi was dead.

CHAPTER 1

Mercy Hospital
April

The nightmare was relentless.

Like a vaporous shadow it seemed to slip under her door and through the window casings, shifting and swirling through the hospital room before steadfastly pushing into Cassie's brain, infiltrating her dreams as she desperately tried to sleep.

No amount of medications or willpower could stop the nightmare from sliding a kaleidoscope of painful pictures through her subconscious. Tonight, in her mind's eye she saw it all again. Lightning sizzled across the sky. Thunder clapped. Rain poured from the heavens.

She and Allie, her little sister, were running frantically for their very lives.

Bam!

The crack of a rifle exploded and she jumped, startled, the noises and visions racing through her head so real, so damned real. "No more," she whispered, and let out the breath she hadn't been aware she'd been holding.

Slowly she opened her eyes and saw the digital readout of her clock. Three AM. Again. Every damned night. Jittery as always from the nightmare, she slid off her hospital bed and walked to the window where rain ran in jagged rivulets against the glass. Her room was located on the fourth floor of this wing, part of the original building built over a century earlier. She peered into the darkness, past the parking lot flanked by hundred-year-old rhododendrons. Farther down the hillside the city of Portland stretched in myriad lights that pulsed along the snaky blackness that was the Willamette River. Bridges linked the river's shores and streams of lights blurred as cars and trucks sped across the concrete and steel spans connecting the city's sprawling east side to its hilly west. Atop this hill, Mercy Hospital was afforded a breathtaking view of the city. If one chose to be inspired.

With her index finger, Cassie traced the path of a raindrop on the pane, the glass cool to her touch. Slowly, as it always did, her heartbeat returned to normal and the nightmare thankfully withered into the hidden corners of her subconscious again. "Just leave me alone," she muttered as if the dream could hear. "Go away!" She was sick of being trapped here in this damned hospital, plagued by the nightmare and exhausted from lack of sleep.

Angry at herself and the whole damned situation, she made her way to the bed, slid between the sheets, and drew the thin blanket to her neck. Sleep would prove elusive, she knew, and she considered picking up the book she'd tried to read, a mystery novel that was lying on the table beside her plastic water container and a phone that looked like it had come straight out of the eighties, or maybe even an earlier decade. But her gaze wandered back to the window where, in the glass, she spied a watery reflection, a dark figure backlit by the illumination slicing into the room from the doorway.

Her heart nearly stopped.

She swung her head around and expected the room to be empty, that the image she saw was imagined, a play of light and dark, a figment of her imagination, but she was wrong. A tall woman in a nurse's uniform stood in the doorway, garbed in an outfit straight out of the fifties or early sixties: crisp, pointed cap; white dress; pale nylon stockings; heavy-duty shoes; and tiny red cross earrings. In her hands, she carried an old-fashioned clipboard and a medical chart, and she ignored the computer monitor mounted near the bed. The thin scent of smoke followed her into the room.

It was all weird as hell.

"You work here?" Cassie asked, not completely sure she wasn't dreaming. What *was* this? The nurse was almost ghostlike in appearance, her skin pale and sallow, her eyes buried so deep in her skull their color was in question.

Staring down at Cassie, she didn't try to take her vital signs or offer medication or anything.

"Who are you?" Cassie asked, and her fingers moved on the bed rail to the nurse's call button as she searched the snowy uniform for some kind of name tag. None was visible in the half-light.

"Your sister is alive."

"What?"

"Your sister.." The woman's voice was flat, her face with its deep-set, haunted eyes expressionless. "She's not dead."

"How do you know?" God, this had to be a dream. Allie had been missing since the time she hadn't shown up for the final shot of *Dead Heat*. "Have you talked to her? Seen her?"

Silence.

Cassie asked, "Where is she?" And when that didn't garner a re-sponse, added, "Of course she's alive." Allie had to be okay. She just had to. No way would Cassie let the doubts creep in, the doubts that had been shouted across the tabloids, screamed in all those horrid blogs, discussed on fan-based chat and message boards, regurgitated over and over again in celebrity news media that Allie Kramer, one of Hollywood's brightest stars, was missing and feared dead. Specula-tion ran rampant that she'd been kidnapped or committed suicide or been murdered, or come to some deadly fate, but it was all just gos-sip. No one knew where Allie Kramer was, least of all Cassie, and she felt miserable about it. Allie who had been such a sweet, sensitive child until the monster had come. Long ago, in one of the coldest winters on record, their world had been shattered and Allie had never recovered. Nor, she supposed, had she. Now her insides shiv-ered and she twisted the blanket in her fingers.

Cassie's mind wandered a bit. *She's alive,* she thought, before suddenly coming back to where she was. The nurse, if she had ever really been standing near Cassie's bedside, had left, slipping quietly away on her crepe-soled shoes.

Cassie's skin crawled.

That terrible little voice that taunted her at night started nagging again.

The nurse was all in your mind, Cass. You know it. No one dresses like that anymore except in the old movies you're addicted to. Nurse Ratched—that's who she was. "Big Nurse" in Ken Kesey's One Flew Over the Cuckoo's Nest. *Right. All just your imagination running wild again. It's not the first time you've seen someone who wasn't there, now, is it? Or had a blackout? It's not as if you haven't "lost time" or seen someone no one else has. Ever since you were kidnapped, nearly murdered, you haven't been completely able to sort fact from fantasy or even know what you may have done. . . . Remember the sleepwalking incidents? Of course not. But they hap-*

pened. The hospital has the security footage to prove it. You're losing it, Cassie . . . all over again, and God only knows what you're capable of when you're "out."

"Stop it!" Cassie hissed, then glanced wildly to the door. On the other side the nurses convened at a wide desk and they might hear her talking to herself again, or worse yet, to whomever or whatever was just here.

You idiot, no one was here. No ghost. No apparition. No nurse, for God's sake. Pull yourself together.

She struggled, her brain at war with her senses. But she knew this time was different from the others, the hallucinations that had landed her here in this mental ward. Didn't she still smell the odors of cigarette smoke and perfume?

Goose bumps crawled up Cassie's arms and she felt a chill as cold as the waters of the Arctic. This was nuts. No way had that nurse really been here. The weird-looking woman's "appearance" was all part and parcel of the bad dreams, the result of exhaustion and fear. She was just stressed out. That's all. Her guilt-laden mind was playing tricks on her. Again. And if the hallucination wasn't caused by her own neurosis, then it was probably caused by the medication they were force-feeding, the stuff that was supposed to keep her "calm" and "stable." Cassie wasn't going crazy. Of course not. Just because the tabloids said—

"Miss Kramer?"

She looked up sharply. The door had swung open and this time a nurse in pale blue scrubs, a staff member she recognized as Leslie Keller, RN, stepped into the room.

"Are you all right?" the RN asked, glancing from Cassie to the monitors surrounding her bed, checking her vitals. Tall and willowy, with springy black curls and smooth mocha-colored skin, Nurse Keller was all business. "I heard you speaking with someone." Nurse Keller's gaze swept the semi-dark room. It, of course, was empty.

"Bad dream," Cassie said.

"Another one?" The nurse sighed and shook her head. "While I'm here, let's get your BP." She was already adjusting the cuff over Cassie's arm.

"Has anyone called? Or asked about me?" Cassie queried.

Nurse Keller's plucked eyebrows shot up and she gave Cassie an *are-you-kidding* look. "At three in the morning?"

"I meant earlier."

She shook her head, wild curls dancing around her face as her features drew into a scowl. "A little elevated," she said to herself, taking note of the blood pressure reading.

"The dream. Got me going, I guess," Cassie said.

"Hmm."

Before she could stop herself Cassie asked, "No one around here wears any of those old uniforms, do they? You know, the white dress and pointy cap?"

"Oh, God. And retro blue and red cape?" She shot Cassie a wry glance of disbelief. "Not in like forty or fifty years, I guess. Why?"

"No big deal."

"Welcome to the twenty-first century, the age of scrubs, thank God." Quickly she typed some information into the keyboard positioned near Cassie's bed. Cassie desperately wanted to ask more questions about the nurse in white, but realized it wouldn't help her cause to appear more confused—that was the term they used—than ever. She cleared her throat and faked a yawn. Better to end this conversation before she said something she'd regret. That was her problem, well, one of them, she was too inquisitive, too forthright, too eager to say what was on her mind. People, especially the doctors and nurses at Mercy Hospital, didn't appreciate her overabundant curiosity and quick tongue. So she held it. For now.

"Do you need anything else?" the nurse asked.

"I don't think so. I'm . . . I'm fine."

Nurse Keller didn't seem convinced and Cassie held her breath, hearing the rattle of a tray from the hallway and the gentle hum of a whispered conversation from the nurses' desk. "Okay, so, if you do need anything, just call."

"Got the button right here," Cassie said, lifting the electronic paging device attached to the rail of her bed.

"Good." A quick smile as the nurse turned to leave.

"Uh, wait. There aren't any cameras here, right? In the room?"

At the reknitting of the nurse's brows, Cassie instantly knew she'd made a mistake.

"I mean monitors, you know?" Oh, she'd stepped into it this time. "Just . . . just to keep an eye on patients, make sure they're okay. For medical reasons."

"Mercy Hospital is very concerned with patient privacy and patient rights. Private rooms are just that: private."

"Oh, good. I thought so," Cassie said with a smile she didn't feel, then pretended to yawn again.

"Is there something wrong?"

"No, no. Just wondering."

Nurse Keller wasn't buying her excuse for a second, Cassie could tell. She hesitated, then with an almost unnoticeable shake of her head, said, "Well, try to rest now," and was gone a few moments later, her footsteps padding down the hall.

This was all so very wrong. Through the crack, she saw Nurse Keller approach the nurses' station. From her elevated bed, she had a view of the curved desk that molded beneath the chest-high counter. Phones, equipment, and monitors were tucked beneath the counter and desk chairs on wheels moved from one station to the next.

Wide hallways fingered like tentacles on an octopus from the nurses' station to the patient rooms. A bank of elevators was positioned across from control central. She couldn't see them from her room but they were close enough that she heard the soft ding of bells announcing the elevator cars' arrival on this the fourth floor, all day and deep into the night.

Cassie's gaze followed Nurse Keller as she joined two other graveyard shift nurses. Tom was tall and lanky. His once-red hair was starting to gray and somehow, despite the constant Oregon drizzle, he boasted a perpetual tan. The third nurse was in her twenties, a pudgy blond woman whom Cassie didn't recognize. They whispered among themselves and glanced in her direction, then the blonde giggled.

Cassie exhaled heavily. She was a celebrity of sorts. Both her sister and mother were far more famous than she, each an actress who had found the public's favor, while her attempt to conquer Hollywood had been pretty dismal, but here, at Mercy Hospital, she'd finally found fame.

Not that she wanted it.

She'd heard her name whispered between the staff and sometimes people Cassie didn't recognize, people she hoped were part of the medical community. She'd caught bits of conversations and had gleaned that there was more discussed than just her physical or mental condition—not that both weren't juicy grist for the gossip mill on their own. But with Allie missing and her own hospitalization, Cassie had probably gained more fame, or notoriety, than she'd experienced in all her years of work in the film industry. Not that she really gave a crap right now. Her fame meant little with her sister gone missing and another woman dead in the freak accident on the movie set.

A soft, persistent ding caught the group of nurses' attention and

Tom and Nurse Keller hurried off, leaving the blonde to answer a phone, which she did with her back turned to Cassie's doorway. Good.

From the bed, Cassie stole a glance at the window again. The rain had stopped, only a few lingering drops visible on the glass. The room seemed to lighten again and in the reflection she saw the door crack open farther, thin light seeping into the room from the hallway.

A stealthy figure slipped into the room.

Her heart clutched.

She whipped her head around just as the door shut with a soft thud. "What the—?" Her body tensed and she grabbed the nurse's call button, but stopped before depressing it when she recognized Steven Rinko.

She let out her breath. Rinko was the weird kid who had been here longer than she and had the ability to move between rooms on stealthy footsteps, the staff rarely noticing. Around thirteen, with a shock of blond hair and skin starting to show signs of acne, he rarely spoke, but when he did, he seemed more genius than mentally challenged. Though usually silent, when prodded, Rinko could tell you every feature on every make and model of car ever designed in America or around the world, or he could rattle off the most insignificant baseball stat about anyone who'd ever played the sport in college or professionally. He hung with a small group of boys who were forever bickering. Why he was at Mercy Hospital, she didn't know, nor, she supposed would she ever as she planned to spring herself by tomorrow or the day after. Enough with this place. She'd checked herself into the hospital and planned on checking herself out.

Now, Rinko sidled to her bed. He knew how to get around the security cameras, guards, and nursing staff, traveling the halls on stealthy feet, almost a ghost himself. "She was here," he said in a whispered voice that cracked.

"Who?"

"I saw her too."

Cassie's skin seemed to shrink on her scalp as he reached forward and grabbed her hand. She bit back a scream as he turned her wrist over and dropped something into her hand. A bit of red, she saw, then recognized a tiny cross, one of the earrings the weird nurse had worn.

"Where did you get this?"

"The nurse," he said, and before she could ask him anything more, Rinko was already sliding out of the room on noiseless footsteps, slipping into the hallway, disappearing from view. Her heart clamored as she curled her fingers around the tiny bit of metal, feeling it press into her skin. It was real, and that meant she wasn't dreaming or hallucinating from the high-octane psychotropic medications that could easily be the reason she blurred reality with lies, fact with fiction, all because she believed something horrid had happened to her younger sister.

Allie, the innocent.

Allie, the sweet.

Allie, the liar.

How had she grown from a naive girl to a self-serving bitch? A once-shy teenager who would now step on anyone in her path to fame? A beloved sibling morphing into an archrival?

Cassie drew in a long breath, fought her jealousy, reminded herself that Allie was missing, perhaps dead.

This was all so wrong—her life, these days.

The little bit of metal in her hand cut into her flesh.

She closed her eyes and let her breath out slowly, calming herself, telling herself that she wasn't losing her mind, that everything would be all right. She just had to check herself out of the hospital.

Tomorrow. You'll leave this psych ward and Mercy Hospital forever. And you'll find Allie . . . you will.

Unless she's already dead.

"Oh, God," Cassie whispered, cold to the bone as she opened her eyes to the sterile room.

She was alone.

Again.

So why did the rocker in the corner sway ever so slightly?

All in your mind, Cass. You know it. All in your damned mind.

CHAPTER 2

Whitney Stone had two things going for her, she thought as she drove through the spitting morning rain. Her first noticeable asset was her looks. She knew it. Everyone knew it. Her features were even, her eyes large and dark fringed, her heart-shaped face compared to the animated Snow White in that ancient Disney flick. Yeah, she looked great. But her second asset wasn't something so obvious and that was her brain. She was smarter than anyone knew, because she downplayed it. Oh, she came off clever, even cunning and Lord knew people respected her dedication to her job, her doggedness, her ability to sniff out a story and track it down. In a good ol' boys network, she was one of the few women who had blazed her trail, even if she'd had to do a little lying, a bit of sleeping around, and just a smidge of illegal phone taps and camera work. Otherwise she wouldn't have made it as far as she had in the cutthroat business of journalism.

Whitney hadn't only survived or made her way, she'd thrived. Because she'd been cagey and smart. Used her good looks and acting ability to her advantage. Had she slipped in and out of roles?

Of course.

But this . . . this was a little trickier.

She had to be careful because damn it, she wasn't getting any younger. Now, she needed her career to take off, to go farther. Much farther. She needed to be catapulted onto the national stage and she had just the ticket: Allie Kramer.

Heading into town, she smiled at the thought as her SUV twisted through the Terwilliger curves on the freeway. Speeding past a moving van that was drifting into her lane, she blasted her horn and the idiot at the wheel yanked back, nearly overcorrecting and fishtailing through a final turn. Wasn't that the same truck she'd followed, with a question printed on the back of the trailer? *How's my driving?* Well, it was shitty, that's what it was. If she had a second to spare, she would ease off the gas, let the damned truck pass, then crawl up its backside and take a picture of the stupid question about the driving along with the number to call to report any infractions.

It would serve the moron right.

But she didn't have time.

She never had enough.

Through her windshield, she caught a glimpse of the Willamette River and the city sprawled upon its wide banks. Bridges connecting the east side to the west were visible through the trees. High-rises had sprung up closer to the heart of the city and she noticed morning mist rising from the water as she spied the aerial tram that connected the waterfront campus of OHSU to the huge hospital built high in the West Hills. Oregon Health and Science University wasn't too far from Mercy Hospital, where Cassie Kramer was currently a patient.

Again she smiled, thinking of Cassie in a mental ward.

A perfect place for her.

And one more juicy element in her story.

All in all Whitney liked Portland. It currently had a cool vibe ascribed to it, but, truth to tell she was sick to her back teeth of the gloomy weather and the constant traveling from PDX to LAX in Southern California.

It will be all worth it.

Soon.

She warmed inside at the thought, clicked on her blinker and edged her way toward an off ramp that would dump her near the Hawthorne Bridge with its metal grating and vertical lift, which allowed large ships to pass beneath it.

She was running late to a meeting with a source on the Eastbank Esplanade, a bicycle and pedestrian path on the east shore of the river. The source was supposed to have information on the rift between the missing Allie Kramer, her nutcase of a sister, Cassie, and their reclusive mother, Jenna Hughes. Whitney expected the guy to be a no-show, one more in a series of irritating dead ends, but she wouldn't let an opportunity pass to gain more information, more insight into the Sisters Kramer and their famous mother.

This was her chance, she thought, as she found one of the few remaining parking spaces, grabbed her microphone and cell, then dodged a speeding bicyclist to wait for the informant.

In the meantime, she made calls and did research, studied the skyline of the west side of the river, where skyscrapers rose against a backdrop of forested hills. After an hour, her irritation growing with each passing minute, she finally gave up. One more time a promising source had turned out to be a dud and she was stood up, once again.

She walked back to her car and flopped inside. As she twisted on the ignition, she decided that she would do whatever was necessary to nail this story and if she had to be . . . uh, creative? . . . so be it. She wasn't above bending the truth a little, or even staging a little drama.

Within reason.

There were lines she wouldn't cross, of course. She had her ethics. But she also had a story to tell, a story that promised her a new echelon of fame.

And she deserved it, by God.

Life hadn't been fair to her, and this time she wasn't going to let the brass ring slip through her fingers. Not when it was sooo close.

Licking her lips, she plotted her next move.

How far would she go to get what she wanted?

Again, her lips twitched.

Pretty damned far.

"But you're not well, not strong enough to leave," Dr. Sherling said to Cassie after breakfast. She was a kind woman, who never wore makeup, her white hair a cloud, her cheeks naturally rosy, her skin unlined though she had to be in her seventies. Slim and fit, Virginia Sherling had been a competitive skier in her day, according to the nurses' gossip. Beneath her bright, toothy smile and soft-spoken, easygoing demeanor lay a will of iron. Cassie knew. She'd tested the psychiatrist several times during her stay here and had witnessed the color rise in the older woman's face and her slight English accent become more pronounced. Now, however, upon walking into Cassie's room and finding her packing, Dr. Sherling was calm. At least outwardly as she stood next to the rocker in the room.

"I'll be okay," Cassie assured her.

"Have you talked to your family? Your mother?"

Cassie threw her a glance. "Have you?" she asked, double-checking that her phone and charger were tucked inside with her clothes and makeup bag. Everything was where it should be. Except for the bottles of meds that were tucked into a side pocket. No need for those. She grabbed the three bottles, read the labels, then threw them all into a nearby trash can.

The doctor's lips tightened. "You can't just stop those," she said. "You need to taper off. Seriously, Cassie, I strongly advise you wean yourself carefully." She walked to the trash, scooped up all three bottles, and dropped them into Cassie's open bag. "These are strong drugs."

"Exactly."

"Please. Be responsible." The doctor's eyes behind her glasses were serious and steady. "You don't want to come back here on a stretcher."

Cassie's jaw tightened.

"Have you talked to your mother?" she asked again.

The answer was "no," of course, and Cassie suspected Dr. Sherling knew it and was just making a point.

When the older woman spoke, her voice was softer, more conspiratorial, as if they shared something personal. "Jenna's concerned."

For a second Cassie flashed on her mother. Petite. Black hair. Wide green eyes. A once-upon-a-time Hollywood beauty, Jenna Hughes had been a household name years before either of her daughters had tried to follow in her famous footsteps, before a monster, a deranged serial killer, had tried to destroy them all. Cassie shuddered, knew that the terror from all those years before had chased after her, unrelenting. Those memories, the horror, fear, and gore, were the dark well from where her blood-chilling nightmares sprang. For years she'd kept the terror at bay. Until the near-murder on the set and Allie's disappearance. Now they'd come back again, with a vengeance.

"You entered the hospital voluntarily," the doctor reminded her softly, as if she could read Cassie's thoughts. That much was true, though she'd felt pressured into the decision. "You know you have unresolved issues." A slight rise of the doctor's white eyebrows punctuated her thought. "Night terrors. Hallucinations. Blackouts."

"They're better." Cassie zipped her bag. Thought about the nurse she'd seen in her room. Not a hallucination; she had the earring to prove it. Still, she'd decided not to mention the visitor; nor would she rat out Rinko. There was no reason to make more trouble.

"Are they?" the doctor asked, her eyes narrowing behind her rimless glasses.

"Mmm." A bit of a lie. Well, maybe more than a bit, but she nodded, pushing aside her doubts. "I was freaked out after the near-murder on the set. You know that. It's why I came here. Voluntarily. To sort things out and get my head right." She stared the doctor squarely in the eyes. "I'm still convinced someone was gunning for Allie."

"It was an accident," Dr. Sherling reminded her, a theory Cassie didn't buy. There was an ongoing investigation after the "incident," of course; the actor who'd pulled the trigger more shocked than anyone, the prop gun having been tampered with. So how was that an accident? This was the kind of thing that was never supposed to happen. Never. There were fail-safes in place.

And yet, Lucinda Rinaldi, who had miraculously survived after nearly two weeks in a coma, was recovering. She was now out of the hospital and, according to a mutual acquaintance, had graduated into a rehabilitation center on the other side of the river, where she was putting her life back together, all the while contemplating a lawsuit against the production company and anyone attached to *Dead Heat*.

An accident?

Cassie didn't think so, but then she'd always been one to buy into conspiracy theories. She would keep her thought to herself for now. What she needed to do was get out of the hospital. She'd admitted herself voluntarily, she was going out the same way.

"Thanks," she said to the doctor, swinging the strap of her bag over her shoulder.

"Seriously, Cassie, I think you should reconsider. Hallucinations? Blackouts? These are very serious issues."

"Duly noted." And then she walked out of the room. She wasn't coming back. Period.

"Remember our appointment next week," the doctor called after her.

Right. Cassie hurried past the information and admittance desks. Through an atrium with a soaring glass ceiling, she made her way outside where she felt the cooling mist against her face. She then hastened down wide marble stairs to the waiting cab, where the cabbie was smoking a cigarette and talking on a cell phone. At the sight of her, he abandoned both activities and climbed out of the car to toss her bag into the trunk of a dented cab that was definitely in need of a wash.

She caught sight of Steven Rinko on the front lawn. "Just a sec." Rinko was a few steps away from a group of young men playing ringtoss.

"Meter's runnin'," the cabbie muttered.

"I'll be right back."

Cassie cut across the dewy grass to the spot where Steven stood in jeans and a white T-shirt and used a bathrobe as a coat. "You're leaving," he said sadly, his gaze traveling to the idling cab.

"That's right."

"Will you be back?"

Never. "I'm not sure. And so I need to know where you got the earring," she said.

"The nurse."

"Last night? The nurse you saw?" She caught one of the other teenage boys holding a plastic ring staring at her. He was tall and reed-thin, an African-American with haunted eyes and a sorrowful expression. Jerome.

"Yeah." Rinko was nodding.

"She was in blue scrubs?" Cassie said, testing him.

He shook his head. "White."

Her knees nearly buckled. Rinko had seen the same vision she had? Then it definitely wasn't all in her mind! "Do you know her? Her name? Does she work here?"

"Hey, Butt-Wipe, you playin' or what?" a third player, with skin that matched his bad attitude, yelled at Rinko. He was scrawny, with a sunken chest and hate-filled eyes, his baseball cap turned backward. "You're up, Romeo."

"Shut up, Fart Face," Rinko said to the kid, then to Cassie, "Look, I gotta go."

"Do you know her?" Cassie wanted to shake the answer from him.

"Nurse Santa Fe?" He shook his head and shrugged. "No one does."

"Her name is Santa Fe? Like Santa Claus? Or saint in Spanish? She works here?"

"1972."

"Hey, Stinko Rinko! You forfeit," his opponent called just as the cab driver honked his horn impatiently, and Rinko stormed back to argue about the game.

"I do not forfeit, you idiot!"

"Steven! The nurse worked here in 1972? How do you know that?" Rinko wasn't born in '72. Nor, for that matter, was she. But the nurse's outfit could have been from that era.

Another impatient beep of the cab's horn. "Lady, I don't have all day," the driver called.

She returned to the cab and gave him the address before settling into the well-worn seat. As she pulled the door shut, she hazarded one last glance over her shoulder to spy Mercy Hospital, a blend of old brick and new glass, perched on its hill. *Good riddance,* she thought, her gaze drifting up to the fourth floor and the older part of the building where she'd spent the last few weeks. She thought she spied her room, saw a shadow within, and for just a second imagined she spied the taciturn nurse from another generation in the window. Before she could really focus, the cab turned and headed downhill, passing trees that blocked her view of the brick edifice.

She didn't have much of a plan, just knew that she was getting better in the hospital and that the cops' search for Allie hadn't turned up anything so far. Cassie chewed on her lower lip and tapped her fingers against the window of the cab. Where was her sister? What had happened? How had she disappeared? And how would Nurse Santa Fe, or whoever she was, know that she was alive? It seemed unlikely and yet Rinko had produced the earring. God, it was all so bizarre and surreal.

Her mother was frantic with fear for her younger daughter. Robert, too, was worried about Allie. Cassie knew because she'd talked to both of her parents at length. And she knew how they felt. She, too, was obsessed with finding her sister.

A headache formed behind her eyes as she considered her splintered family. Her mother and stepfather, a sheriff, no less, resided in Oregon, while her much-married father lived in LA with his current wife, Felicia, twenty years his junior and, of course, a gorgeous would-be actress. As they all had been.

Not that it mattered.

Closing her eyes, Cassie tried to place her thoughts in some kind of order. For months she'd been a zombie. A patient in a hospital, who'd been told what to do, when to do it, and where to be. Now, she was on her own. No more hiding away and licking wounds and feeling bad. No more coddling herself. It was time for action and answers.

First order—she needed a place to crash. She didn't know for how long. A car would help. Also, she had to get her cell phone up and running. Right now the battery life was nil.

You need some kind of plan, she told herself as the cab driver negotiated the narrow street that wound down this section of the West Hills. Fir, maple, and oak trees canopied over the pavement where a walking path was cut along the roadway. Intrepid joggers and bikers vied for space along the steep asphalt trail. Every once in a while, through gaps in the forest, she caught peekaboo views of Portland sprawled along the banks of the Willamette.

She was no longer an actress. She'd given up that dream once her younger sister had come onto the scene and literally upstaged her. Cassie didn't need harsh reviews to remind her of the fact, and Allie had been a natural while she'd struggled. The camera loved Allie and she shined bright, whatever residual shyness from her youth disappearing as she lost herself in a role. The irony of it all was that it had been Cassie who had lured her younger sister to the bright lights of Hollywood. Cassie who'd suggested she move out of Falls Crossing, Oregon, as soon as Allie graduated from high school.

So all of this was, in some way, her fault.

Get over it. Wallowing in guilt and self-pity won't help anything, now, will it?

The cab reached the bottom of the hill and found the freeway, a wide swath of concrete that ran the length of the westernmost states and beyond. Here in Portland I-5 was often a snarl, the traffic not a whole lot better than the loaded freeways of LA, but today they lucked out and the cab was able to sail across the wide span of the Marquam Bridge to the east side of the river.

Fifteen minutes later she was filling out paperwork for a rental car, a compact that turned out to be a white Nissan. Tonight, she'd stay in a hotel. Tomorrow, worry about something more permanent.

And then she was going to find out what the hell had happened to her sister.

CHAPTER 3

The hotel room was basic—two beds with matching quilts, a couple of pictures, a TV, desk, and chair with an ottoman. The bathroom was fitted with a tub/shower and toilet and sink, all squeezed into an impossibly small space. The "suite" would do. For now. Cassie eyed the phone on the bedside table, thought about calling her mother, then shoved aside the jab of guilt that cut through her heart. She'd wait to tell Jenna where she'd landed, otherwise she'd be sucked into that maternal vortex that didn't seem to let go. It wasn't that Jenna played the guilt card, or at least not very often, it was that Cassie couldn't really deal with her mother and stepfather and their ranch sprawling along the banks of the Columbia River. It was all too bucolic or rustic or Podunk for her, and the place brought back a never-ending tidal wave of memories she'd rather keep buried—the bloody, brutal images that were better off forgotten, or at the very least tamped down, until they reared up in horrific, ugly Technicolor in her nightmares.

"Head case," she muttered, grabbing up her cell phone. It was barely alive after being charged for less than fifteen minutes, but it was all the time she could afford. Ever since leaving the hospital she felt that time was slipping through her fingers. She'd been cooped up for what seemed like forever but had only actually been a few weeks, and now she needed to get moving.

Once behind the Nissan's steering wheel, she Googled the name of the rehabilitation center were Lucinda Rinaldi was recovering. Allie's body double had pulled through several surgeries, which included removing part of her spleen, and some liver damage, along with spinal injuries, all of which were on the mend, thank God.

She negotiated the grid of streets that were East Portland and found Meadow Brook Rehabilitation Center, where there seemed to be no meadow, nor brook, anywhere nearby. The long, low, tan building just off Fifty-Second had been constructed in the fifties or sixties from the looks of it, a bank of glass windows facing the street, the reception area under a jutting peak in the otherwise unbroken roofline. An asphalt parking lot in need of resurfacing flanked one side of the sidewalk, a rose garden gone to seed on the other.

Cassie was met by a hefty receptionist with a gravelly voice and easy smile who checked a computer screen and asked, "You're a relative?"

"Friend."

"Don't see your name on the visitor list."

"I've been out of town."

"She's in physical therapy now."

"I'll wait," Cassie said brightly. Before the woman could argue her phone rang, her concentration broken as whoever was on the other end of the connection commanded all of her attention.

"Now, hold on," she said into the phone. "Who is this? What kind of emergency?" Her brow knitted and she started typing on her keyboard, so Cassie pretended to be taking a seat on one of the worn chairs near the window. As soon as the receptionist's back was turned, she hurried down a short hallway and followed the signs to physical therapy. If the receptionist figured out that she'd been thwarted and chased Cassie down, or called security, Cassie would deal with it then.

For now, she stepped quickly through the doorway into a large room that smelled of sweat, plastic, and antiseptic.

Lucinda, dressed in sweats, was working at walking between two parallel bars, a therapist at her side. Her hair was scraped back with a headband, unkempt curls showing dark roots. She was concentrating hard as she inched her way down the length of the apparatus. Her face was flushed, sweat making her skin sheen under the fluorescent lighting.

As if sensing someone's presence, Lucinda looked into the mirrors lining one wall and caught sight of Cassie's reflection. She stumbled, but the aide who was with her was quick to grab her as Lucinda caught her balance again, her lips flattened with unrepressed fury.

"Get her out of here," she gritted.

"Lucinda, wait." Cassie stepped farther into the room as Lucinda made it to the far end of the bars and with the aide's help nearly fell into a waiting wheelchair.

"I don't want to talk to you."

"Really?" Cassie was flummoxed and tried to skirt the thin woman in nurse's scrubs who was attempting to block her access.

"I think you should leave," the woman said firmly. Her name tag read Louise-Marie and she was tough-looking, her expression brooking no argument.

Ignoring her, Cassie said to Lucinda, "I just wanted to see how you were doing, that you were okay."

Lucinda shot her an *oh-sure* glare. "I was nearly killed, all because your stupid sister didn't show up on the set again, and they thought they could get away with shooting the film without her, meaning using me. Shooting *around* her," she stressed, her lips curling as if she'd just tasted something foul. "And I get shot in the process. Ironic, don't you think?" She caught a glimpse of herself and frowned. "God, where's Laura Merrick when you need her?" she muttered, mentioning the makeup person who'd been on the set of *Dead Heat*. Another glance in the mirror and she blinked quickly as if fighting a sudden spate of tears. "How could anyone do this?"

"It was an accident."

Again, the dark glare. "I was almost murdered, but I think they meant to shoot Allie. Or maybe even you. Not me, for God's sake!" Reading the protest forming on Cassie's lips, Lucinda held up a hand. "I'm not talking about that Neanderthal Sig," she said, meaning Sig Masters, the actor who had fired the prop gun on the set. "He was just a pawn. Like me. In the wrong place at the wrong damned time." She yanked the headband from her hair and mopped her forehead. "Y'know he actually sent me flowers. They came with some kind of sympathy note that said 'Sorry.' Can you believe that?" She rolled her eyes. "I mean who does that? Almost kills someone and sends them roses and carnations and shit?"

Cassie shook her head. The truth was no one, not even the cops, thought Sig Masters was behind the accident. His record was clean and he had no ax to grind, no motive to harm Allie or Lucinda or her.

"I just want to find my sister," Cassie said.

Lucinda snorted through her nose. "I didn't think you two ever got along. I heard that the only reason you had a bit part in the movie was because she threw you a bone, or that she thought it would be good for publicity or something."

"Wow."

"Oh, come on. Everybody knows." Lucinda lifted a dismissive shoulder, then wiped her forehead with her sleeve. "As for trying to find your sister, she's probably already dead somewhere." Cassie made a sound of protest but Lucinda went on without a hint of emotion, "I kinda thought you might have an idea of what happened to her." She unlocked the brakes of her wheelchair and began rolling closer to the doorway where Cassie stood, still blocked from entering farther by the intractable Louise-Marie.

"Why would you think that?"

Lucinda gave a humorless laugh. "Everyone knows you were jealous as hell of her success, and then after she goes missing and I get shot, *you* end up in the nuthouse?" She was close enough now that Cassie didn't have to shout. "That's convenient."

"What're you saying?" Cassie asked, stunned. "You think . . . that I know where she is?"

"If the Manolo Blahnik fits . . ." she said tartly as the wheel of her chair caught on the corner of a mat sticking out from where it had been tucked under the parallel bars. Lucinda had always had a chip on her shoulder the size of the Rock of Gibraltar. "Jesus," she growled, irritated, before she was able to push around the obstacle. "I don't know what you're doing here," she said, rolling to the door and edging out the aide.

"I want to know where Allie is, that's all."

"Really? She stole your husband, didn't she?" Lucinda reminded, and Cassie felt as if she'd been slapped. But she couldn't deny it. Heat stormed up the back of her neck as she thought about Trent, whom she'd once considered to be the love of her life, her husband, her damned soul mate, and then his jarring betrayal. Deep inside she felt something break, the dam holding back her raw emotions. She didn't want to but she thought suddenly of Trent's rugged good looks, his strong jaw, deep-set eyes, and thin lips that could twist into an irreverent smile with little provocation. She'd loved him. Wholeheartedly. Stupidly, and as it had turned out, wretchedly . . .

Forcing his image from her mind, she focused on Lucinda's avid gaze. "Trent and I were already over," she lied.

"You know, I'm surprised the cops aren't looking at you for Allie's disappearance. You're the logical choice."

"I didn't have anything to do with—"

Lucinda cut her off. "Yeah, right. Of course not." She let out a short laugh.

Cassie's fingers tightened over her keys and she tried vainly to tamp down the wave of emotion that had started deep inside and was boiling upward. Anger and rage, fury and fear, all threatening to erupt.

"You know what? I'm tired of this," Lucinda muttered, as if she sensed the change in Cassie's mood and didn't want to witness the storm. "I'm not supposed to talk to anyone associated with *Dead Heat*. My lawyer's advice." To the aide, she said, "Can we go now?" then pushed past Cassie and rolled indignantly down the wide tile corridor.

"This isn't a legal thing," Cassie called after her.

Lucinda stopped and deftly turned her wheelchair a hundred and eighty degrees. "What planet do you live on? Hellooo. This is Earth, for God's sake! America. *Every*thing is a legal thing." Then, with a quick movement, she was rolling away again, her head held high, as if she'd just won a chess match.

Check and mate.

Great, Cassie thought, her jaw sliding to one side. She considered storming after Lucinda, demanding answers, but knew it would get her no further than being tossed out of Meadow Brook Rehab on her ear. Besides, Lucinda probably had no better idea than she about what had happened to Allie.

Turning to leave, she nearly tripped over another woman in a walker. "Sorry," she said as the woman stopped short.

"Watch where you're going," was the gruff response.

She couldn't get out of the rehab center fast enough. Pushing open the front door, she drew in a long breath of damp Portland air, then made her way to the parking lot. As she did, Lucinda's accusations followed after her. The truth was, they didn't ring false. She and Allie had always had a love/hate relationship, one that drove their mother crazy. In her teenage years, Cassie had been rebellious and thwarted Jenna at every turn. She'd been angry and hurt over her parents' separation and divorce, had never adjusted to life away from Southern California, and generally hated everything to do with Falls Crossing, Oregon. Aside from her boyfriend, Josh Sykes, who was three years older. Jenna, of course, hadn't approved of the relationship, but she wasn't exactly a shining example when it came to finding Mr. Right.

Allie, too, hadn't liked their parents' divorce and her mother's subsequent move north, but she'd been more introverted, more of a baby in Cassie's estimation, more of an "odd duck" who had hated anything to do with Harrison Elementary. It wasn't until she'd entered high school that she'd turned on to education and spent the next few years outshining all of her peers.

Cassie had been flummoxed. Suddenly, shy, babyish Allie had become a stellar student and athlete, with college prospects and scholarship opportunities. Their mother had been so proud and Cassie, struggling to make it in Hollywood, had been more than a little jealous. Even now, she felt it, that burning rage that boiled up when she remembered their mother bragging up her younger child, mentioning the schools to which Allie had applied.

It had been surreal.

And just plain wrong.

Cassie had intervened, and it had probably been a mistake.

Allie might have been content to live a more "normal" life if Cassie hadn't butted in. As Cassie thought about that now, how stupid she'd been to insist her younger sister follow her, she felt the old rage raise its ugly head and her blood begin to boil. All her plans had backfired! Allie, too, had anger issues with her sibling. There had been times when they'd loved each other and other times when their feelings had bordered on hatred.

"Story of my life," she said as she climbed into the rental car and threw the little Nissan into reverse. A horn blasted and she jumped, standing on the brake pedal and jerking to a stop. In her mirror she caught the blur of a smart car flash by, the driver obviously using the parking lot as a cut-through to avoid waiting at a traffic light.

Cassie wanted to flip the driver off, but didn't. Her hands clenched over the wheel and her heart rate was still somewhere in the stratosphere. "For the love of God. Don't lose your cool. Do not." Drawing a deep breath she scanned the area again and caught sight of the gravel-voiced receptionist walking along the sidewalk as she smoked a cigarette. She threw Cassie a suspicious glance, which Cassie steadfastly ignored as she backed out of the slot. Ramming the Nissan into drive, Cassie drove to the exit. The smart car was long gone and Cassie melded into the flow of traffic without any other problems.

Visiting Lucinda Rinaldi had been a total bust, she decided. She consulted the GPS app on her phone before heading back to the hotel to regroup and come up with a better plan to locate her sister.

CHAPTER 4

Cassie's phone rang the second she turned into the lot of the hotel. She glanced at the caller ID and recognized her mother's cell number displayed on the small screen. She let the call go to voice mail as she parked around the corner from the main entrance. She'd caught sight of a Starbucks on her way, so she'd waited in line at the drive-through window, ordered a latte and a raspberry scone, and had nearly finished her drink by the time she reached the parking area of her temporary home.

"Very temporary," she reminded herself as she took the elevator to her room, where she turned on the television, managed a quick shower, then once she'd thrown on clean jeans and a sweater, ate the scone at the small desk where her cell phone was plugged in and charging. She was still hungry when she threw the wrapper and bag into the trash, but she'd deal with a real meal later.

She needed a better plan than her hastily-put-together notion of leaving the hospital to find Allie. She'd accomplished phase one, the hospital was in her rearview, but discovering what had happened to her sister would take some serious doing, if locating Allie were even possible. There were dozens of cases of people who had just disappeared, seemingly to vanish off the face of the earth. But she didn't believe for a second that her sister was one. First of all, the timing was too perfect. It was almost as if Allie had known there would be some kind of accident on the set of *Dead Heat* that day, that she was a target and that's why she hadn't shown up.

Far-fetched?

Maybe.

But with Allie, Cassie had learned, anything was possible. Even faking her own disappearance.

You don't know that. Sure, Allie's capable of a lot of things, but would she really vanish intentionally? Because she had advance knowledge about the attack, or "accident" as it was being called? Who would try to kill her and why?

The questions, without answers, buzzed through her brain, like darting insects that never quite landed, never settled, never slowed down long enough to be examined and understood.

And there was no getting around that it had been Cassie's fault. Along with her father, she'd encouraged Allie to give up her academic dreams, those scholarships and dorm rooms, or at least put them on hold, for the glitter and allure of Hollywood. Robert had insisted that they could become a successful team, the three of them, and Cassie had been so eager for his attention, she'd gone along with his plan. The ink had barely dried on her own high school diploma when Cassie had turned her car south, hit the accelerator, and drove with only two stops in eighteen hours. Filled with dreams of stardom and anxious to shake the dust of stupid Falls Crossing from her shoes, she'd beelined down the Five.

She'd landed in LA ready for her big break and ended up with big disappointment. Her roles had been few and far between. And then she'd talked Allie into joining her in California and things had only gotten worse.

She flopped down on one of the beds and considered calling her mother back, but decided she wasn't in the mood. She needed to calm down before she dealt with Jenna, or, for that matter Shane Carter, her stepfather. The ex-sheriff. She'd never liked him, still didn't. Too backwoodsy. And come on. A cop? Who marries a cop?

Your mother, that's who!

"Yeah, yeah, I know," she said aloud, her mind returning back to the sibling rivalry that escalated when both she and Allie vied for the same roles, which Cassie inevitably lost.

Even now the old jealousy raised its hateful head, and she punched the extra pillow. She had to rein in her rapidly escaping control over her emotions and she couldn't risk that, didn't want to return to the hospital on the very day she'd signed herself out. She had to avoid hallucinating again and couldn't afford to black out and lose hours of her life.

With an effort, she closed her eyes and concentrated on her breathing. She'd been out of the mental hospital less than twelve hours—hell, less than six—and she couldn't let the fear take over, wouldn't allow it to gnaw away at her tentative hold on reality.

Breathe in.

She settled back on the pillows.

Breathe out.

She imagined the air flowing out of her lungs, taking the bad memories and her fears with it.

Inhale.

Drawing in fresh air, she cleared her mind.

Exhale.

Again, she pushed out the pain.

Slowly she opened her eyes. It'd been rash thinking to toss her meds out earlier this morning, but thankfully, the doc had saved her. She slid a glance at the overnight bag and the pocket, still zippered, where the plastic bottles were tucked.

Not now.

Not yet.

It's only been a few hours and you were so sure you didn't need them, that you would get along just fine without any medication. Already you're tempted?

She turned her attention back to the TV. Just because she had the bottles of antianxiety meds and antidepressants in her bag didn't mean she had to take them. They weren't crutches, just helpmates, she reminded herself. Kind of like the therapist who'd been working with Lucinda as she learned to balance and walk again. Tiny little aides.

Oh, yeah, just like that Rolling Stones' song Dad loves, "Mother's Little Helper." Weren't those lyrics written about diazepam or some other tranquilizer half a century ago? There had been dozens of references in other songs as well, though they escaped her now.

Sighing, Cassie thought about Allie with her pixieish face and hair that shined between gold and red, thick tresses that curled and waved and caught the sun's rays to look as if they were on fire. Her freckles were faint, her eyes bright and expressive. Though Allie's coloring was more like their father's, she was as photogenic and alive on film as her famous mother. Another irony, Cassie thought, as she had been told from the time that she could remember that she was the spitting image of Jenna Hughes. Cassie's hair was lighter than Jenna's, but her eyes were the same shade of green and her facial structure of high cheekbones, arched brows, and sharp chin were much the same. But it hadn't helped.

The camera loved Allie. It caught her inner spark. That's all there was to it. And Cassie? Not so much. Allie had shown up in LA, and with a little help from their father, who had once been a Hollywood producer, landed her first commercial. That success was followed quickly by a bit part on a nighttime drama. And that small part had been a stepping-stone to another, bigger role on television, and within the year, she had a contract for a movie, the script of which was altered for her, her role expanded. *Voila!* Allie Kramer, not her older sister, became the daughter who followed in their mother's glittery footsteps.

Cassie had struggled on for a while, then finally had turned to writing. To her surprise she'd found that, as her English teacher at Falls Crossing High, Mrs. Crosby, had predicted, she had a knack for script writing.

Which was something.

And this . . . Allie's disappearance . . . was one hell of a story. The disappearance of an ingenue who had taken Hollywood by storm? It was golden. So, okay, that was stretching it a little. Allie was far from a wide-eyed innocent, and she hadn't wowed producers and directors all at once, had actually kind of crept in the back door her father had opened, but she had gained some fame and she'd narrowly escaped an assassin's bullet. . . . Well, that was definitely stretching the truth, but who really knew? She had indeed disappeared without a trace. Somehow Allie had pulled off the impossible.

Or she's really dead.

Cassie felt a sharp pang, one of real worry. However, she didn't believe Allie was really gone. No. Her sister was alive. She had to be. There was no death scene at the end of her screenplay.

"You're a true bitch," she said to her reflection in the full-length mirror mounted on the wall near the bathroom. She was capitalizing already on her sister's troubles. She'd been searching for a new idea for a screenplay and Allie's story, as told by her older sister, was a gift. Though she'd pushed these thoughts to the back of her mind while she was in the hospital, her destiny now seemed clear.

And Allie was *not* dead. She just had to find her.

Grabbing up her phone, she felt a jab of guilt about not calling her mother, but pocketed the cell anyway and headed out again. She had work to do and for some reason she felt as if the clock was ticking, not just the seconds of her life, but the time to solve this mystery.

Solve a mystery? You?

"Oh, shut up!" she sputtered. She made certain the privacy sign was positioned over the door handle of her room, then double-checked to see that the lock engaged.

Her next stop? Allie's apartment, the one she'd leased during production of *Dead Heat.* The cops had already been through it, of
course, but Cassie hadn't been since the last time she'd seen her sister.

In her mind's eye, she caught a glimpse of Allie as she'd last seen
her. Small, scared, but angry enough to glare at her older sister. "This
is all your fault," she'd said, in a barely audible whisper. Her face had
been devoid of makeup, tears streaming from her expressive eyes,
wetting her lashes. She'd seemed, at that moment, so much younger
than her years. "If something happens to me, Cassie, you're to blame."
She dashed the teardrops from her face. "Remember that. Okay?
You. And you alone. You're the reason!"

Trent heard the familiar rumble of Shorty O'Donnell's half-ton
truck grinding its way down the lane. He turned, a carton of roof
shingles balanced on one shoulder, and spied Shorty hunched over
the wheel of his twenty-year-old pickup, the older man squinting
through the windshield. Originally painted red and tan, the Chevy
was now equipped with a faded green front panel and black tailgate,
replacements for original parts that had been dented so badly they'd
been scrapped long ago. New dents had appeared over the years.

Trent didn't have to check his watch to know that Shorty was late.

Then again, Shorty was always late. Had come into the world
three weeks overdue according to his mother and hadn't caught up
since. As long as Trent had known him, over three decades, Shorty
had always shown up long after he was due. Today was no exception.
No big surprise there.

Trent walked into the barn, stacked the final carton on top of the
others he'd hauled from the local lumberyard. By the time he was
outside again, the rain that had been threatening all day had begun
in earnest. No more misting drizzle, now the heavy drops poured
from the thick underbellies of the clouds huddling overhead.

Shorty parked and hopped down from the cab of his truck to the
gravel spread between the outbuildings. "Sorry about the time. Damned
cows got out at my place. Sheeeit, I'm gonna have to patch that fence
again." He looked up from beneath the brim of his Oregon Ducks
cap, rain drizzling from its bill. The ranch hand was half a foot shorter
than Trent, whip-thin, and tough as nails when he wanted to be. He
was wearing his usual outfit: a short yellow slicker, jeans, battered
boots, and the University of Oregon cap, though Trent was certain
Shorty had never set one booted foot on the campus in his life.

Shorty asked, "You need help with the load?"

"Just finished." Trent slammed the tailgate closed, heard the lock click, but gave it a tug, just to be sure it would stay latched.

"So I guess I should get to work inside?" He hitched his grizzled chin toward the machine shed where the old John Deere was waiting for a part that was due into town within the week. So far it hadn't shown up.

"Yeah." Trent eyed the weathered barn with its attached grain silo. He'd love to start roofing the sucker, but rain was forecasted for the next three days, so it was best to wait as it would be easier and safer to peel off old shingles and walk on the sloped roof when it was dry. He scowled, hated to be held up by the weather, Mother Nature, or God Himself. His cell phone vibrated in his pocket, but he ignored it. Probably just another reporter looking for a new angle in the Allie Kramer mystery. As Allie's sister's husband, he sometimes got calls where nosy members of the press asked questions he'd rather not answer.

Trent whistled for his dog, who'd sneaked inside and curled up on an old horse blanket the barn cats usually claimed. "Hud. Come." The mutt, a speckled shepherd who had wandered here as a half-grown pup, bounded into the rain, then beelined for the porch, where he sat and waited near the door, his feathery tail dusting the old floorboards.

"He don't like the rain much," Shorty observed. "Seems as if maybe he should be a California dog or an Arizona dog. Somewhere where it don't drizzle all the damned time."

Trent pulled the barn door shut, the casters screeching a bit.

"Could use a little lubricant on them wheels."

Trent nodded.

"Think I saw a can of WD-40 in the equipment shed," Shorty went on. "I'll give 'em all a squirt today."

"Good idea."

"So, guess what I heard in town?" Shorty said, returning the conversation to where he'd begun. "It's about your wife."

Trent tried not to change his expression. "I'm not married."

"Ain't 'cha?" Shorty questioned.

"We're separated." Shorty already knew this, he was just yanking Trent's chain. "It's just a formality."

"A legal formality."

"Okay, I'll bite. What did you hear?" Trent asked impatiently.

"Well, I had to stop in town, for some wire to patch the damned fence and, well, decided to have a quick one before I came over. It was all the talk at Keeper's," he said, mentioning a favorite local pub.

"Something about Cassie?" Trent's voice was clipped. Cassie Kramer was out of his life. Again, he reminded himself. He'd been seriously involved with her twice: first when they were dating and she was too young for him; the second time, when they'd both matured some and he'd thought marrying her was what he wanted.

His jaw clenched a bit when he thought of their breakup. Lies. Accusations. Mistrust. On both sides. But now he was single again—almost—and the less he knew about his ex, he figured, the better.

"I guess she's out of the hospital," Shorty stated evenly, as if he'd just said it was a wet April day, which, of course, it was.

"And you know this how?"

"Oh, I've got my ways," Shorty assured him with a sly smile that showed off teeth yellowed by tobacco and far too small to fill his gum line. "I guess the doctor wasn't ready to release her, but she just walked out. Someone at the hospital called Jenna, and she was fit to be tied. Already upset with the other girl gone missing, you know." He spat a stream of tobacco juice to the loose gravel. "Weird thing that. How does a person, make that a *famous* person, just up and disappear?" He wiped his mouth with the back of his sleeve.

"Don't know."

"But you knew her, right? She was your sister-in-law?"

Hell yes, he knew Allie. All about her. Far more than he should. "We weren't all that close." That was a lie and he figured Shorty knew it. Trent squirmed a little inside, but he didn't so much as blink. He was used to the curiosity. Jenna Hughes was Falls Crossing's biggest celebrity, even if she'd given up acting years before. When her daughters followed in her footsteps and began making their own movies, the townspeople in the area took notice and liked to claim that Cassie and Allie Kramer were locals, though they'd both spent most of their years growing up in California. It didn't matter because both of Jenna Hughes's striking daughters had graduated from the nearby high school and therefore were considered Falls Crossing's own.

"If she was alive, you'd think she'd at least have the decency to call her folks and tell 'em she's okay."

"You'd think," Trent said, though deep down, he wasn't convinced that Allie Kramer had a whole lot of decency in her.

Shorty wasn't going to leave it alone. "Didn't you and her—?" He wagged a finger back and forth.

"Didn't we what?"

"You know."

"I don't."

"I thought you two were an item. You and the younger one. One of them other times you and Cassie were 'separated'?" Shorty's pale eyes sparkled. He'd always loved needling Trent.

"You thought wrong. Look after those casters, would ya?" Trent said, and headed into the house, where the dog, spying his approach, did a quick twirl of excitement at the door. "And then come on in." He opened the door and glanced over his shoulder. "I'll buy you a beer."

CHAPTER 5

Lunch, if you could call it that, consisted of a cup of watery coffee and a Big Mac. Not a great combo on a strong stomach, even worse on a queasy one like Cassie's, and she was paying for it, her insides gurgling as she pulled into the covered parking lot of the apartment building where Allie had rented a suite of rooms while filming *Dead Heat.*

Located in the Pearl, a hip district tucked beneath the West Hills of Portland, the three Art Deco buildings that comprised the Calista Complex were nearly a hundred years old, but had been renovated recently.

Parking was a bitch in this area, so she was lucky Allie's space was empty, the car Allie had used in Portland, a sporty BMW, towed away by the police in their search for clues to her disappearance.

At that thought Cassie felt a pang of dread. "Where the hell are you?" she whispered as she parked and listened to the engine tick once she'd switched it off. The lot was underground and dark, a few pipes overhead dripping condensation from the low cement ceiling, just a handful of cars sprinkled between thick pillars that supported all eight stories of the Calista.

Cassie was one of the last persons to see Allie before she vanished. They'd fought, which she'd admitted and a nosy neighbor had confirmed, so the police had been interested in her for a time, either thinking she'd been in cahoots with her sister, or worse, that she had somehow been integral in Allie's disappearance.

"Yeah, right," she muttered, unbuckling her seat belt before getting out of the car and locking it remotely. Her skin crawled in this wide space with its weak overhead lights and tire marks on the floor. No one else was around, which was a good thing, right? And there were cameras mounted in the corners of each level of the garage, so if anything happened . . .

They didn't help Allie though, did they? No camera lens caught anything unusual on the night she disappeared.

Ignoring her jittery nerves, Cassie made her way to the elevator and with the key Allie had given her, she ordered the elevator car that was already waiting, its doors opening with a *hiss*, no one inside. She punched the button for the eighth and uppermost floor and was grateful the car didn't stop on its ascent. Again, she was aware of the camera mounted somewhere overhead in the elevator carriage, but didn't look up until the car slid to a smooth stop and the doors parted again. Then she sneaked a peek and wondered about the tape of Allie's last journey in the car. The police had it, she knew, but she hadn't yet viewed it. Wasn't sure she was ready for that.

Feeling like she was trespassing, she slid her key into the lock and, glancing over her shoulder to make certain she wasn't observed, she opened the door of Allie's apartment. Inside, the faded scent of her perfume still lingered, bringing back memories of the last time she'd been here. "Not now," she reminded herself.

As she reached for the light switch, she heard the scrape of a shoe against hardwood. The hairs on the back of her neck raised. "Allie?" she called as she stepped inside and peered into the living area.

The silhouette of a tall man was backlit against the window, his dark form visible in front of the thin lines of gray light piercing through the slats in the blinds.

Cassie's heart nearly stopped. "Oh, God."

"Not Allie," he said as she fumbled frantically for the light switch. "Nor God."

She hit the switch, and the ultramodern apartment was suddenly illuminated.

"What the hell are you doing here?" she demanded, her heart thumping as she recognized Brandon McNary, not only Allie's costar in *Dead Heat*, but a man with whom Allie had once had a very public and torrid affair. Their fights, splits, romantic trysts, and reconciliations were tabloid fodder, one of Hollywood's most watchable and gorgeous couples. Standing in front of a sleek sectional, McNary had the audacity to smile at her, as if he knew he'd scared the living crap out of her.

"Cass." He was wearing a black shirt, beat-up jeans, and glasses. His usual three-day beard stubble looked closer to five or six and made him appear more intellectual than he actually was, like he was trying on his Johnny Depp vibe. At five-ten, he was lean and well muscled from hours working out in the gym, and every bit the image of a leading man in Hollywood. His tousled dark hair, deep-set eyes, strong jaw, and slightly off-center smile had helped make McNary a definitive male A-lister.

And he was an ass. A real ass.

Cassie knew.

Hadn't she once, stupidly, almost fallen for him? *Almost,* she reminded herself.

"So?" she said, and repeated, "Why are you here?"

"Probably doing the same thing you are," he said with a shrug. "Trying to figure out what happened to Allie."

"You have a key?" She stepped into the living room with its gleaming hardwood floor.

He hitched his chin toward the front door. "My place is across the hall, so we thought it was best to be able to check on each other's apartment. I'm moving out at the end of the month. The film's wrapped and it's time to move on. Got another gig. Action-adventure. New genre for me."

If he thought she would congratulate him or even comment, he was wrong and the silence stretched until he said, "But, you know, I thought I'd take one last look around."

"With the lights off?"

"I was just leaving. Already turned 'em off."

"Most people do it at the door, you know, so they don't bump into anything on their way out."

"I know my way around," he said, and crossed the living space to stop in the entry, close enough to Cassie to make her want to back up a step. "I'm not 'most people,' am I?"

"No, you're not," she agreed coolly. God, he was smug, and though she hated to admit it, a decent, maybe even more than decent, actor. For a few weeks, before he met Allie, she'd even dated him. She'd been an idiot, but he was charming, in a self-serving manner, and when he focused on a woman, you could feel the heat. She certainly had. But now she knew there was a little snake oil running through his veins. "You were here looking for some clue to help you find Allie?"

He frowned. "Well, yeah . . . and . . . I just wanted to, you know, occupy her space. We did have a thing."

"I thought you two had broken up again."

A shoulder lifted and fell. "With Allie, it was tough," he admitted in a moment where he seemed to let down his guard. "I don't have to tell you that. Half the time she was a woman in control of her destiny, the other half she was an emotional child looking for someone to save her."

"Like you?"

"Exactly." He hesitated, then added, "And sometimes . . . it was like I didn't even know her. As if she really was someone else. You know what I mean, right?" He stared at her hard.

She did, but wasn't going to admit it. There were many sides to Allie. The bookish nerd. The successful Hollywood actress. The insecure little girl. The hateful, jealous bitch. But Cassie wasn't going to voice her opinion. She didn't trust his motives. They were always self-serving. She motioned to the interior of the apartment. "So, while you were playing detective, did you find anything?"

A quick shake of his head.

Her gaze swept the neat interior. "Who cleaned up? Not the police."

"Your mom, I think."

She felt another stab of guilt that she hadn't yet called Jenna. "You talked to her?"

"A while back, once the cops had done their thing and were done. I don't think Jenna could stand it, the mess, I mean. And well . . ." He shrugged. "All of it."

Again the bad feeling that she was being a stubborn, uncaring daughter wormed its way through her brain. "I take it you haven't heard from Allie?"

He looked up quickly, anger flaring, his gaze drilling into her. "If I had, would I be here?"

"I don't know. Would you?"

Shaking his head, he muttered, "You never let it go, do you?"

"What?"

"Everything and anything." His tone was sharp, his famed mercurial temper showing itself, his too-handsome face flushing in an instant. His fists actually balled before he stretched his fingers. "No reason to tiptoe around. You have trust issues, Cass."

She couldn't deny it. "And you have anger issues."

He opened his mouth, then snapped his jaw shut and glanced to the kitchen. "Sometimes."

"Most times."

"I'm working on them."

"Hard, I hope. Working on them hard."

His eyes gleamed. "What is it with you? Why exactly is it you're out of the wacky ward?" he asked, then heard himself and amended, "The hospital."

"It was time."

His thick eyebrows shot up. "Your doctors released you?"

"I'm out, aren't I?"

"For now," he said under his breath, and moved to the door.

"What's that supposed to mean?"

He hesitated, hand on the knob, then turned and walked so that he was close enough that he could touch her. "Cut the bullshit. You might have been the last person to see your sister before . . . whatever it is that happened to her took place. The cops are looking at you, Cass. I figured that was why you ended up in the mental ward."

"I had a breakdown."

He stared at her hard. "A breakdown."

"Yes." When he just continued looking at her, she asked, "What? You think I faked it?"

His eyes narrowed a bit. But he didn't argue.

"Well, now that's crazy."

"There ya go." He stepped back, and in less than a second his expression changed, the tension in his body dissipated. "I gotta run." A beat. "Nice seeing you again, Cassie," he said without a drop of emotion, then flashed his famous smile. So well practiced, so sterile and cold. "Always a pleasure." And then he was gone, the door closing softly but firmly behind him.

She threw the deadbolt, even though she knew he had a key. Just turning the lock made her feel better.

The man was a bastard. She closed her eyes and mentally counted to ten, all the while pushing all thoughts of Brandon McNary out of her mind. He just wasn't worth the effort.

Yes, she'd made the mistake of dating him a few times before he turned his attention to Allie. And of course she'd felt rejected and hurt, but that had just been her pride talking, and really more about Allie than Brandon. She hadn't even been all that attracted to him. The truth was she'd rebounded with him after her last breakup with Trent, which had, of course, also involved Allie.

Allie. *Always* Allie.

Now missing.

Cassie stared at the closed door wondering just what, if anything, Brandon knew about his costar and sometime girlfriend's disappearing act.

Not an act, Cass. You don't know what happened to Allie. She could have been kidnapped or worse.

And yet, she sensed that she might have been played. By Brandon McNary. As if he knew more than he was saying. But what? She felt a tiny niggle of fear for her sister, but refused to fall victim to the chilling idea that Allie could already be dead.

"So get on with it," she told herself, and stepped into Allie's living room with its modern furniture in somber gray tones that reminded her of death. "Get over yourself." Even the splashy, bright pieces of art on the walls, and the geometrically designed rug beneath the glass coffee table couldn't dissolve the disturbing feeling that overcame her.

Cassie had been here before, of course, a handful of times, the last visit having occurred on the day that Allie fell off the face of the earth. Her stomach clenched at the memory and the ragged remnants of the bitter fight that had ensued. Their argument had escalated, tempers flaring, egos rising.

"You hate me," Allie had charged, her hair still wet from her shower, a robe cinched around her waist. Without makeup she looked so much younger. "You've always hated me."

"Of course I don't—"

"Liar!" Tears had tracked down her face. "You always hated me. From the time we moved to Oregon when we were kids!"

"I did not."

"Save it. I know," Allie had choked out, her round eyes wounded.

"If I hated you so much, why did I ask you to come down to Hollywood?"

Allie had swiped at her face with the back of her hand, the sleeve of her oversized robe drying her tears. "You thought I would fail. That's why you wanted me to come." Conviction had set her jaw. "But that didn't work out for you now, did it?"

"No, it didn't," Cassie whispered now, wishing she could replay that argument again, could convince her sister that despite their deep rivalry and their petty jealousies that had started when they were teenagers, she loved her. She blinked hard and felt a lump fill her throat. If she could live her life over, she swore, she wouldn't have been so wrapped up in herself, her own needs, her own damned pride.

Sure, Cass. Don't delude yourself. Allie was right; she knew that you always felt the need to prove that you were the better sister.

With an effort Cassie shoved the nagging voice back into the dark hole where she kept it and turned her attention to Allie's apartment again.

This penthouse unit had come furnished as Allie had only intended to inhabit it during the filming in Portland. Though she snapped the blinds open the apartment felt lifeless, the bedroom reminding Cassie of an upscale hotel suite decorated in the same tone-on-tone shades of gray. The bathroom and walk-in closet were bare. The place had been cleaned and all of Allie's personal items had been removed either by the police or Jenna.

There was nothing here to see, not even a solitary picture of Allie. *It's like walking through a tomb.*

Her skin prickled as she made her way to the front door. Her cell rang as she reached for the handle and she nearly jumped out of her skin. Glancing at the screen, she saw it was her mother.

Then she noticed the text. Again from Jenna: Call me.

"Okay, okay." Walking out of the apartment, she glanced down the corridor as she locked the door behind her. It was empty, but she couldn't shake the feeling of being watched. She carefully looked all around. No one was walking the hallway or waiting for the elevators or at the wide spot in the hallway where two side chairs, a table with a lamp, and a potted palm with bristling fronds created an alcove for sitting or reading, or catching a glimpse of the Portland skyline through tall floor to ceiling windows. The chairs were unoccupied and no one was lingering nearby.

Cassie was alone, yet she had the sensation that someone was silently observing her.

Your imagination. She slapped the elevator call button and was startled when the doors opened immediately, as if someone else had pressed the button before her.

No one was in the car and she gratefully sped down to the lower parking lot without the car stopping on any other floor. She wasn't in the mood to talk to anyone, though, of course, she had to call her mother. Jenna was worried about her or, Cassie thought, she might even have news about Allie. Unlikely, but maybe.

She winced as a stabbing pain cut through her skull, a headache that was nearly blinding and sometimes preceded a loss of time. She was aware of the symptoms and fought them. She'd find a dark room, maybe some coffee or a cola, something with caffeine, pain reliever, and food, yes . . . that's what she needed.

Ouch! Another jab that made her blink. If she could just get home before . . . "Oh, God." The edges of her vision began to blur and her heart pounded. She leaned against her car for support and waited.

The pain would pass.

It had to.

She had too much to do to be compromised or incapacitated.

"Not now," she whispered and took in long breaths as the blackness threatened and the pain sliced through her brain. "Not now."

Cherise Gotwell slipped out from between the sheets. She hazarded one last look at the smooth back of the man in the bed. What was his name? Ryan? Or Riley? Or Reed . . . something that started with an R.

She was pretty sure.

The guy, whom she'd picked up in Vintner's House, a Portland bar Allie Kramer had been known to haunt, had found her beautiful. (Of course.) Interesting. (No surprise there.) And witty. (Well, that was a bit of a stretch.) But then he'd learned she'd worked for Allie Kramer and he'd been hooked.

How sick was that?

He probably pretended the whole time they were screwing that she was actually Allie. It had happened before and yeah, there was some resemblance. But it always left her feeling a little empty inside and like now, as she picked up her clothes to put them on in the living area of his bachelor pad, she knew she'd been playing the game as well.

Didn't Ryan or Riley or whoever look a little bit like Brandon Mc-Nary, who just happened to be her new boss? Okay, so yeah, it was all a little sick, head games if you will, but she didn't mind.

Until she could have the real thing, why not have a little fun?

And she didn't want to be just another score for Brandon, she wanted all of him, heart, body and soul. The trouble was, she thought, slipping on her panties and hooking her bra in the half-light of the apartment, she thought Brandon wasn't over Allie. Oh, sure, they'd split for the bazillionth time again just before *Dead Heat* went into production, but Cherise had wondered about that. The timing seemed a little too perfect for public fodder, a way to propel the on-again, off-again couple onto the front page of the tabloids, movie magazines, and Internet gossip. Brandon loved nothing more than to be "trending" and Allie was no better.

Also, Cherise had seen the way they'd looked at each other when they'd thought no one was looking; not so much with anguish and longing, but as if they'd shared some huge private secret or joke.

Or had it all been in her head?

She'd been in love with Brandon since like for-ev-er. It was all she could do not to fall into his bed and fuck the hell out of him. God, she wanted to. So badly. But she needed more. So much more. And she was willing to sacrifice to get what she wanted.

Hadn't that always been the way? Since she was a little girl. She'd been the pretty one, the ambitious one. Her sister? Not so much. She'd been the daring one, always ready to take a dare or a risk.

She still was.

She slid on a pair of tight jeans and a sweater. Well, not just any sweater, but one that had been Allie's from the costume department, one that Cherise had decided to "borrow," a sweater people might recognize as belonging to or being a knockoff of one Allie had worn in a famous scene where she'd pulled it slowly over her head while straddling her male lead on a picnic table.

Yep. Memorable.

Riley or Reed or Randy had noticed. The sweater was definitely an ice-breaker and nearly any red-blooded man in America would love to see it pulled off by Allie Kramer, or someone who looked like her, while being straddled.

Ryan or Whoever certainly had been turned on. Nearly came before he'd even kicked off his jeans.

She loved that kind of power over men. Hey, it wouldn't be bad over women either, a power Allie wielded as if it were her God-given right.

Yeah, she thought, slipping outside without a second glance at the bedroom and the sleeping male within. She was glad Allie Kramer was gone.

Glad, glad, glad! She hoped she never came back. Working for Allie had been like being in some kind of indentured servitude or worse. Cherise had been a slave to Allie's whims, fantasies, frustrations, and ambitions. The woman had called her at any time day or night and yeah, she paid well, but if you figured out that Cherise had been forced to be available twenty-four/seven, she wondered if she'd even made minimum wage.

All for the sake of being the "fabulous, beautiful, incredible Allie Kramer's" assistant. Well, no more.

She took the stairs and stepped outside to the vibrance and pulse of the city at night. Now that she'd let loose some of her frustrations, she wasn't ready to call it a night. Not yet.

There was still plenty to do, she thought, the dampness in the air invigorating, the prospect of the rest of her life exciting.

"Mrs. Brandon McNary," she said aloud. Not for the first time. She loved the sound of it. As long as Allie Kramer didn't reappear, Cherise figured she had a good shot at making all of her dreams come true. "Mrs. Brandon McNary," she repeated, a little louder, and tingled inside as she walked on the sidewalk.

She would do anything. Any damned thing, to make certain she became Brandon's wife. Allie Kramer didn't stand a chance.

ACT I

She walked onto the balcony of the bed and breakfast. From the second story she heard the hustle and bustle of the city and viewed pedestrians walking briskly into the trendy restaurants and unique shops of this section of town. As a car passed on the street below, she narrowed her view to the West Hills, then leaned over the railing to gaze down the side street where the final scene of *Dead Heat* had been filmed, to that very spot where Lucinda Rinaldi had been shot and nearly killed.

A pity about that, she thought. The "accident" had turned out wrong.

In so many ways.

In her mind's eye she saw them, the two women running. Her skin dimpled with the thrill and the first drops of rain falling from the leaden skies. She imagined the sounds of feet slapping against pavement, the darkened set, the hushed tones, the intensity of the scene and the actress, her heart racing, glancing over her shoulder, making certain . . .

"Sssh." She sucked in her breath and gripped the railing as she re-created the scene in her mind. A buzz sizzled through her blood again and she fought the urge that seemed to be her ever-present companion.

"Not today." With an effort she released the rail and stepped backward, across the wet flagstones into her bedroom. Surprised at how wet she was, that her hair was curling around her face, her shoulders drenched, she pulled the French door shut. How long had she been out there? Had anyone seen her? Dear God, she was getting reckless.

Be careful, she silently warned herself as she stepped into the bathroom where she found a towel and dried her hair and skin, only catching a glimpse of her reflection in the mirror now and then. She smiled at the brief images. She knew she was drop-dead gorgeous. How many times had she been told as much?

Still toweling her hair, she returned to the bedroom, dropped onto the thick duvet covering the bed, and saw the picture, one she'd placed so carefully near her pillows. The three of them were walking. A much younger Jenna Hughes was crossing an LA street with her daughters, holding each of their hands.

Her heart hardened as she noticed again that while Jenna was dragging the older one, who had turned to look at a puppy on a leash, she was half bent down to listen to what the younger girl was saying.

This snapshot taken by a member of the paparazzi said it all.

Sisters. As if they cared for each other. As if they had some special bond. Ridiculous. She knew all about sisters.

A slow-growing rage overtook her and she felt hot inside. Her lips tightened, her jaw ached. Her head pounded and her thoughts turned dark. Again. No matter how hard she wanted to kill it, the fury within was a dark seed that had sprouted, grown, and twisted itself over her heart for so many years now.

Beginning to shake, she spied a tube of lipstick on the table. Blood red. Though she knew it was a little crazy, she succumbed to her anger, flipped off the top of the tube, and smeared it across the glass, marring Jenna's well-known features. In her haste the picture dropped.

Glass shattered.

A spiderweb of cracks formed over the threesome.

Allie's face was obliterated by the broken glass.

Something within her broke.

Still trembling, she carefully used the lipstick to moisten her lips, then picked up a shard of glass from the table and ever so slowly sliced across her wrist. As a drop of blood appeared she squeezed her hand into a fist and it fell. First one. Then another. And another. Dripping over the photograph until the people in the shot were covered in her blood and unrecognizable.

She felt a lump in her throat as she whispered, "It's all an act."

It was well after dark when Cassie drove to the motel. Once in her room, she bought a ticket to LA on the Internet. Then the next morning, she headed to the airport where she said good-bye to the Nissan at the rental car return.

Once she was through security, she found a relatively quiet spot in Concourse B and stopped to dial her mother.

"Hello?" Jenna answered anxiously before the phone could ring a second time. Cassie's gut twisted as she realized her mother was sitting by the phone, half freaking out while waiting for news of her girls.

"Hi, Mom."

"Cassie!" Jenna's voice actually cracked. "For the love of God, I've been so worried about you."

"I'm fine, Mom." A lie. She felt like a heel for not returning her mother's calls earlier.

"Doctor Sherling said you left the hospital."

"True." *Here we go.*

"She couldn't talk to me too much about it because of all the legalities involved, but it sounded as if she wasn't sure you should be released."

"I know. But I'm fine." The image of the nurse in the white uniform floated through her mind. Real? Or imagined? *Real, damn it. Rinko gave you the earring!*

"I hope so."

"Has there been any word on Allie?" she asked, and mentally crossed her fingers.

"No." Jenna couldn't hide the sadness in her voice.

"What about the police? Do they have any leads?"

"None that they're sharing."

"Can't Shane get info?" she asked as other travelers rolled bags past her on the way to their gates. "I mean, he *was* the sheriff."

"Not on the force any longer. Just Joe Citizen."

"But, doesn't he know someone who will talk to him?"

There was a slight hesitation and then, "You know Shane, everything by the book."

In her mind's eye, Cassie saw the man who was her stepfather. Tall and kind of rugged-looking with a thick dark mustache and eyes that didn't miss anything. "This might be a time when he ignores the rules."

"There's just nothing to tell."

"That sucks," she said, moving into the pedestrian traffic.

A voice behind her asked, "Excuse me, is this the A Concourse?"

Cassie glanced over her shoulder to spy a woman who appeared to be in her late seventies or early eighties. A tiny, birdlike thing dressed in layers that included a down vest, she was peering at Cassie intently through magnified glasses that made her eyes appear owlish. She was holding a boarding pass in one hand and the handle of a tapestry-print roller bag with the other.

"This is C."

"Not A?" Gray eyebrows knitted as the older woman struggled to keep up with her.

Cassie pointed down the wide corridor. "A's over there. Past security, and the restaurant." Into the phone, she said, "Just a second, Mom."

"You're sure?" the woman asked, biting the edge of her lip. "I'm going to Seattle to see my great-grandson. Just born two weeks ago. I don't want to miss my flight." Her expression changed. "You look familiar, oh, I know, like that actress . . . oh, what's her name?"

"Jenna Hughes," Cassie said automatically. She'd heard the same remark time and time again. No one remembered her endeavors, but her mother was a different story.

"That's who it is!" She stared at Cassie long and hard. "A shame about her. So much tragedy in her life." She clucked her tongue as they passed a kiosk filled with University of Oregon Ducks clothing and paraphernalia. "Now I see it. Concourse A and B. Thank you!"

With a wave of the hand clutching the boarding pass, she hurried off, joining the flow of other travelers pulling roller bags and hauling large totes toward the A Concourse.

"Cassie? Where are you?" Jenna demanded, an edge of panic in her voice. "The airport."

She'd hoped to keep that tidbit of information under wraps. For now. "Look, Mom, I gotta go. I'm fine."

"What're you doing at the airport?"

"I'm going home."

"But your home's here . . . no, wait a minute. You're heading to LA?"

"I need my car and personal things," Cassie said as she threaded through the throng milling around security on her way to her gate.

"Are you sure that's a good idea?"

No, I'm not positive of anything. "Pretty sure."

A beat. "I would've come with you."

That's just what you need. Jenna wringing her hands, coming up with different ideas, her worry infecting you. "Aren't you in the middle of production of a play or something?" Ever since moving to Oregon, Jenna had helped out at the local theater, which Cassie thought was about as boring as it could get. Putting on plays in Falls Crossing, Oregon?

"Cassie," her mother reproached.

"And you'd have to leave Shane—"

"Cassie!" More sharply this time. "Nothing's more important than you and Allie, you know that."

She did know it, but right now, it wasn't enough. "Look Mom, I'm about out of battery for the phone. I'll call you once I touch down and power up."

"Cassie—"

"Later." She clicked off. She didn't have time to deal with Jenna or anyone else, for that matter. She was going to LA. Alone. And damn it, she was going to get some answers about her missing sister.

CHAPTER 6

Someone was following her! All the way to Southern California. Cassie had experienced the eerie feeling in the baggage claim area of LAX and then again, while waiting for a cab. Unseen eyes had followed her every movement.

Someone watching.

Someone waiting.

Her paranoia kicking into overdrive.

Don't buy trouble, she told herself, as she was dropped at her apartment without anyone accosting her. *Remember: It's all in your head.*

She watched the taxi pull from the curb, then walked around the huge stucco mansion to a private walkway. Still unnerved, she passed a manicured hedge then she hurried up the tiled steps to her apartment. After unlocking the door she stepped inside the space she'd rented for the past two years. Only then did she breathe a sigh of relief.

A quick look inside told her everything was as she'd left it except that now a fine layer of dust covered the coffee tables and counters. The potted ficus tree near the slider had given up the ghost, judging from the dry leaves littering the floor. Spiders had nested near the shower and the interior was sweltering, the air stale.

She'd thought she would feel some tug on her heartstrings upon returning, but found she couldn't grab her things and get out fast enough. The charm of this little one-bedroom unit, once a nanny's quarters tucked into an Old California–style home with arched hallways, red tile roof, and wrought-iron accents, was now lost on her. What had once been her haven, a place where she could get away from the noise of LA and the emotional stress of her family, now appeared tired and worn with the dust and dead insects trapped in the cobwebs in the corners, months-old magazines strewn over the coffee table.

Closing the door, she had a quick flash of the last time she'd seen Trent. He'd pounded frantically on the carved panels of the door, his fist banging loudly on the heavy wood. Watching him through the sidelight, she'd actually worried that he might break the window. As if he'd read her mind, he turned his attention to the old panes, his fist curled and raised. She'd held up her phone so that he could see her, that she was threatening to call 911, intending to place the call and have him hauled away by the cops. His jaw had been set, his knuckles bleeding, his eyes sparking fire as he glowered at her through the panes, but he'd hesitated.

She'd backed up a step, put the phone to her ear, and watched as he'd sent her a hard, killing look, uttered something she couldn't hear, then threw his hands over his head and walked stiffly away.

For damned ever.

"Good," she said now, though her voice sounded a little uneven. She hated herself for her weakness where he was concerned, but wouldn't even give herself the excuse of having just been released from the hospital. She'd always been a moron when it came to Trent. What kind of fool gets her heart broken not once, but twice, by the same man? What idiot marries the bastard after the first breakup and thinks things will change, that he'll love her forever, that he won't cheat on her? And especially with her own younger, more famous sister? "Stupid," she muttered under her breath and spied a framed picture on the narrow table near the door. The 5x7 was of Trent on their wedding day.

Maybe she'd toss it later.

Then again, maybe not.

She was still legally married to him.

Why hadn't she gone through with the divorce she'd threatened?

She cleared the sudden lump forming in her throat and decided she'd chalk up her inability to end an already-dead marriage to one more mental problem on her ever-growing list. Her eyes grew hot and she blinked hard rather than let a single teardrop fall. She'd cried her last tear for Trent Kittle. Her very last. Against her will she remembered that last fight, how his anger had radiated off him in waves and his fury had been etched in all the sharp angles of his face.

Shaking off his memory, she walked through the small apartment, which now seemed just an empty space with no heart, no soul. She probably should have let it go and moved months ago, during the filming of *Dead Heat*.

While Allie had moved to Portland and found her own place during shooting of the movie, Cassie, who was in far fewer scenes, had flown back and forth to LA or camped out at her mother's house in Falls Crossing, or sometimes, when she was beat, rented a room in a hotel located a few blocks from the set.

When she'd checked herself into the hospital, the few things she'd left in the hotel room had been transferred to her mother's house in Falls Crossing, to the very bedroom she'd occupied as a teenager. What had been a convenience at a low point in her life now seemed completely wrong. Uncomfortable. As soon as she figured out where she was going to end up, even temporarily, she'd get things moved, but she wasn't certain where she'd land. Back here in this retro apartment in LA? Or somewhere else entirely. Of course it depended upon what had become of Allie.

For what had to be the zillionth time, she tried to call her sister and for just as many times she heard that the voice mailbox associated with the phone was full. She texted her again. **Call me.** But she figured this text, like all of the other ones she'd sent, would show on the screen of her own phone as delivered but not read.

What had she expected?

She walked into the kitchen area where a yogurt container with a spoon sticking out of it was growing mold. She rinsed them both and put them into the dishwasher. After this small nod to housekeeping, she checked the refrigerator to find two bottles of chardonnay, a few bottles of water, and a cube of butter. Not much sustenance here. Next, she gathered her things: makeup, a few clothes, the mail, and her laptop, then locked the door behind her and wondered when she'd return for the rest. Her future was unclear, but it would stay that way until she found out what had happened to her sister.

Outside, she located her car, a seven-year-old Honda Accord parked where she'd left it, in the shade of a palm tree. With over a hundred thousand miles on the odometer and a crack in the driver's seat, the car was well used, but it didn't matter. What did was its ability to start, and it did that without a hiccup, the smooth little engine turning over on the first try.

Her first break.

The gas tank was half full, so she took off. As she entered the main street, she turned on the window spray and wipers to clean off the dust, bugs, and bird droppings from the glass. LA was a clogged network of side streets and freeways as usual and she had to wear sunglasses against the glare from the California sun. Soon she was at Allie's condo. The building was super-chic and modern, a direct opposite to her own residence.

She parked in an empty spot in the garage, one marked RESIDENTS ONLY, and took an exterior elevator to the third floor. Using the key she had made when Allie had once entrusted her to water the plants and pick up the mail while she was on location, Cassie stepped inside and drew a breath. The place was a mess, left so by the police as they'd searched the unit looking for clues to Allie Kramer's disappearance. Drawers and cupboards had been left open, furniture moved, fingerprint dust covering most surfaces, closet doors ajar.

As she walked through the spacious unit, Cassie felt as if she were walking on Allie's grave.

What're you doing here? What do you think you'll find? Something the police missed? C'mon . . . With their manpower, technology, skill, and expertise?

The simple truth was she was curious. Yes, she was searching for some clue as to the sister she desperately wanted to find, but there was also a morbid curiosity factor embedded inside her. She could get a closer glimpse into Allie's life, a glamorous existence that she, Cassie, had never experienced and never would. And the writer in her wanted more information. Unwittingly Allie's vanishing act had given her fodder for her next story and whetted her screenwriter's appetite.

She walked through the connecting rooms. Long, low couches were huddled around a sleek tile fireplace where gas flames appeared to float upward through clear glass stones. The fire was off now, but Cassie remembered sitting near it and reading lines with Allie, in one of their few moments of civility.

The mental images came in bits and pieces, some painfully sharp, others blurred and nearly forgotten. Then there were those that were missing altogether, like the night that Allie disappeared. Yes, they'd fought—there were images of the struggle burned deep into her brain—but a lot of that night was foggy at best, some hours simply unaccounted for. God, how could she forget . . . and why? Usually her periods of missing hours were preceded by emotional anguish, but she just couldn't remember, certainly not everything. She hated to think of the reasons, couldn't go there. Even for Allie.

Her heart squeezed a little, but she carried on, noticing, not for the first time, that on every stretch of wall space, pictures of Allie were framed and mounted, the smaller photos collected together, the larger portraits dominating a wall in the dining area or hung over the fireplace. More photos were placed on side tables and shelves, to the point it seemed as if Allie were immortalizing herself in some kind of shrine—an homage to vanity and narcissism. But a few spaces on the wall were empty. Noticeably so. As if taken down. By Allie? Had her sister told Cassie that she was having some of her favorites, the bigger ones, retouched or remounted, that she needed better frames? It seemed so, though Cassie was fairly certain she'd never been in the condo since they'd been taken down. Or maybe the police had needed them, or, more likely, someone on the force had been a fan and helped himself. Whatever the reason, it made her uncomfortable, gave her a weird vibe that didn't leave.

Down a short hallway, she entered Allie's bedroom with its gold star pressed into the door. A joke? Allie's wacky sense of humor?

Cassie didn't think so.

A messy king-size bed dominated the room. But the mattress had been stripped, the pink and silver duvet with matching sheets gone. As Cassie remembered, there had been a huge array of pillows atop the modern four-poster, but they, too, were missing, probably compliments of the police. Again, pictures of Allie filled the walls, but there were others on the dresser. And possibly some missing. Or was she wrong?

Several framed shots of Brandon McNary and Allie were on the nightstand and dresser. Cassie studied the photos and wondered if her sister had ever gotten over her costar. Theirs had been a volatile relationship and the tabloids had eaten it up. She, the daughter of Jenna Hughes; he, the only son of a wealthy, southwestern family. Allie had sworn she'd finally broken it off for good, but now Cassie wondered.

The attached bath was empty and the second bedroom was used as a closet where Allie's clothes and shoes were stored in massive floor-to-ceiling shelving, drawers, and racks. Positioned near the wide window, with its view of the Hollywood Hills, was a vanity complete with multiple drawers and mirrors that, despite the lights surround-

ing each reflective panel, could be adjusted to catch the right illumination and offer differing views.

She sat on Allie's stool and wondered what it would be like to be
the brainy-turned-beauty sister rather than the screwed up one? Catching her own reflection in one of the mirrors that had been turned in,
she saw her image repeated and repeated, getting smaller and more
indistinct in the echoing reflections until they disappeared in a tiny
blur. She was turning away when she saw something in the mirror.

A shadowy figure loomed behind her.

Her heart jolted and she jumped, knocking over a glass jar of
makeup brushes with her hand.

Biting back a scream, she twisted to find nothing but a gray curtain
draped to the floor. No person. No dark figure. Just an innocuous
length of fabric that her willing mind conjured into an evil presence.

Pull yourself together!

Shaken, she righted the jar, stuffed the brushes into it, then
stood.

Her cell phone buzzed.

Heart still pounding she glanced at the number on the screen,
digits she didn't recognize, couldn't place.

She let the call go to voice mail as she left Allie's home with no
more answers than she'd had when she'd entered. Making her way
to her car, she found a nasty note on the windshield about respect-
ing that the parking spaces were for "tenants only," then wadded the
note and climbed into the car. Geez, she'd been in the spot for less
than an hour and someone got pissed? But someone was probably
monitoring the surveillance setup in the garage, she thought as she
heard the ping indicating she had voice mail. She spied a camera
mounted high on a pillar, a red light winking to show that it was
monitoring this level of the lot.

"Fabulous," Cassie said tightly, and an urgency took over, a need
to get away from this place with its dark memories of Allie and the
prying eyes of hidden cameras. Shuddering, she zoomed out of the
exit, barely braking as she drove her Honda into the street, pigeons
fluttering out of her path as she squinted against the high intensity of
the sun.

"I thought you might know why she'd be at the airport." Jenna's
voice was filled with worry, a concern that came across the wireless
connection all too clearly.

Driving into town and talking on the phone illegally, Trent felt that tightness in the back of his neck that always accompanied conversations about Cassie. He wouldn't have answered his cell, but had seen that the caller was Jenna Hughes, so he was willing to risk the ticket. Cassie was always trouble—or in trouble—and because he hadn't yet pulled the trigger on the divorce, he felt she was still his responsibility. Kind of.

"Don't have a clue," he said, taking a corner a little too sharply and wondering why the hell his not-yet-ex-wife was taking a trip so soon after leaving the psychiatric ward of a hospital. The windshield wipers were slapping away the rain pouring from the heavy clouds overhead and the truck's wheels hummed against the wet asphalt, but Trent's thoughts were now centered on Cassie.

"I thought she may have talked to you."

Fingers curled over the steering wheel in a death grip, he turned off the highway and angled his old pickup into the outskirts of Falls Crossing. "Not for a while."

"You didn't see her at the hospital?" Jenna asked, but he suspected she knew the truth.

"Cass wouldn't see me. Refused to let me near her. I was, and am, persona non grata."

"But you're her husband."

"Doesn't mean much to Cass." He slowed for a stop sign. A Cadillac old enough to sport fins rolled through the intersection.

"I'm worried about her," Jenna admitted.

"Yeah."

"Aren't you?" The question had a bite to it.

"She's always a worry," he bit back, then mentally kicked himself. Jenna had always been fair with him, no matter how many times he'd screwed up. He pulled into a parking slot near the post office. "I haven't talked to Cassie since she and everyone else came back to reshoot the end of her last movie and Allie went missing. She called me and ranted and railed at me, thought I had something to do with Allie's disappearance and then I hauled her ass—I picked her up from the police station after a particularly rough interview. But you know all that."

Silence.

"Haven't heard from her since."

Jenna said through a tight throat, "She . . . she won't talk to me.

Barely takes my calls. I just thought . . . or hoped that she might have been in touch with you."

"Sorry."

Another long pause and he could almost see his famous mother-in-law pull herself together. "Me too."

Trent felt obliged to ask, "Any news on Allie?" though he knew there wasn't. If Allie Kramer or her body had been found it would be splashed all over the news, tabloids, and Internet. She'd been missing for over three weeks and *Dead Heat* was soon to premiere. Allie Kramer, its star, had disappeared before the last day of shooting, or more precisely, reshooting, of the ending for the film. No one had seen or heard from her since.

A catch in her voice, Jenna said, "Nothing yet."

"Damn."

She sighed. "Precisely."

He felt like a heel. "I'm sorry," he said again. It was a platitude. Heartfelt, but a platitude. As the days and weeks had passed, hope for finding Allie Kramer alive had diminished, though, now that the movie was to be released, interest in her fate and whereabouts was ramping to new levels. He knew from personal experience. As Cassie's husband of record and Allie's brother-in-law, he'd been dealing with the press himself. "Look, I'll give Cassie a call, see if she'll take it and let me know what's up."

"I appreciate it, Trent." She sounded weary. "Good-bye."

He stared at the screen a second or two after the call ended, then speed-dialed Cassie. Might as well get it over with.

The call connected, and he heard it ringing. "Come on," he said under his breath, his gut clenching at the thought of talking to her again. He dropped his visor down where a picture of her was clipped. In the shot her smile curved up on one side, a naughty little grin, her eyes sparkling green, her brows arched, her pointed chin at an angle, her tousled hair tossed behind one shoulder. Sexy. Seductive. Smart.

The line rang again.

His jaw clenched.

He waited through three more rings, but of course, she didn't pick up.

CHAPTER 7

Cassie grabbed an iced coffee from a Starbucks near La Cienega Boulevard and as she sipped it at an umbrella table on the sidewalk, she went through her phone messages again. Since leaving Portland, she'd collected four voice messages: one from her mother; another from Whitney Stone, a reporter who had dogged her before she'd entered the hospital; a third from Holly Dennison, who was a set designer and, if not a friend, an acquaintance; and the last, she noted, biting her lower lip, was from Trent.

Her mother had asked her to call, Whitney wanted to meet, and Holly had said, "Hey, I'm in LA. I think I saw you at the airport. Give me a call."

Finally, it had been Trent's turn. "It's me," and the timbre of his voice touched a forbidden part of her heart. "Jenna called. She's worried. Wants to know what's going on with you. She said you were in the airport or taking a trip." A pause. Cassie held her breath. "Give me a call when you can. Or her." Another pause and then her undoing, "Take care, Cass."

"As if you give a crap," she whispered, her throat instantly thick. That was the problem. If Trent showed her any hint of kindness whether heartfelt or fake, it got to her.

She erased all the messages, then checked her texts. Again, one from that reporter, Whitney Stone, asking to meet. No way. Not when Whitney Stone produced and reported for her own tell-all television show, a blend of Hollywood gossip and unsolved mysteries. Rumor had it *Justice: Stone Cold* was already in production with the Allie Kramer disappearance story. Cassie wanted no part of it. *Delete!* Another from her mother asking her to call. *Delete.* A third was from Holly, suggesting they get together since they were both in town.

That message she didn't immediately delete. Since Holly had worked on *Dead Heat* and was an acquaintance of Allie's, it made sense to meet her.

Still, Cassie hesitated. She sipped the coffee, watched people hurrying in and out of the coffee shop, or sitting like she was, laptop on the table or phone in hand or both as they drank from paper cups.

It was late afternoon now, a few clouds creating a haze over the lowering sun. She needed a plan. She'd left the hospital with no clear idea of what to do, how to locate Allie, how to go forward with her life. Her first impulse had been to check out Allie's apartment in Portland, fly south, grab her own things and her car, and snoop around a little down here, see what she could dig up.

And now as the sun sank lower in the sky and she watched the little birds pluck at bits of scones and whatever dropped near the tables, she wondered what her next move was. She knew she'd probably return to Portland, if only temporarily, as that was where, presumably, Allie had last been seen.

By you.

According to the police, you were the last person known to see her before she'd disappeared.

"Tell me about that night," Detective Rhonda Nash had asked in the stuffy, cinder-block interrogation room. In her forties, Cassie had guessed, she wore short, frosted hair that spiked above an oval face with no apparent laugh lines. Her gray suit was crisp, her open-throated blouse pressed. From the way she'd held herself, Cassie guessed Detective Nash was no stranger to the gym. "The last night you were with your sister."

"Nothing much to tell."

"What did you discuss?"

"The movie," Cassie had said. "We were both involved in *Dead Heat*."

"She was the star."

Behind rimless glasses, dark eyes had stared pointedly at Cassie, who guessed the detective had been searching for a reaction. "Yes." This was a fact the whole world knew, an unnecessary question.

"And you had, what? Four lines?" Had there been an underlying sneer in her question?

"Yes." Cassie had nodded as she'd somehow managed to keep her irritation from showing.

"She's become a pretty big name."

Cassie had waited.

"So, you talked about the movie." She'd glanced down at her notes. "What was the nature of the discussion?"

"We were both a little upset that we had to return to shoot the final scene."

"And why was that?"

"Because there was a test audience who didn't like the ending as it had been written and shot, so everyone involved in that last scene had to reschedule everything to come back here, to Portland."

"I meant why were you upset?"

"Allie wasn't thrilled that I made a minor adjustment to a scene."

"You made an adjustment?"

"I'm a writer, so I had an idea that the director liked."

"But this adjustment bothered her."

Big time. "She said so, yeah. And she was irritated because she was going to take a break from acting for a few months. Go over screenplays that were offered to her, make sure she found the right . . . 'vehicle.' That's what she said."

"And you?"

"I'm a screenwriter now and I was anxious"—*Wrong word! Wrong word!*—"eager to jump into a plot I'd been playing around with."

"So you'd rather write than act?"

Cassie had fielded this one before. "A lot of actors think they'd rather direct or produce or write. I chose writing."

"Because your acting career wasn't taking off."

"That's one reason," she'd admitted. "Yes."

"Unlike your sister's."

"I guess."

"Ever since her breakout role in that film . . . oh, what was it?" She'd actually snapped her fingers as if she'd forgotten the name of *Street Life*, a blockbuster hit in which Allie played a teenage prostitute who, a drug user, had found herself pregnant by a sixty-year-old john and, despite all the cards stacked against her, prevailed. The role had been gritty and dark, one Cassie had auditioned for but had been cast aside as "too old," in her early twenties. Allie had been eighteen but had been able to pull off the scared, desperate actions of a girl three years her junior.

"*Street Life.*"

"That's right." Nash had nodded. "You tried out for that role, didn't you?"

"I did."

"But Allie landed it."

"Yes."

"And there was talk of her being up for an Oscar, I think."

"She wasn't nominated."

"But the buzz was that she should have been."

"Her breakout role," Cassie had agreed as the detective had scribbled a note to herself even though the session was being taped.

"It had to be difficult for you that your kid sister got it and you didn't."

"She was better suited. Younger." Cassie's palms had begun to sweat and she'd stuffed them under her legs, kept her face relaxed, though Detective Nash had hit a sensitive nerve. That role of Penelope Burke was an actor's dream. In fact it had been Cassie's dream. Allie had only learned of it from her older sister and then decided to audition.

"I understand she beat you out of roles more than once," the detective had said as she scanned some pages from the file she'd brought into the small, airless room. "Three times?" She looked up expectantly.

"Uh . . . yes. Yes, I think that's right."

"You can't remember?" Skepticism. "Boy, I would have known, if it had been me."

"Three parts," Cassie had clarified, keeping the edge out of her voice. Obviously the cop had been badgering her, looking for a way to get her to explode and say something she'd regret.

"There were signs of a struggle at her apartment. A broken wineglass on the floor. Furniture slightly moved. Since you were the last one there, I thought you might tell me about it."

"We argued over the change to the script, and she got upset and dropped the glass."

"It wasn't more personal?"

"No." Another lie. She'd wanted to expand, to blame it all on sister stuff, sibling rivalry, but she'd thought it best to keep her answers short and to the point. Her lies and equivocations simple. So she could recall them when necessary.

Detective Nash's eyebrows had pinched together as if she were deep in thought. "Your sister and your husband had gotten together, hadn't they?"

Cassie had seen red and her fingers had curled over the edge of her chair, her fingertips glancing off wads of gum. "While we were separated, Allie and Trent had gone out," she acknowledged though Trent had insisted it had all been platonic, both parties concerned about Cassie. All bull, but she hadn't admitted it in the interview. In fact, she hadn't admitted to much, not when the questions had gotten more personal about her marriage nor when the detective had probed about her relationship with each of her parents. Detective Nash had even brought up the horrid ordeal she and Allie had gone through at the hands of their mother's stalker, but Cassie had held on to her cool.

It had been obvious they considered her a suspect in her sister's disappearance. She'd been one of the last, if not *the* last, person to see Allie before she vanished. The fact that she had no alibi, that she'd been alone on the night Allie had seemingly evaporated into thin air, had made her a "person of interest" in Allie Kramer's missing person's case. As such, she'd been under surveillance, had felt people following her, watching her, and knew the police were discussing her motives and opportunity to do away with her sister. Paranoia had become full-blown.

Was it any wonder she'd checked herself into Mercy Hospital where she was under constant observation and psychiatric care? The staff at Mercy had been employed to help her, not be suspicious of her.

As she took her final sip of her coffee, her phone vibrated across the table and she snagged it. Another text from Holly.

In Santa Monica. How about drinks near the pier? Love to get together.

She could have a drink. She would talk to Holly, then head back to her condo. Her plan, loose as it was, included cleaning out the apartment, giving her notice, poking around LA for a few days, and finally heading north. Maybe at night. Traffic would be easier then, and she could start her drive up the coast, take the PCH toward San Francisco and chill out, enjoy the view of the Pacific lapping along the California shore, then cut over to the Five, sometime along the way. Or she could freeway it from here and the drive would take sixteen hours or so.

She tossed her empty cup into the trash and climbed into the heat of her car where she second-guessed herself. What good would meeting Holly do?

Maybe it will do nothing, not help at all, but it sure as hell won't hurt, will it?

Before she could talk herself out of the meeting, she texted:

Sure. How about The Sundowner? I can be there in 20 min or so. It's still happy hour.

Before she could jab her keys in the ignition, her phone chirped and she read: I'm there!

Cassie glanced at the rearview mirror. Worried eyes stared back at her.

What're you doing? You don't even like Holly. If she knew where Allie was, she would have told the police already. She can't help you.

"Yeah. Well, no one can," she said aloud.

Jamming her car into reverse, she backed out. A silver Mercedes that had been hovering grabbed her spot, nearly hitting her in an effort to park near the café. Cassie restrained herself from flipping off the driver as she pulled out of the parking lot. Instead, she scrounged around and found a pair of dusty sunglasses in a side pocket of the car and slid them onto the bridge of her nose.

She prayed the gods of traffic would rain grace on the 405 heading north.

Otherwise, the drive would be a bitch.

CHAPTER 8

Judging by the empty glasses, Holly was deep into her second mojito—or was it her third?—when Cassie arrived at The Sundowner. Half a block from the beach, the bar filled part of the basement of a trendy hotel in Santa Monica. Already the after-work crowd was starting to gather, people knotted in groups inside the darkened interior, standing room only, the noise of conversation escalating.

"Hey, I thought you were going to ditch me!" Holly accused as she spied Cassie wending her way through the tightly spaced bistro tables packed between a wall of booths and a long, glass-topped bar.

"I would have called or texted if I wasn't going to show," Cassie said. She eyed the table. A tiny copper-colored mug with a slice of lime perched on the rim sat on the table in front of the only empty seat. Obviously the drink was intended for her.

"A Moscow Mule," Holly said, licking a bit of mint from her upper lip. Petite, with her hair spiked on end, the current color being jet black, she waved Cassie into her seat. Her makeup was perfect, full lips glossy, skin smooth, eye shadow glittering a bit. Holly had an impish charm about her and had, she'd admitted, played the character of Tinkerbell more times than she wanted to admit. She'd started her career at Disneyland and over the years gotten into acting, primarily commercials, before the roles had dried up and she'd been forced to turn her attention to set design. A true artist, she'd worked her way up through the ranks to eventually become the lead designer on *Dead Heat*.

"For me?" Cassie asked.

"Umm-hmm."

Cassie slid onto the padded bench.

"Basically it's vodka and ginger beer and . . ." Holly's neatly plucked eyebrows drew together as she thought, her gaze falling onto the drink again. "And, oh, yeah, lime. Duh!" She mock-slapped her forehead, then had another sip of her drink. "Thought you might like it."

"I've had 'em before." She glanced at Holly's mojito. "Why aren't you having one?"

"Vodka's not my thing." A forced shudder. "One too many martinis on New Year's Eve a few years back." She rolled her expressive eyes. "Man, was that a hangover? God. It seemed to last forever. I switched to gin and . . ." She lifted her glass, hoisting it in a toast. "Rum. Yum."

Holly seemed to be already starting to feel the effects of her drinks. Her smile was a little off-center, some of her words slightly slurred. "So," she said, eyeing Cassie, "what're you doing back here anyway?"

"I live in LA."

"But it's been a while since you really lived in California," she said. "Ever since you and Trent . . . you know." She ducked her head into her shoulders and waggled it as if she couldn't quite find the right word. ". . . split, I guess you'd say, you haven't stuck around much."

"I was busy."

"Yeah . . ." Another long swallow. A quick check of her phone as over the noise of the bar it had pinged, indicating texts had come in.

Cassie wasn't going to argue, nor explain her relationship or non-relationship with her husband to Holly Dennison or anyone else for that matter.

As if she hadn't noticed Cassie's discomfiture Holly said, "So, I was kind of surprised when I saw you at LAX. I didn't even know you were out of the hospital."

"I was just released." A bit of a fib. Not exactly "released."

Holly waved her hand as if flitting aside any excuse. "Anyway, I was waiting for my bag there in the claim area. Just got back from Phoenix visiting my mom. Talk about a trip. I swear she's losing it. So I'm waiting and waiting for my damned bag, texting my boyfriend and out of the corner of my eye, I see you walking out the doors. I yelled and waved at you, made myself look like an idiot, but . . . I guess you didn't hear me. I couldn't just leave my bag on the carousel, y'know. It's the only Louis Vuitton I'll ever own." She made a face. "Anyway, by the time I grabbed my bag and tried to catch up, I saw you getting into a taxi. And that was that."

"I didn't hear you."

A waitress was serpentining through the tables and Holly, catching her eye, twirled her finger, signaling another round.

"Hey, no. I just started this," Cassie said, and thought of all of the drugs she'd recently taken while in the hospital. How much was still in her bloodstream? Should she mix alcohol and God-only-knew what else?

Holly grinned. "Then you'd better catch up."

The waitress, a willowy blonde in a white shirt and black skirt, appeared. "Two more?" she asked.

"I'm good," Cassie assured her while Holly shot her a disgusted look.

"I'll have another. Of these." Holly hoisted her glass and when the waitress cast another glance at Cassie, she shook her head. After she moved to the next table, Holly turned to Cassie and said, "I just don't get why anyone would voluntarily check themselves into a nuthouse."

"Pressure. Stress."

"Because of the Allie thing, yeah, okay . . ." Holly nodded, her head wobbling a bit. "Whoa . . . maybe I'd better slow down." She let her drink go untouched as she leaned back in the booth. "So what do you think happened to her?"

Cassie slowly shook her head and stared at the copper cup. "Don't know. It's upsetting, to say the least." She thought about her mother's grief, her fears, and once again, felt as if she were the worst daughter on earth for not communicating more with Jenna. She grew silent and Holly was quick to fill the ensuing lapse in the conversation.

"I wasn't that close to Allie, but if you ask me, she was a head case . . . oh, sorry, that's probably a sensitive subject."

"I'm okay."

"Good. Good. But it was the whole man thing with Allie, y'know? From one to the other. I mean, I'm not one to judge, hell, who wouldn't want to hop in a few of the beds she warmed, you know what I mean? This isn't a judgment call—God knows I'm no saint—but it wasn't just casual sex with her, was it?"

"What do you mean?"

"I don't mean to get too personal, but didn't she go after some of your boyfriends, even your husband?" Holly held up her hands, palms outward, stopping any answer Cassie would make. "Sorry . . . sorry . . . I should leave Trent out of it. But Brandon McNary? She swore she was over him, right? I mean, I heard it over and over again, and they barely spoke on the set of *Dead Heat.*"

"They'd broken up just before it started shooting."

"I know, but I got this feeling, call it a vibe or female intuition or whatever, that she was still in love with him."

"McNary? Nah . . ." Cassie was skeptical, but she recalled the pictures of Allie and Brandon in Allie's bedroom.

The waitress deposited the new drink and Holly actually smacked her lips. "She still had a thing for him," she insisted.

Cassie shrugged and nursed her Moscow Mule as customers continued to drift into the bar. The decibel level had risen to the point that Holly was nearly shouting in order for Cassie to hear her. After Holly downed her last drink, they paid their tab, splitting the lopsided bill, and the minute they stepped away from their table, two couples who had been eyeing it descended. Each claimed ownership rights, and a squabbling match ensued.

Outside, the sun was dipping into the Pacific, the sky striped in vibrant hues of orange and pink. A cool breeze blew inland and rustled the fronds of the tall palms guarding the entrance to the hotel, and Cassie was reminded why she loved this part of California as she watched Rollerbladers, dog walkers, and runners vying with pedestrians on the long stretch of sidewalk raised above the beach.

"You ever talk to anyone from the movie?" Holly asked.

"I've been kind of out of it."

They were walking along the sidewalk toward the parking space that Cassie had claimed.

"Yeah, but not totally, right?"

Cassie wasn't sure where this was going, but admitted, "Recently I spoke to Lucinda Rinaldi. I visited her in a rehab facility."

"She gonna be okay?"

"I don't know. She was still struggling to walk, so it's going to be a while."

"I bet she'll sue."

"Maybe. It was sure as hell traumatic."

"For everyone," Holly said. "God, I still have nightmares. I can't imagine what she's going through." She rubbed her arms as if experiencing a sudden chill.

As they rounded a corner Cassie added, "I saw Brandon McNary, too, well, actually I ran into him at Allie's apartment building in Portland. Turns out he lives across the hall. Or he did while they were filming."

"Wow, he still has the place?" Holly fumbled inside her bag and found her phone, quickly scanned her texts again, then pulled out a pair of oversize sunglasses.

"I guess."

"Convenient." She slid the shades onto her nose. "You haven't talked to Arnette? The man thinks he's God, y'know. Got one nomination from the Academy and suddenly, his head swells up and he's like above everyone else."

Cassie shook her head. "Not since right after the shooting on the set."

"You were there," Holly remembered.

"One of my few scenes had to be reshot and so, yeah, I talked to him that night, but it's all kind of a blur. He called me the next day and also my mom. He was trying to get hold of Allie . . . but . . ." She shrugged, felt the dying sun's warmth against her back. ". . . by then she was missing." She slid Holly a glance. "For what it's worth he said he was concerned."

Holly snorted. "His star flat out disappears and someone's shot on his production and he's 'concerned'? He's a prick. Ask anyone who's ever worked with him."

"Have you run into anyone from *Dead Heat*?"

"A few, but everyone's into their own thing. Little Bea's out of the country, I think, on location in London. At least that's what Laura Merrick says. She still does my hair and makeup sometimes, so I get some info from her." She shot Cassie a glance as Cassie pulled her keys from her purse and hit the keyless lock for her Honda. The little car responded with a chirp and a flash of lights. "And I heard that Sig Masters's lawyer told him to keep quiet. Since he was the, you know, 'shooter,' it could have been big trouble. Or bigger trouble if Lucinda had died. And she could have. I think the bullet just missed her heart or aorta or something."

Cassie hadn't heard that. "Sig thought the gun was the prop."

Holly lifted her shoulders and dropped them again. "Who really knows? Anyway, because of the ongoing investigation and his role, whether intentional or not, and the threat of a lawsuit, he's keeping his mouth shut." She pretended to zip her own lips closed.

"Probably good advice."

"You know, I wouldn't put a lawsuit past Lucinda to sue everyone she can. She's such a freakin' bitch and she's always after money, that's why she came to Hollywood, to make a fortune and when it didn't turn out that way, she tried dating rich guys. Then, she discovered lawsuits. She's already been involved with a couple. Don't think she got much, though. If she did, she didn't say and there's like no new Ferrari in her garage or anything. Everyone in this goddamned town is so damned paranoid, so worried about saving their own skin, and your sister is missing! Maybe worse." She was still slurring a little, but she seemed steady on her feet.

"Are you driving?"

They paused at Cassie's car. Holly added, "You know I ran into Cherise at the fitness center. The one where we all go. Well, Allie went there, too."

Cherise Gotwell had been Allie's personal assistant.

"And get this—" Holly touched Cassie on the forearm and teetered on her four-inch heels. Her fingers tightened and she righted herself. "Sorry. I guess I had one too many and before you ask again, no, I'm not driving. My apartment is only a few blocks off the beach. You're gonna drive me."

"Fair enough. Get in."

Holly wobbled around the back of the car and slid into the passenger seat. Again she checked her phone.

"Someone trying to get hold of you?"

"Not really. Just, you know, talk." She sighed. "Well, that's not really the truth. I might've told a couple of people that I was meeting with you and they're curious, like about how you're doing and if you've seen Allie . . . crap like that."

Cassie did a slow burn. "Who?"

"People who know you."

"Who?" Cassie demanded.

"Like Cherise."

"Anyone else?"

"People you don't know."

"Oh, great. Gossip. Thanks so much, Holly."

"Hey, no offense."

Cassie's stomach was churning. "They could talk to me themselves instead of talking behind my back. Especially Cherise. Damn it." Angrily Cassie flicked on the ignition and pulled down her visor.

Holly nodded and seemed a little rueful, but it didn't last long. "I saw Cherise after yoga class and she casually mentioned that she's going to work for Brandon McNary. Just like that. Like it was no big deal." Struggling with her seatbelt, Holly glanced up at Cassie and gave her a *can-you-believe-that-crap?* look. The seat belt clicked. "She always was a bitch."

Cassie didn't comment. As she backed out and took directions from Holly to her apartment that was considerably more than "a few blocks" from the beach, her companion rambled on about how everyone in Allie's entourage from bitchy Cherise, her assistant, to Laura, the makeup and hair stylist, had been searching for new jobs, backstabbing each other as if it were necessary to find one, probably all calling Holly for any gossip she had on the Kramer sisters. Cassie forced her voice to be level, for the anger to dissipate. "Everybody needs to work," Cassie muttered.

"Not for pricks, bitches, and dickheads. Oh, wait." Holly paused dramatically as if struck by a sudden truth. "I'm one of the bitches." Barely able to see over the dash, she pointed a manicured finger at the glass and steel apartment building that rose seven floors into the sky. "That's it. Home sweet home. Just pull in there, to the side entrance." She indicated a back alley and Cassie nosed her Honda around a planter with lavender plants so lush the blooms scraped the side of the car. "A little close, aren't you?" Holly complained.

"Shut up," Cassie teased. "You got a ride, didn't you?"

Holly giggled.

Cassie let the car idle as Holly reached for the door handle. As she clambered out, she said, "Hey! Have you seen the trailer? For *Dead Heat*?"

"It's out already?" Cassie asked, a chill running through her as she thought about seeing Allie on the screen. She didn't want to think it, didn't want to believe it, but there was a chance that the movie might be the last time Allie's image would ever be caught on film. *She's not dead.*

The nurse in the old uniform's words came back to her and she clung to them.

"Just out," Holly was saying. She looked over her shoulder as she pushed the door open and stepped outside. "I caught it last night, before one of the late shows."

"And?"

"It was okay. Even good, I think." She leaned into the interior. "But it was weird, you know. Seeing Allie up on the screen. So . . . vibrant. So alive." Holly appeared to sober up a bit as her gaze met Cassie's for a second. "I just wish I knew what happened to her."

Cassie nodded and her mood darkened even more. "We all do."

"I know, I know." Holly was nodding. She cleared her throat as if she, too, were emotional. "Thanks for the ride."

"No problem."

Holly closed the door, then veered a little unsteadily toward the side entrance.

Attempting to shake her thoughts from Allie, Cassie managed to turn her car around in the tight parking lot and eventually eased her Honda into the steady stream of traffic. Night was falling and in the dusk, streetlights began to illuminate the city, a place she'd called home as a child and then again after she'd fled Falls Crossing. She'd never felt at home in the small town, the horror of her captivity by a lunatic only adding to her hatred of all things Oregon. The night terrors and fears, the feeling of abject vulnerability and, yes, paranoia, hadn't left her when she'd headed south after her high school graduation.

Maybe that's why she'd wanted Allie to join her. Familiarity. Safety. And maybe that's why she'd fallen for Trent, whom she'd met in Oregon. Maybe that's why she'd foolishly ended up marrying him.

"Don't go there," she warned herself, checking the rearview to catch the clouds in her eyes before looking farther back, to the street and the headlights crowding behind her. She felt that same little prickle of anxiety skitter up her neck and burrow into her hairline, digging deep into her brain. Was a car following? Maybe a silver SUV of some kind? Or was she mistaken? How could she tell in the sea of vehicles that swelled around her?

Impossible.

And fruitless. Ten cars could be tailing her and she wouldn't know which they were, not in this throng of vehicles.

"Get over your scaredy self," she warned.

She tried to concentrate on the road ahead but found herself eyeing her rearview mirror several times, making certain that someone wasn't silently tracking. The eerie feeling of someone watching her had been explained, at least when she was leaving the airport. Holly had seen her and tried to chase her down. There was no danger here.

She took the side streets near her home.

No car followed.

No vehicle slowed at the corner, then kept going.

No suspicious van kept a long distance from her, then cruised by the massive house that sheltered her apartment from the street.

No. It was all in her mind.

Letting out her breath, she parked, locked the car on the fly, and felt more at ease than she had in days. She walked back through her apartment door, dropped her keys onto the kitchen counter, then found a glass and poured herself a drink of water from the faucet over the sink. She made a note to herself to get some bottled water as she took a long swallow. Then she took out her phone, leaned against the counter, and listened to the message from Trent again.

The sound of his voice called up memories best forgotten. The deep timbre, the slight bit of a drawl reminding her of his Texas childhood, his inflection.

Her hand tightened on the phone as she reminded herself that she despised him. When the message finished, she considered playing it once more, just to hear him and allow herself to be taken back to a time when they'd been happy. Before he'd been tempted by Allie. Before he'd admitted as much. Before she'd realized their marriage had no chance. Before her sister had disappeared. Her throat thickened. Unshed tears burned behind her eyes.

"Idiot," she whispered, not knowing if she was thinking of him or herself as she quickly erased the message. It irritated the hell out of her that he had the gall to phone on behalf of her mother.

Nonetheless, before her cell's battery completely gave up the ghost, she punched in the digits of a familiar number.

It was time for that talk Jenna wanted so desperately.

CHAPTER 9

"I'll be fine," Cassie reassured her mother for what had to be the dozenth time in their telephone conversation. She was standing in the kitchen, one hip resting against the counter near the sink and staring out the window where in the coming twilight she spied a black cat on the top of the fence near the bougainvillea. Of course Jenna was worried, she thought, watching as the cat, ever patient, stalked a tiny bird fluttering in the blooms. With Allie missing and Cassie checking herself out of the mental hospital and hopping a flight to LA, Jenna was obviously attempting not to freak out about the safety of her kids.

Because they were both adults.

"I'm trying not to be a mother bear, you know, overprotective and all, but . . . I worry, Cass. You know it. And with Allie missing . . ." Her voice trailed off and, damn it, Cassie imagined Jenna struggling against tears.

Cassie turned away from the window and closed her eyes. "I know. I get it." She felt bad. Her mother, who had been famous and yes, rich at one time, had lost a lot in her life. Jenna's sister, Jill, had been killed in a freak accident while filming *White Out,* a movie produced by Jenna's husband, Robert Kramer, a film that, because of the tragedy, had never been released. Losing Jill had been a horrible blow. Losing Allie would devastate Jenna. "I'll be back soon."

"Promise?"

"Yeah."

"How soon?"

"Couple of days. I'll keep you posted."

A pause. Probably Jenna was remembering all the times Cassie, as

a rebellious teen, had lied through her teeth and broken more promises than she could recall.

"All right," Jenna acquiesced.

Cassie envisioned her mother's face, worry lines evident between
her eyebrows, green eyes clouded with concern, upper teeth gnaw-
ing at her lower lip. "I'll let you know when I'm close," she said.

"You're sure your car will make it?"

"Positive," she answered too quickly. Another lie. She had no idea
how dependable the car would be, but she covered it up. "Hey, it's a
Honda. They run forever. Come on, Mom, don't freak out about that."

"Okay. I'll check that one off the list." Jenna actually chuckled
weakly. "I'll see you soon then."

"Yes. And Mom?"

"Yeah?"

"Next time, don't call Trent, okay? He and I are over."

"You say so, but—"

"Don't bring up the marriage thing. I'll take care of it. But now he
doesn't need to know anything about me. It's . . . what I do is none
of his business."

"Got it." Jenna waited a beat. "So listen, when you get up here, to
Oregon, you can camp out in the space over the garage until you find
a place, if you don't want to stay in your old room."

"I'm not seventeen."

"I know. That's the problem," Jenna admitted.

The conversation stalled again before Cassie said, "Listen, I've
gotta run."

"Sure. Me too. Love you."

"Love you, too," Cassie said automatically and cut the connection.
She plugged the phone into its charger and attempted to shake off
the oppressive feeling that she wasn't good enough, hadn't mea-
sured up, had always been a problem for her mother. The feeling was
like a bad taste that lingered, something you couldn't rinse away or
spit out no matter how you tried. And the fact that Allie had come to
LA at Cassie's urging and had ended up missing only made that sensation dig a little deeper, like needle-sharp talons slicing into Cassie's
brain, making it bleed with guilt. Jenna would be horrified if she realized how Cassie felt, so, Cassie promised herself, her mother would
never know. And somehow, she, Cassie, would solve the problem.
First step? Locating Allie.

Making her way to the postage-stamp-sized bathroom shower,
she stripped off her clothes and let them fall, then turned on the

spray. The old pipes creaked a bit and a fine mist, the best her ancient showerhead could deliver, started to steam up the bathroom that felt small enough to be configured for an airliner. She cracked the tiny window, then let the water wash over her.

In her mind's eye, she saw her sister on the set of *Dead Heat*, playing the terrified, deranged heroine of the film. Allie's skin had been pale, her big eyes round with fear as she'd understood that her lover, played with a feverish passion by Brandon McNary, might kill her. The image was from a poster made specifically for the movie with Shondie Kent, Allie's character, staring into a broken mirror, her lover visible between the cracks.

Allie and Brandon had been perfectly cast, their on-screen chemistry palpable as they'd made love or fought, their combustible relationship offscreen exploding during filming. Though they'd avoided each other when not on the set, while the cameras were rolling, they'd come alive, their interaction believable, the sparks flying. Brandon's sizzling looks coupled with Allie's sultry sexuality created a passion the viewer could almost feel.

Cassie shook the vision from her head, letting the spray of the water rinse the day's sweat and frustrations from her body. Of course she knew Allie was a remarkable actress. Her talent was obvious. That wasn't the issue, nor really was Cassie's lack of success. The problem was their relationships with Jenna. Both daughters had "mommy issues" where Jenna Hughes was concerned. Never had it been more obvious than the last time the sisters had collided, the night before Allie's disappearance. Cassie had made the fateful mistake of wanting to discuss the tweaks to the script of *Dead Heat* before the final day of the reshoot. Allie had already voiced her concerns, after all Cassie had a bit part in the movie and hadn't written the script, but both the writer and director had liked the subtle change. Sure, Allie had lost a little screen time and Cassie, cast as the heroine's sister-in-law, had picked up those precious minutes.

Allie had perceived it, as always, as a way for Cassie to garner favor at Allie's expense.

All of which was a lie.

Cassie had driven to her sister's Portland residence through the driving rain, second-guessing herself, all the while wondering if she'd made a huge mistake. As the windshield wipers struggled with a deluge from the heavens, Cassie had squinted against the glare of headlights and told herself she needed to have it out with her sibling once and for all. She'd intended to straighten out any misconceptions and

had hoped beyond hope that all their adolescent insecurities and unresolved issues would be put to bed.

What a pipe dream!

The meeting started off rocky as it was immediately obvious that
Allie had somewhere else she would rather be. Though she didn't admit
as much, she'd continually glanced at the decorative clock mounted
in the dining area. At least three times she received texts on her cell
phone. She responded quickly to them, all the while trying to end
her conversation with Cassie.

"This isn't a good time," she said even before admitting Cassie
into the suite. "I'm really tired." As Cassie hung her dripping jacket
over the arm of a modern hall tree, she added, "I just haven't been
feeling all that well." A lie. One she didn't bother keeping up herself
as she offered Cassie a glass of red wine. Cassie had declined while
Allie poured herself a hefty glassful. From the open bottle on the
table, Cassie guessed it wasn't her first drink of the evening.

It was after eight when they started the conversation. Cassie said,
"I wanted to talk about the change to the script."

"What's done is done. Everyone including Arnette is on board."
Allie had sounded so damned flippant.

"Everyone but you."

"Yeah, well, who cares what I think? I'm just the lead." She buried
her nose in her drink and took a long swallow.

As Allie glowered from a position near the windows, Cassie had
tried to explain why she'd rewritten the scene, how the little change
had improved the ending and added to her character's motive and—

"It's all bullshit!" Allie cut her off. She stalked to the bar separating
the kitchen from the dining area and poured herself another glass.
"This is *not* about adding to the movie, it's about getting the last word.
Literally." She jammed the cork into the bottle and picked up her
glass. "So you can feel good about yourself."

"No, that's not why—"

"Of course it is!" She took back her position near the floor-to-ceiling
windows. One arm wrapped around her slim waist, the other tipping
her glass to her lips, she eyed her sister. "It's always what it's about."
Rain drizzled down the windows behind her, blurring the lights of
the city and distorting the faded reflection of the interior.

"Why do you always make this a competition?" Cassie demanded,
growing irritated.

"Because it fucking is. Always." Another long gulp.

"Only if you make it—"

"No, if *you* make it one. It's you, Cassie. Always you who pushes me." She was getting agitated, her eyes avoiding Cassie's, her lips twisted down. "Face it. You're selfish and self-centered and . . . mean."

Cassie struggled to hold her tongue, glancing meaningfully at the pictures of Allie lining the walls, shelves, and slim wooden mantel mounted over the stones of the fireplace.

"Don't even go there," Allie sniped.

But it was too late. Cassie rose to the bait. "Yeah? Well, it sure sounds as if you're describing yourself."

Allie's eyes flashed. "You're just jealous. I made it big. And that bothers you. That I'm a . . ."

"Star?" Cassie interjected as Allie, in an uncharacteristic bout of humility, couldn't finish what was obviously on the tip of her tongue.

Allie hesitated. "Well, yeah, I guess I'm a celebrity."

"You guess?"

"What about you? You're a . . ." She shrugged dramatically, letting the incomplete sentence hang in the air as she took a long swallow from her glass.

"Say it," Cassie encouraged as her own temper had flared hotter. "I'm a what?"

Allie remained quiet.

Cassie advanced, stepping around a chair. "A what?" she said again.

"Fill in the blank." Allie drained her glass and her hand trembled.

"Say it."

Allie swallowed hard. She looked as if she were fighting a losing battle with emotions she didn't want revealed. Surprisingly her eyes sheened and for a second Cassie remembered Allie as she had once been, a scared little girl caught up in a monstrous scheme that nearly killed her mother. Cassie's heart twisted, but she didn't fall victim to her own raw feelings as she saw some other emotion lurking beneath Allie's teary facade, something that ran far deeper and darker. Something dangerous.

"Just get out," Allie ordered.

Cassie closed in on her sister. "Not before you say it. I'm . . . what?"

"I don't know. Doesn't matter."

"Say it, damn it." The air crackled, but when Allie wouldn't respond, Cassie said, "Loser?" Allie's glass slipped from her fingers to crack and bounce against the hardwood. "Or maybe just plain old failure?" Cassie pushed.

"That's a start," her younger sister finally got out.

"Maybe a bitch?"

Allie's lips twisted, her facade slipped for a millisecond. But Allie was an uncanny actress, one who could easily turn her emotions on and off and she recovered with, "*Definitely* a bitch."

That sounded more like Allie. "Then maybe we're not just sisters, maybe we're more like twins," Cassie said tightly.

"*Puleeez*. We are not alike," Allie insisted, pointing at Cassie. "You know the difference between us?" She'd paused for effect, her elfin face expectant, her chin tipped upward. Without much makeup a fine dusting of freckles still bridged her perfect little nose.

"I'm sure you're going to tell me."

Cassie could click off the traits that distinguished Allie from her. Allie had been shyer as a young woman and blessed with a nearly photographic memory, which made it as easy for her to quote Shakespeare as find applications for the Pythagorean theorem or whatever in the third grade. Allie had been a brainiac turned computer nerd who'd hated school as it had bored her. Improbably, she'd blossomed into a beauty and eventually conquered Hollywood and was on her way to captivating the American public. Cassie had been, for the most part, a failure. Though tougher and bolder than her little sister, Cassie didn't have the drive and the all-consuming ambition that were both integral parts of what made up Allie Kramer.

Allie reminded Cassie, "You were practically a dropout in school and after barely graduating, you left, not because of some big dream you'd had to follow in Mom's footsteps and become an actress. Uh-huh. You ran away, not *to* something, but from your shitty life in Oregon." Bingo. The truth. Ugly as it was. Inwardly Cassie recoiled but tried not to show how much her words hurt. "So, Cassie, how did that work out for you?" Allie's voice shook a bit and her eyes glistened with unshed tears, but she stared hotly at her sister.

"I—"

"What?" She turned her palms to the ceiling, silently suggested she had no clue as to what her sister was about to say, but before Cassie could speak, Allie went on. "And don't bring up the writing, okay? That's insulting to those of us who can act. Writing's just an excuse. Every damned actor who can't make it thinks he or she will write or maybe direct. And you know what?" she asked, her perfect little chin projecting, fury radiating from her. "Most of them fail. Even if they end up writing a book about their own pathetic lives, it's usually ghosted. Someone else does all the real work, the real composing. So face it. You're a mess, Cassie. A mental case. A weak woman who can't even keep her own husband from straying."

Cassie's jaw had hardened. That was below the belt.

But Allie wasn't finished. "Trent and you? You know it's a joke!"

"He's my husband."

"And he wants to fuck me."

Cassie's guts clenched. "And that's what you live for, isn't it? Making men, *any* man, want you. Even the married ones. What does that say about you?"

"What does it say about them?" she countered. "Or their wives? So who's really to blame?"

"Not you, obviously." Cassie's voice had been low and menacing. She'd felt her eyes narrow as her temper took over. "Never you, right?"

"Don't turn this around. Don't blame me. Okay, finally, we've hit what you're good at: blaming me."

"Untrue."

"Ask Mom."

"Leave her out of it." So now they were down to the bones of it. Their mother. No, make that their beautiful, successful mother who was at the heart of all their disputes. Not that Jenna hadn't been fair to each of them, loving both of her daughters equally, if differently. And truth to tell, Cassie had been a lot more difficult a daughter to raise. She knew that.

"I wish to hell that you weren't my sister!" Allie suddenly shouted, her voice rising.

Cassie had wanted to strike out, to knock her down, to wipe that superior attitude off her face and grind it into the ground. She would have loved to let loose and get into one of the fights they'd had as children. When she'd been bigger than her younger sister, when she'd always prevailed, when she could make Allie with one look go running to their mother.

"Maybe I'd just better go," Cassie said woodenly. "I wanted you to understand why I made the suggestions I did to the script, but you're not interested. It's just making things worse, so forget it."

"You made those changes to prove a point. Because you hate me."

"You've got to be kidding."

"You've always hated me. Been jealous as hell and regretted the day you suggested, no, *begged* me to come down here. But then I took you up on the dare, started auditioning for parts against you and blew you out of the water! Dad saw it the minute I took my first screen test and he dropped all of his interest in you because of me. *I was his chance to revive his own career as a producer.*" Her smile was almost evil. "Until I ditched him. Just like he dumped us."

Cassie's heart was pounding in her ears. "This is ridiculous," she whispered, all the while knowing Allie wasn't completely off the mark as far as her original intentions of getting Allie to come to California. Cassie had begged her to come, then regretted it when Allie's celebrity had skyrocketed. But over time Cassie had mellowed, accepted that Allie was the better actress, the true star in the family. She didn't want the argument to escalate, so she tried to back down. As rain pummeled the windows, Cassie used every device she'd learned from years in therapy to walk away before things got worse. She backed up a step, mentally counted to ten, then said, "I'm outta here," and headed for the entry hall and her jacket.

"Sure," Allie mocked. "Run away. That's what you're good at."

Cassie fought the urge to bite back. This was childish. Stupid. Like all their dumb sibling stuff. She jammed her arms into the jacket's sleeves.

"You're absolutely pathetic," Allie charged.

"I guess we're even," she stated flatly. "Because I wish you weren't my sister, either."

At that last salvo, Allie hurried after her, standing only inches from her as Cassie cinched the jacket's belt tightly around her waist. "Get out and don't come back."

"You've been a pain in the ass forever, Allie." Reaching for the door handle, she made the colossal mistake of adding, "I wish you'd never been born!"

Slap! Allie's palm struck.

Pain exploded in Cassie's head as it spun.

She stumbled back a step, recoiling in shock.

"Bitch!" Allie cried, her features twisted.

Anger pulsed red inside Cassie's head. Every muscle in her body bunched. Without thinking she struck back, pushing her sister so hard Allie stumbled backward into the living room, her calves colliding with the edge of the coffee table, her feet coming out from under her. She'd landed on the floor, her head glancing off the arm of the sofa, her legs sprawled.

"Shit!" Allie cried. "You're a freak. A fucking freak!" Frantically she scooted into a sitting position and rubbed the knot that was forming on the side of her head. "Something's seriously wrong with you!"

The words rang far too true and they'd stung.

That instant Cassie's rage ebbed.

Allie caught the change and realized she'd hit her mark, deep into the soft center of Cassie's insecurities. "You need help. Serious help," Allie charged. "I mean it. You should see a shrink. I mean a real psychiatrist, not Dr. Feel Good or whatever her name is. She's not helping. In fact, I think you're worse from seeing her!"

Pulling herself to her feet, Allie held on to the back of the couch for support, keeping the piece of furniture between them. "Do yourself and Mom and *Trent* and the whole damned world a favor, Cassie. Commit yourself! Or have the state do it! You've never been right since that creep nearly killed you!"

Allie's anger had dissipated and she was shaking. Pleading. She'd wounded Cassie, yes, intended to hurt her, but she'd also made a painfully true point.

Cassie had backed away and wondered at her sister's deep-seated hatred of her. Somehow she'd left. Cassie didn't remember much about the drive home. Had she gone straight back to her hotel room? Or had she driven aimlessly around the rain-washed streets of Port land before returning to her suite and flinging herself onto her bed? Had she returned to Allie's apartment? Lost track of time? Done something unthinkable, something she'd regret for the rest of her life? No! She couldn't have. Yet, she shuddered. All she really recalled was that she'd woken up hours later with a serious migraine that had nearly kept her from the shoot.

She'd arrived on set to find out that Allie's assistant, Cherise, had called Little Bea and claimed illness. Lucinda Rinaldi had stepped into Allie's costume for the reshooting of that final, fateful scene. It appeared that Cassie had been the last person to see her sister before Allie had fallen off the face of the earth.

"Where are you?" Cassie whispered now, leaning against the slick tiles of the tiny shower stall. Not for the first time she wondered if she were somehow at fault, at least partially. The fight. Allie hitting her head. Emotional and physical trauma that she, Cassie, had inflicted. The black hole of missing hours.

And now this. The not knowing.

She started to cry, tears mingling with the drizzle running from the showerhead over her body. Just like the guilt. Always the guilt. The truth was that she loved her sister and yes, there was envy and pain involved, even jealousy and anger, but she still remembered the scared little girl Allie had once been, the nerdy kid who'd been so shy. The girl Cassie had felt an intense need to protect. Before everything had gone so far downhill. God, what had happened to them? Angrily she swiped the salty drops away and pulled herself together. She was no use to herself or Allie or anyone by falling into a billion pieces.

Drawing a breath, she washed her hair and lathered and rinsed her body, scrubbing hard as if the very act could scour away any remaining bits of self-loathing and doubts. Once she was finished, she stepped out of the tile and glass enclosure and realized she hadn't brought a towel with her.

Dripping, she padded to the hall closet, leaving a trail of wet footprints behind her. She found a bath sheet and wrapped herself in the thick terry cloth before returning to the bathroom and swiping at the fogged-over mirror.

Her phone rang as she was staring at her reflection, and she quickly made her way to the kitchen, where her cell lay charging on the counter. She'd missed the call and saw that no number registered on the screen. All that was listed was: **Private call**. She felt a moment's fear, the old worries returning, but told herself it was no big deal. Probably just a wrong number. Or a telemarketer. Whoever it was, if they wanted something, they would call back.

She checked the screen again. Another call had come in, a number she recognized as belonging to Trent. This time he didn't leave a message and she was surprised that she felt a prick of disappointment, but there it was, a tiny new rip in her already fragile heart. "Fool," she whispered, and then noticed the face-down picture on a side table in the living room. She and Trent noticed. So much in love. She picked it up. The glass was cracked, a scar from a fight she'd had with Trent when she'd hurled the wedding photo across the living room they'd shared. Her temper had always run white-hot and the fact that she'd caught him having drinks with her sister had sent her over the edge. When he'd tried to explain, she hadn't listened. Instead she'd thrown the wedding photo across the room, aiming for his face. After he left she'd tossed the picture into the trash only to retrieve it the next day.

She looked at it now. In the photograph, she was wearing a short white dress. Trent was in jeans and an open-throated shirt. It was night, they stood near the street, the lights of Las Vegas blurring behind them. They were so happy, Trent's crooked, irreverent grin in place, her smile as bright as the future stretching before them. She'd been certain at that moment their life together would be worry-free and guaranteed to have a happy ending. She'd been so naive. Such an idiot to start dating him again after their breakup in Oregon. Granted, they'd separated mainly because of distance and family pressures: She was leaving for LA, and he was staying in Oregon. Her mother had been worried, Cassie had endured so much, she was concerned about the relationship. And though Trent hadn't given a rip about Jenna's feelings at the time, Cassie had been confused.

Well, wasn't she always?

Nothing had changed much there. Maybe her fury at Trent on the night of the fight had been misdirected. She knew now that Allie had targeted her husband, not the other way around. How sick was that, her own sister actually wanting to sleep with him? It was really messed up, but, of course, Cassie's relationship with Allie had always been difficult and weird.

She hefted the only photograph of Trent she'd kept and considered throwing it away. Permanently. But she didn't. Couldn't. She wasn't as rash as she once had been, at least she hoped that was the case. She set the picture face down on the table. He was just another bastard who'd crossed her path. One of a handful. Her taste in men had always been less than stellar, probably due to "daddy issues." After all, Robert was always leaving his current wife for the next best thing. Not exactly a candidate for Father of the Year.

"Get over it," she told herself.

Allie, as it turned out, had been right: Cassie was a screw up and a mental case.

Still, she wasn't going to let paranoia stop her. Nor would she allow Allie's questionable morals where Trent was concerned veer Cassie from her course.

Maybe she should start looking now. She wasn't tired. In fact she was antsy, needed to do something to calm herself down and think clearly. Maybe she needed a drink? Or a walk? Even a drive? Risky, but then what in life wasn't?

She dropped her towel.

Somehow, some way, she was going to find Allie.

Then the little princess could eat her words.

CHAPTER 10

Jenna felt a sudden chill, as if a ghost had just walked over her soul. It was silly really, but as she stepped into the attic and snapped on the light, she went cold inside. It was night, Shane was working in the den downstairs and she needed time alone. To think. To consider her life. To silently pray that her daughters were safe. She'd used the excuse of looking for her grandmother's recipe box, lost when it had been packed away during the kitchen remodel.

The attic was cold, its sloped ceiling uninsulated, the sharp tips of roofing nails visible between the rafters. One of the light bulbs had burned out, leaving just one small bulb to illuminate the vast space with its dormers and peek-a-boo windows. She pulled her sweater around her body a little more tightly. Here, she thought, was the detritus of her life, the pieces and things that no longer fit into her daily routine.

Boxes, broken tables, a broken lamp, pictures and frames stacked in a corner. The wind was blowing hard outside, whistling through the rafters in this section of the rambling old house, one of the few places she hadn't renovated over the years. She ran a finger across the edge of a box, felt the dust collect on her skin and saw a book-case filled with old electronic equipment and wires connected to nothing. Here were stashed the remnants of her life, boxes of possessions from her school days, college, and her marriage to Robert, things she'd never had the heart nor time to dispose of. Each of her children, too, had a collection of papers, trophies, clothes, books, and toys that had settled in the attic for years.

The scratch of tiny claws suggested she wasn't alone and she scanned the ceiling for bats, then avoided the darkest corners that could be home for mice or rats or squirrels, even raccoons.

Not exactly the most peaceful or comfortable place to think. She dusted off an old rocker wedged between two stacks of plastic cartons and sat, letting the chair sway of its own accord. She'd rocked her babies in this very rocker, now forgotten and stained. She thought of her children and worried about them. Tears burned the back of her eyes as she saw a picture of Allie, distorted slightly in the dim light, her image just visible through the side of the plastic bin. She'd been around eight, her adult front teeth just showing through her gums, her smile wide and still innocent. Jenna moved some of the boxes, then opened the tub to extract Allie's second grade school picture. Allie had been such an awkward girl at the time, an innocent if introverted kid who had no idea the beauty she'd become.

"Oh, baby," Jenna whispered, her throat thick, the frigid air in the room burrowing deep into her bones. "Where are you?" Sniffling, she looked up to this attic where Allie had played as a child, where she'd hidden or built a fort or spent hours reading. Alone.

What had happened to change things so?

A divorce, yes, to Allie's ultimate bewilderment.

A move that she didn't comprehend. Both she and Cassie had loved LA and hadn't understood Jenna's reasons for taking her children to a place she thought safer, a ranch in Oregon out of the fast-paced life, the glitter of Hollywood.

Then in Oregon came a monster. A deranged fan who had terrorized them all.

Also a stepfather she'd accepted if not embraced.

And a sister. Older. More rebellious. One who required most of Jenna's attention. Cassie and Allie's relationship had always been strained and it had only gotten worse, much worse, after the attack ten years ago.

She shuddered at the thought of the madman who had killed senselessly and brutally, then set his sights on Jenna and her girls. Cassie had not only lost her boyfriend, but nearly her own life and had been traumatized, nearly committed at that time. Jenna had focused on getting her daughter mentally well and in the process, she now assumed, ignored her younger, more serious and stable daughter. Had the rift begun then? At the time Allie's relationship with her father was nearly nonexistent and Jenna had been wrapped in guilt about inadvertently putting Cassie's life in danger. Looking back, she had probably ignored Allie's wants and needs, or at least put them beneath Cassie's. And then there was the fact that Cassie had been much more popular with the boys. Probably her irreverent attitude had attracted them like flies, while bookish, "I'm bored" Allie hadn't gotten a second glance. She'd matured late and always, Jenna had sensed, envied her sister's appeal to the opposite sex. Being Cassie Kramer's younger sister in school had resulted in a grudge that hadn't eased with time, not even when the tables had turned as adults and Allie had been lavished with all of the attention once she'd been "discovered" in Hollywood.

But childhood despairs ran deep. Never completely evaporated. She knew it herself.

Deeper in the plastic tub she found the stuffed elephant that had been Allie's "go to" cuddle toy as a toddler and into school. Jenna smiled and stroked the once-blue trunk, while noticing one of the eyes was missing and there was a rip in the seam of the elephant's belly.

She remembered telling her girls to clean out their rooms and haul all their things up to the attic during the remodel of the bedroom wing. Apparently this box was never retrieved and returned to Allie's room. Like so many things, she thought.

Footsteps heralded Shane's approach.

"Jenna?" he called up the stairs. The first step creaked with his weight. "You up here?"

"Coming," she said, and reluctantly left the old rocker with its memories behind. She hesitated for a moment beneath the single burning bulb and cast one final look around, all the while thinking of her daughters.

"Please," she prayed under her breath as she clicked off the light, "wherever they are, keep them safe."

ACT II

In her darkened room she waited impatiently. She'd intended to leave earlier, but remembered the television program, so she'd lingered.

Lying on the mussed bed, a half-drunk glass of chardonnay on the nearby table, she reached for the television remote, which lay on the night stand. The scratch on her wrist was still purplish red where she'd run the edge of the broken glass across her skin. Lips twisting, she switched on the TV just as *Justice: Stone Cold* was being aired. In tonight's edition, there was supposed to be a teaser for future programming, all concerning the disappearance of Allie Kramer.

She waited as the advertisements tried vainly to sell her products. "Come on, come on," she said, her eyes narrowing, her patience running thin.

Suddenly, big as life, a head shot of Allie Kramer, the start of a trailer for *Dead Heat.*

Her insides clenched and she felt a little frisson of anticipation.

The clip from the movie started with a close up of Allie playing the character of Shondie Kent, first her full face, then moving to one hazel eye where a bit of refracted light showed in her pupil. Finally, as if through Shondie's vision, the tiny spot of light became larger, filling the screen with blurry images that sharpened into the scene of two frantic women running through the rain-washed streets of Portland, Oregon, panic and fear evident in their expressions.

The mood was dark.

Eerie.

Nearly perfect.

Craaack!

A gun went off.

The second woman stumbled as the scene faded to black.

Watching spellbound, she felt a deep sense of satisfaction. No one would ever guess how it happened, how the bullets in the prop gun had been exchanged, and who was the real target. She took a sip from her wine. That part, the mistake with the victim, still bothered her. Needed to be fixed.

On the screen, the scene changed again and the earnest and beautiful face of investigative reporter Whitney Stone appeared. Her hair was dark, cut at a sharp angle, her eyes large and sincere, her chin pointed and her attitude one of incredible concern. She started speaking intimately into the camera's lens.

For the truth.

For justice.

For the public's right to know!

Even better.

Whitney promised a complete exposé on what really happened to Allie Kramer. Was the wildly popular actress alive or dead? Or maybe being held captive? Used as some kind of sex slave? Or bargaining chip? Or was this all an elaborate publicity stunt foisted on the American public by Galactic West Productions, the company that had produced the movie? Too many questions had no answers, but Whitney Stone vowed to uncover and dissect the truth for her viewers during Mystery Week on the cable station on which her program aired. What more intriguing mystery could there be than what had happened to America's Darling, Allie Kramer?

"America's Darling?" Like Allie was Shirley Temple or Sandra Bullock or Reese Witherspoon or whoever the current sweetheart of the week was?

Her insides curled.

Even though Whitney Stone's interest was all part of the plan.

Stone insisted that in following installments what had happened to Allie Kramer would become crystal clear.

Now, she picked up her stemmed glass and twirled it in her fingers. Staring through the clear liquid, she viewed the television and the distorted image of Whitney Stone's face. Perfect. She took a sip.

Stone was gazing so intently into the camera and reminding viewers that the star of *Dead Heat*, Allie Kramer not only had gone missing, but her disappearance had occurred just ten years after she and her sister, Cassie, as well was their mother, Jenna Hughes, had survived a horrific and brutal attack.

Pictures of the three women filled the screen.

Her fingers tightened over the stem of her glass.

Whitney Stone posed the questions:

Was this Hollywood family cursed?

Was another psychotic fan on the loose?

Could Jenna and her daughters never find a "normal" or "peaceful" life?

"Of course not," she said to the flat screen. Another sip as anger sparked deep inside.

A montage of pictures rolled across the screen, short clips of Jenna Hughes in her starring roles. For a few seconds Jenna Hughes became Anne Parks in *Resurrection*. One by one, there were more quick tidbits, glimpses of other roles Jenna had played as the heroines of *Beneath the Shadows* and *Bystander*. Then, to top off the collage, the last clip was of Jenna as a naive teen in *Innocence Lost,* the movie destined to become an overnight success and elevate her to stardom.

The screen suddenly split and Jenna's image filled one half, while Allie Kramer, at around the same age, was on the other. Both mother and daughter had been catapulted to fame, as teens at the center of a darkly sexual coming-of-age film.

The comparison was obvious. Though Allie couldn't pass for her mother—too many of her father's genes were evident in her features—the resemblance to Jenna Hughes was noticeable.

Watching the quick little clips, she felt her insides churn. She barely heard Whitney Stone's promise of a soon-to-be-aired "explosive interview" that would "shatter" the image of the reclusive Jenna Hughes and her family. A family portrait of Jenna, Cassie, and Allie came into view and as the camera zoomed in closer, Whitney Stone's voiceover assured the viewers that, "The daughters of Jenna Hughes are not who they seem to be!"

"No shit," she whispered, alone in the dark room. Anger coursed through her veins and her jaw hardened. She watched the image of Jenna and her daughters fade into individual pictures, first Jenna, then Cassie, and finally the missing Allie, before they slowly vanished from sight.

That damned bitch, Whitney Stone, pulled the teaser off beautifully. Perfectly. Stirring the pot, adding to the mystery surrounding the Kramer sisters and promising a full-blown exposé on the secretive little family. Whetting the viewers' appetites for more info on Allie Kramer's disappearance, Whitney Stone had also created the illusion that she was actually the star, a heroine fighting for truth and justice.

Because Whitney Stone knew far more than she was telling.

She clicked the television off and silently congratulated herself for a job well done. The wheels had been set into motion. And it was just the beginning. Closing her eyes, she leaned back against the headboard of the bed and tried to calm herself. Her headache pounded painfully, the demons inside hitting their sharp fists against her skull, demanding to be set free. "No," she said aloud. But, oh how they wanted to get loose. She'd named them. Pride and Invincibility were the most vociferous, their talons scraping through her gray matter. But their companion, Fury, deep-seated and ever growing, was the worst. Fury would be her downfall, she'd been told by more than one shrink. Fury would push her over the edge of sanity.

She thought about a drive along the coast. Something to calm the nerves. Wine hadn't helped and she could drink a little more, but then she'd be over the edge and she couldn't afford to lose her perspective.

The need inside her grew, began to thrum, a desire to hunt. She told herself to fight the feeling, that this kind of obsession was what the psychiatrists had warned her about, but her whole body ached to do something, *any*thing to scratch the insidious itch. And why not?

She'd already picked out who would be the perfect victim, who would play her part.

The shrinks she'd seen would disapprove. "Tsk. Tsk."

A half-smile played across her lips and she opened her eyes to the thick darkness. "Save me," she whispered to the empty room and then laughed out loud.

The doctors were idiots.

She clicked off the TV and changed, then headed out the door. Cool air brushed her skin as she found her vehicle and, driving through the deserted streets of the city, she headed west.

She was keyed up. Eager. Her nerve endings alive. Adrenaline pumping through her veins.

It was dangerous being out where someone might see her, where a traffic cam, security camera, or even the camera app on a cell phone of someone who, like she, was up so late, but she didn't care. The night was thick, clouds gathering overhead. The closer she got to the ocean, the freer she felt. She rolled down all of the windows, letting the scent of the sea into the car's interior.

She felt tense.

Needy.

The wind tugged at her hair. She should feel free. Exhilarated. But she didn't. Deep inside, anxiety roiled, coupling with a base, dark, and pulsing need, a desire she couldn't fight much longer. Whether she admitted it to herself or not, she was on the hunt. It felt good, yet scared her to death. That's where the rush came into it. She licked her lips in anticipation and hated herself for it.

Few cars passed her, their headlights glaring, but she didn't think she'd be recognized as they flew past. No one was looking for her at this late hour. No one knew, and that gave her power, the fact that she was inconspicuous.

It also ground her guts.

Finally she reached the beach. With her first glimpse of the dark waters of the Pacific she considered driving up the PCH, catching views of the ocean. Maybe then she'd calm down. Maybe then she could tamp down her secret urges. Maybe the serenity of the ocean would help her fight the warring feelings of Invincibility and Frustration.

Of course it was too late.

She knew it as her fingers gripped the wheel, and the roar of the surf reached her ears. She was already on the search and, deep down, in that dark place in her psyche she didn't like to acknowledge, it felt damned good to finally be doing something, to start assuaging the ache that drove her.

The soothing waters of the Pacific stretched darkly to an invisible horizon, but it didn't matter.

Rain began to sprinkle on the windshield, a few drops falling into the interior. As she reached upward to reluctantly close the sunroof, she caught a glimpse of her eyes in the rearview mirror, eyes so like her mother's.

She didn't want to go there, not now. Not when she was already on the hunt. But there was no stopping the burn in her stomach and the taste of bile rising in her throat when she thought of her patchwork of a family, sewn together but always falling apart.

It was all that bitch's fault.

CHAPTER II

Ineesha Sallinger knew she should never have agreed to meet with Sig Masters. The man was a mess. A complete, bumbling mess. Or worse. A damned freak show. She had to distance herself from him. So, the sooner she could get out of his dump of a house tonight, the better.

"It's your fault," he was saying for the fourth—or was it the fifth?—time since they'd agreed to meet at Sig's house, which was kind of a dump, really, at this god-awful hour in the morning. Five AM, because she had a meeting with her trainer at six and a full day stretched out in front of her?

So she'd agreed to come to this . . . fixer-upper. Sure the house was in LA, and that was something, she supposed, but it was tiny, probably no more than eight hundred square feet, enough for Sig and his damned dogs, built in that cute Old California Spanish style, but it was going to seed. Not that Sig wasn't trying to improve it. There were ladders and paint buckets and sheets of plastic creating new walls or taking the place of old ones, she couldn't really tell which. It was weird, that was all, and Sig, almost chain-smoking, was angry, upset, and a physical wreck. He looked like he'd dropped fifteen pounds since the last day of filming for *Dead Heat*. Ineesha was always impressed when someone was able to peel off some weight, but in Sig's case, it was a tad too much.

"My fault," she repeated, picking her way between paint cans and nearly stepping on some little fluff of fur that growled at her. God, the dog couldn't weigh five pounds, but it snarled and snapped as if it thought it was an alpha wolf. "How's that?"

He picked up the growling little beast and petted its tiny head. It was comical, really, this tall man, over six-two, gently stroking the mottled Chihuahua or whatever it was. "You were in charge of the props. They were your responsibility! Now the cops . . . they think I did it. Oh, fuck, I *did* do it, but I didn't mean to." He drew hard on his cigarette. Set the dog down. It scuttled away to peer out between the sheets of Visqueen suspiciously. "Lucinda Rinaldi?" he asked, as if Ineesha didn't know who the woman was. "She's going to sue me. Well, probably you, too."

"I can't stop that."

"How the hell were the guns switched? How the hell was there live ammo in a prop gun?"

"I don't know."

"But you should! It's your goddamned job!"

This was getting them nowhere and was a huge waste of time. "So I've heard. Look, Sig, what's done is done. I can't explain it and I can't do anything about Lucinda Rinaldi or her lawyer. But I can try to keep my cool and I suggest you do the same."

"But I'm innocent!" he cried and from somewhere in the back, possibly the kitchen, came a deep-throated "woof" that made Ineesha jump. Whatever was hiding back there was definitely *not* a Chihuahua.

"For Christ's sake, aren't you even worried? I mean, I almost killed a woman. Shit, shit, shit!" Over the smell of paint, Ineesha caught a whiff of alcohol.

She should never have come here.

She should have followed her attorney's advice and kept mum about everything.

She didn't want the cops digging around in her life as she did have a couple of old drug charges that had been dogging her for years. For the love of God, when would people quit reminding her of a couple of mistakes *fifteen fucking years ago!*

Her blood pressure started to elevate and she decided she'd stop by the gym on the way home. If intense exercise didn't calm her down, then there was yoga and meditation, if, at this time of night she could get her instructor . . . Georges the Gorgeous as she silently called him . . . to help her equilibrium.

First things first though. She had to escape this death trap of paint fumes, hidden Cujos, and a big man who looked about to snap. God knows what he could do. She took a step backward and ran into a metal ladder. Jesus, this was nowhere to be.

"Look, try and calm down, Sig. This will all sort itself out."

"How?"

"I don't know, but it will."

"How do you know?"

"Okay. You got me. I don't."

"Right." He looked around for an ashtray, found an empty roller pan and frantically jabbed out his filter-tip.

"What else can we do? You've got a lawyer."

"Yeah, and he's costing me an arm and a leg. They're all blood-suckers!"

"Or lifesavers."

"I didn't do anything wrong. I got the gun that you locked in the prop closet. It was ready to go and . . . And I fired it on the set . . . and . . . Oh, Jesus, do you know how many nightmares I've had about Lucinda going down? She could have been killed. I could have killed her. Allie Kramer's damned lucky she wasn't on the set that day." He buried his face in his hand and the dogs, now it sounded like a third, had started baying from behind the plastic, began to howl.

"Yeah, Allie was lucky," she said and despite her show of bravado felt a deep-seated fear. She, like Sig, was under investigation. It was all so crazy. She picked her way past the paint can with a drizzle running down its side of some gawd-awful mustard color, to the front door. "Look," she said before stepping outside, "take my advice and listen to your lawyer. Make sure he's the best one you can find." And then she left Sig with his Marlboros, hideous paint, and miserable dogs. She found her way to her car and slid inside.

She'd done her duty.

Now, Sig was on his own.

Scraape!

Like fingernails scratching a chalkboard, the screeching sound echoed through Cassie's brain. What was it? Where was it coming from? Fear crawling up her spine, she sat up in bed and peered into the half-light. Was it her imagination? She strained to listen. Something had caused her to waken so sharply and she had the uneasy sensation she wasn't alone.

Her door was cracked, a sliver of bluish incandescence filtering in and offering a weird illumination.

Still, she saw nothing.

Scraape!

She jumped. Bit back a scream.

What in God's name was *that*?

The screeching sound was so close. But from where?

Heart in her throat, she tossed back the covers.

Her bare feet landed on the cool tiles of the floor. In only her hospital gown, she crossed the room and pushed the door open a little farther.

Beyond, the corridor was empty, the eerie light seeming to move, like the play of shadowy light on water, the hallway long and austere. Her pulse was deep and hard. Fear collected in her gut.

Where was everyone?

This was a hospital, wasn't it? There should be nurses and aides, doctors and patients, even if it was late at night. The corridor seemed to stretch for miles, but she walked silently toward what appeared to be the source of the light, a brighter end of the hallway far, far away. Identical doors lined the hallway.

She tried the first.

Locked.

Frantic, she pushed on the one on the opposite side of the hallway. It didn't budge.

Nor did the next or the next or next.

Were there footsteps behind her?

She broke into a jog and threw a glance over her shoulder, but saw no one, just the never-ending hallway that seemed to disappear into nothing. Fear rising, she ran on, checking each doorway, knowing before she pressed on the levers, that the locks were in place.

As she ran, she felt, rather than saw, someone . . . no *something* . . . moving stealthily behind her, giving invisible chase.

Fear iced her blood.

She ran faster.

The air became colder until her breath was fogging with her uneven breaths, her skin prickling.

Was that a footfall?

Why couldn't she see anyone?

Dear God, help me!

She wanted to cry out, to call for help, but she didn't. Not when she sensed an evil presence a heartbeat away, a demon breathing his icy breath against the back of her neck.

Don't go all paranoid. This is weird, yes, but there is nothing, not a thing following you. To prove it to herself, she glanced over her shoulder again and the corridor was as empty as before, stretching out endlessly behind her.

What kind of weird place is this?

Mercy Hospital with its bland walls and polished floors? No— that didn't seem right, and yet the corridor had the feel, the scent of a long hospital wing in an abandoned building.

Scraape!

She broke into a sprint, the locked doors flying past, fear driving her onward.

Finally the end of the hallway loomed, a white brick wall with double doors, frosted windows reinforced with wire mesh cut into the smooth metal.

She flung herself against the wide lever and stopped short.

Over the ragged sound of her breathing she heard footsteps. With a glance over her shoulder she saw no one.

All in your mind, Cassie, just like this weird place. Paranoia settling in.

"Shut up!"

She bit her lip and threw all of her weight against the lever again.

It didn't move.

Scraape!

The sound came from the other side of the doors. Cassie's throat turned to sand. She should leave, run back the way she'd come, seek solace in that weird room where she woke up.

She took one step backward and spied a fat button on the wall near the doors.

The release!

Before she could hit the button, the doors clanged loudly and opened inward. Quickly she stepped into a wide, windowless room with white walls and tile flooring. A mist seeped from a nearby stairwell where an exit sign pulsed red. Within the center of the room were rows of wheeled stretchers, twenty-one beds, all of which were draped and hiding what appeared to be bodies.

Is this some kind of bizarre morgue?

Heart thudding wildly, Cassie started to back up, but the swinging doors banged shut. No! She pushed on the lever, but the doors were locked tight, and though she looked desperately on the wall for a release button, there was none.

Like it or not, she was locked in.

Dear Jesus . . .

Why, oh, why had she come here?

But it was more than just idle curiosity that had lured her down that long hallway. She'd felt as if she were being lured to this chilled room.

Rotating slowly, anxiety tightening her muscles, she eyed the unmoving beds. Were they all occupied by the dead? Or were some alive? Were they even human? She didn't want to find out, didn't want to know. On quiet feet she quickly edged to the stairwell. All the while she was tense, feeling as if she were running out of time, that if she didn't get out now, she might lose her opportunity.

She reached the stairwell and found another locked door with no release.

"Damn it," she whispered through clenched teeth, and tried again, slamming her weight against the levers. Cold metal rattled loudly but didn't give.

"Son of a—"

Scraape!

The horrid sound was right behind her.

She whirled.

There in the far corner the nurse in her white cap and uniform, her blue cape stark against the white walls, materialized as if from vapor. "She's alive," the nurse whispered in a low, raspy voice.

"Your sister is alive."

Cassie backed up. Oh. Dear. God.

From the nurse's earlobes, the red cross earrings glittered before turning into tiny red globules. The red drops splashed from her lobes to the shoulders of her uniform, running down her white dress, staining it red.

Shivering, Cassie swallowed hard and kept inching backward.

Scraape!

Wheels loose, one of the gurneys began rolling, hard metal casters scratching loudly against the tile. As it wheeled by, the draped body's head and shoulders raised, the sheet sliding to the floor.

Allie's bloodless face stared straight at her. "Cassie," she hissed through blue lips that barely moved.

No!

"Help me . . ."

A scream echoed through the morgue.

Cassie blinked awake.

Her heart was trip-hammering. The scream she'd heard had come from her own lips. Sweating, nearly hyperventilating, she was lying on her own bed in her apartment in LA. Dear God, it was five-thirty in the morning, not quite dawn. The shadowed room slowly sharpened into view and she told herself to calm down. It was just a bad dream, a nightmare, nothing more.

But the vision had been so real and surreal.

She let out her breath slowly, her hands fisting in the sheets as she forced herself to think rationally, to not freak out, to take control and—

Scraape!

She shrieked, spinning on the bed as the sound seemed to reverberate through the walls. "What the hell?" Leaping from the mattress, she stared at the window positioned over her headboard and heard the sound again, but this time she saw the tree branch moving to scratch the glass.

Her shoulders slumped in relief.

That was all.

Nothing sinister.

Nothing evil.

Just a damned branch moving in the wind.

And the reason she was so cold? The air conditioner was working overtime, blowing cold air through the room. That was one of the problems with this place, the temperature. Always either hot or cold.

"You're a freak show," she muttered as she walked into the hallway and flipped the switch to turn off the cool air. Now fully awake, she made her way to the kitchen, where she opened the refrigerator and reached inside for a bottle of water.

Thud!

The noise came from her living room.

She dropped the bottle. "Who's there?" she called out immediately, then closed the refrigerator door, the kitchen once again cloaked in darkness.

No response.

But she *felt* a presence.

"Who's there?"

Nothing.

Her throat was dry and hot.

Stealthily she let her fingers crawl across the counter top until she found the block holding her knives. Her heart was in her throat as she withdrew a long blade and then noiselessly moved from the kitchen to the archway leading to the living area.

The apartment was still.

Without the air from the air conditioner, all Cassie could hear was the crazy knocking of her heart accompanied by her own shallow breathing. But someone was inside, she knew it.

Her fingers clamped around the knife's hilt so tightly that they began to ache. She gazed over the counter, into the darkened living room and thought she spied movement, a darker shadow in the surrounding umbra.

She hardly dared breathe.

Where was her cell phone?

She needed to call 9-1-1.

She flashed on the cell hooked to her charger it on the night stand in her bedroom.

Too far. She'd have to pass by the living area again and now the intruder knew she was onto him.

Panic rose. Who was inside? What did he want? Why was he here? *Think, Cassie, think!*

Get out. Get out, now!

If she could just get around the corner of the kitchen, to the front hall where she could hit the switch and race out the door . . . Oh, God, were those eyes staring back at her, reflecting the barest of light filtering in from the living room window? She didn't wait to find out.

Adrenaline firing her blood, she tore around the refrigerator, her feet landing on the tile of the small entry. Clutching the butcher knife in one hand, she flipped on the lights in the foyer with the other, and opened the door.

The *unlocked* door. She knew she'd thrown the bolt before heading to bed. Oh, God, oh, God, oh God!

The ceiling fixtures flashed on. Bright light nearly blinded her. Holding the knife in front of her with both hands, she fell back a step onto the porch but saw no one in the apartment. No malicious figure appeared. No killer with murderous intent showed himself. For a second she thought she'd imagined it all, that her nightmare had confused her.

So here she was, standing on her porch, butcher knife in hand feeling like a complete idiot and—

She saw the eyes, peering out of the open closet door. Unblinking. Near the floor. Glaring.

Her heart stopped as she tried to imagine what it was.

An *animal?*

"SSSSssss," the black creature hissed, back arching, teeth showing. *The cat?*

Quick as a lightning bolt, the black fur ball shot by her.

She almost laughed. How ludicrous that she was standing on her front porch in her night shirt, a huge knife clutched in her hands, when all her fears had been about a stupid cat.

Oh, for the love of St. Peter. Really? An animal of less than twenty pounds had instilled the fear of God in her? Caused her to arm herself? Sent her into panic mode and probably shaved a year off her life?

You are *crazy, Cassie!*

Sagging against the doorjamb, noticing the sky lightening to the east, she was berating herself for being such a fool when she remembered that she'd locked her apartment. When she'd gone out earlier in the day, and then before she'd turned in for the night. She recalled throwing the dead bolt.

So how had the neighbor's cat ended up inside?

Gooseflesh rose on her arms.

A new fear slithered through her as she examined the door and found no forced entry. But the cat had gotten in somehow . . .

It probably snuck in behind you when you weren't looking, then it hid in a dark corner until the sound of the tree branch woke you up and—

Who was she kidding? The cat had *not* sneaked unnoticed into the apartment and the door had been *locked.*

She started to pull the door shut when she heard a car's engine start about a block away from the house.

Coincidence?

Or had someone been watching?

Her throat turned to sand as the car passed on the street in front of the main house, headlights illuminating the drive for a second as it passed.

Had someone been inside her home?

Had the cat followed whoever it was inside?

If so, how did they get in?

Her mind was racing, trying to figure it out, trying to stay rational, when all of her instincts were to panic. Inside the apartment again, she threw the deadbolt then placed a chair under the door knob and checked all the windows. Shut tight and latched. There was no back door, just the one entrance to her unit. So how . . . ?

Who else has a key to your place?

"No one," she said out loud. "No—" Oh, hell.

Hadn't she loaned a key to Allie a few months after she'd moved in? Allie had needed a place to crash when her place was being painted and Cassie had thought it was time they mended some seriously broken fences. Allie had never stayed in the apartment, nor had she bothered returning the key.

Allie?

In here?

Skulking around?

No, no, that didn't make sense. But, if someone had abducted Allie, there was a chance that he had control of whatever possessions she had on her, which would, of course, include her key ring.

And the "borrowed" key.

CHAPTER 12

Insomnia had become Detective Rhonda Nash's best friend. One she hated. It crawled into bed with her each night and wouldn't let go. Even though she worked long hours, exercised her butt off whenever she had a minute, tried her best to meditate in what little free time she had, felt exhausted when she tumbled into bed, Ronnie just couldn't fall asleep until the wee hours of the morning.

Her damned brain wouldn't shut off. No amount of warm milk, counting sheep, deep breathing, clearing her mind, or swearing and punching her pillow could change her routine or keep insomnia at bay.

Last night had been no different from those of the past three months, she thought, as she found an open slot in the parking structure, then cut the engine of her Ford Focus. Her mind already on the day stretching before her, she grabbed her laptop, locked the car, then hurried down four flights of stairs. Emerging from the open-air building she flipped up the hood of her raincoat. A soft Oregon drizzle was falling from the heavens. As it was not yet seven in the morning, the sky was still dark, streetlights glowing, the city starting to come alive. Buses rumbled down the one-way streets while bikes sped past, tires hissing on the wet pavement as the riders cut through the few cars, trucks, and vans already moving through the west side of the Willamette River.

Nash jaywalked quickly, crossing the street between the lights to dash through the doors of the Justice Center, taking the elevator up to the Homicide Division.

As the rain puddled onto the lift's floor she thought she probably should find a different, less stressful job, should give up all the cop crap and the tension that came with it, but she couldn't. Becoming a detective had been her life's ambition. So here she was pushing forty, married to a career that wouldn't leave her alone at night, one that invaded her dreams and chased her out of bed before dawn while her friends were busy balancing their careers and home life, husbands and children, school and work schedules.

But she couldn't see herself as a nine-to-fiver, or a doting stay-at-home mother and wife. "Diff'rent strokes for diff'rent folks," she said under her breath.

Besides, she loved her job, especially in the early morning, which was the most peaceful time of day in the office after the crazies of the night had been dealt with and before the morning shift got into full swing. This was a time when she could think and plan her day, a time before her partner showed up, or many of the other desks in the large room cut up into cubicles were filled with other cops on phones, writing reports, questioning suspects, or generally taking up space.

Nash hated the lack of privacy involved. She would have preferred her own office complete with walls, maybe a window, and a door that she could open or close depending upon her workload and mood.

As she stepped into the division, she noticed that she wasn't alone. A few other cops were already seated at their desks, on their phones, reading files, or keying info into their computers. A couple of them were standing together, a newbie named Trish Bellegarde was trying not to be rude to Kowalski, who had trapped her into a conversation. Nash had been there. Kowalski was a decent enough detective, the "old man" in the department. He sported a white crew cut, jowls, glasses that he was always polishing, and a good ol' boy attitude that was a pain in the butt. Retirement loomed for Kowalski and for that Nash was grateful. She just didn't like the guy.

After hanging her coat in a locker and leaving her bag in a drawer at her desk, she went into the lunchroom, found a carafe of coffee, and poured herself a lukewarm cup. Good enough, for now. Back at her desk she discovered she'd already acquired a dozen or so e-mail messages since she'd left the office sometime after six the night before. As she sipped from her cup with her free hand, she scrolled through the missives, sorted out reports and filed them along with autopsies and statements, then saw a more personal note from Whitney Stone.

Oh joy.

Stone had worked her way up as a freelance reporter and now produced and starred in her own reality-type mystery show. Nash had watched a couple of episodes and thought Stone was long on innuendos and short on facts. Worse yet, Stone, originally a native of the Southwest, maybe Arizona or New Mexico, Nash thought, had lived in Portland for a while, and since Portland had achieved a newfound "cool" status, Stone had adopted the city as her own. Now she was always nosing around, looking for a juicy story she could sink her teeth into and, sometimes, at least in Nash's opinion, exploit.

The woman was photogenic enough to be a model, so she made crime reporting look good.

Now, she was sinking her investigative teeth into the Allie Kramer case, asking for an interview with Nash.

"Forget it," Nash said under her breath, but noted that Stone had mentioned in her e-mail that Cassie Kramer had left Mercy Hospital.

This was news to Nash and it shouldn't have been, since Cassie Kramer was very much a person of interest in her sister's disappearance. The day was starting out just great, she thought grimly. It wasn't yet eight and already Nash was irritated enough to reach for a bottle of Tums to calm her nervous stomach. After popping three chalky tablets, Nash dialed the hospital and met roadblock after roadblock in the form of a taciturn receptionist who could quote HIPAA compliancy rules and hospital regulations without the least inflection in her voice. Biting back her frustration, Nash persevered and after cutting through what seemed to be reams of red tape concerning privacy, was told, "Miss Kramer is no longer a patient at Mercy Hospital." A few more inquiries to a local cab company and she learned that Allie Kramer's sister had been driven to a car rental agency. More telephone calls ended up revealing that Cassie Kramer had, indeed, left the gloom of Portland for the sunnier climate of Los Angeles.

Nash made a call to the LAPD and a note to herself.

Then she searched through the rest of her never-ending in-box of e-mails. Once she'd dispensed with the ones she could, she picked up her phone and checked her voice mail. Fortunately it consisted of only a few calls. Again, Whitney Stone had recorded a similar message to her e-mail. She wasn't alone. Two other reporters had left their name and number. Nash didn't bother to call them back. If they were professional, then they knew the protocol, which was to go through the Public Information Officer.

Besides, she didn't have any answers. The Kramer case was a puzzler, the primary reason Nash was losing sleep, even though there wasn't a homicide, at least not a proven one yet. A famous person was missing under suspicious circumstances, but her stunt double had been shot on the last day of filming, when the cast and crew had been called back to Portland to reshoot a scene. Had those shots been accidental? Or had Lucinda Rinaldi been the intended victim? Maybe Allie Kramer, who hadn't shown up that day, had been the ultimate target? Had she known she was in danger, been tipped off somehow and made herself disappear, putting another woman in danger? That was hard to believe. Why stay away so long? Why not reach out to family, friends, or the police if she'd felt so threatened?

Nash thought hard, swallowing coffee by rote. She wondered if it were possible that the killer had found Allie Kramer and kidnapped and/or killed her when he realized his mistake at targeting the wrong woman. That was a possibility. A long shot, but a working theory because Nash was certain that Sig Masters, the actor who'd actually pulled the trigger, hadn't intended to shoot Lucinda Rinaldi or anyone else. Nash remembered questioning him and the man had broken down and cried, shaking his head, swearing he'd gotten the prop gun from the locker; and the woman who had the key, Ineesha Sallinger, the prop manager, corroborated Masters's story and swore her key to the prop locker had been with her for the entire time it took to film the scene. Though the room where the locker was located had been left open during the shoot, the locker itself had been secure. Sallinger had sworn that no one could have exchanged the guns.

But someone had.

The pistol used in the shooting looked identical to the prop, but it had been armed with real bullets. The only fingerprints upon it were Masters's. Not even Sallinger's had been found anywhere on the barrel, trigger, or grip. That in and of itself was odd. A prop gun should have several sets of prints on it. The prop manager, maybe someone who had loaded it with blanks, and the shooter, to start with. The gun seemed to have been wiped clean until Sig had received it. Sallinger explained that question away by saying that she'd been wearing gloves that day. The Portland wintry weather had been cold and wet.

So where the hell was Allie Kramer? Or her body?

Dumped into the Willamette River? Buried in the wooded slopes of the West Hills? Shoved into a trash receptacle beneath a concrete slab? Rotting in a dark room or under a house somewhere?

Or alive and held captive by a nutcase, an over-the-top, possibly homicidal fan?

Nash chewed on the edge of her paper cup as her mind whirled with questions she couldn't answer. The furnace rumbled, blowing warm air into the department, as other detectives began to report for duty and start their shifts. Computer keyboards clicked and phones began to ring in other cubicles, but Nash was lost in thought, caught in the mystery that was Allie Damned Kramer.

Nash had other cases to deal with, of course. Over the past weekend there had been a knifing near the waterfront and there was always escalating gang violence that a task force was dealing with, but this, the disappearance of Allie Kramer, was the one that kept nagging at her, digging into her brain, teasing her. Was it because Allie was a celebrity, a local girl who'd conquered Hollywood? Or was it just that the elements were all so intriguing, a puzzle not easily solved?

And now Cassie Kramer, very much a person of interest in her sister's disappearance, had flown the proverbial coop. There was the rumored jealousy and fights between the sisters. Cassie, the last person to see or communicate with Allie, had admitted that she and Allie had "argued" on that fateful visit.

What had happened? Nash wondered, not for the first time. The broken wineglass, the furniture that had been moved according to impressions on the throw rug, the yelling that a neighbor had attested to.

She fidgeted at her desk, playing distractedly with a paper clip as she considered the multifaceted sides to this case. Not only had Cassie Kramer had a fight with her sister, but she'd also suffered a mental breakdown on the day after the shooting on the set. She'd actually committed herself. Why? Was she really that unstable? What exactly was her diagnosis? Paranoia? Schizophrenia? Was she seriously depressed? Was she afraid of harming herself? Or others? Or was it some other condition? Nash couldn't help but wonder if checking into the psychiatric wing of Mercy was all part of Cassie's plan, just in case she needed a quick insanity defense should her sister's body show up.

Too many loose ends for Nash's satisfaction.

"Watch out." A deep voice interrupted her thoughts, and she looked up to see Kowalski passing by the opening to her cubicle. His work space was located across a passageway with an eighties glamour shot of his wife, Marcia, situated on the corner of his desk, angled so that Marcia, in a glittery boa, looking over hands folded under her strong chin, seemed to be staring at Nash. "Wouldn't want you to hurt yourself." He started a rumbling laugh that was rough from years of cigarettes.

Nash dropped the paper clip as he walked into his own cubicle and settled his heft into a desk chair that groaned in protest.

Asshole, she thought without heat as she turned back to her computer.

A few minutes later, she heard her partner arrive before she saw him. Talking into his cell phone in one hand, balancing a cup of coffee in the other, Tyronne Thompson, or Double T as he was known around the bureau, strolled into the Homicide Division. With a nod to Nash, he plopped himself into his desk chair, his cubicle catty-corner from hers, and took an experimental sip from the cup which, she knew, was usually filled with something like five shots of espresso from the coffee shop down the block, what he referred to as his "high-octane kick start" for the morning.

His head was shaved, his bald pate gleaming a deep mocha color under the lights strung high overhead. With the build of an NFL tight end, Double T was usually affable, but had a temper that could spark when crossed. Fortunately he didn't lose control all that much. He peeled off his jacket and draped it over the back of his chair before stepping into the opening to her work area. "Guess who checked herself out of the hospital?"

"Let me see . . ." She pretended to think. "How about our infamous actress who swears she doesn't have a clue as to what happened to her sister?"

A wide smile stretched across Double T's defined jaw and his dark eyes gleamed. "You already heard," he charged.

With a shake of her head she said, "We only have one person we're interested in who was in a hospital." She lifted one side of her mouth. "See. I'm just displaying my awesome powers of deduction. By the way, Cassie Kramer booked herself on a flight to LA as well."

"More awesomeness displayed," he said, leaning a hip against her desk. "You can't seem to control it."

"Oh, I know."

"And you're a liar. What tipped you off?"

"Who. Whitney Stone." When he didn't respond, she added, *"Justice: Stone Cold."*

Recognition flared in his eyes. "Oh. That one. Just what we need."

"Mmm."

"So what do you think our runaway is doing?"

Nash shrugged. "Good question. Cassie Kramer does live in LA, or at least she did. Maybe she's just going home and trying to rebuild her life."

"As an actress?"

"I don't think so. Unless all this publicity about her missing sister gives her more Hollywood cred, she's not getting any parts. Nothing major anyway, for quite a while. She's trying to be a writer, got a couple of scripts written." Double T's eyebrows raised but Nash shook her head. "Hasn't sold anything that I could find."

"She any good?"

"Who knows? The jury's still out."

"And there's still that missing sister."

"Uh-huh."

Double T asked, "You got a tail on the sister? In LA?"

Nash felt herself smile. "What do you think?" She then pulled up a link on her computer. "Take a look at this," she said, indicating the monitor where a close-up of Allie Kramer's beautiful face appeared along with a tense music score. Her expression was coy, a sly smile, eyes flashing with mischief, her skin appearing flawless as the camera pushed in more closely to focus the reflection of light in one of Allie's eyes, the striations of color becoming clearer, the pupil enlarging and the speck of light growing, showing colors and movement within. Blurry images sharpened, then the screen was filled with the image of a frantically running woman, racing as if terror-driven, her shoes pounding the wet pavement, her breathing ragged, her face twisted in horror as heart-pounding music swelled.

The woman was Allie Kramer.

A shot rang out.

Abruptly the image on the screen faded to black.

With the sound of following shots, letters began to appear, spelling out DEAD HEAT. A final bang and the date of the movie's release came into view and then the blackness behind the lettering evaporated into gray skies and Allie Kramer's watery image before fading completely.

Double T leaned back in his chair. "It's almost as if whoever put this together is playing off the star going missing in real life."

"Ya think?" They'd already gone over the possibility that Allie Kramer's disappearance was staged to generate more interest in her and the film, but if so the production company, or whoever was behind her vanishing act, was taking the law into its own hands.

Unlikely.

People had been known to pull outrageous stunts for publicity, but the idea seemed far-fetched. Yet they were getting nowhere with the missing person's case. No one had heard from Allie Kramer since the night before the reshooting of the final scene. She'd called her assistant, Cherise Gotwell, and said she didn't think she'd make the morning shoot, had wanted to make sure her stunt double was available, and had said that she would confirm in the morning.

She hadn't. No more calls had come in from her. In fact that was the last bit of communication of any kind. Her cell phone records indicated that she'd received one final call from her sister, Cassie, but then nothing. No one had seen or heard from her since.

How the hell could someone with a face recognized by most of the people in America disappear?

"This is just one of the trailers for the movie. There are a couple more—variations of the same. I've got a call in to the producer and the director. Maybe I'll get lucky and one of them will call me back," Nash said.

"Yeah, right. And maybe I'll go pick us up some Voodoo Doughnuts and there won't be a line."

She smiled at the idea, but her good humor faded as she turned her computer screen to face her and replayed the video one more time to stare at Allie Kramer's earnest face. "Where the hell are you?" she whispered under her breath, then tamped down the feeling that the woman was already dead. Until a body was located, Allie Kramer was presumed alive.

But deep down, Rhonda Nash thought the chances of finding Allie Kramer living and breathing were slim.

And getting slimmer by the second.

CHAPTER 13

When Cassie roused to look at the clock near her bed, it was nearly ten. Her bedroom was flooded with sunlight as she'd forgotten to pull the drapes shut the night before.

Stretching, she raised up on one elbow as she shook off the cobwebs of a night teeming with nightmares.

After weeks in the hospital room, hearing the sounds of murmuring voices, rattling carts, and soft dings of the elevator, the relative peace and quiet of her apartment should have brought on a slumber deeper than any sleeping aid could deliver, but it hadn't. She was tired to the bone and felt as if she'd run a marathon. Or maybe two marathons.

Yawning, she pushed her hair from her eyes and found her computer where she'd left it, on wrinkled sheets next to her on the bed, its screen dark.

So now she was sleeping with electronic devices.

Instead of Trent.

In her mind's eye, she saw a glimpse of life as it had been. She used to awaken to Trent stretched out beside her on the bed, one tanned arm flung over her waist, his hair tousled, his breathing rhythmic and deep. She would stare at the curve of his spine and muscles of his back, his taut skin showing a few scars.

God, how she'd loved him.

"It's over," she reminded herself, and rolled over to pick up the earring on her nightstand, the one Rinko had found in her hospital room.

For the next hour she searched the Internet for earrings in the shape of a red cross, scouring hundreds of images and comparing them to the little bit of jewelry she'd collected from the hospital.

Some had dangles, others made of glass or rubies, still others in the wrong configuration. Eventually, though, she'd discovered several pictures of red crosses on posts that seemed to be a match. From what she could glean, the earrings were made sometime after World War II, and weren't expensive, nor rare. At least they hadn't been in the 1950s. Now, of course, they were little more than a cheap collector's item that, due to the passage of over half a century, had become harder to find.

As she sat cross-legged on the messy bed, staring at the bit of jewelry in her palm, she realized the earring wasn't a clue to who had worn it in her hospital room, but it was the only hard evidence that the nurse had really existed and visited her. No one would believe that she had actually seen the nurse, not in her state of tentative rationality. The same could be said of Steven Rinko, as no one at the hospital nor his parents trusted him since he had been diagnosed with some kind of neurological disorder in which, at least at some times, he hallucinated and couldn't distinguish between reality and fantasy. Though he claimed his IQ was off the charts, and that's why he saw things others didn't, Cassie wasn't quick to believe him. But she did think he actually believed his own warped view of the world, even though it was slightly altered from that of the general public.

She studied the earring for the hundredth time, then slid it into a compartment in her purse and made her way to the bathroom. She brushed her teeth, threw on her clothes, and twisted her hair onto her head. A slap of lipstick and sunglasses was her makeup as she grabbed the overnight bag that she kept with a change of clothes and headed out the door and into the bright morning.

A flock of tiny birds chatted and flitted in and out of the bank of bougainvillea that separated the parking area from the main house. The sun was high, sharp rays bouncing off the windshield of her car as she slid inside. She rolled down the windows and started the ignition.

As she backed up, she glanced at the door of her condo, the place she'd sought sanctuary after her last split with Trent. The unit had been available and she'd been able to rent it month to month, but it had never felt like home, had always been a place to crash when she was in LA, nothing more. The truth was that there was nothing to come home to here. No pets. No children. No husband. No reason to stay. Which is just as well as she intended to drive to Oregon the following morning.

If she could get through another night.

She'd already called the owner of the apartment and explained about the key going missing and asking that the locks be changed at her cost. Doug Peterson, who lived in the main house and was retired, was a handyman and promised to replace the dead bolt. Thankfully, he hadn't asked a million questions about Allie.

As she drove to the local post office Cassie's stomach growled. Somehow she'd missed dinner, opting instead for the Moscow Mules Holly had ordered and which had, as far as she could see, zero nutritional value.

Her plans for the day were simple: First grab her mail, then find coffee followed quickly with food. Next, she planned to double-check with a jeweler about the earring. Then the rest of the day she would spend trying to connect with acquaintances of Allie's, people Cassie hadn't talked to since entering the hospital. She knew her chances of finding out anything new, anything the police could have missed, were nearly nonexistent, but she wouldn't be satisfied until she'd reached as many people as possible. Why? Because she loved her sister. Oftentimes it was a love/hate relationship, sibling rivalry at its worst, but she did care about Allie. That was a fact.

And, of course, there was the story surrounding her disappearance and the fact that Cassie was already blocking it out in her head.

At the post office she went through her mail, tossed the junk in a recycle bin, and kept the bills and anything that looked important before grabbing coffee and a scone at a drive-through coffee shop. She pulled into a park and rolled down the windows to let in a soft little breeze, eased her seat away from the steering wheel, then made several phone calls, starting with the people who had recently worked with Allie.

As she watched a nanny playing with toddlers at a slide, Cassie dialed Little Bea, then Dean Arnette, followed by Cherise Gotwell. No one answered. "Great," she said, leaving voice mail messages and texts for each of them. She then tossed her phone onto the passenger seat and opened the paper bag she'd brought from the coffee shop.

Picking at her scone, she kept her eyes on the scene in front of her, the group of little children running, skipping, and screaming with glee as they darted in and out of the play structure. With an effort she ignored the emptiness that threatened to crawl through her soul. A boy of around four and a girl a couple of years younger prattled at each other as they took turns on the small slide, then, with the nanny pushing the empty stroller, they ran for the fountain, which was little more than a grid of spouts shooting jets of water high into the air. The kids giggled and screamed in delight as they tried to anticipate where the next stream would appear.

They were wet, happy, and adorable.

Cassie smiled and took a sip of her coffee. Being the oldest she could remember playing with Allie at that age, here in California. Her sister had been a toddler, cute, plump, and delightful, and their parents had been, at that time, happily married. Before Robert had started cheating, or at least before Jenna had realized it. God, it seemed like ages ago, another lifetime.

Nearby the nanny lit a cigarette, blew smoke away from the children who were paying her no attention, then checked her cell phone as she sat on a bench, just out of reach of the spray. She was young. Maybe twenty. Maybe not quite. Her hair was pulled into a messy knot, and she wore tattered jeans, a T-shirt, and a bored expression, but she kept her eyes, for the most part, on her charges.

Cassie glanced at her own cell. Of course there were no new messages.

She wondered if anyone she'd called would phone or text her back.

Unlikely. Very unlikely.

How could she ask questions or find out *any*thing when no one would give her the time of day?

Figure it out. There has to be a way.

As if she were in the throes of trying to quit smoking or hide her habit, the nanny quickly dropped her cigarette onto the concrete and crushed it with the heel of her sandal. Then, while the kids were distracted, she walked to a trash can situated near the restrooms and discarded the butt.

Cassie watched while a thirtysomething man in shorts and a T-shirt jogged along a path. He passed by on the opposite side of the fountain, where beneath a shade tree an older woman sat on a bench. She was busy breaking a crust of bread and tossing crumbs to a few small birds and a crow that inspected each morsel before pecking quickly and cawing for another tidbit. "Enough," the woman yelled as if the bird could understand her. Then she crumpled her sack and stuffed it into her collapsible shopping cart, dusting her hands. "Tomorrow," she said, then climbed off the bench and, rolling the cart in front of her, headed to a little Volkswagen Beetle parked in a handicapped space.

Cassie's thoughts were still on how she could possibly find her sister as she watched the woman leave. She finished her scone and tapped her fingers on the steering wheel. Someone knew something. She was sure of it. Allie had to confide in someone. Probably Cherise, who was MIA. *Damn it all to hell. If only—*

Like a lightning bolt, inspiration hit.

Who would be Allie's most likely confidante? Someone who knew her moods inside out, someone who had worked with her for years. A smile spread across Cassie's face as she picked up the phone again, scrolled through the menu, and touched Laura Merrick's name. There were several numbers listed, one being her personal cell, which Cassie had gotten from Allie. In her mind's eye she conjured up Laura's face. Sharp features, big eyes, smooth complexion, and someone who might just know something.

Laura the makeup artist.

Laura the hairdresser.

Laura who had been with Allie since her first role in *Street Life.*

Who else would Allie spend so much time with, be inclined to share secrets with? Cassie pressed the number and waited. One ring. Two. Three and then a real voice, not a recording.

"This is Laura."

Thank God. "Hi. It's Cassie," she said, testing the waters.

No response.

"Cassie Kramer."

Another pause. "Yeah?"

Not exactly encouraging and Cassie didn't want to take a chance that Laura would simply hang up on her if she started asking questions, so she said, "Look, I'm in town for a day or two and I was wondering if there was any chance you had room to squeeze me in for a haircut?"

Again the pregnant pause, then, "You want an appointment with me? And like immediately?"

"Well, yeah. That would be so great."

"Well . . . you know, Cassie, I'm booked solid."

"It's . . . it's just a quick trim. Really. I don't need a shampoo or color or anything."

"Today?" Laura actually laughed. "Seriously?" And then, before Cassie could respond, "You're here? In LA? But I thought . . ." She let the sentence trail.

"I thought that you were in a psych ward somewhere." That's what she was about to say. Of course. "I just got back into town and I won't be here long." Cassie forced her voice to sound cheerful. "I knew it was a long shot, a really long shot, but I thought I'd call. Allie

raves about you." Cassie crossed her fingers, knowing she was playing on Laura's relationship with her sister, but she didn't feel bad about using every possible trick in the book. Laura, as Allie's hair and makeup person, was likely to know more about Allie's inner feelings than anyone. Sitting for hours in a chair while the stylist tended to you created a sense of intimacy. Secrets were often shared.

"Have you heard from her?" Laura asked.

"No. I . . . we don't know anything."

A long sigh. "Look, I'm not joking. I'm scheduled for like eternity. Most of the time I'm on a set somewhere. I'd like to help you out, but everyone who works in my salon is crazy busy."

Cassie hid her disappointment. "The truth is I'd like to talk to you. About Allie."

"You said you hadn't heard from her."

"That's right, but I was hoping you might know something."

"Sorry. I don't know what happened to her. It's weird, y'know?" There was another pause, then Laura said, "Look, Cassie, tell ya what. I've got to run, but if anyone cancels with any of my hairdressers, they're all spectacular, by the way, then I'll text you, okay? We'll work something out. Are you here for a while?"

"I was planning to leave in the morning."

"You thought you could get in *today? Just today?*" Laura laughed again. "You don't ask for much, do you? I'll do what I can, but don't hold your breath. As I said, on the off chance someone in the shop gets a cancellation, I'll let you know. But you have to understand it's really unlikely. Like probably not going to happen." And then she was gone. Cassie stared at her phone and felt defeated. Laura wasn't just Allie's hair and makeup person, she had other big-name clients as well. There wasn't a snowball's chance in hell that Cassie could speak to her alone. Not that it really mattered, she thought, staring out the windshield. Hadn't Laura just said she didn't know anything?

A text had come in while she was on the phone, from a private number she didn't recognize:

santafe07.

What? She texted back:

Who is this? What do you mean?

She hit send before realizing someone had probably texted the wrong number.

Or not?

What did anything having to do with Santa Fe, New Mexico, have to do with her? And 07? Did something happen there in 2007? Or was the 07 part of another number? Had Allie had a movie out in that year? Been on location in Santa Fe . . . no, her career started after that.

"It's nothing," she warned herself. She didn't even know the person who'd texted. Still, it bothered her, so when no one responded immediately to her text, she dialed the phone number, which she could tell from the first three digits had originated in Oregon. Maybe if she knew who'd called?

A recording stated: "You have reached the voice mail of Dr. Virginia Sherling. Please leave your name, number, and a brief message and I'll get back to you."

Dr. Sherling? Cassie's own psychiatrist at Mercy Hospital? Why would she send a cryptic text? That couldn't be right. But there was no way Cassie was going to leave a message back and risk talking to the doctor who would try to convince her to return to the hospital.

At the sound of the beep, Cassie disconnected.

Through the windshield she watched the older boy push the little girl into the water with enough force to send her sprawling. The girl screamed bloody murder, then got up and gave him a reciprocal shove while the nanny, caught up in her texting, looked up sharply. Scowling, the nanny reluctantly slid the phone into a huge bag then marched her charges out of the spurting fountain while they both cried and balked, blaming each other in true sibling fashion.

Like she and Allie had done.

Rather than take a melancholy trip down memory lane, Cassie finished her coffee, wadded up her empty bag and cup, then climbed out of her car in search of a trash can. The nanny was bundling the kids into their double stroller. The breeze had died, and in the distance Cassie heard the steady hum of traffic on the freeway. She thought she caught a whiff of smoke, but the nanny was long over her cigarette and halfway to her car.

Odd.

She made her way to the garbage can the nanny had used that was positioned near the restrooms and a covered picnic area. Glancing around, she searched for the source of the scent. No one else was in the park except two people who were seated in a silver SUV, a Toyota with tinted windows, and parked several spaces away from her Honda. It must've pulled up when she was lost in thought, she decided, as she hadn't noticed it pull in. She shot a look its way and noticed that the driver was a woman in sunglasses who, like Cassie, had been staring through the windshield observing the action, or now, lack thereof, in the park. The SUV's windows were rolled down.

Cassie caught a glimpse of the occupant in the passenger seat, a burly man whose hairy arm was stretched through the open window, a cigarette dangling from his fingers. His eyes, too, were shaded.

The hairs on the back of Cassie's neck rose. She sensed both occupants of the Toyota were staring at her, following her with their shaded eyes, not moving their heads, not saying a word.

Cassie checked the park and her heart sank. The nanny and kids had almost disappeared through a far entrance, the jogger long gone, the woman who'd been feeding the birds already driving away.

Stop it. It's no big deal. Weren't you just doing the same thing? Sitting in your car, observing everyone else. The park is a public place, for crying out loud.

Still, she felt uneasy as she headed back toward her car.

As she did a door clicked open and the woman stepped out of the SUV.

She was slim. Attractive. With thick black hair cut at an angle, her oversize sunglasses hiding her face. She raised a hand. "Cassie?" she called and her voice was vaguely familiar. "Cassie Kramer?" Two inches shorter than Cassie, she walked purposely across the spaces separating their vehicles. Before she said, "Whitney Stone," Cassie recognized the reporter.

And her heart nosedived.

She braced herself.

Whitney Stone was smiling, white teeth flashing above a pointed chin, her arm outstretched as if she and Cassie were long-lost friends or at the very least acquaintances.

Cassie ignored the friendly hand reaching for hers and saw the tiny tightening of the corners of Whitney Stone's mouth. In her free hand was a microphone. "I'm the producer and reporter for *Justice: Stone Cold*."

Cassie didn't need to know what the reporter wanted. She could guess because the subject of interest never changed: Allie. Always Allie. Interest in Cassie was limited to the fact that she was Allie Kramer's sister and, of course, Jenna Hughes's daughter. Now that Allie was missing, even Jenna had become an adjunct to the real matter of interest, the "story."

From the corner of her eye Cassie witnessed the guy in the passenger seat toss his cigarette out the window, climb out of the SUV, and, while crushing the smoldering butt with his shoe, head their way. A bruiser in jeans and a black T-shirt, with huge biceps, receding hairline, and a swagger, he was carrying a shoulder camera as if it weighed nothing.

"I'd like a few minutes with you," Whitney was saying as her companion hoisted his camera to his shoulder. "We're doing a series on the mystery surrounding Allie Kramer's disappearance."

"No, thanks." Cassie was firm.

Whitney Stone barreled on, "Since you're Allie Kramer's sister and are rumored to be the last person to see her before she vanished, I think your input is necessary."

"Not interested." Cassie started moving toward her car.

Whitney offered that well-practiced smile again as she eased between Cassie and her car. "I'd just like to talk to you about your sister. It could be helpful, I think, in finding her." Whitney Stone was scrambling now. "I know you want to know what happened to her and together we could—"

"I said I wasn't interested and I'm not." By now Cassie had angled to her car but she saw that the cameraman had positioned his camera so that it was focused on her, its red light a beacon warning that he was filming. *Bastard!*

"The public wants to know—"

"About Allie? Yeah, I know, but I have nothing to say." She was aware of the cameraman, moving in closer, focusing on her face. "Don't," she warned him.

"Nothing?" Whitney repeated as a gust of wind kicked up, pushing a bit of trash across the parking lot and causing Whitney's sleek hair to ruffle. "You don't want to say anything to the public, to find a way to locate your sister?"

Cassie ignored the barb with an effort and kept walking.

"Come on, you two were close at least at one time, that's what I'm told."

"Who told you that?" Cassie blurted while trying and failing to hold her tongue. She was tired and cranky from lack of sleep and she didn't need Whitney Stone's questions or her innuendos.

"Common knowledge."

Was it? Cassie didn't think so and there was something smarmy about Whitney that really got under her skin. And wasn't she based out of Portland? Cassie thought she'd heard that from someone, a producer who had worked on her show. "Why are you in LA?" she asked. And then she got it, everything that wasn't making sense fell easily into place. "Oh, God, no. You're here at this park because of me. You found out that I . . ." She was going to say "checked out of the hospital," but caught herself. Instead she swung her arm in a wide arc to include herself, her car, and the park in general. "How did you know I'd be here?" When Whitney wasn't quick with an answer, Cassie guessed the answer. "You followed me here? To California? You . . . what? Flew down here? Staked out my place?" Her mind was running now, imagining how the reporter had located her at this random park.

Again she was met with righteous silence, as if Whitney Friggin' Stone had the right to invade and stomp on her privacy. "I can't believe it," Cassie whispered, stunned. It hadn't been Holly Dennison she'd felt eyeing her at the airport at all. It was the woman standing before her, microphone in hand. Damn! And that silver SUV she'd caught a glimpse of in her rearview mirror? Hadn't it been identical to the Toyota 4Runner parked a stone's throw from her own car?

"I called," Whitney said.

"I got your messages," Cassie shot back, "but I thought you were in Portland."

"What does it matter? I'm mobile."

"You're right. It doesn't, matter that is. I don't have anything to say. No interview." But it might have already been too late as the goon was filming away, the tiny red light glowing steadily on the shoulder cam.

"But I've already started the series."

"Your problem, not mine." She turned on the stocky cameraman. "Don't film me," she said. "Did you hear me? I'm serious. Turn the camera off!"

"This is a public park," Whitney reminded her, as if she were playing by some kind of legal rules.

"Turn it off!"

"Are you afraid to talk to me, Ms. Kramer?" Whitney persisted.

"No."

"Do you prefer to be called Ms. Kramer or Mrs. Kittle? You're still legally married to Trent Kittle, right?"

"Leave him out of this," she said, horrified that Trent's name had come up. Oh, God, what if this aired? What if he saw the program? She knew that Whitney Stone was already airing segments about Allie. God, what a mess! What if Whitney edited her pieces to make it look like Cassie was somehow a part of Allie's disappearance? That *Trent* was? She told herself not to panic, but she felt a wave start to envelop her as the camera kept rolling, catching her doe-in-the-headlights look while Whitney twisted the truth.

"But you are still married to him," Whitney pressed.

"I don't want to talk about—"

"And it's been reported that he was with your sister, Allie Kramer, as well, that his relationship with her is the reason you two separated."

"There was no relationship between Trent and Allie," she shot back before biting her tongue. There was an almost imperceptible smile on the reporter's lips. This had to end.

"But he was seen at her apartment. Alone. During the time she was broken up with Brandon McNary."

"As I said, I have nothing to say to you."

"Your marriage failed because of your sister and then she goes missing."

"For the love of God . . ." Cassie tried to step away.

"Isn't it true that your sister, your *baby* sister, was having an affair with your husband?"

"No!" The word felt like acid on her tongue. Whitney Stone was voicing her own darkest fears that Trent, like everyone else in America, had fallen in love with Allie Kramer. She needed to stop talking and end this interview, but the hook had been set and Cassie's temper, always a problem, took over. "I warned you not to—"

"Warned me not to what?" Whitney asked innocently.

Don't let her bully you into a confrontation, not more than it is, and do NOT give her what she wants. She's looking to fan the fires, and she'll twist your words to make it look like you made Allie disappear in some kind of jealous rage, that maybe you even killed her. She will edit this interview and turn it all back on you. On Allie. On Trent.

"I'm just trying to help," Whitney wheedled.

This was about ratings and scandal and promoting Whitney Stone's career!

Cassie withdrew her own phone and hit the camera app. "Then you won't mind me filming you, like you're filming me." She depressed the button to start recording the entire interview, turning the phone's camera toward the reporter.

"What're you doing?"

"Just ensuring that your reporting is accurate," she said, rotating slightly to show the intimidating cameraman before returning to Whitney Stone. "I asked you not to film, and you ignored me. I told you I know nothing more about Allie Kramer's disappearance, but you kept at me. So I repeat: I don't have anything to say to you."

For a moment Whitney looked stunned, but the reporter quickly got hold of her unspooling composure. "Your sister disappeared under suspicious circumstances. You and your family must be devastated."

"Any questions you have about my sister's disappearance should be directed to the Portland Police Department. Detective Nash is investigating the case. Now, we're done." She moved around the reporter and, with her phone still aimed at Whitney Stone, opened the door of her car.

"You went through a horrific tragedy before, when your mother was stalked by that maniac. You were nearly killed and Allie witnessed—"

"Don't even go there!"

"It's part of your history. Of Allie's history. Certainly of Jenna Hughes's history, and there's a new interest in what happened then."

"No," Cassie said through clenched teeth. Her darkest fears were coming to light. She couldn't relive the horror.

"You lost a boyfriend," Whitney went on, and Cassie felt a numbing cold when she realized the story had already been researched. "He was murdered."

"I don't know why you want to bring this up now."

"Because the public wants to know and they're going to. I'm doing a report on what happened ten years ago."

Knowing it would do no good, Cassie couldn't help herself from begging. "No . . . please. There's no reason to dredge all that up again." Images of ice and snow, blood and freezing water, frozen visages of Jenna in her most popular roles sped through her memory. But the image that was most indelibly painted in her mind: Josh, slumped behind the wheel of his truck, a dark oozing gash visible on his throat. She could still hear the loud music pulsing through the frigid night, still recall the pure fear and shock she'd felt.

Her knees threatened to buckle. She felt suddenly cold to the bone as she thought of the madman who'd terrorized them, how close she and Jenna had come to becoming his final victims. She was shaking so badly she leaned against her car for support.

Watching her, Whitney seemed to pull back with genuine concern. "The story about Jenna's stalker airs this week. I just thought you might want to add something that I could edit in."

"Go to hell," Cassie ground out, pulling herself together. "Leave me and my family alone, you bloodsucking bitch."

"Wait!" Whitney Stone raised a hand. She was irritated as hell, but tried to hide it under a smooth coat of civility. "Okay, I get it, you don't want to talk to the press, but I just have a few questions. As I said, to help. And really, come on, it'll be good publicity with the movie coming out in a couple of months."

Cassie slid into the driver's seat. "I've said all I'm going to."

Whitney grabbed on to the open driver's window. "I thought you might want to tell your side of the story. You know, what happened then. What's happening now. I'm going to run it, you know, as I've already started airing my investigation. So, with or without your input the story will air, but I would love to hear what you think, to try and work with you."

"I have nothing to say." She jabbed her key into the ignition.

The car started but Whitney was still hanging on. "The police questioned you for hours. You were reportedly the last person to see your sister before she disappeared. And it's common knowledge that you two had your ups and downs."

Cassie tried to keep her cool, but the woman was irritating the hell out of her and the cameraman had positioned himself so that if she backed up, she might hit him. "How long have you been following me? How did you know that I'd be here? Now. In this park?"

A tiny muscle worked in the reporter's jaw. "I was going to talk to you at your house and I got there just as you were leaving so—"

"You know where I live?"

"Of course."

Cassie mentally reviewed the stops she'd made before landing here. "You followed me to the post office and through the coffee drive-in . . . For God's sake—" She snapped. "All the way from Portland to LA? You're unbelievable." She glanced at the hulk who was blocking her exit. "Get out of my way and leave me the hell alone." Before waiting for an answer, she shoved her Honda into reverse. "You'd better move," she told the cameraman.

"I know you want to find out what happened to your sister," Whitney pleaded. "I do, too."

"For a story."

"Maybe we could help each other."

"Tell your boy there to watch out. I'm not stopping."

Whitney was still talking as Cassie rolled up her window and eased backward, certain her back tire would roll over the toe of the big galoot's boot. Well, tough. She kept reversing. At the last second the cameraman moved slightly away, and she kept right on backing up until she could maneuver her car around the bastard. "Idiot," she muttered under her breath as she tore out of the lot.

She didn't know if she was talking about Whitney Stone, the man with the shoulder cam, or herself.

CHAPTER 14

"I, um . . . I don't suppose there's any word. About Allie Kramer, I mean." Her eyes wide, the girl behind the antique cash register at the hardware store looked up at Trent expectantly. She had layered red hair, a turned up nose spattered with freckles and braces, and she smiled a bit anxiously as she handed him his sack of nails, his receipt, and change.

"I haven't heard." He stood on the worn floorboards at the counter in Bart's Hardware, an iconic Falls Crossing establishment that had sat on Main Street for over a hundred years. Inside, labyrinthine corridors were lined with shelves that climbed to the ceiling, accessed by dusty, rolling ladders and holding containers of just about any hardware known to man in the past century or two. Some of the tools on display were probably older than the gray-haired men who still played checkers, poker, and traded insults around a wood stove in the barnlike building's basement.

"So, you don't know if she's okay? She's like a local celebrity, y'know?"

He did. Oh, how he did.

"I mean like a really big star. From here! Can you believe it? Falls Crossing?" She sighed. "*Nothing* ever happens here, but Allie Kramer grew up here, went to the same schools I did. You know, Harrington? I probably, like, sat in the same desk she did. I saw her picture in one of the old yearbooks. It's soooo awesome."

The girl was practically swooning, which was ridiculous when considering Allie Kramer's personality, which, of course, was at odds with any of her on-screen personas. Allie Kramer was *not* like any of the heroines she portrayed so convincingly on-screen.

"Yeah," he agreed, scooping up the change she'd laid on the scarred counter. "But really, I don't know anything about what happened to her." He folded the ones into his wallet.

"I thought. I mean, I heard from like everybody, that you're married to . . ." Her eyebrows pulled together in confusion as if maybe her information was faulty. "You were married to her sister, I thought. Casey."

"Cassie."

Her head bobbed in agreement. "Cassie. She was in some movies, too, I think. I never saw any of them."

Not a lot of people had, he thought.

"I watched Whitney Stone, y'know? She's reporting on it on TV, but—" She shrugged her slim shoulders. "She didn't really say anything. So you don't know what happened to her? Allie, I mean." Disappointment clouded her big eyes.

How many times did he have to say it? He slid his wallet into the back pocket of his jeans. "That's right." He smiled through clenched teeth. The girl at the counter meant no harm—she was just curious—but he was sick to death of questions about Allie's disappearance, his estranged wife, her mental condition, and the whole damned circus surrounding both of them. For the love of Christ, he'd even gotten calls from the press himself, none of which he'd taken, but they bothered him just the same.

It was like stepping into a field of nettles with no way out . . . you just kept getting stung over and over again.

Worse yet, he'd fought his gut instinct to find Cassie—take the next flight or drive the whole damned sixteen hours straight to LA. He was still fighting it.

Carrying his small sack of roofing staples and nails, he made his way out of the store. "Son of a bitch," he muttered under his breath as the door closed sharply behind him.

The air outside was heavy with the threat of more rain, gray clouds hanging low. Whitecaps churned on the dark water of the Columbia, while the streets of Falls Crossing were still wet and shimmering from an earlier cloudburst. Trent turned his collar to the wind and made his way to his truck, where Hud was waiting. Bouncing on the driver's seat, his head out the open window, the dog spied Trent and let out an enthusiastic yip.

"Yeah, glad to see you, too," Trent said as he opened the door. Tail wagging wildly, Hud hopped onto the passenger seat.

It had been ten minutes since Trent had left the dog alone and the shepherd acted as if he'd been waiting for years.

Another sharp yip.

"Settle down, boy." Scratching Hud behind his ears, he added, "Let's go home." The words echoed through his mind and for a second he hesitated, key in position over the ignition as a memory sizzled through his brain, a white-hot image of Cassie, after two glasses of wine, draping her arm around his shoulders, rising on tiptoes and whispering those same words.

They'd been married barely a month and had gone to a restaurant in Malibu for dinner and drinks at an outdoor table where they were able to watch the sun settle into the Pacific. Before the check came, Cassie kicked off one sandal and beneath the table had inched her bare toes up his leg. He'd immediately felt his damned cock harden and had sent her a warning glare. But her mischievous gaze had met his and she'd whispered in a sultry voice, "I love you, you know, Trent Kittle. So let's go home and do something about it."

He'd left cash, including an overly generous tip, on the table, taken her hand, and they'd wended their way quickly through the tables packed tightly onto the patio. Once in the car, Trent had ignored the speed limit. When they'd reached their apartment she'd taken off before he'd put the car into park and, laughing, led him through the garden and front door. He'd chased after his wife as she ran into their unit and through their small apartment, both of them laughing and tossing off their clothes on the way to the bedroom, where he'd caught her, pulled her close, and kissed her with a fervor he'd never felt with any other woman. It had been ninety degrees in the apartment, only a fan to move the air, but they hadn't cared. They'd tumbled onto the bed, half-dressed and entwined, somehow managing to peel off the remainder of their clothing and make love until long after midnight.

His muscles tensed at the memory and even now, seeing her in his mind's eye, her streaked hair wet from perspiration, her breathing rapid, her eyes dilated in the darkened room, he felt an erection in the making.

Annoyed, he turned his thoughts away from his missing wife.

Jabbing his key into the ignition, Trent switched on the engine, then he backed out of the badly marked space and put the Ford into drive. He hit the gas a little too hard. The truck leaped forward and he eased off the pedal as he nosed his pickup into the heart of Falls Crossing, the Oregon town he'd called home except for his brief stint in LA. Traffic was light along a street where retail stores and offices were crowded together, windowed storefronts lining the sidewalks, pedestrians dashing under awnings to protect them from the rain that had begun to spit from the dark sky. Turning on the windshield wipers, he only had to slow to a stop at one intersection where, while his truck idled, he checked his cell phone.

No one had called him, which wasn't a surprise. He told himself it didn't bother him that Cassie hadn't phoned him back; he hadn't really expected her to. But deep down, in a place he refused to acknowledge, he had hoped she would reach out to him, had wanted to hear her voice and determine for himself if she was okay. He slid the phone onto the console and waited for the light to change, then drove out of town.

Cassie was still his wife, at least legally, and he still worried about her. No matter how many times he reminded himself that she'd walked out on him, wouldn't listen to his excuses, explanations, or reasons, just called him a "stupid ass son of a bitch," before leaving him and moving out permanently, he couldn't completely eradicate her from his thoughts.

The phone calls and visits he'd attempted to make after their last fight had been ignored or rejected, even after the accident on the set of *Dead Heat* and her sister's disappearance.

While the dog kept his nose to the cracked window and the town gave way to farmland, Trent told himself that he should just leave well enough alone. Cassie had made it more than clear that he should back off. His jaw tightened as he remembered how he'd panicked upon hearing that an actress had been shot while filming a final scene for *Dead Heat*. He'd flipped out, fearing for Cassie's life, only to discover that the victim had not been either his wife or his sister-in-law. For a second he'd felt relief, then he'd learned Allie had disappeared.

Once more he'd tried to reach Cassie, but she hadn't returned his texts or calls. So he'd decided enough was enough, that he needed to talk to her in person, to actually set eyes on her and hopefully get some answers. He'd driven to her hotel in Portland to no avail. She'd left specific instructions with the management and staff of the hotel to allow no one, not even her husband, to know her room number. No information about her was to be mentioned to anyone.

Insisting on seeing her had proved impossible and a real pisser, his arguments with the receptionist escalating to the point that he'd been threatened with being forcefully escorted by security to the street and the police contacted. Grudgingly he'd given up. He'd stood in the cold rain and stared angrily upward at the tall edifice and thought that he'd caught a glimpse of her on the balcony of a room on an upper floor. His eyes had narrowed but he'd been jostled by a threesome of teenagers half running down the sidewalk. "Hey, look out, man," one of the boys had grumbled as they'd passed, and for a second Trent's concentration had been broken. When he looked up again, he realized he'd been mistaken. Cassie wasn't standing on the balcony. He'd only seen the play of light and shadow and a curtain moving inside an open sliding door. He'd conjured up her image. Of course she hadn't been outside in the rain.

He'd left then, but hadn't been satisfied, especially when within two days of Allie's disappearance, amid rumors that Cassie was the last person to see her alive and was considered a person of interest in the missing person's case, rumors had swirled that Cassie had checked herself into Mercy Hospital. He'd called, of course, and once again had run up against the wall of her privacy. She'd refused to communicate with him in any way, shape, or form.

After six or seven phone calls to various people, including the hospital administrative staff and her mother, who also hadn't been able to get him through to Cassie, he'd once again driven to Portland. As he'd wound up the tree-lined street that led to Mercy Hospital he'd told himself this time he wasn't going to take "no" for an answer.

So thinking, he'd determinedly walked through the front doors and asked for a visitor's pass. The receptionist had been a stout woman whose gray roots showed in her flat, black hair and whose chin and jaw had disappeared into her neck. Seated at a desk, she'd looked over the tops of her rimless glasses when he'd stated that he was there to visit Cassie Kramer. With a frigid smile, she'd pleasantly but firmly refused him entrance. Even pulling the "I'm her husband" card hadn't worked.

She'd made it very clear that he'd been persona non grata.

He'd then asked that someone tell Cassie he was waiting and had camped out in the waiting area of the hospital, while he had leafed distractedly through an out-of-date magazine filled with last year's summer salad recipes and beach getaway ideas while the wintry rain sheeted down the windows.

As he'd thumbed past what had to be the fifth article on weight loss, a teenage boy with wild blond hair and bad skin had approached him.

Trent had looked up.

The kid, in khakis and a long-sleeved Yankees T-shirt, had announced, "She says, 'Go away.'"

"Pardon?" Trent had dropped his magazine. "Who said, 'Go away'?"

"You're looking for Cassie," the boy had said and it wasn't a question. "She doesn't want to talk to you and you should go away."

"And you are?"

"Steven. Steven L. Rinko," the kid had said. "The *L* stands for Leon. He was my grandpop. He's dead now."

"I'm sorry."

Unblinking eyes had stared at him. "Why? Did you know him?"

"No, I'm sure I didn't."

"Then you couldn't be sorry."

"I guess not. It's just what people say."

"So they're liars because they can't be sorry." He'd shrugged with the innocence of a child telling the simple truth.

Deciding the conversation was going nowhere, Trent had clarified, "So 'Cassie'? Cassie Kramer? She told you to give me the message?"

"That's what I already told you. She said, 'Go away,'" he'd repeated without expression and only the merest hint of irritation in his voice.

"Look . . . Steven—"

"Steven L. Rinko. The *L* is for Leon. He was my grandpop. He's dead."

"I know, but you tell her—Cassie—I'm not going anywhere that—"

"You drive the truck?" Rinko had walked to the window and stared outside to the parking area where Trent's pickup was one of the few in the lot. "Eighty-six Ford-150 half-ton?"

"That's right."

He'd looked over his shoulder to pin Trent in his gaze. "'Course it is," he said flatly. "Bad mileage. Sometimes not enough power. Paint job can be a problem. Most owners say they are satisfied."

"Most owners?"

"Yes."

Who was this kid?

Before he'd been able to ask, the boy had nodded curtly, as if agreeing with himself, then slipped through a side door marked NO ADMITTANCE. When Trent had tried following Rinko, he found the door was locked and all he got for his trouble of pushing repeatedly on the lever was a rattling noise and the evil eye from the receptionist. Pursing her lips she slowly shook her head in disapproval and actually made little tsking sounds.

He'd left the building then.

But he'd been foolish enough to sit in his parked truck and stare up at the windows of the hospital as he'd wondered in which room she'd taken up residence.

She really hadn't wanted to see him.

Pissed, he'd finally gotten the message and started the damned truck. If she'd been peeking out a window, or standing on a veranda, or peering from behind a corner, tough. He'd done what he could. Telling himself it was over, he drove down the winding hillside through the trees, determined to contact his lawyer and end the marriage once and for all. He didn't need the grief nor the aggravation. Obviously his "wife" wanted nothing to do with him.

By the time he'd crossed the Marquam Bridge and melded into the traffic heading east, he'd cooled off considerably and decided that instead of filing for divorce he'd drive home, find his good old friend Jack Daniel's, and have himself a sit-down.

That's where he'd left it. Drinking too much, suffering from a hangover the next day, and resolving to never contact Cassie again. He'd half convinced himself she was not the woman for him. Maybe not for anyone. Her emotions had always been a little edgier than those of most people. She just never held back. That's what had attracted him to her from the get-go, her quick tongue, flashing eyes, ability to hold her own in a verbal debate, all tempered with a quick sense of humor. Life with Cassie had never been dull, which had been fine with him as Trent wasn't the kind of guy who liked things planned or even-keeled. He believed that every road should have a few bumps. It kept things interesting. He'd always lived a little on the edge himself and he'd thought he'd found a kindred spirit in Cassie Kramer.

He should have known better.

The first time he'd seen her she was on the side of the road, her car pulled onto the gravel shoulder as she'd tried to change a tire by herself.

He'd been intrigued then and damned if he still wasn't.

Now, frowning as he turned into the lane leading to his ranch, he remembered the first day he set eyes on Cassie Kramer, on the road not far from here, at twilight on a wet spring evening.

He'd been home less than a year after his stint in the military when he'd seen her little car pulled into the gravel of the road's shoulder, her left rear tire flattened. He'd parked his truck behind her, turned on his emergency flashers, and offered to help. Until she looked over her shoulder, he hadn't realized who she was. Then he

knew. She looked too much like her famous mother to miss the resemblance. It was a little eerie and, truth to tell, that part of her had
intrigued him, too. He'd had a major crush on Jenna Hughes as a
teenager. Hell, who hadn't? Every teenage boy he knew thought she
was beyond hot.

However, that day in the driving rain, he'd seen something more
in Cassie, something real, something tangible. She wasn't just some
horny schoolboy's fantasy, but a real girl on the brink of woman-
hood, a girl who had grown up famous, whose childhood had been
part of a Hollywood circus, and later suffered unimaginable horror at
the hands of a madman.

Her hair had been plastered to her head, her jacket and jeans
soaked, no makeup on her face. Determination had been evident in
the set of her jaw and when he'd offered to help, she'd declined at
first, was a little bristly. But he'd smiled and reasoned with her.

"Got the tools and the know-how," he remembered telling her.
She'd hesitated, her gaze narrowing on him, then finally stepped
aside and allowed him to do the dirty work of changing the tire and
making sure the spare was good to go before tossing the flat into her
trunk.

In the end, her suspicions softened, and she thanked him, and then
they'd both stood awkwardly in the Oregon downpour. She'd been
young and innocent, with a hint of sexuality in eyes that were identical
to those of Jenna Hughes. Noticing a smudge of dirt on her cheek,
he'd slowly wiped the mark away. She hadn't stopped him and probably he'd let his thumb linger a little too long on the arch of her cheek.

Instead of drawing away, she'd met his gaze, then impulsively
stood on her tiptoes and brushed her lips across his beard-stubbled
jaw. "Thanks," she said again, a breathless quality to her voice. "Really."

Before he could respond, she'd turned and walked to the front of
her car, slid behind the wheel, and driven off, never once looking
back. He'd watched her leave in a spray of gravel as she'd hit the gas.

Yeah, he'd been hooked.

Now, all these years later, he was having a helluva time letting go.
The ring on his left hand was proof of it.

Cassie's fingers were tense on the wheel. If she never saw Whitney Stone again, it would be too soon. All her talk about helping her
find Allie was little more than a ploy to weasel out more information
from Cassie, get some kind of inside scoop or something.

Her heart was still pounding from the confrontation. There was a chance she'd handled her face-to-face with the reporter all wrong. What if Whitney, with all her contacts, was able to help in locating Allie? What if Cassie had let her temper do the talking and the reasoning?

"No way," she said. Stone was an opportunist.

The light changed and Cassie waited impatiently for pedestrians to cross the street two cars ahead of her. Tapping her fingers nervously on the wheel, she glanced in the rearview and for a heartbeat, she didn't see her own reflection but that of Allie as she had been in the nightmare, her lips blue, her haunted eyes pleading.

I'm alive. Help me.

She blinked and the image was gone, replaced by her own worried gaze.

Could she? Help her sister? But how?

Beep!

An angry blast of a horn behind her brought her back to the present and she hit the gas, her Honda's wheels actually chirping as the driver behind her, a woman with a blond ponytail driving a Corvette, moved into another lane and shot her a look and an obscene gesture as she zipped past.

"Nice," Cassie muttered under her breath as she ran the next yellow light and headed to the 110, merging into the freeway traffic. She smiled when she noticed a big black SUV, like a Chevy Suburban or something, too, charge through behind her. At least he'd catch the ticket if there was a cop around.

She'd left Stone and her goon and headed straight to Galactic West Productions in Burbank. GW, as it was familiarly called, was the place where Little Bea worked and was owned by Dean Arnette. Since no one had bothered returning her calls and texts, she'd decided that showing up in person might be more effective.

To what end? she asked herself. If anyone had known anything about Cassie's sister, surely that person would have contacted the police.

What the hell do you think you're doing?

"Shut up!" she said to that stupid, nagging voice in her head. She'd spent weeks in a hospital, hiding, doing nothing, while her little sister was . . . God, who knew? That was the problem. Someone had to find out. It might as well be she. But what did she have to go on? A ghost nurse? An earring in the shape of a cross? Connections in the movie business? Did she really think she could find her sister over the police? Had her hastily planned trip to California been of any use in locating Allie? How had she ever thought she could find her sister when the police hadn't? If she'd thought she could get information from people who knew Allie, that they might confide in her when they hadn't to a detective, she'd been dead wrong. So far. There was a good chance that her trip south was a great big bust.

Pushing her doubts aside, she drove on toward the studio. The flow of traffic was smooth, cars flying past her though she was five miles above the speed limit. A glance at the rearview convinced her that no silver Toyota was following her. A larger black SUV was a few cars behind, but so what? Even if it was the guy who'd flagrantly run a red light or two, it wasn't that unusual and the boxy SUV hadn't been lurking near the park; she would have noticed. The important thing now was that it seemed Whitney Stone had given up trying to interview her.

But she'd be back.

No doubt about it.

The woman was relentless.

Cassie relaxed a little, her hands loosening their death grip on the steering wheel.

Whitney Stone had jangled her, ramped up her already escalated case of nerves. But at least for the time being, she'd given the reporter the slip.

Angling her Honda onto Interstate 5, she flicked her gaze to her rearview and saw no signs that anyone had her in their sights. Again, no silver Toyota and the black SUV she'd seen several times behind her hung back.

It's nothing. Just your imagination. Whitney Stone sent your case of nerves into overdrive.

A slew of traffic turned off at Burbank, but as she wound her way through the streets, she still didn't notice anyone lagging behind and tailing her. Still, she made a few extra turns and doubled back on her route, just to be sure that the reporter or the Suburban weren't following.

Telling herself she was more paranoid than even Dr. Sherling suspected, she finally drove up to the offices of Galactic West Productions, which was located in an inauspicious office building shaded by a line of tall palms.

A white Mercedes was pulling out of a parking spot on the street and she slid her Honda in behind it, parked, and was inside the familiar building within two minutes. She took the stairs to the third floor and walked through seamless glass doors to a reception area. Then she was stopped cold, blocked entry to the private offices by a receptionist who was barely five feet tall and not a day over twenty. The girl's smooth complexion, youthful innocence, and bright smile belied the fact that she was an immovable object. Obviously she regarded her job of obstructing passage to the inner sanctum of Galactic West as gospel, as if God Himself had assigned her the task of stopping anyone from entering. Maybe she, too, believed Dean Arnette was omnipotent, a god to all of Hollywood and beyond.

Cassie even tried the "But-I'm-Allie-Kramer's-sister" card, to no avail.

"If you don't have an appointment, then I'm sorry," the girl said without a hint of remorse in her huge blue eyes. "You'll have to make one, an appointment, I mean, if I can even get you in to see him. Mr. Arnette is a very busy man."

When Cassie said she'd be satisfied talking with Beatrice Little or Sybil Jones, the producers who worked with Arnette on the film, she was met with the same implacable resistance and a wide, orthodontically improved smile. "They're not in and even if they were, you'd need an appointment. If you leave your number, I'll have someone call you." For the moment, Cassie felt as if she had no options. She glanced at the door she knew led to the private offices and even considered bolting around the receptionist's massive desk, but decided she'd rather not deal with someone from the building's security staff, or the police hauling her outside. At least not yet. No reason to give Whitney Stone more grist for her gossip mill. The simple fact was Cassie already had a history of mental issues and the cops in Oregon were already looking at her closely in conjunction with her sister's disappearance. It just didn't make sense to draw attention to herself by causing trouble or in any way encouraging Detective Nash to move Cassie from "a person of interest" to her "A #1 suspect."

Still, she was irritated. She left her name and number, which seemed redundant. Dean Arnette, Little Bea, Sybil Jones, and just about everyone else in the production company already had her personal information. Not that it mattered, though. She knew as well as the big-eyed receptionist that no one was going to call her as no one had bothered returning her personal voice messages or texts to date.

God, it was irritating.

She was just trying to find Allie, for God's sake. You'd think the production company about to release its star's latest film would be doing everything in its power to find her, and that included talking with Allie Kramer's sister. Unless the people involved at GW were running under the same impression as the damned police, that Cassie Kramer was a certifiable nutcase and a person to avoid.

She made her way out of the building and found a parking ticket on her windshield. She hadn't even seen the meter.

Grabbing the ticket, she climbed into the car and pulled away from the curb, then made an illegal U-turn.

Why not?

Things couldn't get much worse.

Right?

CHAPTER 15

The muscles in Trent's shoulders tightened as he drove over the final rise to the heart of his ranch and spied Shane Carter's Jeep parked near the garage. The ex-lawman was out of his truck and leaning over the top rail of the fence, staring at a field where broodmares were grazing. He was obviously waiting. For Trent. To deliver bad news?

Cassie! Oh, Jesus.

He should have called her again or flown down to LA after her! His heart was thudding. Whatever had propelled Carter here, it couldn't be good. As far as Trent could remember, Shane Carter had never stepped foot on his property except in times of trouble.

Mind-numbing images rolled through his head—Cassie in a plane crash, Cassie in an automobile accident, Cassie in a mental hospital being restrained, Cassie in the clutches of a madman or . . . damn it all to hell, Cassie on a slab in the morgue.

When Trent had been a wild-ass teenager, Carter had come onto this ranch to arrest him. Later Trent had shown interest in Cassie. Carter had again come knocking, this time to warn him to be careful with his frail stepdaughter, and when he and Cassie had announced they'd eloped, Carter had driven to this place and glared at Trent as if he'd like to shoot him where he stood while his wife, Jenna, had tried not to crumble at her husband's side. That time Cassie had squared off with her family, reminding them that marrying Trent had been her decision and they could butt out of her life.

But there wasn't a lot of love lost between Trent and Carter.

Now he threw the pickup into park, yanked the keys from the ignition, and was out of the truck practically before the engine stopped running.

"Hey!" he called, Hud bounding ahead of him.

Carter wore a black Stetson and a long coat. He'd turned at the sound of Trent's truck's engine and was already waiting for him.

"What's going on?" Trent asked, his jaw so tight it ached. "Is it Cassie? Is she okay?"

"Far as I know."

Trent felt instant relief.

Hud, wiggling his butt, sidled up to Carter, a virtual stranger. Some guard dog.

Shane bent down to scratch the shepherd who was wriggling at his feet, as if they were long-lost friends.

"Allie?"

A shake of Carter's head. "Heard nothing."

"What the hell, then?"

"It's killing Jenna." Carter straightened as the dog trotted toward the porch and his water bowl.

A few more lines than Trent remembered were etched across the older man's forehead and the crow's-feet fanning from his eyes were deeper. Unspoken accusations lingered in his eyes, questions concerning Trent and his involvement with Jenna's youngest daughter, but he didn't voice them. Trent didn't offer up any apologies or explanations about Allie.

"Good to see ya," Carter said a bit grimly, extending a hand.

Trent shook it. "You too." Courtesy. But a lie. He dropped Carter's hand.

"Just wonderin' if you'd heard from Cass, but obviously you haven't."

"I phoned her. Left a message."

"She hasn't called you back?"

Trent shook his head and studied his stepfather-in-law for a second. Then he, too, looked at the broodmares. A small herd of seven, three bays, two chestnuts, a paint, and a Kiger mustang. All were heavy-bellied, due to foal soon.

"She didn't get hold of Jenna?" Trent asked, his insides tensing as he considered the possibilities. Was Cassie in some kind of trouble? But Carter had just said she was "fine" as far as he knew.

"She did. Called last night."

Trent relaxed a little, but didn't understand why Carter was here.

"Jenna wanted you to know, didn't want you to worry. In case you hadn't heard from her." A sidelong glance.

"Thanks." But there was more. Trent sensed it as surely as he knew that rain would pour from the heavens before nightfall.

"She's coming back. Probably tomorrow."

So there it was, the reason for the visit. Next, he expected, would come the warning to back off again. Judging from Carter's attitude it would be couched in a bit of family concern, not quite as harsh as it might have been, but he'd be told to "stay away." Probably for the sake of Cassie's emotional and mental state.

However it turned out Shane was through. "Jenna wanted me to thank you. She was busy with the local theater today, but she'll try to give you a call. If we hear anything else, we'll let ya know." He hitched his chin toward Trent's small herd of mares. "Good lookin' horses," he said, thumping a fencepost with his fist before heading to his Jeep.

Helluva thing, now that his marriage was nearly over, his wife's family was treating him with some kind of guarded respect. *Son of a bitch.*

As Carter drove away, Trent's thoughts turned to Cassie. It pissed him off that she didn't have the decency to return his phone calls. Carter had said she was returning to Oregon in the next couple of days.

Trent wasn't about to wait.

Shorty would see to his place and the livestock. He'd make sure of it just as soon as he booked the first available flight to LA.

Striding to the house, he pulled his cell from his pocket, punched out Shorty's number and glanced at the sky just as the first drops of rain began to fall.

Enough with the unanswered phone calls and texts.

He was going to see his wife face-to-face.

Whether she liked it or not.

The day had been a bust.

Cassie had driven all over LA and beyond, adding another hundred or so miles to her odometer but getting nowhere. No one had been available to talk to her, no one had returned her calls. She'd spun her wheels trying to get answers and had come home with the feeling that she was some kind of pariah. She'd left voice and text messages with anyone she could think of who might know something about Allie, and in the end she'd only connected with Sig Masters, who had actually pulled the trigger and shot Lucinda. He had refused to meet with Cassie. On the phone, he'd sounded freaked beyond freaked.

"For the love of God, Cassie, I can't talk!" She'd heard the click of a lighter and the quick intake of breath as he'd lit a cigarette. She'd just filled her tank with gas and had pulled onto a side street, parking in the shade of a tall building, when she'd finally gotten through to him. "My lawyer has advised me that I shouldn't say a word to anyone. Not to any of my friends or anyone I worked with on *Dead Heat* or the police or . . . oh, shit . . . every fuckin' person on earth! It's a nightmare, y'know. I didn't mean to shoot Lucinda Rinaldi and I certainly didn't mistake her for Allie Kramer, and I'm not a murderin' bastard. I didn't even know Allie. I'm sick of being hounded, y'know? No one will hire me, but the press . . . shit . . . they're all over me. But . . . fuck it. Just leave me the hell alone." He'd hung up abruptly.

Rebuffed, Cassie had considered calling back, but figured she'd get nowhere. Instead she had stopped at her apartment, picked up her mail and changed into shorts and a T-shirt, then headed to a fast-food restaurant where she grabbed an iced tea. After that she drove to the athletic club where Ineesha Sallinger worked out. Knowing that the prop manager was a gym rat who worked out two hours or so a day, often after work, she parked in the shade on the street with a view of the club's front entrance. Then she settled down into the driver's seat to wait.

She spent the time on her phone accessing the Internet before sorting through the snail mail that had been left at her apartment. Most of what she had were bills, but there was one envelope she hadn't spied earlier, this one hand-addressed. She opened it with a fingernail and found an invitation for the members of the cast of *Dead Heat* and the media to a party celebrating the premiere of the movie. The event was to be held at the Hotel Danvers in Portland, where several scenes of the film had been shot, and the party was hosted by Dean Arnette and Galactic West Productions. It was slated for the coming weekend—only a few days away—and an RSVP card was enclosed.

As soon as she discovered the invitation she tried to RSVP by phone, but that didn't work. She decided her first chance to talk to Arnette would probably be at the party and that was only if she could get him alone for a few minutes.

It was weird to think that the party would be held despite the fact that the status of the star was unknown. Cassie tossed the envelope aside and focused on the front entrance to the gym again.

Two long hours later, she was rewarded when Ineesha's classic Karmann Ghia pulled into the circular drive, and Ineesha, toting a gym bag, unfolded herself from behind the wheel of the red convertible. She dropped her keys into the hands of a waiting valet before disappearing through the front door.

Cassie considered her options. Should she wait for Ineesha to exit in a few hours, or should she accost her during her workout? She opted for the latter.

Climbing from her car, she then lingered until a group of three women were walking inside just as two couples exited through the wide doors. Fortunately only one desk clerk had been on duty and while the eighteen-year-old was distracted by someone with a problem with their key to the exclusive locker room, Cassie slipped past the desk and walked briskly inside. The interior was familiar, as she'd come here often when she'd been a member.

She hurried past the entry to the pool, spa, and the locker room, then through a wide corridor flanked by glass walls and smaller rooms. One of the spaces housed a spinning class and another was filled with yoga mats and members attempting downward-facing dog poses.

She didn't spy Ineesha in any of the classes, which was good, but Cassie silently prayed that the prop manager wasn't involved in a session with her private trainer. No. She needed to find Ineesha alone.

She walked through an open area filled with exercise equipment. Muscle men were working out on the weights and various machines that looked as if they'd been designed for human torture. A group of women were clustered together in a private Pilates class while cyclists spun to the beat of frantic music.

Cassie checked out all of the rowing machines and treadmills, eyeing earnest personal trainers working with clients and thinking she'd made a big mistake until she caught sight of her target. Ineesha Sallinger was sweating profusely on an elliptical machine. Perfect. Or as good as it could get.

Hopping onto the machine next to her, Cassie caught the older woman's eye and said, "Hi."

Ineesha glared at her. Lips pinched, eyes narrowed suspiciously, she said loudly, "I'm not talking to you." Attached to her cell phone, thin, white cords hung from her ears as she pumped with her arms and legs. Her skin glistened and her hair, pulled into a ponytail, was separating from perspiration, her carefully matched yoga pants and T-shirt dripping. "I don't know anything. How did you get in here anyway? This is a private club."

And one to which both she and Allie had once belonged. "I used to be a member."

"Used to be doesn't cut it. Leave me alone or I'll have you thrown out." She focused on her monitor, which showed a steep hill. Gritting her teeth, she poked her earbud deeeper into the shell of her ear and turned her attention away from Cassie. "I'm not kidding. I'll call security."

"I just want to know about the prop gun."

"You and the whole damned world. Including me." Rather than keep shouting, Ineesha yanked out one of her ear buds.

"Somehow it was exchanged."

Ineesha, struggling on the elliptical, shot her a no-shit-Sherlock look. "Duh."

"But you were in charge—"

"Of the prop closet. Yeah, I know." She kept on pumping. "God, don't I know. But I have no idea how it happened, okay? I followed protocol. The cupboard was locked. I double checked. I always double check."

But she didn't seem to be as sure.

"Who else has a key?"

"To the cupboard? No one . . . unless I specifically loan it to an assistant, but no, I didn't that day."

"What about to the room?"

"Several people in the department and the producers," she said, thinking aloud and then caught herself up short. "Oh for the love of Jesus, why am I talking to you?" Her eyes were fierce. "My lawyer told me to say nothing to anyone without him, so this interview is O-V-E-R! I wasn't kidding about calling security. I mean it, Cassie, leave me the hell alone!"

"What about Sig?"

"Masters? That moron? You think what? He exchanged the guns? Even he isn't *that* stupid. He couldn't switch batteries and get away with it, much less firearms." Ineesha rolled her expressive eyes. "The man's a twit. IQ of fourteen, I think. Well . . . okay, maybe he's just dumb enough to exchange the weapon, real for fake, and shoot, almost kill Lucinda Rinaldi." She snorted through her nose. "No, that doesn't make a helluva lot of sense, but I suppose that's not surprising, coming from you." Breathing hard, she sent Cassie a pitying look. "Again, what is it you want from me?"

"I'm just trying to find out what happened to my sister."

"Oh, save me. Like you care what happened to her! The way I heard it she was after your husband." A little smirk.

"I don't think so."

"Whatever."

"So what do you think happened?"

"How many times do I have to say, 'I don't know'?" She grabbed her water bottle from a cup holder, twisted off the lid without breaking stride and took a long swallow. "Your sister didn't show up that day, right? Have you ever wondered about that? Like maybe she knew something might happen?"

Cassie didn't reply. Of course she had.

"Okay, so I'll take that as a 'yes.'" She put the bottle back in its holder just as the landscape on her monitor flattened out again. "Look, this is over. I said more than I should. My lawyer told me not to talk to anyone and that includes you." Visibly irritated, Ineesha turned off the machine, grabbed her water bottle and towel, and stalked toward the center area where there was a wide desk manned by several trainers and reception people.

Rather than risking making a scene and being thrown out on her ear, Cassie, frustrated and discouraged, feeling as if she was getting nowhere, made her way between two rows of treadmills, some occupied by runners, others standing idle.

She hadn't learned much more than that Ineesha was definitely testy, but it was no use to try and stick around. Ineesha, if she did know something, wasn't going to crack, and Cassie doubted if she did have any idea what had happened to Allie anyway.

But while she was in LA, Cassie wanted to talk to as many people as possible, hopefully glean some information about Allie, and talking to Ineesha had seemed important. She had been in charge of the prop room and cupboard. And somewhere, despite "protocol," the weapons had been exchanged. On Ineesha's watch. No wonder she was so defensive. Did she know more than she was saying?

Someone knew something. Cassie only hoped she could locate that someone who might eventually lead her to Allie.

Unless she's already dead.

A chill raced down her spine and her thoughts started to turn down a desperate, painful path, but she fought the fear that it could be true and turned her thinking around. For now.

She left the gym and headed home, parking near the bougainvillea hedge again. After stopping at the main house and picking up a new set of keys from Doug, she hauled her purse, mail, and a bag of fish tacos she'd picked up on her way home, to her apartment. As she was unlocking the door, her cell phone chimed with a text. The key stuck a little, then the lock twisted open.

Hallelujah!

Inside she dropped her things on the counter, then checked her messages.

The first was from Brandon McNary:

"I'm in LA. Heard you were in town. Looking for Allie. Thought we could combine forces to find her. Let's talk over drinks."

"As if," she said. Was it a little weird that Brandon was now back in Southern California? Of course not. He lived here, worked here, but still she found it a little unsettling that she'd seen him in Portland and now he was trying to contact her again in Los Angeles.

But throwing in with Brandon seemed a bad idea. As much as she wanted to locate her sister, she didn't think Brandon could help. She hit the delete button. Almost immediately she second-guessed herself. Brandon *might* be able to help. He had been close to Allie. But they'd already had that conversation. "Forget it," she said after a moment of indecision, then scrolled to the next message from Laura Merrick:

Have a cancellation. Call me.

Really? After all her talk about being booked to eternity and back again? Nonetheless, Cassie immediately phoned her.

Laura picked up on the third ring. "Can you believe it?" she said, and it was obvious she was angry, almost incensed. "This woman . . . she's a client of one of my stylists. A real big deal around here and she . . . she has the *gall* to cancel the day before!" Acrimony was mingled with disgust in her voice. As Laura was a makeup artist to the stars, few people dared change an appointment once it was made. Even with one of her underlings. "Sorry . . . You said you needed a trim and you'll still be in town tomorrow morning, is that right?"

"I'm leaving tomorrow."

"Well, can you come in at nine? I cannot tell you how pissed I am."

Before Laura could go off on another rant, Cassie said, "I'll be there."

She rattled off the address and Cassie hung up. She had to start packing, figuring out what she was taking with her, how long she would stay. Her plans weren't to live in Oregon, at least not permanently.

Her life was down here.

Or was it?

As a writer, she could set up shop anywhere. With wireless connections and the Internet, she didn't have to be in LA to be close to the industry, to do her job. She could keep this apartment another month or two, and maybe once Allie was found, Cassie would have more direction in her life. She hoped so. She packed one roller bag and left it by the front door, took a break by zapping the tacos for a few seconds in the microwave, then plopped onto a barstool at the counter separating the kitchen from the dining area.

She'd just gingerly opened the wrap from around her first taco when her phone rang. She glanced at the screen. It was her father. Great. Obviously he'd gotten the word that she was out of the hospital and in the area. She considered not answering, told herself she was a *horrible* daughter, and guilted herself into taking the call.

"Cassie!" her father bellowed as she answered. "You're in LA? And you didn't phone or text or whatever?"

"Not yet."

"You were going to let me know you were in town?"

Guilt became a knife that sliced deep. "Probably. Sure." *Eventually*.

"So how are you feeling? Would you like to come over? Or . . . I'd love to take you out. I'm busy tonight, important clients, but maybe sometime next week?"

"I'm leaving in the morning."

"But you just got here, right? I mean your mom called me and said you'd checked yourself out of the hospital and flown down here."

"I want to find out what happened to Allie." She didn't even ask if he'd heard anything about his daughter because surely he would have mentioned it. Robert Kramer wasn't one to hold back.

"I know," he said soberly, genuine sadness in his voice.

She pictured him in her mind's eye, his once-thick hair thinning, his waist thickening, his face freckled from hours in the sun playing golf. She knew he loved her and Allie, always had. She also realized that he wouldn't be afraid to make a buck off either of his daughters in the film industry.

"But I was asking about you."

"I'm fine," she lied. Would she ever be? And why couldn't she trust her father enough to admit she was a mess? "Hey," she said as a thought crossed her mind. "Do you know if Allie was ever in New Mexico? Santa Fe? Maybe around 2007?"

"New Mexico? No . . . or did she go to a doctor there?"

"Why would she go to a doctor in Santa Fe when she lived in LA?"

"Privacy."

Cassie's ears pricked up. "For what?" A baby? Had she been pregnant and was hiding it, didn't want anyone to know?

"A little nip or tuck."

"Allie? She's perfect." And young. She would have been far too young for any kind of plastic surgery. No, her father had to be mistaken. It didn't make sense.

"I'm not sure I'm even right," he said. "Maybe it was Phoenix. And 2007 doesn't sound right either. More like a year ago."

That didn't help. "Did she have any connection in Santa Fe? A friend or some kind of business?"

"Sorry, honey. I don't remember. Your sister didn't exactly fill me in on her personal life. As public as her image has become she's a pretty private person."

True enough, Cassie thought, though still wondered why she was left with the cryptic text message . . . and from her psychiatrist, no less. The text bothered her enough that she'd have to break down and call her doctor.

"So why go back to Oregon?" her father asked. "Because of your mom?"

"No."

"Ahh. Trent, then?"

"No!" she said sharply. Too sharply. "Trent and I are over."

"Are you?"

She bristled. "It's just something I have to do."

"Okay, no judgment call. Whatever you want to do. It's probably a good idea to be closer to your mom." He didn't sound convinced, but at least he left Trent out of the equation. "You know, what with Allie missing, Jenna needs you more than ever."

That guilty knife twisted in her gut again. She leaned back on the barstool and eyed her open roller bag. "Dad, I've got to go. Really. I'm only half packed. But I'll call you the next time I come here. Promise."

"And if you learn anything about your sister?"

"Absolutely."

"All right, then." There was a glitch in the conversation, as if he had something more to say but couldn't find the words. "I'll catch you later, Cass. Take care."

"You too, Dad." Her throat was suddenly thick and she cleared it as she hung up. There was a time when they had been a happy family, when she and Allie had been their father's "girls." That's what he'd called them. "My girls." Until he'd found a new, younger wife.

She stared at the phone, felt a wash of nostalgia and, as always, ignored it. She didn't have time to get hung up on old memories and could-have-beens. The past was over and gone and tomorrow morning, depending upon what, if anything, she learned from Laura, she was heading north.

CHAPTER 16

Holly Dennison paid her tab and collected her debit card from the bartender of the Pinwheel, a hot spot not far from the beach. After taking a final swallow from her daiquiri, she licked her lips and slid off the barstool. As her feet hit the ground she wobbled a little, cursing her shoes, the heels that were a smidge too high for her to walk steadily, especially after three—or was it four?—drinks.

She'd come to the bar alone because she'd heard that Luca Valerio, the Italian heartthrob who was in LA to promote his latest film, liked to hang out here, so she hadn't bothered calling any of her girlfriends to meet for a drink. She'd hoped to "run into" him, strike up a conversation, and hit things off. The truth was that Holly had nursed a crush on him for years. But of course he hadn't shown.

While she'd waited, she'd sampled everything rum on the menu and when she realized Luca probably wouldn't be arriving, that her information, as usual, had been faulty, she'd tried to hook up with a couple of other guys. They all had girlfriends whom they were meeting, so she'd backed off, even though the cute one had suggested he call her "later." Uh, no thanks. Holly had a hard and fast rule when it came to dating and other women's men: They were strictly off-limits. At least, if she knew about the woman. She'd overstepped her bounds a couple of times because the jerk who'd picked her up had neglected to tell her that he was married. But she always asked, although if a guy was willing to step out on his wife, what were the chances of him not lying about it?

She decided to go home. She was tired. It was after midnight and she needed to be up by six thirty or seven as her sister Barbara was dropping off her little niece for the day. Holly couldn't wait. Though she wasn't ready for kids herself yet—hell, she didn't even have a boyfriend at the moment—she adored watching little three-year-old Adele for Barbara. On those days when Barb had to run errands, or get her hair colored, or go to a doctor's appointment or whatever, Holly stepped in. That is, when Barb allowed it. Which wasn't all that often. Sometimes her sister could be such a bitch. Fortunately Barb's jerkwad of a husband, who wouldn't give up golf, poker, or work, in that order, to watch his own daughter, was always relieved that Holly was quick to babysit. She figured it was her brother-in-law's loss even though Frank had been, and always would be, a self-centered egomaniac. And that was on a good day.

So she was giving up searching for Mr. Right for the night.

Making her way to the front door was a trick. The rum hadn't seemed to have much of a kick as she'd sat on the barstool and sipped her drinks, but now, as she wended through nearly empty tables, the liquor had definitely found its way into her bloodstream, making walking steadily a trick.

Outside the wind was cool, a stiff breeze blowing in from the Pacific, the smooth sound of the tide drowned by the few cars rolling past. Above the streetlights, Holly could barely make out the stars overhead, not that she really cared. She wondered if Marlie Babcock had intentionally sent her on a wild goose chase. Marlie was just mean enough. Holly should never have trusted her, another set designer whose connection to Luca had been a previous film they'd both worked on.

Big deal, she thought now, wobbling a little.

It crossed her mind that she probably shouldn't drive because she was a stage or two beyond buzzed, but the thought of calling a taxi or Uber or phoning a friend and leaving her car, a leased BMW convertible, in the parking lot all night freaked her out. And she didn't dare dial Barb, who would look at her disapprovingly and probably revoke her babysitting privileges. Besides, it was only a few blocks to her apartment, less than a mile, really, and she'd be careful behind the wheel.

Of course she would.

As she reached the parking lot, she thought she heard her cell phone ring. At this late hour? Not good news. She fumbled a bit, found the iPhone in an inner pocket, and checked the screen. No call. She'd been mistaken, but she did notice that she'd missed two texts from her sister saying that she was canceling on the babysitting gig in the morning. Little Adele was running a fever of 103. "Poor baby," Holly said, disappointed. Well, this way she could sleep in. As she was sliding the phone into the side pocket of her bag, she thought she caught movement out of the corner of her eye, a play of light and shadow that seemed out of place.

She blinked and saw that there was definitely someone in the lot. A dark figure lurking between the parked vehicles. The hairs on the back of her arms came to attention and her heart jump-started, pounding erratically before she decided it was probably a drunk guy taking a leak. Gross. But it happened. In fact, she'd seen it here more than once before.

She turned away and found her car, the locks opening as the signal from the key fob in her purse came into range. She nearly stumbled again and from the corner of her eye saw that the guy was moving, probably zipping up—well, she *hoped* he was pulling up his zipper—as she reached for the door handle.

"Holly?"

What? A woman's voice?

She twisted her head and realized that "the guy" she'd first seen was really a woman who definitely had not been relieving herself. And she was walking briskly through the parked cars, her footsteps distinct against the asphalt. "You're Holly Dennison."

"Uh-huh." Wasn't the voice familiar? If so, why was she suddenly uneasy again? The parking lot instantly seemed darker and more isolated than it had moments before.

"I thought so." The woman was drawing nearer, her face still shadowed, still unrecognizable. Dark hair. Or a hood?

But that voice. Holly definitely knew it, but couldn't place the name and now the other woman was only a few feet away. Holly squinted, ignoring the little drip of fear, a warning, that rippled through her blood. "Do I know—?"

A loud motorcycle roared past the lot.

Holly jumped, her attention switched to the street.

In that split second, the woman in black pounced.

Bam!

Her body weight knocked Holly off her feet. Holly slammed against her car, her head cracking against the driver's door, and then her body slithered to the ground.

Pain slammed through her brain.

Shit! What the hell?

She dropped her purse, her phone skittering out, the screen illuminating.

No! This couldn't be happening! This stranger, this *woman* couldn't be attacking her! She started to scream.

A gloved hand, a *strong* gloved hand, slammed across her mouth and muffled any sounds she could make as her attacker forced her onto her back and straddled her chest.

Oh. Dear. God.

Fear crystallized in her brain.

Blood froze in her veins.

This was happening! Holy crap. No!

Squirming wildly she clawed and bit and tried to scream, but her attempts were drunken and clumsy, her arms flailing, her blows landing in the air.

Help me! Oh, God, please let someone help me! Surely there were people on the street, someone who could see that she was being abducted. She screamed into the leather glove but heard only a muted mewl.

"Bitch," the woman growled as she twisted her free hand into Holly's hair, grabbing a thick clump, nearly pulling it out by the roots as she lifted Holly's head from the pavement.

What?

Her attacker shifted suddenly. Using her body weight she slammed Holly's head against the pavement.

Crack!

Agony ripped through Holly's head.

Pain exploded behind her eyes, nearly blinding her.

Her skin ripped and she began to bleed. Chipped pieces of asphalt clung to her, matted in her hair.

No, no, no! Frantically she tried to peel her assailant from her. Kicking and bucking, scrabbling in the air, she felt woozy, her coordination failing her, the wicked, horrid mass of humanity atop her not budging. Who the hell was this maniac? Why was this happening?

Help me!

Her thoughts were ragged. Cut painfully through her gray matter.

This woman, whoever the hell she was, planned to murder her. Right here in this horrid little parking lot.

Tears ran down her face with the dark realization.

Take my purse, my phone, my cash, the damned car but please . . . please . . . stop. Let me live . . . oh, Jesus . . .

She couldn't see straight. Her head throbbed. Panic screamed through her body. Why was this happening? *Why?* Wedged between two cars, where no one could see her, she focused on the sky above, invisible over the weak light from a streetlamp on the sidewalk.

"Stop! Help! Someone help me!" she tried to scream, but her voice was muted, little sound escaping as her head was lifted, hairs sticking to the pavement, glued due to her own blood.

Oh, God, no. Don't! Her eyes were wide. Fear curdled deep inside.

Bam!

Once more her head was smashed against the asphalt.

Pain erupted, sending shock waves through her body.

She felt a new gash on the back of her head, the blood flowing warm and wet.

Blackness threatened.

Feverishly, knowing it was a matter of life and death, *her* life and death, Holly fought to stay conscious. Blood rushed in her ears and fear clutched her heart. Her movements were now sluggish, ungainly, her arms not obeying her brain.

Her attacker leaned closer and in the dim light from a faraway security lamp and the screen of her phone, she caught a glimpse of the fiend atop her.

It couldn't be!

Allie?

Allie Kramer?

Oh, God, oh, God, oh, God. Could this deranged woman astride her actually be Allie Kramer? Or . . . God, why did she look so weird and distorted?

Even as the crazy thoughts slid through her brain she denied them. No way. Allie was many things, some of them not so nice, but she wasn't a killer . . . or was she?

Desperately Holly blinked, tried to stay aware, felt herself slipping away, the image looking more warped, Allie's features blurring into a monstrous caricature of herself.

"Allie?" Holly vainly tried to speak but only managed to mouth the woman's name.

The woman's face, distorted, filled her vision. This maniac wasn't Allie Kramer, couldn't be. Just someone who looked a lot like Allie, who was dressed like Allie, but is really . . . shit, was it Cassie? No. Yes? There was something wrong . . . for the love of Jesus, what the hell was wrong with her face?

A new fear curdled through her.

Cassie!

Using all her strength Holly tried to throw herself upward, to buck off her assailant, but her efforts were too feeble. Trying to get her bearings, she stared at her attacker and the weird image in front of her.

And then the woman above her moved, letting go of Holly's hair, reached behind her, and pulled something from her coat pocket.

A pistol?

What? No! Oh, God, no. With a supreme effort she tried to wiggle away but it was too late.

Within a second Holly felt the cold muzzle of a gun pressed to her chest.

"NO!" she tried to scream, as the woman pulled the trigger. There was a muffled *pffft* and then she felt liquid inside as the attacker stepped off her and the lights began to dim.

In her last desperate moments Holly told herself that this all had to be a dream, a horrible nightmare, that the blood blooming on her chest was nothing but a wild-ass memory of Lucinda on the set of *Dead Heat,* that the weird sensation, the pain and her floating mind were all because of the booze.

For a second, she caught a glimpse of her attacker, the pistol with its silencer in her gloved hand. As Holly's eyes began to shutter, her assailant leaned close. She smelled of a perfume Holly recognized over the metallic scent of her own blood. Familiar . . . ? Then felt herself start to lift, her soul rising.

The pain slipped away as Holly looked down on her body and her assailant from a distance, high over the street lamps and the rooftops. Dear Lord, it was so damned dark, so hard to tell what she was witnessing.

Was the woman peeling off her own face?

No . . . couldn't be.

Cold to the bone, Holly felt a blindfold being placed over her eyes, and she could no longer see her own image, though she still felt as if she were floating. She wanted to strip away the blindfold, but she couldn't find the strength to peel it off.

Thankfully, as she tasted metal and salt on her lips and gurgled up something warm and liquid from her lungs, a quiet blackness converged over her and her last thought was that she was dying, that a murderous bitch had succeeded in killing her.

She just didn't know why.

Mitch Stevens's bladder was about to burst. He'd been thrown out of the Pinwheel and most of the bars were shutting down, so he didn't have a chance at another men's room. Shit. He'd never make it home.

But it was pretty dark here in the parking lot, the streetlights not really falling on all the nooks and crannies between the scattered cars, no security camera visible, so he slipped between two vehicles, a sweet-looking Jag and a Chevy sedan, faced the side of a neighboring building, unzipped, and took aim at a dandelion growing up through a crack in the pavement.

Almost immediately he felt relief and with his immediate discomfort over, he kept up his stream and wondered if he might be able to locate a bar that would let him slip inside even though it was *slightly* after last call. Not the Pinwheel, unfortunately. That loser of a bartender had been gunning for him all night and so, with just one little slip where he'd fallen against a girl who was dancing, and in trying to stay on his feet had *accidentally* brushed her damned boob with his hand, he was out. No matter how hard he'd protested that he'd needed to use the john, the bartender had signaled to a bouncer with a Mohawk and goatee who had to be pushing three hundred pounds and who had silently but effectively shoved him sprawling onto the sidewalk. It was a damned miracle he hadn't pissed all over the cement in front of the door.

"Hey, loser!" a male voice catcalled from the street, and Mitch froze. "This ain't a latrine, for fuck's sake!"

Go to hell. Still, he finished quickly, tucking his cock into his pants as he looked over his shoulder. The fucker was walking on, jogging across the dark street to a car that was parked on the other side. "Dickhead," he mumbled under his breath as the car's lights blinked and its horn gave off a soft honk when the sanctimonious prick hit the remote unlock button to his van. Probably a "soccer dad."

Making sure his fly was completely zipped, Mitch moved furtively and quickly rather than hear about his public urination from another ass, or a mugger, or worse yet, a cop. He made his way around the front of the Chevy, careful not to step in his recent puddle, and then nearly tripped again when the toe of his boot hit something soft and giving.

He caught himself and looked down.

In that instant he felt the blood drain from his body.

He was staring at a woman lying faceup on the pavement.

"Hey!" Startled, he jumped backward a step. He blinked. Tried to focus.

What the hell was wrong with her?

Tentatively he asked, "Are you okay?" But he knew she wasn't. Hell, he wasn't certain she was even alive. Freaked beyond freaked, he backed up and tried to think. All he could do was stare at her.

Spiky black hair stood on end around a face that was distorted, as if it were eerily melting off her body. Horribly disfigured.

Jesus Holy Christ!

Fear slithered through him. His throat went dry. If he hadn't just peed, he would have pissed himself right then and there. He backed away fast, around the Chevy again.

Oh, God. Oh, shit. Oh, *hell!*

Frantically he scrabbled in his pocket for his phone, yanked it out, then promptly dropped it on the wet asphalt. The damned cell skated away from him, but he managed to scoop it up while scraping his fingers on the rough pavement that was still wet and warm with his own damned urine.

He didn't care.

Heart thudding with fear, the alcohol in his bloodstream seemed to dissipate as he heard a footfall behind him. He turned quickly, fear making his breath come in quick, shallow breaths.

"I need help," he said to the darkness, but the parking lot was empty, the footstep all part of his wild, frenzied imagination. "Help! Someone! I need help here!" he yelled.

With shaking fingers, he ignored the acrid stench of piss and punched in 9-1-1. His gaze slid back to that white, grotesque face.

"Nine-one-one," an operator answered. "Please state your name and nature of your emergency—"

"Get someone here. Now! Do you hear me? Get them here."

"Sir, if you would tell me where you are and what's happening—"

"I don't know what's happening. But she's dead! She's fuckin' dead!"

"Who's dead, sir?" the firm voice asked. "Where are you?"

"I don't know her . . . She's a . . . freak. Oh, my God, just send someone!" In a full-blown panic he looked around, trying to focus on a street sign but he couldn't think straight. "Shit, where am I? By the Pinwheel. The bar. In . . . Venice on Pacific and . . . crap, I don't know what the cross street is. But she's in the parking lot. I'm telling you, there's a fuckin' dead body on the floor—I mean on the ground. I was taking a whiz, for fuck's sake, I nearly tripped over her." His voice was rising and he backed away from the body, the freaking dead body. "Get someone here," he screamed. "NOW!"

CHAPTER 17

Detective Jonas Hayes stared down at the body.

At three in the damned morning.

He'd seen a lot of weird shit in his years on the force in LA, but tonight's crime scene was right up there with the most bizarre.

Three police cruisers blocked the entrance of the parking lot, their light bars strobing the area in bright flashes of red and blue, making the scene even more eerie. The air was as still as it ever got in this part of town, little traffic, the smell of the ocean faint in the luminescence of streetlights and a few thin clouds. The ME was on his way, several techs already working the parking lot, looking for trace evidence and snapping pictures. Even at this unholy hour a handful of onlookers had gathered, mostly barflies who had been kicked out as the establishments had closed. The looky-loos talked among themselves, speculated drunkenly, probably were piecing together what was going on due to a passing interest in *CSI, Law & Order*, or in one older guy's case *Murder, She Wrote* or *Dragnet* or some such crap.

Hayes paid them no mind as he took in the crime scene.

The victim's purse held a driver's license for Holly Dennison, though ID hadn't been completely established as the victim, left sprawled on the pavement, a gunshot wound to her chest, had been wearing a mask, a bizarre twisted image of Allie Kramer, the missing movie star who had recently disappeared. The dead woman's identification was still unconfirmed, but probably could be surmised. If she was Holly Dennison, her most recent employment had been with Galactic West Productions as part of the set crew for *Dead Heat,* the movie starring the missing Allie Kramer.

As Hayes had been working on the disappearance of *Dead Heat*'s lead actress, he recognized her head shot, even though the picture was distorted, the eyes cut to allow vision . . . maybe. Had Holly been wearing the mask before she was killed, hence the eyeholes? Or had the mask been placed over her head postmortem?

But why?

And who?

"Who found her?" he asked one of the beat cops who was standing guard near the entrance of the lot.

"Guy by the name of Mitch Stevens. He'd been at the Pinwheel next door and according to the barkeep had been cut off and thrown out. He'd come over here to take a leak and literally stumbled over her." The cop hitched his head to a small group standing near a parked Camaro with a bold racing stripe. Two cops were talking to a twenty-to-thirty-year-old who looked like he wanted to be anywhere but in this parking lot.

"Stevens have trouble with the law?"

"Nah. Clean as a whistle," the cop said. "A couple of parking tickets. That's it. Nearly tripping over the vic must've scared him sober because he's freaked, coherent, and just wants to get the hell out of here."

Hayes nodded once. "I want to talk to him."

"Figured."

"Let him cool his jets for a couple of minutes."

"Got it." The beat cop motioned to the corpse. "Who would go to all this trouble?"

"That's what we have to find out." Hayes crouched near the body and waited until the crime scene photographer had taken pictures of the dead woman from different angles.

As the digital camera flashed, Hayes saw more distinctly the dark red stain on her T-shirt, a thick bloom that soaked the cotton then ran off her rib cage to pool on the pavement beneath her. Had she known her attacker? Was it a stranger? What the hell was with the mask?

Life-sized, the altered photograph had been laminated and cut precisely around Allie Kramer's hairline and held in place with what looked like a thin elastic band. Pieces of the victim's hair had been arranged around the mask, to make it appear more lifelike. Some thought had gone into the process, but not a lot of effort. The picture could have been downloaded from the Internet, then maybe an app used to distort the image before the resulting art was enlarged to the size of a human head, printed, laminated, and cut. The elastic holding the mask in place could have been purchased at any fabric, craft, or other store, if it hadn't been retrieved from Grandma's sewing kit that had been stuffed in the attic.

Yeah, the artwork was crude, almost something that could have been created by a kid in grade school. Hayes had better pieces displayed on his refrigerator by his own daughter, Maren, when she was in the third grade.

Strange as hell.

But he'd seen worse.

Hayes pulled on a pair of gloves, then lifting the vic's head carefully and not moving the position of the body, removed the mask by unwinding bits of hair clinging to the elastic band holding the mask in place and pulling it away from her face.

Carefully, he turned the mask over.

A single word had been scribbled across it in erratic, blood red letters: *Sister.*

"Gawd A'mighty!" the beat cop whispered. "What the hell does that mean?"

"Don't know," Hayes admitted, but his mind was racing. Was Holly someone's sister? He'd check that. But his gut told him the word *Sister* had to do with the mask itself, that of Allie Kramer. It was common knowledge the rising star had a less-famous sister, another daughter of Jenna Hughes, and Hayes already had notes about her as she was the last person known to have seen her sister before Allie Kramer's disappearing act. He only hoped Cassie Kramer could shed some light on the whole blasted affair.

Leaving the mask with a crime-scene tech, Jonas straightened and walked toward Mitch Stevens. The man visibly shrunk into his own skin at the sight of him. It wasn't uncommon. Jonas Hayes was a six-foot-four African-American who had once been a running back for UNLV. Though heavier than in his football days, he was fit and, he knew, more than a little intimidating, which he sometimes used to his advantage.

"I'm Detective Hayes," he said to the shorter man who managed a weak, fleeting smile. "Why don't you tell me what happened?"

"Nothin'," Stevens said. "I mean I was just mindin' my own business, takin' a whiz, y'know, and I like was zippin' up and there she was. Fuck!" His eyes strayed reluctantly toward the corpse again.

"You with anyone?"

"No. Shit. Just me." He was trembling. "I told the other cop, I was just . . . you know . . . relievin' myself. Jesus!" He shrugged and reached into his pocket for a pack of cigarettes and lit up again. "I mean, it's weird as hell, man," he said as he sucked on the Camel as if nicotine would be his salvation. He exhaled in a cloud and added, "Weird as fuckin' hell."

Somehow, some way, Cassie finally fell asleep in the wee morning hours and didn't wake up until after seven. She'd been frustrated by not being able to reach anyone on the phone again and wondered if she'd been blackballed by everyone who worked on *Dead Heat,* or knew Allie. It had gotten so bad she'd almost called Brandon McNary and told him she had reconsidered and they could work together on trying to locate her sister, but she'd resisted.

So far.

Surfing the Internet hadn't helped much either. From hours on the computer, she'd learned little more about red cross earrings, or nurses' uniforms from fifty years prior. She'd also searched Santa Fe, New Mexico, but she had no idea what she was looking for there. She'd even Googled her sister and hoped she'd find some crumb, a little speck of knowledge about Allie that she hadn't known before.

Her searches weren't entirely altruistic, of course. Though she desperately wanted to locate her sister, to find out what had happened to Allie, there was another side to it. The more she delved, the more she realized what a great screenplay she could write, and she'd scribbled notes to that effect.

But of course the screenplay was secondary, she told herself. Allie's whereabouts and well-being came first.

Last night after getting home late, she'd stayed up until her eyes had blurred. She'd felt as if she'd been running in circles when she'd finally dropped off, most likely because the night before had been such a madhouse with its outré nightmares, glowering black cat, and uneasy feeling that someone had been inside her home.

This morning, aside from running later than she'd hoped, she felt a little better, a bit more ready to take on the world, and, she reminded herself, start over. She showered, twisted her hair onto her head, dabbed on lipstick and mascara, and grabbed her roller bag in case she needed a quick change. She would come back for the rest of her stuff, which was half packed into three more suitcases, after her appointment at Salon Laura. Though she was set to have her hair trimmed by another stylist, she hoped she'd be able to track down Laura Merrick. She had a gut feeling Laura could help her, no matter what the stylist had said.

She stepped outside to the brilliance of another sunny LA day, then nearly stumbled as she caught sight of Trent-Damned-Kittle leaning his jean-clad hips against the passenger side of her car. She blinked, slack-jawed, but there he was in faded jeans, a black T-shirt, cowboy boots, and aviator sunglasses. Two days' growth of beard shadowed his jaw. The twist of his blade-thin lips was the only sign that he'd seen her. Worse yet, the black cat that had scared the liver out of her two nights before had the audacity to sun himself on the Honda's roof. At the sight of her, the cat scrambled down to the hood, then leaped away to slink quickly into the shrubbery.

"What the hell are you doing here?" Cassie asked tightly, walking straight up to him, dragging the roller bag behind her, its wheels scraping on the uneven asphalt.

"Waitin'."

"For?"

"You."

She swatted at a bee that buzzed near her head. "Well, you found me."

A dark eyebrow cocked, silently asking why else would he be camped out here.

"I thought you were in Oregon on your ranch or . . . whatever." She glared at him. She didn't need the aggravation of her husband, make that soon-to-be-ex-husband, this morning.

"I was. Flew down late last night."

"And . . . what?"

He hitched his chin toward a Ford Explorer parked next to the owner's garage. "Spent a few hours there. In the rental."

"You slept in your car?" she asked as she stopped a few feet from him and squinted, trying to read his expression behind the shades. "You could have knocked on the door."

"Uh-huh." He nodded, agreeing. So damned affable. All an act. "And you could have not answered. Just like you didn't respond to my calls and texts." He stretched to his full height, casting a shadow across the hedge. "This way I figured you'd have to talk to me."

"I still don't have to talk to you."

"I'll buy coffee."

"Don't try to charm me."

"You're still pissed."

"Extremely so. But I don't have time to discuss it or anything else. I've got an appointment at nine."

"Somewhere close, or . . . ?" He glanced pointedly at her roller bag.

"Hair. With Laura. This is just the first bag I packed for the trip back to—" Hell. Why was she telling him anything?

"To where?"

"Does it matter?"

He shrugged. "Maybe not."

She checked her watch. "What did you want to say?"

"I want to work things out."

"What do you mean?" she asked automatically. "No—wait." She held up a hand. "I'm not in the mood for this."

"I came down here for you."

"Come on." Enough. Tugging on her bag she made her way to the driver's door of her Honda. She didn't know what Trent's game was, if he even had one, but she didn't have time for it, not now, most likely not ever. "Go to hell."

"You keep saying that," he said, infuriatingly unconcerned.

"I really have to go." She tugged the door open, then tossed her bag into the passenger seat.

"And you'll be back?"

"For the rest of my things."

One eyebrow raised. He didn't believe her.

"You don't trust me," she charged, and slid into the driver's seat.

"I think it's the other way 'round."

"I have a reason." She yanked the door shut.

"You never gave me a chance to explain."

Rolling down the window, she said, "Look, Trent. I don't even know why I'm talking to you. You had plenty of chances and I'm not doing this."

"Cass—" His voice was low and when he said her name like that it just killed her inside.

"Don't. Just don't, okay?" A thunderstorm of emotions was threatening her, but she couldn't deal with them so she pulled herself together and turned on the ignition. As the little car sputtered to life, she added, "I said I'll be back and I will."

"I'll be waiting." For the briefest of seconds she thought of canceling with Laura and having things out with him, once and for all, but she changed her mind. This was her one chance to catch up with the person who could be Allie's closest confidante, and she wasn't going to blow it on rehashing the problems in her marriage with Trent. At least not at the moment. Telling herself she was being a damned fool, she found her new key on her ring, unwound it from the others. "Go inside. I'll be back in an hour, maybe two." She handed him the key and didn't let her fingers linger on his. "If you want coffee, you'll have to go get a cup at Starbucks or Java Buzz, two blocks south. There's nothing in my place. Now, I've really got to go."

She didn't wait for him to argue, just tore out of the lot. A glance into the rearview mirror showed that he was still standing where she'd left him. Long legs shoulder-length apart, jaw rock hard, shaded eyes turned in her direction.

She dragged her gaze away from his all-too-sexy image. That was the trouble with him, he was innately sensual and didn't seem to know it, that's why he was so attractive. She let out a sigh. She'd sworn that she was over him, but, obviously, she'd been lying to herself.

CHAPTER 18

At three minutes to nine, Cassie stepped through the doors of Salon Laura.

The spa-like business was located a couple of blocks off Rodeo Drive, tucked into the first floor of a stucco and glass building in the high-rent district. Behind a sleek black counter a big-eyed, too-cool-to-smile receptionist, whose platinum hair was short and carefully mussed, told her what she'd already guessed, that, "No, Miss Merrick isn't in today, but I see you have an appointment with Verna."

An appointment she didn't need.

Cassie wanted to speak to Laura.

"But Laura, er, Miss Merrick is coming in, right? I thought that's what she said."

She was offered a bored expression and a single raised skeptical eyebrow. "That's not what she told me. Or like anyone else here." Then, with a word to another girl, the receptionist grudgingly guided Cassie through a frosted glass door and down a tiled hallway lit by sconces. Soft Asian-inspired music played from hidden speakers and the scents of lavender and eucalyptus seeped into the hallway from double doors leading to the day spa.

Around a final corner the hallway opened into a brightly lit area designated for hair stylists. Along one wall were individual stations, separated by half walls, each with a chair, sink, mirror, and private closet.

Verna's space was on the end of a row of eight stylists. "Laura said to take good care of you," she said as Cassie dropped into the chair and yanked the band out of her hair before shaking it loose.

Tall and thin, with an asymmetrical hairstyle in multiple shades of brown and blond, a nose ring, and a tattoo climbing up one arm, Verna eyed Cassie's hair. "Just a trim?" Obviously she thought a lot more work was in order. Her eyes met Cassie's in the mirror and she physically started. "Wait a second, you're Allie Kramer's sister, aren't you? How could I not put two and two together? You really look like your mom."

"So I've heard."

"Hey, I'm sorry . . . really sorry about your sister, I mean." She shook her head and reached for a comb. "I don't suppose anyone has any idea . . . ?" She left the sentence unfinished as if she were unsure how much she could ask.

"No," Cassie said, not wanting to go into it with a virtual stranger. Besides, she was on edge, well, more on edge than usual, especially with Trent in her house. The thought of him hanging out in her apartment without her bothered her and she mentally kicked herself again for handing over her key so readily.

"Bummer." Verna was already touching Cassie's hair, pulling it away from her head, testing it as an assistant came by with the offer of drinks, everything from herbal tea to regular coffee and cucumber water.

Cassie declined. She'd just come here for information, but it seemed her idea had been foolish.

"You know, I think some red streaks would be cool," Verna was saying. "Nothing too noticeable. Maybe a deep burgundy or an auburn with a kick would brighten this up. Be nice on you. Kind of contempo."

"Just a trim." Her hair wasn't the issue.

"Okay," Verna agreed with a smile as she met Cassie's gaze in the mirror again. "You're the boss."

This was turning out to be a big waste of time. Verna knew nothing. Of course. In the end, Cassie ended up with slightly shorter hair and a lot less cash in her wallet, but she hadn't found out anything about her sister.

Once again, a dead end, she thought as she found her way out of the building and slid a pair of sunglasses onto her nose. What had she really thought she'd accomplish? She didn't know the first thing about locating a missing person. She should just leave Allie's disappearance to the police. Let the professionals handle it.

And who are they considering their number one suspect in her disappearance? You.

As she reached her Honda, a BMW tore into the lot, wheeled into one of the few open spaces, and in a chirp of tires stopped short. The driver's door flew out and Laura Merrick, blond hair streaming behind her, oversize sunglasses covering her eyes, practically leaped from the car. "Oh, God, Cassie! I thought I might still catch you," she said breathlessly. "I mean I was hoping. Did you hear?"

"Hear what?" Cassie asked, instantly panicked. *Allie! Oh no. It's Allie. Something awful has happened!*

"About Holly Dennison."

"Holly? No . . . I just saw her."

A pause. "When?"

"The other night."

"Not last night?"

Cassie shook her head. "What?"

Laura took in a breath, then said, "She's dead."

"*Dead?*" Cassie said, her insides going cold. *Holly? Bubbly, full-of-life, Moscow-Mule-pushing Holly?* "No."

"It's true. I just heard," Laura said, shaking her head in disbelief.

"Then you must've heard wrong." But the expression on Laura's face said it was true. Cassie went from denial to despair. Could it be? She felt the blood draining from her face and the warm sun beating against the back of her neck.

"Her body was found this morning. Outside a bar in . . . in, oh, God, I can't remember, no . . . somewhere in Venice, I think. It . . . it doesn't matter." Laura ran her hands through her hair. "I need a cigarette." She looked pointedly at Cassie.

"I don't have any."

"Really?"

"Never smoked."

"Figures. Well, come on, Verna or maybe Alana might." She saw that a couple of potential customers had stopped to listen to their excited conversation, and she grabbed Cassie by the arm. "No reason to make a scene." Quickly, she propelled Cassie back through the shop, stopped at Verna's station where, after a quick exchange, she was handed a French cigarette, then she hurried them both through a supply area and break room with a coffeepot and mini fridge to a small outdoor space facing an alley.

A few plastic chairs were scattered around a white table with a faded umbrella. In the table's center was an ashtray overflowing with cigarette butts and some gum wrappers. Laura scooped up the ashtray and poured its contents into a nearby trash can. Then she lit up the Gauloise, drew deep, and tossed back her head to exhale the smoke toward the sky. "Better," she sighed.

Still in shock, Cassie asked, "How do you know about Holly?"

"Internet." She wrapped one arm around her waist and held the cigarette near her face with the other. "She was only found this morning. Google it." Another deep drag. Cassie started typing Holly's name into her phone and Laura added, "Little Bea called me when she heard, too."

"I thought she was out of the country."

Laura shook her head. "Where'd you hear that?"

"Holly."

"Don't think so. She had an appointment with me, what? Like two days ago, I think." Another deep drag and after dusting the seat of a chair with her hand she flopped into it. The umbrella shaded half of her face and reminded Cassie of one of Jenna's old movie posters, one she'd hung up in her bedroom where part of her face was in darkness, the other pale.

"Holly told me you said she was in London." Cassie looked down at the screen on her phone where she'd Googled information on Holly Dennison.

"Little Bea and Cherise *were* in London. They came back a week or so ago." She rolled her eyes. "Trust Holly to get it wrong," she said, and then caught herself up as if she'd realized the woman was gone. "Did you find it?" Laura asked.

Cassie looked down at her phone again where a picture of Holly filled the small screen. The back of her mouth went dry. Scrolling down she read the headline: *Set Designer's Body Discovered.* She skimmed the scanty details, heart racing. A man frequenting a bar in Venice had found the woman, who was identified as Holly Marie Dennison, a set designer, in a parking lot. Several of the movies she worked on were mentioned, including the last, *Dead Heat.* The police had limited details but the death was being investigated as a homicide. Anyone with any knowledge should contact them immediately.

Cassie sank into one of the chairs. Sadness enveloped her as she remembered Holly's quick smile and recently spiked hair, how she'd sipped her mojitos at The Sundowner. "I can't believe it." She was stunned.

Calmer now, Laura suddenly looked at her cigarette as if it were the devil incarnate and angrily jabbed it out in the ashtray. "She has . . . had a sister who lived in town. That was her next of kin, I guess, so her name was released and these days, everything, all news is instantaneous." She let out her breath, then looked at Cassie. "I didn't mean to shock you, but I thought you'd want to know and since I knew you were coming here . . ."

"I do. Did." She was still in shock. "God, it's hard to believe."

"Look, I'm glad I caught you, but I have an appointment in like . . ." She glanced down at her phone for the time. "Five minutes ago."

"I just wanted to talk to you. I really didn't need a haircut."

Laura frowned. "About . . . Allie?" she guessed.

"Yeah."

"I don't know anything, Cassie. That's what I already told the police."

"I know. But you were Allie's friend as well as makeup artist. She spent hours with you daily, especially when *Dead Heat* was filming. I thought you, of all of her friends, might have some idea of what she was going through. What was happening in her life. Why she didn't show up for the last day of the reshoot of the movie."

"I have no idea. We talked, sure. But just about normal, everyday stuff. Nothing deep, trust me. It wasn't like I was her shrink or anything."

Cassie pushed, "But everyone talks to their hairdresser because of all those hours in the chair." When Laura didn't respond, Cassie added, "Look, of course you're not her shrink, but maybe her confidante? It's what we all do. People are always talking to, or even dating, sometimes marrying, the person who does their hair and makeup, especially in this business."

"We weren't dating," Laura said with a glimmer of humor.

"But you knew who she hung out with. Who she was seeing."

"Other than Brandon?" Laura shrugged. "He's the last one she was really involved with. It made things kind of awkward on the set."

Not exactly news. Cassie had been there. "So what was she thinking before she disappeared? Was she depressed? Anxious? Did you think there was any reason she would take off? Anyone she was scared of?"

"Cassie, what do you want from me? If I knew anything about Allie, I'd tell the police or you or Jenna."

"Mom?" That surprised Cassie.

"Mothers always worry. So, of course I'd let her know." She shifted in her chair, as if suddenly uncomfortable.

"I didn't know you knew her."

"I don't, not really, but Allie introduced me once, on the set. It was obvious that she really cared about her kids."

That much was true. And it was obvious that she and Allie shared enough of a bond for Allie to feel comfortable enough to introduce Jenna to her. Cassie tried again. "Are you sure Allie didn't say anything to you about what was going on in her life?"

Laura checked the time on her phone once more. She seemed to wrestle with her conscience then said, "Oh, hell. Look, I really don't know much . . ." Again she hesitated, then through the dark glasses her gaze found Cassie's and her voice was almost a whisper. "What I do know, you're not going to like."

"What?"

"It's about you, Cassie." For a second, Laura looked away. "She . . . she was jealous of you."

"Jealous of me?" Cassie barked out a short laugh. "Sure."

"I knew you wouldn't believe me."

"Allie was successful. On top of the world."

"Was she?" Serious.

"Of course she was. She had her pick of movie roles."

Laura let out a sigh. "It wasn't about her work."

"What then? Why would she be jealous of me?" The idea was ludicrous. Allie had always been the baby of the family and as such, both Cassie and Jenna had protected her in their ways and Robert had coddled her. Allie had shined in school and then later in the same profession where she competed with Cassie, always, always crushing her older sister in any audition.

"There's always been some kind of competition between you two, hasn't there?"

"But she always came out on top. Always."

"I guess it depends upon what you're vying for." Laura seemed to become philosophical, her thoughts turned inward. "It happens in every family. My family."

"You have sisters and brothers?"

"Not anymore. I had a sister, but . . . she passed years ago. Freak car accident." She let out a sigh. "I survived. Felt guilty ever since."

"I'm sorry."

"It's okay," she said, though she turned a little pensive. "It was a long time ago. But I remember sibling rivalry." She shot Cassie a look. "It's never any fun."

"No, but Allie and I . . ."

"I just think Allie always wanted what you had."

"But I didn't have anything . . ." Cassie's voice faded away slowly. *Trent.* Allie had never been married. Never come close. Never engaged. A handful of quasi-serious boyfriends, none of which had connected with her until after she'd made her mark in Hollywood, but no one who'd ever wanted to spend the rest of his life with her.

"That's ridiculous."

Laura got to her feet. "You asked. If you don't believe me, talk to Cherise. She was the one who knew her best, who scheduled her appointments, who knew what Allie was doing, who probably even covered for her."

"Cherise hasn't returned my calls. I think she doesn't want to talk to me. Holly said she's working for Brandon McNary."

"Yeah, I think I heard that, too . . . maybe from Little Bea. I can't remember, but hey, I really have to go. I can't help you with Allie." She was already walking through the doorway into the back of the salon. "I have no idea what happened to her."

Join the club, Cassie thought as she followed a step behind.

She made her way through the salon to the front of the shop and eventually to her car. After climbing inside and starting the engine she sat for a second and thought about Holly and how hard it was to believe she was dead. Murdered. Who would want to take her life? Granted, Cassie didn't know a lot about Holly, only that she had a sister, a niece she adored, and a brother-in-law she didn't like. She'd always been looking for Mr. Right and had never found him, though she'd never given up hope.

It seemed strange, more than coincidental, that three people who had worked on *Dead Heat* had suffered tragedies recently. Not only had Allie gone missing and Lucinda been shot, but now Holly, vital, fun-loving Holly was dead.

How odd was that? More than odd, it was eerie. And sad. Fear crawled up her spine as she headed back to her apartment.

And Trent, she reminded herself.

He complicated things.

And confused things.

Somehow she had to convince him and maybe herself that their relationship was over. She should call her attorney, have him dust off her divorce papers, sign them, and be done with it. Why was she just hanging on to a marriage that was dead, had already died a horrible death on the altar of adultery?

With her own younger sister. No, make that younger, more beautiful and more talented and much more famous younger sister.

Could the scenario get any more cliché? Sometimes she felt as if she were in some kind of soap opera.

The old pain twisted deep in her heart.

Somehow, she'd have to get over it.

Jamming her Honda into gear, she drove toward home, dust covering her windshield, sunlight bouncing off the hood of her car. Traffic was heavy and slow. She was tucked behind a behemoth of a vehicle, some old Chevrolet, a pristine two-toned model from the middle of the last century, buffed and waxed so that it gleamed, as the male driver in a little cap tore up the road a good five miles under the speed limit.

Annoyed at the pace, Cassie was already checking her mirrors, just about to pass when her phone jangled. She fished in her purse, plucked out her cell, saw Cherise's name on the display and, risking a ticket, hit the button to answer.

"Cassie?" Cherise said, before Cassie could say a word. "Oh my God, I just heard about Holly. It's awful. Awful!" She sounded breathless as she echoed Cassie's feelings.

"Horrible. I'd like to—"

"Laura just called me and told me you were trying to reach me," she interrupted. "She said you thought I'd blown you off because I took a job with Brandon, but . . . oh, this is so, so horrible. I can't believe it."

"Neither can I."

"I know, I know, it's like the movie's cursed or something. I mean what else could go wrong?"

Cassie shuddered to think.

"Look, if you want to talk to me, okay, I can meet you in half an hour, then I have to be someplace, but I don't know what I can tell you. Laura said you were trying to figure out what happened to Allie and I swear to God, I don't have any idea, and so please, please, please don't be mad at me for going to work with Brandon. I know he's not your favorite person but with Allie gone I needed a job and—"

"Cherise," Cassie cut in. "Tell me where to meet and I'll be there." Cassie explained where she was and Cherise suggested a coffee shop about fifteen minutes away, closer to Cassie's apartment. "Perfect. I'll meet you there." For the briefest of seconds, she considered calling Trent to tell him she'd been held up, but discarded the idea immediately.

She'd only seen him for a few minutes, long enough to have an argument, and already she was acting like a wife, like she needed to report in. "Forget it," she muttered under her breath. At the next opportunity, she shot past the guy in the red and white Chevy straight out of the fifties.

She reached the coffee shop a few minutes before Cherise. Standing in line to order and scouting the crowded seating area in search of a free table, she spied the other woman driving into the lot. Cell phone pressed to her ear, Cherise wheeled into the lot in a champagne-colored Mercedes convertible. Parking spaces were at a premium and she had to wait until another car had backed up, then she squeezed into a slim space, beating another car coming from the other direction. The Mitsubishi's blinker indicated that the driver had intended to claim the spot, but Cherise didn't appear to care or even notice.

Brown hair twisted onto her head in a messy bun, Cherise flew out of her car. In shorts and a long-sleeved T-shirt that slid over one shoulder, she was still talking on the phone and seemed oblivious to the other driver's frustration as she jogged to the front doors.

By the time she burst inside Cassie was at the front of the line and ready to order. Cherise looked around the busy shop, then race-walked past four other customers. "Grab me a triple shot Americano, okay?" Before Cassie could answer, she added, "I'll get a table. God, this place is always sooo busy. Oh! There's one now!" She was off, ignoring the scowls and glares from the people standing in line and hurrying toward a café table being vacated by a couple of teenagers wearing watch caps, army jackets, and shorts while hauling their beat-up skateboards and coffee drinks outside.

While Cassie ordered, Cherise, as if she'd been a waitress in another lifetime, dropped her phone and keys onto one of the tall chairs, grabbed three sugar packets from a counter, then bussed the trash away. Using a couple of napkins she wiped up spilled coffee and muttered about "lame, self-involved, entitled kids who should be in school," before spying Cassie with the coffee. "Thanks!" She took the cup Cassie offered and then pulled some one-dollar bills from a pocket in her shorts as if intent on paying.

Cassie waved away the offered cash. "Next time's on you."

"You sure?" Before Cassie could respond, she tucked the cash away. "Thanks." Cherise took the lid off her cup and blew across the hot brew, then started opening sugar packets and dumping them in. "I can't quit thinking about Holly," she whispered. "Who would do something so awful? And to her of all people? She was so sweet. It doesn't make any sense." Stirring the sugar, waiting for it to dissolve, she stared into her coffee as if she could find answers within the dark depths. "Why?"

"I wish I knew."

A fussy-looking woman with pursed lips who had been in line behind Cassie passed by their table and shot Cherise a hard glare. "There are no cuts," she hissed as if they were in an elementary school lunch line, before bustling importantly out of the shop on wedged sandals.

Cherise paid no attention to her.

The line of customers waiting to order waxed and waned while Cassie and Cherise sipped from their drinks and discussed Holly Dennison for a few minutes. Cassie was about to broach the subject of Allie when Cherise asked, "You're going to the party for the premiere in Portland this weekend, right? It's kind of a command performance, y'know. A big splash. Dean does it before the release of all of his pictures."

"I haven't thought too much about it. But, probably." It might be her only opportunity to talk to Arnette and Little Bea.

"Yeah, me too. It's too bad Allie won't be there." Her smile was pensive. "Maybe she'll show up by then."

"I wanted to talk to you about her."

"That's what Laura said. Have you heard from her?"

Cassie shook her head. "Not a word."

She took another quick sip of her drink. "Me neither."

"But you talked to her every day, you knew her schedule in and out. Was anything unusual going on?"

She half laughed. "There was no *usual* with Allie. Every day was an 'experience.'" Her amusement faded. "But she was kind of acting strangely, y'know, kind of weird and freaky a day or two before. I mean it wasn't a big deal, but she was off."

"Off? How?"

"She was just a little . . . tenser than usual. Like edgy, I guess. I didn't say anything to the police because it was nothing really. It certainly wasn't anything that made me think something out of the ordinary was going on. Then again with Allie, what's normal?" Her smile was feeble.

"What was she tense about?"

"I don't know. The movie? Working with Brandon? They were like fire and ice, always running hot and cold. And I can tell you this, he misses her." She looked quickly away, burying her nose into her cup and taking a swallow.

Cassie was skeptical of Brandon McNary caring about anything or anyone but himself and his own interests.

"I know, I know, he's an egomaniac," Cherise said, reading Cassie's expression. "I felt like such a traitor going to work for him, but it's really been good, I think. And I kind of see things from his perspective now." She glanced out the window then added, "You know your sister wasn't exactly easy to work for."

"Yes." If Brandon McNary was an egocentric male, Allie was his female counterpart. "Do you know if she was ever in Santa Fe, or if she knew or contacted someone who lived there?"

"Santa Fe?"

"Maybe in 2007?"

"I wasn't working for her then."

"But she might have talked about it?"

She rolled that around in her mind and scowled thoughtfully all the while slowly shaking her head. "Don't know. Maybe? But geez, wouldn't she have been a teenager and your mom have to give permission, or something?" After taking a final sip from her cup, she crumpled it in her fist. "I don't remember her mentioning it, but she certainly didn't tell me *everything*." Cherise's cell phone rang musically and she answered, then turned her head away for a little privacy. The conversation was one-sided. Cherise barely said a word but hung up and turned back to Cassie. "Sorry, duty calls."

"Brandon?"

"Uh-huh." She was standing, clearing the table of empty sugar packets and her cup. "So I've got to get going."

"He's in LA?" Cassie just wanted to confirm.

"Flew in late the night before last, I think."

That jived.

She sighed and rolled her eyes. "He's not easy to work for, either, but the only other job offer I got was from Whitney Stone, and it didn't pay as much. She's working on some shows for a mystery week at a cable company. Even asked about Allie—not just what's happening now, but what happened in the past, when your mother was stalked by that sicko up in Oregon."

Cassie's heart froze. "She told you that?"

"She mentioned it just this morning. Can you believe she called me at six thirty? Who does that? Like I would work for a woman that anal. And all of a sudden she has an interest in the nutjob who killed people who looked like Jenna Hughes." Cherise gave a shudder.

Cassie's vocal cords felt as if they'd seized up. She tried to respond, but there was no need as Cherise went on blithely, "All the buzz surrounding *Dead Heat* must've resurrected interest in your mom's story. Whitney was trying to pick my brain, see if I knew anything, y'know, unique. If Allie had said anything to me. She acted like it was kind of a rush job, said something about already having the footage and wanting to air the program during mystery week. It was a little over the top, y'know. Not that tragedy hasn't been used as a means to promote a program before." She glanced at her phone and noted the time. "Look, if I think of anything, I'll call ya," Cherise promised, obviously in a hurry. "But don't hold your breath." With that she turned and racewalked to her car. She drove off with the same pedal-to-the-metal attitude that she'd come in with.

It was almost as if she'd met Cassie because of some kind of duty, like getting through a hated obligatory chore. Odd. But the bare fact of the matter was that as refreshing and energetic as Cherise was, Cassie didn't trust her and felt Cherise might be holding back. Cassie swallowed cold coffee and replayed Cherise's words. *Not that tragedy hasn't been used as a means to promote a program before.* Or to promote a movie. Like *Dead Heat.*

The gears in her mind ground. Was it possible? Could some of the strange occurrences that had been happening be a means to create a buzz around the film? She was so lost in thought she nearly jumped when she heard someone clear his throat. Looking up, she realized that a twentysomething was hovering nearby, a cup of coffee in one hand, an iPad in his other, waiting for her table. Quickly, she picked up her trash and left the shop. It was after eleven by now and she wondered if, when she got home, Trent would still be waiting. A little jolt of anticipation filled her heart and she told herself she was being an idiot.

Again.

But then wasn't she always about her husband? She figured it was a character flaw. One of far too many.

CHAPTER 19

As Trent waited in Cassie's apartment, he figured he might be stood up.

Or, more likely, played for a fool.

It was a chance he'd decided to take.

He'd found breakfast and coffee at a deli six blocks away, returned his rental car, then taken a cab to the apartment to find that Cassie still wasn't home. Her place was small and compact, three half-packed suitcases flung open on her bed, her closets virtually stripped, the bathroom nearly empty of products, the refrigerator not much more than a bare lightbulb.

It did appear as if she were leaving, that she'd returned to LA to grab her things. And play private detective. Trent wondered about that, her quest to find her sister. Maybe it was natural but he doubted a would-be actress, sometime writer, recent mental hospital patient, would have more luck finding out what had happened to Allie than the police with their manpower, sophisticated technology, and training. Allie and Cassie had always had a love/hate relationship, hate being the best-stated emotion recently.

He'd been the cause of that.

Hell, he'd been the cause of a lot of friction in Cassie's life.

While he'd been at her place he'd snooped a little and didn't feel all that bad about it. She was his wife, he rationalized, and she'd just walked out of a psychiatric wing. He hadn't found much of interest except for the single keepsake from their wedding, a picture of the two of them in Las Vegas, the glass covering the photo broken, the frame placed facedown as if she hadn't wanted a reminder.

But it hadn't been in the trash.

Or missing.

Maybe that was a good, if slightly marred, sign.

He was just replacing the photo, standing it up, when he saw her pull into the parking area. Without her roller bag, she was out of the car and heading inside. He met her on the tiny porch.

"So you are still here" was her greeting.

"I missed you, too."

She shot him a dark look. Obviously she wasn't in the mood for levity. "Let's go." Passing through the living room, she spied the photograph, hesitated, then flipped it facedown again before storming into the bedroom.

He followed after her and watched as she opened drawers in her dresser and threw a few more sweaters and jeans into the open bags. Without looking up, she zipped up the first roller bag and said, "Why don't you make yourself useful and help me take these out to the car?"

"Wrong side of bed?"

"Oh, I'm sorry. What I meant to say was why don't you *please* make yourself useful and take these out to the car."

He chuckled. Her head shot up and it looked as if she might let loose again, but all she did was shake her head. "You're just being a little intense," he pointed out.

"I'm busy and . . . you know, it's been kind of a bad day." Then she stopped short. Her face fell and all of the bristly anger he'd witnessed melted into sadness. "Oh, God, you don't know."

"What?"

"Holly Dennison is dead," she said and bit her lip. "Murdered."

"*What?*" He thought he'd heard wrong.

"She was the set designer on *Dead Heat.*"

"I know who she is. You've worked with her before." He was stunned. "Murdered?" he repeated, and the bad feeling that had been with him for the last few days intensified. "When did this happen?"

"Last night, I guess. I just found out a couple of hours ago from Laura Merrick." Calmer, she told him what little she knew and all that Trent got out of it was that Holly was found last night in the Venice area.

"My God, Cass."

"I saw her the other night and . . ." Her voice trailed off and she cleared her throat, blinking rapidly.

"I don't like this."

"Neither do I, but I have to get back to Oregon. I'm sure the police will want to talk to me, but they can damned well do it up there. I had nothing to do with any of this."

"I'm coming with you," he said suddenly.

"No, you're not." She gazed at him as if he'd lost his mind.

"Already took back the rental and took a cab back. I'm good to go."

"What? Why? Did you think you were staying here? With me?" She looked at him as if he were stark, raving mad.

"I came for you, Cass. I told you that."

They stared at each other. He could almost see her calculating, trying to figure out how to ditch him again. But then she just made a sound of exasperation and said, "Come on, then. Let's get out of here."

With that she finished packing quickly and together they hauled the things she wanted to take with her to Oregon to her car. She locked the door of the apartment as he folded himself into the passenger seat and within ten minutes they were on the freeway, heading north.

Neither said a word.

Cassie wondered why she had ever agreed to let Trent ride with her to Oregon. It had been a mistake; she hadn't been thinking, she'd just reacted. So here she was, hands gripped on the steering wheel as if she thought the car was going to run away from her, nerves strung tight as bowstrings, heading ever northward on the Five. They were out of Los Angeles, traffic on the freeway moving along at a good clip. The engine was purring, the wheels humming on the pavement, the scenery of Southern California flying by the windows, and Trent was way too close to her for comfort, his shoulder nearly touching hers, the familiar smell of him teasing her.

Big mistake.

"So, the way I figure it," he said, "we've got fifteen hours or so to sort things out." He slid a glance her way and her heart did a hard little flip. God, she was a moron where he was concerned. "Unless of course you're a lead-foot. Then the trip will be shorter. We'll have to work faster."

"You mean about what happened to Holly and Allie."

"You know what I mean." He focused on the windshield again.

Her chest tightened. She wasn't ready for this. He was too near and there was nowhere she could run or get away from him. "I don't think I want to talk about *us* on a road trip."

"No better time," he said. "No distractions. No way to run away from each other. Just you and me and the miles rolling by."

"Sounds like lyrics for a bad country song."

He smiled faintly. "Isn't that what we've been living?"

She winced. He was right. But the thought of hashing out all of their history right here in the warm car scared her a little. Too many emotions were involved, too much drama. "I don't think it's a good idea."

"Got a better one?"

"Another time."

"Nope." He was firm. "I'm tired of living in limbo. Married, but not married. Having a wife who avoids me at all costs. Thinking I'll be served with divorce papers at any inconvenient minute. It's time to resolve this," he said, turning to stare straight at her. "Either we stay married and try like hell to work things out, go to counseling, the whole nine yards, or we throw in the towel now. But we make a damned decision. Together."

"Don't you think it would be better if I wasn't driving?"

"It'll never happen."

He had her there. No way would she have ever agreed to meet with him to talk things out over dinner or coffee or drinks. Nor would she text, e-mail, or take his phone calls. But still . . . this could get messy, they would surely argue. She might even break down. She thought of the long hours in the car ahead. She was tense already, her shoulders tight, her stomach in knots. "No."

"Cass—"

"Listen. I'm not ready." She shot him a look. "Let's get to Oregon first."

"You're stalling."

"Hell, yes, I'm stalling. I said, 'Not now!'" She let out a sigh, realized she was being unreasonable, but she didn't care.

"You can do this. You're a lot tougher than you know."

She flexed her hands on the wheel. No, she wasn't.

"So listen, I'm going to tell you about what happened with Allie, and you're not going to run us off the road or try to kill me or anything. You're just going to keep driving and more importantly, keep calm."

She didn't think that was possible, but she tucked her Honda behind a green station wagon filled with people, a dog, the cargo space crammed with gear, suitcases strapped to an ancient roof rack. The wagon was moving a couple of miles over the speed limit, which she figured was as good as this part of the trip was going to get.

Just so he was clear about how she felt, she said, "For the record I think this is a crazy idea. And you know, if I don't want to talk about it, I could either crash or pull over and kick you out of the car."

"You could. I hope it doesn't come to that."

This was such a bad idea. "I'll try to keep my cool."

"That would be good."

She shot him a glance, caught his profile. There was an earthiness to him, a pure-male quality that always got to her and she silently cursed it. "No promises." When she felt his gaze on her again, she added, "I said I'd try. It's the best I can do."

"Okay." A pause. Then, "First off, and you have to believe me, I never cheated on you."

Liar! But she didn't say it. Bit back the word. Felt her stomach roil a little.

"I'll admit I thought about it. After all we were separated and you'd made it very clear you wanted a divorce."

"Because of Allie," she reminded flatly.

"*Before* you *thought* I'd gotten involved with her."

Yep. This was a bad idea. Real bad. Her jaw tightened and she found herself driving too close to the station wagon in front of her, so she backed off, slowed down, and caught a glimpse of the car behind her, a black compact that pulled sharply into the next lane to jet around her and the station wagon.

"That's not how it was," she said. "Allie said—"

"Allie lies. You know that. For whatever she wants and she doesn't care who she hurts. Yeah, she's attractive. Yeah, she came on to me."

Cassie died a little inside even though she'd known part of this for a long while.

Trent looked out the side window. "Yeah," he admitted. "The truth is I considered going for it. She was offering and for all intents and purposes I was single because my wife wanted it that way. Why the hell not?" There was a bite to his words. "But before anything happened I figured out why she got to me. Why I was so tempted."

"Because you're like all the other males in America?"

"You really don't know?" He was staring at her again and her skin began to heat, her fingers turning slick.

"But you'll tell me."

"Damned straight, I will. It was because she reminded me of you, Cass. She looks like you, she sounds like you and . . . and you didn't want me."

"I always . . ." She bit her tongue.

"Don't say it. You broke up with me before you went to LA and I figured you needed to go follow your dream, to find yourself, or just run away for a while. You were young, so hell, the only sensible thing to do was let you go."

She swallowed hard, remembering that the only tie that had caused her to doubt her decision to leave Oregon was her feelings for Trent. She'd been ready to leave her mother, her stepfather, and her sister in her dust, but saying good-bye to Trent had given her serious second thoughts, doubts she'd wrestled with but ultimately ignored. "It was hard," she admitted, feeling some of the old pain. "Hard to leave you. But . . . Yeah, I did." The truth was it had happened and she wasn't going to deny it. "So far," she said, "you're right. And then you came to LA."

"Right. I wasn't ready to give up, so I thought I'd see if we could give it a second chance."

She remembered seeing him again. Reigniting what they'd once had, ending up in a whirlwind romance and an elopement to Las Vegas. It had been exciting. Thrilling. And oh, how she'd loved him. She didn't want to consider it now, how he'd made her feel, how he'd turned her inside out with the brush of his lips against her ear or the sensation of his tongue tracing the hollow of her throat.

Once more she was driving too fast and eased off the gas pedal.

"You seemed to be on board."

She couldn't deny that those first few months of marriage were pure wedded bliss. But that was before Allie had set her sights on the rugged cowboy-turned-stuntman who had married her sister. Soon after the wedding, Allie had tried to set her straight about her new husband by warning Cassie that Trent was a player, that within weeks of Cassie moving to LA, Trent had shown interest in her as well as other girls and women around town.

Allie had even insinuated that Trent had cornered Allie one night while Cassie was still living in Falls Crossing and tried to kiss her and "God knew what else." Cassie hadn't believed the story initially, but over time, she'd begun to have doubts.

Had she really been so blind? Had she believed Allie because dealing with Trent and trying to make a relationship work was too difficult? Had she run from her marriage just as she'd run from her life in Oregon?

"I don't know what to believe."

"Maybe you should trust your own instincts." He slid her a glance that she caught.

"You might not like the outcome."

"I'll take my chances."

When he didn't say anything more, she prodded. "That's it? All you have to say."

"For now." He leaned back in the seat. "We've got a long trip ahead of us." With that, he lapsed into silence.

Which gave her a lot of time to think.

She turned on the radio and her favorite LA station was starting to fade, the long road north stretching out for hundreds of miles, the future uncertain.

Rhonda Nash didn't put much faith in "hunches" or "gut feelings" or hypothetical "theories." She was a cold, hard facts kind of cop and those feelings spilled over into her private life, which probably explained why, at nearly forty, she'd never married though she'd gotten close a couple of times. It was just that her bullshit meter was nearly always on alert and a lot of men she'd dated didn't pass the test.

So when she found a connection in a case she was working on, some little piece of evidence that tied parts of the ongoing investigation together, she experienced a little sizzle of anticipation, a spike of adrenaline that fired her blood and, as was the case in the disappearance of Allie Kramer, propelled Nash into action.

Nash had been contacted by Jonas Hayes, who worked homicide in LA. A woman's body had been discovered in a parking lot near a club in Venice Beach. She'd been identified as Holly Dennison, who not only had worked with Allie Kramer and Lucinda Rinaldi on *Dead Heat*, but who had been found wearing a mask, a distorted image of Allie Kramer.

The pictures were disturbing, a set of digital photos of a woman's dead body wedged between a couple of cars in a parking lot. The first set showed pictures of the corpse wearing the mask. The second set was the victim without the mask, a woman's face with fixed gaze and ashen skin tones, Holly Dennison, a set designer, who like Rinaldi, had worked on *Dead Heat*. A third set was of close-ups of the mask, front and back, and the one-word message scrawled on the picture's back.

All in all, weird as hell.

The cause of death wasn't yet official, but a single gunshot wound to the torso, a through and through, made an educated guess simple.

Why had the mask been placed on the victim's face? What connection, other than the obvious movie link, did Dennison have to Allie Kramer?

Now, Nash hurried out of the station house in Portland and felt the slap of cold April rain. At four in the afternoon, rush hour was already in full swing. Cars, trucks, vans, bikes, and buses clogged the city streets, inching from one red light to the next, each vehicle angling around the others in an effort to find a way out of the heart of Portland.

Making her way along the crowded afternoon sidewalk, Nash pulled up the hood of her coat and tried to imagine how Holly Dennison, a dead woman in LA wearing a grotesque mask of Allie Kramer, fit into the case. The connection was obvious. Almost too obvious: the message on the mask's back side.

A single word: *Sister.*

Bingo. Connection.

Who was Allie Kramer's sister?

Cassie Kramer.

Who fought with Allie on the night she disappeared?

Cassie Kramer.

Who felt betrayed by her sister's involvement with her estranged husband?

Cassie Kramer.

And who just happened to be in LA when the murder of set designer Holly Dennison occurred?

Cassie Kramer.

But why would Cassie leave such an obvious clue, almost framing herself? Even though she'd recently been a patient in the mental ward of Mercy Hospital, Cassie seemed coherent. She had a documented quick temper, but was she really homicidal? Could she have found a way to make her sister disappear? Was Allie Kramer, like Holly Dennison, already dead? Then why hide one body and leave the other to be found?

Things weren't adding up.

There were still too many inconsistencies.

Another reason to head to LA and sort a few things out.

From the corner of her eye, she saw Double T, in a baseball cap and rain jacket, fall into step with her.

"Did I hear right?" he asked as they reached the corner. "You're flying to California tonight?"

"In three hours if I can make it to the airport in rush hour."

"Could set you up with a police escort. Make sure you get to PDX in time."

"Funny guy." She checked her watch. Told herself there was plenty of time. "You know there's been an Allie Kramer sighting down there."

"Isn't there always?" This wasn't news. Ever since the popular star's disappearance, the police departments in LA, Portland, and even places in between received "tips" that the missing woman had been seen. "I swear, Allie Kramer's more popular than Elvis these days. And more visible. Didn't we get a call last week from somewhere in Alaska? And don't forget that little town outside of Birmingham. Good Lord, someone even called from Molalla, here in Oregon."

He nodded, drips spilling off the bill of his cap.

"Each time we do a follow-up, it's a case of mistaken identity. Once, the woman spotted was eighty-two years old . . . and then later a man was sure he'd seen her." Both sightings hadn't panned out. "People see what they want to see. You know that. You've interviewed enough eyewitnesses to a crime, each contradicting the other."

"But now you're flying south because some woman who was loosely associated with *Dead Heat* was murdered. The last I heard LA isn't in our jurisdiction."

She almost smiled as she waited for the light to change. "Already cleared it."

The light finally switched and she and Double T stepped off the curb into the swarm of pedestrians crossing to the other side. Once on the opposite sidewalk, she and Double T veered off toward the parking structure.

"You work fast," he observed.

"No one higher up likes all the press the Allie Kramer case is getting, the pressure to solve what happened to her and arrest whoever it was who was behind the Rinaldi shooting. The public wants answers. The press is in a feeding frenzy and the brass are feeling the heat."

"You're convinced the dead woman in LA is linked to what happened up here," he said as they climbed the stairs of the elevated lot.

"Uh-huh. If we didn't now have a dead body, I'd almost think this was a publicity stunt gone bad."

"But we do have a dead body. Or LA does."

"There's more going on than just homicide." Slanting rain poured through the open windows of the stairwell, dampening each landing. Nash barely noticed. "You saw the pictures."

"Yeah."

"Maybe it's not our jurisdiction," she said, remembering the shots of the mask that had been left on the corpse, "but Holly Dennison's murder has bearing on our case. I just need to figure out how."

"And here I thought you just wanted to head south and sip margaritas under the palms."

"I'm saving my frequent flyer miles for the islands. You know, preferably one with scorching sun, white sand, ocean breezes, and hot pool boys."

His lips twitched. "I'll hold down the fort while you're away."

"Do that. It won't be long. Fingers crossed, I should be back by tomorrow night." She found her Ford Focus wedged between a monster truck and an equally large SUV, both parked in *Compact Only* slots. "Doesn't anyone read?" she muttered and clicked her keyless lock before inching between the truck and the driver's side.

"Give 'em a ticket."

"I wish."

With a final grin cast in her direction Double T peeled off in search of his own vehicle.

Nash couldn't open her damned door, so she made her way back to the rear of her Focus, opened the cargo door, and cursing every moronic driver on the planet, crawled over the backseat, then into the driver's side. Worrying that her mirrors might scrape the sides of the encroaching vehicles, she hesitated before firing the engine. Then she thought, too damned bad. If she scraped the nearby rigs, too bad. She eased her way out of the space, took a deep breath, and started down the ramp leading to the street. She planned to pick up something to eat at a local Thai food cart, then head to the airport and hopefully make her flight. With the traffic and the rain, she didn't have a lot of time. She couldn't even run by her house on the east side, but thankfully she always kept an overnight bag filled with the essentials, including a toothbrush and change of clothes, in her Ford.

Just in case she ever got lucky.

So far, at least in recent memory, she had not.

CHAPTER 20

They pulled into a truck stop near Redding to fill up on gas and food. Inside the long, flat-roofed restaurant, they sat on opposite sides of a booth next to a plate glass window. The view was of the freeway, headlights and taillights streaking past, illuminating the night. A few other customers were scattered under the unforgiving overhead lights as a fiftysomething waitress with a forced smile and tired eyes took their orders, then disappeared through swinging doors.

"You okay?" Trent asked. His voice actually had a tender quality to it.

"Fine." That, of course, was a lie. She wondered if she'd ever be "fine" again. She tried to find a smile and gave up, lifting a shoulder and whispering, "I guess I'm as fine as I can be, all things considered."

His eyes, a shade of brown that was almost gold, seemed understanding, even kind, so she glanced away quickly and was thankful when their drinks arrived.

Thinking a jolt of caffeine might help her stay awake, Cassie had ordered a Coke. Trent settled in with his beer and ignoring the frosted glass that was left for him, took a long pull from the bottle.

"I'll drive for a while," he offered, and she nodded. The silence that had been fairly companionable in the car was now awkward and she was grateful when his cheeseburger and her club sandwich arrived. They concentrated on their meals for a few minutes before she decided to be proactive. "Did Allie's mood change?" she asked.

"What do you mean?"

"You know, just before she disappeared?"

His eyes found hers and his gaze wasn't friendly. "How would I know? Did you even hear what I told you before? We were *not* involved. I have no idea what was going on in her mind." He took another long drink, then said, "You just don't give up."

"Not when it's about my sister."

"Or a story," he added, reaching for his beer.

That momentarily stopped her. "You looked through my work? My computer?"

"No computer. I didn't see one." That was right, she remembered, she'd had her laptop with her earlier today. "But you did leave some notes lying around. I read them."

Okay, so he knew about her plans to write a screenplay about Allie. So what? Everyone would know soon enough, including, she hoped, Allie herself, once she was found. A tiny doubt skidded through her mind, a worry about her sister's whereabouts and the possibility Allie might never be found, but she pushed it aside. She picked at her sandwich and persevered. "So, did you know any reason Allie might have gone to Santa Fe? Does she know someone there, maybe a plastic surgeon? Probably around 2007?" The problem was the numbers didn't add up. In 2007, Allie had still been in Falls Crossing. . . .

Trent just stared at her, then with a shake of his head took another bite from his cheeseburger. "I don't know."

"It's just that I got this weird message from Portland. Actually the phone number is my psychiatrist's cell, but I don't think she sent it." She scrounged in her purse, withdrew her phone, and scrolled down to the cryptic text she'd received before sliding her iPhone across the table. He glanced at the display.

"Look, Cass, I don't know how to make you get it. I really don't know Allie, only through you as my sister-in-law. As for this"—he thumped the tiny screen with a finger—"I have no idea what it means. None."

He was so emphatic, she almost believed him. Which sent her back to square one. "Are you sure?"

"Jesus, Cass. I don't know your damned sister! I didn't sleep with her!"

A man in a baseball cap who had been forking a bite of meat loaf into his mouth turned his head. Trent noticed the guy and lowered his voice. "That's it, Cassie!" he warned. "You've got to find a way to trust me."

"I'm trying."

"Try harder." Scowling, he studied the message on her phone and appeared to somehow rein in his anger. "So this is what you've got? Santa Fe 07?"

"Yeah."

"A message from your doctor?" He slid the phone across the table that was topped in Formica straight out of the 1960s, and dug into the rest of his meal.

Cassie nodded.

"Could the text have been sent to you by mistake?"

"I suppose." She'd considered that possibility herself. "Or maybe it's just gobbledygook. You know, maybe the doctor let one of her grandchildren play with it and . . . no, I don't think so." Virginia Sherling didn't seem like the kind of woman who would let kids touch anything associated with her professional life, and Cassie wasn't sure the woman had ever been married or had a child.

"Did you call her? Ask her about it?"

"Called. Didn't leave a message." She frowned. "I'm her patient, her *mental* patient. I didn't want to leave some kind of voice mail she might misinterpret."

"By thinking you were . . . what? Hallucinating about a text? It would show on her phone, too."

"It's touchy with the doctor. Dr. Sherling didn't release me. In fact, she thought my leaving Mercy wasn't the best idea, and she said so." She pushed aside the remains of her sandwich. "I decided to leave it alone for a while. Besides, everything at the hospital was so out of sync," she admitted.

"What do you mean?"

She hesitated.

"Cass? If you want me to help, you have to confide in me."

"Hey, I didn't ask for your help. You showed up on my doorstep. Remember?"

"Okay."

"Okay?"

She might have said more but the lift of one eyebrow, silently accusing her of not acknowledging that she might want his help, no matter how hard she protested, caused her to rethink her position. Knowing she was probably making a mistake of immense proportions, she nevertheless told him about her dream in the hospital, about the nurse from an earlier era telling her that her sister was alive. But she kept the part about the reasons she'd checked herself in, the hallucinations and blackouts to herself. She saw no reason to muddle the issue. At least not yet.

He didn't remark, just kept right on eating while he listened. When he was finished, he pushed his plate aside.

"You think the nurse was real," he said.

"Rinko said he saw her."

"Rinko?" Trent repeated, his eyes narrowing. "The kid at the hospital with all the car stats?"

"And sports statistics," she said, fishing into a side pocket of her purse again. "You know him?"

"I met him. When I came to the hospital looking for you. He said you didn't want to talk to me."

"I didn't. I told him so."

"He conveyed the message very succinctly."

She figured as much and changed the topic of conversation before it turned too personal. She'd spent enough time feeling the pain of the breakup, or trying to trust Trent and believe that he hadn't fallen in love with and taken Allie to bed. That still had the power to make her stomach churn. Nor did she want to consider the fate of their marriage. Doomed? Or repairable? She wasn't even sure what she wanted, so she decided it was best not to go there. Not on this trip. Not again. So she said, "Rinko's nearly a genius, but he's got issues. Severe issues, I gather, though I don't know what they are. Otherwise he wouldn't be in Mercy Hospital indefinitely. But, if you ask him a question about any team in the nineteenth or twentieth or twenty-first century, he's got names, numbers, and RBIs or TDs or goals or three-pointers or assists or . . . whatever. I think it's impossible to trip him up." She found the little earring in the side pocket of her purse and set it on the table between them.

"What's this?"

"An earring. Like the one the nurse was wearing the night she came into the room or appeared or whatever you want to call it. But ghosts don't leave jewelry behind, nor do people in nightmares."

He picked up the bauble and examined it.

Cassie felt bands around her lungs tighten. Would he believe her? Or write her off as a mental case, a conspiracy theorist, or worse? She explained about her research on the earring and he listened, all the while studying the tiny cross and frowning, the wheels in his mind turning.

"You'd better keep it," he finally said, then picked up the tab and paid for both their meals over her protests. "Don't worry, you don't owe me anything," he added as he handed the bored-looking waitress his credit card.

Cassie stopped fighting him and when he offered to drive, she handed over the keys. Despite the jolt of caffeine from her Coke, she was exhausted, the ongoing nights of restless sleep having finally caught up with her. She'd thought she'd be on edge the whole time with Trent in the car, nervous around him, the anxiety keeping her awake, but as the miles of California had disappeared under the Honda's wheels so had her wariness. The idea of maneuvering the car through the winding turns of the mountains in Southern Oregon then onto the long, monotonous stretch of freeway to Portland and beyond wasn't something she looked forward to. Yep, let him drive.

After finding a blanket tucked under her bag in the backseat, she drew it around her body and curled up against the passenger window. Her eyes at half-mast, she observed Trent in the muted lights from the dash.

Did she trust him?

No. Well, at least not completely.

Was she still angry with him?

Yes, but not as violently so. Of course the jury was still out on her emotions and she had the right to change her mind.

Time will tell, she thought. As he drove steadily, keeping the Honda just above the speed limit, she drifted off somewhere near the Oregon border. Her sleep was never deep. At some level she was aware of the sounds of the journey; the radio stations fading in and out, the steady whine of the engine and outside the rumble of trucks passing, or the rush of the wind. All in all, though, she let slumber envelop her. Though she was loath to admit it, the fact that Trent was driving gave her a sense of security, no matter how false it might be.

She was vaguely aware of another filling station, lights along the overhang bright enough to rouse her a bit, the sounds of the pump being activated, the rush of fuel into the tank. Her eyes fluttered open, but she closed them quickly, then rotated her neck before slumber caught up with her again.

Only when the car began to bounce a little, the ride becoming rougher, did she start to surface. "Where are we?" she said around a yawn, stretching her arms as she peered through the windshield. Beams from the headlights splashed upon a rutted lane guarded by fence posts. Raindrops drizzled down the glass, the wipers rhythmically scraping water from the windshield.

"Home."

"Home?"

"My place."

She was instantly awake and trying to shake the cobwebs from her mind. They were in Oregon? In Falls Crossing? At his ranch? "No."

He slid her a glance. "Where else would we go?"

"I can't stay here!" She was squinting into the night as the beams caught a farmhouse with a wide, wraparound porch.

"Who invited you?"

She swung her head around to stare at him.

"It's your car, but I need to be here." He seemed amused at her befuddlement. "I don't recall asking you to stay."

"Oh. Right." *Of course!*

"But, you could stay over if you wanted."

"No, thanks."

He pulled up to the garage and cut the engine, then handed the keys to her. "If you're going to crash with Jenna, you might want to call and give her a heads-up."

"What time is it?"

"Four thirty."

She groaned. Originally, she'd planned to find a local hotel, sleep for however long she needed to, shower, and show up at her mother's house only to start looking for a place to stay, probably finding a hotel or temporary apartment closer to Portland until she figured out what she was going to do with her life. Falls Crossing was sixty miles east of the city, though with WiFi and the Internet and cell phones, for her job, location wasn't critical. Research and information were a laptop keystroke away. Connections with experts—a call or live chat or instant message, at the very least e-mail—were now nearly instantaneous.

Trent climbed out of the car. A stiff, damp breeze infiltrated the interior and the thought of driving one mile farther in the dark and rain sounded miserable.

"Maybe I could stay for a few hours, you know, until it's a reasonable time to show up at Mom and Shane's."

"Your call."

All she could think about was tumbling into bed. No questions. No conversation. No sex. Just crashing. "You got a spare couch?"

"At least one. You need a bag?" He was already reaching into the backseat.

"The smallest one. Thanks." Still a little groggy, she pocketed the keys, pushed her hair out of her eyes, grabbed her purse, opened the car door, and stepped into a puddle. "Did you have to park in the middle of a damned lake?" she sputtered.

"Welcome to Oregon," he said, and she could have sworn he was trying not to chuckle.

"I'm wearing flip-flops."

"It's not like you never lived here."

She made a strangled sound in her throat, first turning away from, then facing the cold bite of the wind against her face, the Oregon drizzle on her bare arms and legs.

"When did you get to be such a pansy?" He hauled the bag from the backseat and slammed the door as she picked her way up a darkened pathway to his house. From the corner of her eye, she saw movement, a fast-moving black shadow streaking toward her. "What the—"

A dog bounded into view, splashing through the muddy puddles and wet grass to leap up on her. Wet paws streaked her with mud, claws scraped. She sucked in a startled breath.

"Hud! Down!" Trent commanded as he reached her side. The wriggling, whining mass of fur instantly was on all fours. To Cassie, he said, "Sorry."

"It's . . . it's . . ." Hud's hind end still gyrated, as the shepherd gazed expectantly up at her. She leaned down to pat his damp head, smiling at the eager dog. "Not your fault."

"I'll get your clothes clean," Trent apologized.

"Truly, it's fine."

"Sorry, he's an escape artist. Hud is really short for Houdini. I'm guessing that Shorty, my ranch hand who was watching the place, must've left the garage door open. Come on." He whistled to the dog and headed toward the garage where a side door was ajar and through which they entered the house. It was two steps into a screened-in porch that led to a back door and oversize kitchen. Following a step behind, Cassie waited while he toweled off the dog and checked to make sure there was water in Hud's large dish.

"This way," Trent told her as he headed down a short hallway wedged between the staircase and the front door to a small closet. From an upper shelf, he hauled out a rolled sleeping bag and pillow. "I'm not overly supplied with sheets and things. Just moved in a while back, about the time I got the dog."

"Doesn't matter."

"You're sure you don't want to sleep upstairs?"

"You've got guest rooms?"

A slow smile spread over his jaw. "There's no furniture in them. I was thinking that since we're still married, you might want to stay with me."

She saw the amusement in his eyes. He *knew* she'd never take that step. "Maybe another time," she said, and couldn't believe it actually sounded as if she were flirting.

"Okay."

Little did he know how tempted she was. It had been so long since she'd slept beside him, heard his deep breathing, felt the weight of his arm flung across her waist, or nestled against the warmth of his naked body, long and lean, spooned up against her. An ache started to swell deep inside her, but before she could change her mind and take him up on his offer, he said, "Suit yourself," then carried the sleeping bag into a den off the front hallway.

"Two options," he said. "The couch there is long enough for you to stretch out on, or that chair in the corner actually folds out to a single bed."

"Don't bother with the fold-out. I won't be here that long."

He tossed the bedding onto the leather divan, then bent on one knee near a wood stove and lit the kindling already stacked inside. "There's a remote for the TV on the table near the chair." As the paper and kindling caught fire, he hooked a thumb toward the back of the house. "Bathroom's around the corner. Should be towels and everything you need in there."

"Thanks."

As the flames started to crackle, a warm glow emanating through the glass door of the stove, he glanced over his shoulder and his gaze touched hers. In a quicksilver instant she remembered another time when they'd gone to the mountains, had secreted themselves into an isolated cabin where he'd lit a fire in a huge rock fireplace and they'd made love for hours in front of the rising flames. She swallowed hard and, as if he'd shared the same intimate memory, he straightened and cleared his throat.

She almost blurted out that she was sorry for how far they'd come from the time when they'd been so much in love, but before she could form the words, he said, "I'm gonna run outside, check on the stock. Be back in a few."

Whistling to the dog once more, he headed for the front door.

She walked to the window, stared through the rain sliding down the panes, and was reminded of another night, not that long ago when she was looking outside her hospital room to the night beyond.

It seemed like a lifetime ago.

And now she was here. Alone with Trent. Her marriage crumbling.

Her sister still missing. One friend murdered, another nearly killed. She was too tired to make sense of it now, so she unzipped her bag and tossed her pajamas onto the couch. She dug past a makeup case for her toothbrush, which wasn't in the usual pocket where she'd always kept it packed. Nor was her e-reader in its spot. Certain she'd just packed the items in one of the myriad pockets, she opened the case that held her laptop and there, on top of the slim computer, was a slick piece of paper with something attached to it.

"What the devil?" she said as she tugged on the laminated paper. It slid out and she found herself staring down at a warped picture of her sister. "Oh my God." Her heart stilled and a newfound horror consumed her.

The photograph was hideous. Allie's eyes had been cut out, as if they'd been gouged, but the face, even distorted, was recognizable as that of Jenna Hughes's daughter. A thin strap of elastic was attached to the face in the back, as if the disturbing thing were a mask.

No! No! No! Cassie gasped and dropped the disfigured photo as if it burned her. As it fluttered to the floor it turned slightly to reveal the back where a horrid damning word, scribbled hastily in red, was visible:

Sister.

"What?" Horrified, she backed up, putting distance between herself and the evil, twisted image. Her heart was pounding, her mind whirling, her stomach churning. How had the horrid thing ended up in her bag? Who had planted it there? Why, oh, God, why? She was breathing rapidly, her heart pounding in her brain, her skin crawling at the thought that someone had actually been in her apartment, had gone through her things, had hidden the mask in her laptop case. She felt the world go dark and leaned against the wall. With an effort she forced a calm that was against her very nature. The intruder had come into her home to do this . . . whatever it was. A warning? A threat? The cat had followed him and been locked inside when he'd left. Who would be so heartless, so cruel, so insidious to do this?

A door opened and she jumped about a foot. Trent walked into the house, his dog tagging behind. He found her with a hand pressed to her chest, her heart a drum, a newfound fear congealing in her blood

"Cass?" he said, his brows furrowing. "Are you okay? I thought for sure that you'd already be asleep by now and—"

She launched herself at him. Without thinking she let out a broken sob and flung herself into his arms.

"Hey."

Squeezing her eyes shut, she refused to cry but she held on fast. Desperately attempting to find some equilibrium, some stability in her unstable life, she drank in the solid male scent of him, felt the strength of his body as he held her, his breath ruffling over her hair.

"What's going on?" he asked. She shook her head but he must've looked over her head into the room and spied the mask because she heard his sharp intake of breath and felt him stiffen. A second passed and then he said, "What the hell is *that?*"

CHAPTER 21

She spent what was left of the early morning in Trent's bed, lying in his arms, telling herself she was falling into a trap, surprised that he'd not tried to kiss or touch her other than to hold her close. She hadn't undressed. The streaks of mud from Hud's eager greeting had dried on her clothes, and she hadn't given them a second thought. She'd struggled to fall asleep with Trent beside her, though, so it took till morning light was beginning to touch the bare windows before she'd drifted off. When she finally opened her eyes, she saw on the bedside clock it was nearly ten and Trent wasn't with her, the sheets on the spot of the bed where he'd lain cool to her touch.

In a flash, she remembered the hideous poster or mask or whatever it was and forced herself not to dwell on it, not let the evil piece of art consume her. "One day at a time," she told herself and pushed off the warm bed.

After a quick trip to the bathroom, she hurried downstairs. The dog was lying on a rug near the wood stove where a fire still burned. As she walked into the room, Hud lifted his head and thumped his tail. "Yeah, you see this?" she teased, pointing to her dirt-smeared pants. Unconcerned, Hud stretched and got to his feet. Quickly she eyed the cozy room. Her bag was still open, but it was now near the couch, and the sleeping bag, along with the horrid mask, was nowhere to be seen.

Following the scents of brewed coffee and fried bacon, she found Trent seated at the kitchen table. His damp hair had been combed, his jaw clean-shaven, his jeans as disreputable as ever, an unbuttoned flannel shirt tossed over a dark T-shirt.

On the table in front of him were a cup of coffee, her cell phone, the red earring, and the dreadful mask. Allie's ghostlike image lay face up, the table's scratched wood surface showing through the empty eye sockets.

"Mornin'," he drawled, looking up as she entered with the dog in tow.

"Oh, God, what is that doing here?" She pointed to the mask.

"Couldn't throw it out." He scraped his chair back. "Coffee?"

Her stomach turned over and she shook her head. "Maybe water first."

He found a glass in a cupboard that was filled with mismatched kitchenware and filled it from the tap, then handed it to her.

"What're you doing with my phone and that . . . that thing?" she asked again, taking a sip of water and gesturing to the distorted picture.

"We need to get to the bottom of what's going on." After refilling his cup from a pot still warming in the coffeemaker, he pulled another mug from a shelf and filled it, then placed both cups on the table. "Then we have to talk to the police." He looked at the mask. "How do you think that got into your bag?"

Setting the water glass aside, she picked up the chipped mug that held her coffee. She explained how she thought someone had placed it in her bag when she'd been out, how she'd felt someone had been inside her apartment and that the cat had been trapped inside, and finished with, ". . . before the hospital, I'd been going back and forth from Portland to LA during the filming of *Dead Heat,* so I'd never really emptied my bags. I didn't check to see what was inside before I packed, just threw in some more clothes and personal stuff, things I thought I'd need. Unless someone was in my apartment another time that I don't know about, that's when it happened." She looked out the window over the sink. Dark clouds roiled over the forested hills surrounding the ranch, but the rain had stopped, at least for now. "What about my phone? What're you doing with it?" she asked.

"Snooping, obviously."

She saw that he was kidding around, trying to lighten the mood. Cocking an eyebrow, she waited, silently suggesting he explain.

"I think you should call your doctor again. See if she texted you."

She took another swallow. He was right. Of course. Before she could change her mind, she dialed and waited. One ring. Two. Voice mail picked up and Cassie forced herself to leave a simple message. "Dr. Sherling, this is Cassie Kramer. Please call me back." She left her number and clicked off. "Mission accomplished."

"Not until you actually speak with her. Even then we'll have a lot more to do." He went to the stove and opened the oven door. The scents of bacon and fresh bread erupted. Cassie's stomach growled. "Let's start with breakfast."

For once, she didn't argue.

Standing in the living room of Cassie Kramer's LA apartment, Rhonda Nash did a slow burn. The place, obviously, had been left in a hurry. There were a few clothes left in the bedroom closet, a couple sweaters tossed onto the bed, and the trash, what little there was of it, hadn't been taken out. Some mail, mostly junk, was scattered on a small desk. The bed hadn't been made. It was as if Cassie Kramer had gotten a call in the middle of the night and blown town, which wasn't exactly what had happened according to the landlord. Still, it was becoming more evident by the second that Nash's trip to California might have been, if not a wild goose chase, then too little, too late. The apartment was in minor disarray and, if the landlord were to be believed, Cassie Kramer had barely touched down before she'd fled LA, as quickly as possible. From what Detective Nash could determine, she'd been in California just long enough to ask questions about her sister, ruffle some feathers, then race out. Cassie had been seen with Holly Dennison the night before the set designer's murder and she was still a person of interest in her sister's disappearance. If nothing else, she was guilty of being in the wrong place at the wrong time. As she eyed the living room and bedroom of the apartment, Detective Nash wondered if Allie Kramer's sister's culpability ran a little deeper than that.

"She said she was going back to Oregon for a while. Didn't know exactly when she'd return, but wanted to keep the apartment," Doug Peterson had told her. Pushing seventy, with thinning white hair and a bit of a paunch, Peterson owned the large home on the property and rented out this little apartment.

Currently, Peterson was hovering on the tiny front porch and holding a black cat while stroking its fur and keeping an eye on Nash and Hayes as they poked around. He didn't set foot in the apartment, just hung near the open door. She sensed he wanted them to leave things be, but didn't have the guts to take on the police. "She's been a good tenant, Cassie has," he said. "Quiet for the most part. Respectful of the property. Always pays on time. Even when she isn't in town."

Yeah, yeah, Cassie Kramer is effin' fantastic, Nash thought sourly, but kept her opinions to herself. "Good to know."

She'd already seen Holly Dennison's corpse and the mask that had been left at the crime scene. She'd talked to the LA techs and cops who'd been at the scene, but had spent most of her morning with Jonas Hayes who had brought her up to date on his investigation.

Glancing around the apartment one last time, she figured her next move was to have another face-to-face with Allie Kramer's sister.

And she hoped to do it in Oregon, if that's where she'd flown.

"I don't know what you're talking about," Virginia Sherling insisted across the wireless connection. "I never texted you. I don't text." There was irritation in the doctor's voice.

"Could someone else have?" Cassie asked. She was standing on the porch off of Trent's back door and staring at the dreary day. The sky was gun-metal gray, the clouds low. Cattle lumbered in the fields separated from other pastures where horses plucked at the grass. A cool wind slipped through the screens, to tug at Cassie's hair.

"My phone is always with me or in my office or my house, so I don't see how." Her tone changed. "How're you doing, Cassie?" Was there an undercurrent beneath the solicitous tones, a hint that Dr. Sherling thought she was making up the story about the texts?

"I'm fine."

"That's good to hear." Again, Cassie sensed a falseness to the psychiatrist's words. "I think it might be a good idea if we had a session. I'd like to hear how you're doing, what you're working on, where your life is heading. Your thoughts on everything. You did leave abruptly."

"I'll call you," Cassie said. "Right now, I don't have time, but thank you. Good-bye." She hung up before the doctor could say anything else.

"Not her?" Trent asked, as she stepped inside.

"No."

"I have a theory," he said slowly, his gaze careful, his eyebrows drawing together as they always did when he was thinking.

"All right . . ." she responded cautiously.

"The kid who knows all the stats? Rinko? What if he got hold of the doctor's phone and texted you quickly, then erased the message so Doctor Sherling wouldn't find out."

"The message about Santa Fe?"

"He knows everything about sports and cars, right? That's what you said and he sure as hell knew every detail about my truck. He'd spied it in the lot at the hospital and figured it belonged to me."

"That sounds like Rinko," she said. "He's amazing."

"Okay. So maybe Santa Fe isn't about the city, but about the car, an SUV. And the 07 is the model year of the car. Maybe he's talking about a 2007 Hyundai Santa Fe."

"That's kind of a stretch," she said, but felt as if she'd stepped into a time warp. How many times, while she was in the hospital, had Rinko gone on and on about the cars he'd seen in the parking lot? He knew what type of car each member of the staff drove and remarked when one of the nurses, aides, or doctors came in something new, or a loaner or their spouse's vehicle. With his near-photographic memory, Rinko could remember most vehicles that had ever wheeled onto the tree-lined lot of Mercy Hospital.

"It could be. But what does it mean?" she asked. "An SUV made in Korea?"

"The vehicle was unusual, probably. My guess is it wasn't normally in the lot, or he wouldn't have felt compelled to send the text. I'm guessing it might belong to your nightmare nurse, the one who dropped her earring." He carried his cup to the sink and added it to a stack of breakfast dishes. "Why don't we go talk to Rinko?"

She withered inside at the thought of returning to the hospital. She was certain to run into someone who would alert Dr. Sherling that she was on the premises.

"Come on," Trent said, and he was already reaching for his jacket. "We'll make the rounds. First to visit Jenna, assure her you're all right, then to Rinko to have a little chat with him, see what else he might be able to tell us about the Santa Fe."

"If that's what it is."

"Easy to find out."

She recalled that Trent had been in military intelligence, though his stint in the army had lasted less than five years and had occurred before he'd met Cassie. "If I have to I can call one of the guys who was in the army with me. He ended up with his own detective agency. High tech. He has connections with the police."

"Don't tell my stepfather. He thinks everything should go through the proper channels."

"For once I agree with Carter. That is, until the channels are clogged. After talking to Rinko, I think we'd better go to the police station to visit Nash and show off the fun gift that was left in your suitcase."

Her good mood evaporated at the thought of seeing the detective. "Nash thinks I did it, you know. That somehow I made Allie disappear."

"Maybe the mask will change her mind."

"She'll probably think I was behind it as well."

"Maybe they can get some prints off it."

"Let's hope. But . . . let's not let Mom know that someone was in my apartment and left it there. She'd freak." She thought of Jenna and how she'd become paranoid for her children after the trauma that had occurred ten years earlier.

"She's going to find out soon enough."

"No . . . I don't think that's such a good idea."

"Then at least let me talk to Shane."

"He's not your biggest fan," Cassie reminded him.

"I know, but let's pull him in. He's an ex-sheriff who still has major connections with the department. He can decide how much your mom can handle."

She hesitated, but at least she knew she could trust her stepfather. Unlike Detective Nash, he didn't think she was a suspect in her sister's disappearance. "Deal."

Trent smiled and gave her a wink. His grin was infectious and despite the trauma of recent days, Cassie returned it even though the last place on earth she wanted to be was anywhere near the Portland Police Department, well, unless you counted Mercy Hospital. But he had a point. "Okay," she acquiesced. "Fine. I'll go to the hospital and we'll talk to Carter, but I'd like to avoid dealing with Detective Nash as long as possible. That woman has it in for me."

Before he could argue, she added, "Just give me time to walk through the shower and change. Fifteen minutes and then we'll go."

"That's my girl," he said automatically, then caught himself.

His words burned in her brain. As cozy as being here with him had been, as comfortable as the ride from California had turned out to be, she was definitely *not* his girl or woman.

But she was still his wife.

The pregnancy test was negative.

Again.

Sitting on the edge of her bathtub, Jenna Hughes decided she was done with the whole baby-making idea. Maybe God was telling her that she was too old, that she should be satisfied that she had healthy children who now were grown women. For a second she thought of

Allie, still missing, and Cassie, who had so recently been a patient in a mental ward. She clenched her hands into fists, worried enough about them and probably didn't need a new baby in the mix.

Still, it was hard to accept.

Yes, she was no longer a young woman. She'd passed forty a few years earlier, but it was hard to give up the dream of sharing a child with Shane. Now, glancing in the mirror, she saw a feathering of small lines near her eyes that hadn't been there a few years earlier, and there was more than one silvery thread stubbornly showing in her black hair.

Jenna bit her lip, a new habit that had come with the strain and concern over her daughters.

Shane didn't have children. Not biological. Not adopted. Just the stepchildren he'd inherited when they'd married. He hadn't wanted children with his first wife, Carolyn, and it had been a deep fissure in that marriage. Once he and Jenna had married, he'd changed his mind. However, he'd never been as disappointed as she when she hadn't gotten pregnant.

Obviously another baby wasn't meant to be.

She could be okay with that.

Maybe.

If her daughters were safe. She thought of her previous pregnancies, the births, the joy of life and the sadness, of the mistakes she'd made, the guilt over decisions that hadn't turned out well. God knew she hadn't been a stellar mother, and more often than not she'd second-guessed herself. But being a parent meant making errors that sometimes came back to haunt her, one of many being that she'd hoped neither Cassie, nor Allie, would turn to Hollywood. She hadn't wanted them to follow in their mother's footsteps.

However, the bright lights of Hollywood had beckoned them, her daughters' desires amplified by their father's own dreams.

Rubbing the kinks from her neck, she reminded herself it was all part of being a parent: heartache and joy, happiness and pain. And always, inevitably, guilt.

God knew she had enough on her plate with the children she already had. She threw the test strip into the trash and told herself, "No more," then checked her watch as she passed through the bedroom she shared with Shane. Cassie had called and said she'd be coming by.

The dog started making a ruckus, barking her fool head off. Jenna hurried down the stairs of this old ranch house with its log walls and paned windows. She'd bought it when she'd relocated from California and Shane had moved in as soon as they'd married, now nearly ten years ago.

She racewalked through the hallway, threw open the front door, and, with the dog galloping ahead of her, spied Cassie's little Honda appearing over a slight rise in the lane to her house. "Thank God," she murmured. She hadn't bothered with a coat and rain was lashing from the sky. Jenna didn't care as she ran across the wet grass and muddy puddles only to stop on the gravel drive at the spot where Cassie stopped her car and flung open the door. Relief washed over her at the sight of her daughter and damn, if a lump didn't form in her throat when Cassie climbed from behind the wheel.

"Cassie!"

"Geez, Mom, you're getting wet."

Jenna threw her arms around her daughter and desperately tried not to cry. She'd been out of her mind with worry. Allie was still missing. Cassie had been distant, her mental health fragile. Jenna felt a gap widening between herself and her two children and she hated it. She clung to Cassie as if to life itself. "I've been so worried."

"I'm okay."

"Good." Jenna squeezed her eyes shut and wished she could believe it. God, how she prayed that her daughter was healthy and strong.

"And we'll find Allie, Mom," she said as the wind blew cold down the Columbia Gorge.

How? How can we find her when the police haven't been able to?

Jenna nearly broke down. Her throat closed, her eyes burned, and she held Cassie tight. "Of course we will," she whispered, her voice cracking a little. What she would give to have Allie with them right now. Memories of moving to Falls Crossing assailed her, memories of carving out a new life for herself and her two girls on this very patch of land, this ranch nestled near the shores of the river.

Fighting a losing battle with tears, Jenna finally released Cassie and realized that Trent Kittle had been in the passenger seat and now was standing on the opposite side of the car. She'd never thought she would approve of Kittle, but found herself grateful he appeared to be in Cassie's corner. "Come on. Let's go inside. You're moving back, yes? Into your old room?"

Cassie and Trent exchanged glances over the top of her car.

"Silly of me," Jenna said, catching the eye contact and feeling a moment's confusion mingled with relief. "You're with Trent. Married. Together."

Cassie appeared uncomfortable and it seemed that rather than answer, she turned her attention to the dog, petting Paris's wet head. Were they together again? It seemed so, but the last Jenna had heard, before Cassie had checked herself into Mercy Hospital, was that she was ending her marriage. Maybe the divorce had been tabled. Maybe they were working things out. Though Jenna had never been on board with the relationship.

He'd been too old and experienced when they'd first started seeing each other in Falls Crossing. Cassie had been recovering from the trauma of being nearly killed by a stalker who had his sights set on Jenna and her daughters, and she'd also been dealing with the pain of her most recent boyfriend's murder. She'd witnessed Josh die, so Trent—older, more mature, kind of a bad boy who'd been through the military—didn't seem to be the right guy at the right time. At least not to Jenna. But once Cassie took off for Hollywood and had been on her own a bit, she'd hooked up with Trent again and that time Jenna hadn't been as against the relationship. Now, standing in this cold rain, she was grateful her daughter had someone who, it seemed, still cared for her. Cassie took a long time to pet the dog, then both she and Trent followed Jenna into the house. In the living room, Cassie dropped her purse onto the floor and tumbled onto the couch, taking over the very spot she'd claimed as a teenager. The dog, muddy feet and all, hopped up beside her and wiggled close. Trent sat nearby, in a leather recliner, and Jenna dropped into the rocker by the window, the chair that had become her home while sitting and waiting for news of her missing daughter. A fire glowed in the hearth, red embers nearly dead, the smell of wood smoke heavy.

"Whitney Stone's been calling me. Well, along with the others," Jenna said, switching on a table lamp. "So many reporters or paparazzi or whatever these days!"

Cassie made a sour face. "Whitney Stone actually tracked me down in California."

"I'm not surprised. She's pretty . . . determined."

"Ruthless," Cassie said, before launching into her story about the reporter chasing her down and trying to film her at a park. She ended with, "I nearly ran over her goon of a cameraman. Geez, what's wrong with that woman?"

"Greed. Ambition. Whatever. She feeds into the public's fascination with the minutiae of celebrity life. That's why I ended up here."

"And how did that turn out for you?" Cassie tossed out, then seemed immediately rueful. "Sorry."

"I got Shane out of the deal," Jenna reminded. Then, "The trouble is Whitney Stone wants to not only talk about what's going on now, she's putting out a 'special report.' I think it's about what happened in the past. The stalker during the ice storm." Cassie's eyes looked bruised and Jenna added, "None of us want to live through that again. I'm just giving you a heads-up in case you didn't know."

"She told me," Cassie said.

"I'm sorry," Jenna responded, heartfelt.

Trent stood and walked to the fire, then bent down and added a log to the already burning pieces of oak. Flames caught quickly on the dry moss to crackle and burn hungrily, all the while casting the room in a shifting golden glow.

Cassie said slowly, "I want to show you something."

Jenna noticed Trent's hand tightening over the fireplace poker. He shot Cassie a warning glance that her daughter ignored as she scrounged inside her purse.

"What?" Jenna leaned closer as Cassie extracted a small plastic bag and handed it to Jenna. Inside was an earring, blood red and in the shape of a cross.

"Ever seen it before?" Cassie asked.

"No . . ." Jenna surveyed the bit of jewelry, then started to hand it back. "No wait . . . maybe. God, a long, long time ago. I had a bit part in a soap opera when I was first starting out. *North Wing.* The show was only on for two seasons, then died. And my part was nothing, a foot in the door to get into the business, you know? My character, Norma Allen, barely spoke. Really, I was little more than an extra who played a nurse who was always in the background."

"Was the show set in the 1950s?" Trent asked.

"Sixties or seventies. It was a little retro at the time and didn't catch on."

Cassie's face drained of color.

"What?" Jenna asked.

"This was found when I was at the hospital. I thought it was a bad dream, a nightmare, and that the nurse who visited me was a figment of my imagination."

"What're you talking about?"

Cassie explained about being visited by a nurse dressed in an old-fashioned uniform, that she had woken to find the woman in her retro costume in the room.

"What?" An icy talon of fear slid down Jenna's spine.

"She must've dropped the earring." Cassie swallowed tensely. "Somehow she knew that Allie was okay."

"When did this happen?" Jenna demanded.

"The night before I left the hospital."

"And you didn't tell me?"

"I thought it was all in my imagination. Except for that." She indicated the bit of jewelry.

Jenna was stunned. This was so bizarre! But maybe . . . could the nurse actually know where Allie was? Or was this some kind of cruel prank or, worse yet, something her daughter's fragile mind had concocted?

But there was the evidence of the earring . . .

She handed it back to Cassie and tried to stay calm. What did it mean? What the hell did it mean? "I haven't heard anything about your sister," she admitted, moving the rocker slowly back and forth. "Shane's talked to the Portland police but if they have any new information they haven't shared it. I assume they don't." She rubbed her hands together, caught herself, and grabbed both arms of her chair. "Have you shown them this?" She motioned with a finger toward the bagged earring.

"Not yet," Trent interjected.

"Detective Nash thinks I'm crazy or worse." Something unreadable passed behind Cassie's eyes.

"What?" Jenna stopped rocking. Her trouble radar, now on alert, ratcheted up a couple of notches. "You know something?"

"No."

"Cassie?" She could always tell when her children were lying to her and right now Cassie was hiding something. "What is it?"

"Is Shane around?" Cassie asked. She'd turned deathly sober as she and Trent exchanged glances.

"He's on his way home. I texted him when you called and said you were coming by. But what is it?" Then her heart stilled. "Is it Allie?" she whispered, fear knotting her insides. "Oh, my God."

"No, no, no . . . I don't know about Allie. I don't. But . . ." She looked at Trent just as the sound of a truck reached their ears. The dog lifted his head, leaped from the couch, and began whining at the door.

"We've got something we'd like to show him and you," Trent explained. "I'll go get it." Following the spaniel, he was outside in an instant.

"What?" Jenna asked, her pulse pounding. "What's going on, Cassie? What's he got to show me?"

Cassie's expression turned even more serious and her lips barely moved as she spoke. "A mask, Mom. A mask of Allie that was left in my bag. I think someone broke into my apartment and left it there, you know, to freak me out." Cassie's eyes held Jenna's. "Mission accomplished."

"For the love of God, what're you talking about?"

Cassie climbed to her feet and stared out the window. Rotating her chair, Jenna watched the two men approaching the house, Shane and Trent, both head-bent against the rain, the dog running circles around them. Trent was carrying what appeared to be a legal-size zipper pouch. Their boots echoed on the porch before the door swung open and the dog streaked inside.

For once, Jenna didn't care about the dirty paw prints visible on the hardwood. "Show me," she said, on her feet and walking toward the entry hall. Her gaze was fixed on the pouch Trent carried.

"In here," he said, heading into the dining room. Jenna's heart was thudding, her pulse pounding in her brain. She barely heard Cassie's footsteps behind her as they collected around the dining room table and Trent unzipped the black pouch to retrieve a clear plastic bag. Inside was a thick piece of paper, an obscene twisted picture of Allie from one of her movie roles. Her mangled face was lifesize, the paper trimmed around her hairline, and her eyes had been cut out for viewing holes.

"Oh, God." Jenna's hand flew to her mouth and she backed up a step, but she still stared at the horrid mask. She barely felt Shane's arm around her shoulders as she sank against him. "What the hell is this?" she whispered, quivering inside. "Dear God, what?" She felt as if her soul was being shredded.

"Some sick bastard left this for you?" Shane demanded of Cassie.

Jenna felt rather than saw Cassie nod. She couldn't drag her gaze from the table and its wretched display.

Her stomach churned.

Sweat tickled the back of her neck.

Bile crawled up her throat and she knew in that instant that she was going to throw up.

Beginning to retch she frantically stumbled away from her husband, from the dining room, from the marred visage of her youngest daughter. She ran half-blind to the powder room where she heaved over the toilet, hot tears filling her eyes, her stomach emptying again and again. For the love of all that was holy, where was Allie? Where was her baby? Why had the horrid mask been left at Cassie's apartment?

A new fear slithered through her: Would Cassie disappear as well? Was this a warning?

For a few seconds she stood, bent over the toilet bowl. Until she was certain nothing else was coming up. Then, unsteadily, she flushed the toilet and stepped to the sink where she bent down again and rinsed her mouth with water from the tap. Her body's shaking had stopped, she was no longer trembling, but the fear still gnawed at her as she splashed water over her face. A floorboard near the doorway creaked and she caught sight of Shane's face in the reflection. A tall man, with an intimidating stature, he met her gaze. "We'll get him," he told her. "We'll get the bastard."

Her knees threatened to buckle and she clung to the edge of the pedestal sink for support. "Promise?"

Big arms surrounded her again, the scent of wet leather from his jacket over the smell of his aftershave and a deeper, earthier male scent. Familiar. Calming. Safe. The smells she associated with him that caused her heart to tick a little faster. Today they weren't calming. Nothing was. Rain peppered the small window in the room, and she saw Shane holding her in the mirror's reflection. Her face was thin and drawn, devoid of makeup. His eyebrows were pulled into a line of concern, his lips a thin, hard blade as he tried to soothe her.

It was all she could do to not break down completely.

"I want twenty-four-hour protection for Cassie," she whispered. "And she should live here with us. We'll get a bigger dog and have an alarm system installed and . . ." She let her voice trail off. Hadn't she tried all those techniques ten years before? And still the monster had easily breached the walls of her fortress.

"I'll take care of things."

How? Jenna wondered, and knew his statement was little more than a platitude, just as Cassie promising to find Allie was only to ease her mother's mind. Well, nothing could. At least no words were the bromide for her deep-seated worries. She blinked back the damned tears that had been threatening all morning, then set her jaw. She could not, would not collapse. Not now.

She swallowed hard. Stiffened her spine.

First things first: They had to find Allie. And she had to remain sane. Not fall apart.

In the past few weeks, Jenna had been so desperate to locate her daughter, so unhinged at the thought of Allie being stalked by a crazed fan, being abducted or worse, that her mind had been playing tricks on her. Twice she'd thought she'd caught a glimpse of Allie, always at a distance, but when she'd tried to call out to the woman, reach her, she'd disappeared. It had happened once in the supermarket and another time when she'd seen "Allie" getting into a car. Each time the look-alike had appeared to stare straight at her, only to ignore her and leave.

Had those sightings been tricks of her imagination?

Wishful thinking?

Or something deeper, a mental weakness that seemed to run in her family? Cassie's mental state had been fragile for the past ten years, ever since the unthinkable had happened. Her grip on reality had faltered, and she claimed to have seen things that hadn't existed. Sometimes Cassie swore she couldn't remember hours of her life. So what about herself? Or Allie? Couldn't they, too, be affected by the trauma they'd suffered? Couldn't their mental states be weakened, allowing paranoia or worse to creep in and take hold?

Don't go there, she warned herself. *Nothing good will come of it.*

She couldn't have Shane thinking she was unraveling.

"It'll be okay," Shane said now, kissing the top of her head.

She muffled a little choking sound.

Okay? Things would be okay?

She hoped to hell he was right, but deep down she didn't believe him for a second.

CHAPTER 22

The digital clock on her dash indicated it was after three when Cassie and Trent finally drove across the Marquam Bridge and wound their way to Mercy Hospital. Cassie had spent most of the day at Jenna's house bringing her mother and stepfather up to speed on what had happened to her and where she was in her own amateur attempts at finding Allie.

Jenna had been freaked, of course, and Cassie didn't blame her. Over coffee and eventually lunch, Jenna, Cassie, Trent, and Shane had mapped out a loose game plan. While Trent and Cassie were visiting Mercy Hospital, Shane would call Detective Nash and later they would converge at the police station with the mask.

Cassie wasn't looking forward to the meeting with Detective Nash. Now, her car lugged down and she had to step on the accelerator to climb the steep hill to Mercy Hospital. Fir and maple trees lining the road shivered with the rain, the windshield wipers scraping water off the glass and the car's heater working overtime to clear condensation from the windshield.

"I hope you're right about this," Cassie said to Trent, who had called his ranch hand, Shorty Something-Or-Other, to take care of the place while Cassie and Trent drove into Portland. The street was rain-washed, asphalt shining, headlights reflecting off the pavement in the gloom of the deep cloud cover.

As they rounded a final curve, the entrance to Mercy Hospital came into view. Cassie's hands clenched over the wheel and though she fought it, she felt her pulse elevate a notch. She hadn't left the hospital under the best of conditions and she expected nothing more than a frosty reception.

Which she got at the front desk when she asked to see Steven Rinko.

"Miss Kramer," the woman seated importantly behind the counter said. "You of all people should know hospital policy. When you were a patient here, and you specifically asked for your privacy, we ensured it." Her beady eyes, intense behind rimless glasses, drilled straight into Trent, who was standing next to Cassie, but Trent's gaze had drifted to the reception area.

Cassie said, "If you asked him, I'm certain Steven would want to talk to me."

"His family has asked for his privacy." Staunch. Unmoving. A gleam of satisfaction in her eyes that she had this authority, the keys to the kingdom, as it were.

"We can wait while someone contacts him," Cassie said.

The woman flashed a grim, unyielding smile. "I'll contact his doctor and then we'll see. Unfortunately Dr. Sherling is out of the hospital now, in clinic, I think, so you might be waiting a while and even then . . ." She lifted her slim, stiff shoulders. ". . . you might not be in luck." Again the cold grin with no hint of teeth showing. "Why don't you leave a message for Dr. Sherling and go out and go shopping or grab a bite? Portland's known for its great restaurants, you know, farm fresh, organic and all that. Then call back. I'll see what I can do."

Cassie's temper started to boil. "Just tell Steven we're here."

"I'm sorry." She folded her hands, fingers neatly manicured. "Are we going to have a problem, Ms. Kramer?"

Cassie's temper went through the stratosphere. "No problem, Connie," she gritted out, knowing the woman always went by Constance.

The receptionist's lips pulled into a knot of disapproval. "I can call security, if you'd like."

"What I'd like is to talk to Steven Rinko. Now tell him we're here to see him and—" She felt Trent's hand on her shoulder and stopped midsentence.

"And?" Constance prompted, raising her plucked brows above the tops of her rimless glasses.

"We'll be back," Trent replied calmly.

Cassie was having none of it. "I want to see Steven." She tried to shrug off Trent's hand, but his grip tightened. He was folding? Just like that? After he'd come up with this wild theory and they'd driven over an hour to get here? He was ready to just walk out the door?

"Let's go." He started pulling on her arm a little too hard.

"Ouch!" She actually winced.

"What?"

She started to answer, then said, "Nothing." She didn't want to go into it about the cat scratches.

"Come on." He said the words through a taut smile, and his gaze, when she found it, drilled into hers as if he was sending her some unspoken message. What the hell was wrong with him?

"I need to talk to—"

"Rinko. I know. We *will.*" With an iron grip he ushered her to the front door and down the steps.

"We came all this way—"

"I *know.*" He marched her all the way to the car and she wanted to slap him, but obviously something was going on. "Get behind the wheel."

"For the love of God, Trent." But when he opened the Honda's door and released her, she slid inside and waited until he climbed into the passenger seat. "Are you going to tell me what the hell's going on? Or have you just decided to be a moronic brute all of a sudden?"

"Start the engine."

With an effort Cassie fought her natural inclination to argue and switched on the ignition. The motor sparked to life as she said, "Happy now?" sarcastically.

He didn't answer, just rolled down his window. As soon as the glass lowered, from out of nowhere Steven Rinko's head popped up, his face framed in the open space. He was crouched down beside the car, his body hidden from view of the hospital by the SUV.

Cassie physically started before she recognized him, his hair wet, rain running down his face. She turned her gaze on Trent. "How did you know?"

"He gave me the high sign in the reception area," Trent said quickly, then turned to Rinko and said, "You sent a message to Cassie using Dr. Sherling's phone, didn't you?"

"Yes." He said it as if it were common knowledge.

"Why didn't you tell me it was you?" Cassie asked, but Trent held up a hand, cutting her off.

"The message was about a Hyundai Santa Fe? Right? The SUV?" Trent asked.

A curt nod. "Most customers are satisfied, some complain about the fuel gauge and sun visors, but overall they like the vehicle."

Cassie tried not to be irritated with his review. "So this car—"

"The 2007 Hyundai Santa Fe is an SUV."

"Yes." She fought back her frustration and said more calmly, "I know. Why did you text the information to me? Is it because the car, er, SUV, wasn't usually in the lot?" She knew he observed what vehicles parked near the hospital.

"The nurse drove it." Blond hair plastered to his head, he stared through the open window at her as if she were a complete idiot.

"The nurse? The one who came into my room?" Cassie questioned. "With the white shoes and dress. And that blue cape. The one who lost the earring?"

"She drove the 2007 Hyundai Santa Fe and parked it in the lot." His gaze moved from Cassie's face to Trent's. "I saw her leave in it."

He knew this? And didn't say anything? Cassie couldn't believe it. The car, idling, was beginning to warm, the windows fogging a little.

Trent asked, "What color was it?"

"Arctic white. Beige interior. Automatic transmission." Without expression, Rinko repeated the information as if reading the data from an ad in the classified section. "V-6. Mag wheels."

"Did you notice anything else about it? The license plate?" Trent asked.

Rinko nodded. "Oregon plates. Man on a bucking bronco."

"That image was part of the plate?" Trent asked.

Rinko didn't reply, just stared with that same faraway look that sometimes came over him. As far as Cassie knew, there was no image of a bronco rider on plates issued by the state. There had been different plates over the years, some decorative, but none Cassie remembered with images of a rodeo rider. Then again, it was possible that Rinko could be wrong. It could all be a figment of his imagination.

"How about the number?" Trent asked. "On the plate?"

Steven, who was getting soaked, shrugged. He was shivering in the cold, his lips turning blue, but he didn't seem to notice.

"Maybe the SUV had some identifying marks on it. Like a broken headlight, or damaged window, or some dents?" Cassie suggested, leaning over Trent. When Rinko didn't respond, she added, "Maybe a bumper sticker?"

"Kill Your Television."

"That was on the Hyundai?" Trent asked.

Rinko's eyebrows drew together in concentration. Rain dripped from the tip of his nose. "A map of Oregon with a green heart in the middle of it."

Cassie had seen that one, a white background, the black outline of the state's shape surrounding a forest-green heart. Trent glanced at Cassie. "That should narrow it down," he said.

Cassie asked, "Has the nurse, the one with the car, been back?"

He shook his head. "She only came to see you."

"You're sure?"

He didn't bother to answer. Of course. When Steven Rinko said anything, it was a fact. At least in his mind.

She and Trent asked a few more questions, but Rinko had no more information to share, and the poor kid was obviously freezing. She couldn't keep him a second more. "Thanks," she said. "Now, go inside, and get warm. Dry off and make an aide bring you cocoa."

He smiled a bit. "With marshmallows."

"Definitely. Oh, and Steven, how did you get Doctor Sherling's phone?"

"I have keys to all the rooms. All the lockers. All the doors. All the cupboards."

"How?"

He hesitated. "Sometimes Elmo's not so careful."

Elmo was in charge of maintenance. Cassie had seen him play chess with Rinko. Once in a while, he even won.

Then again, maybe he never had. Maybe Rinko had lost on purpose. Cassie wouldn't put it past the kid.

Before she put the car into gear, Cassie finally asked Rinko one last question. "Why didn't you tell me all this before?"

He stared at her and said, "Because you didn't ask."

Then he took off, keeping near the shrubbery, sprinting through the wet grass and up the steps to the side of the building where he disappeared and, presumably, crept inside the same way he'd exited minutes before.

"How did you know he'd be out here?" Cassie asked.

"I saw him peeking through the same door he'd come through before, around the corner from the receptionist, not visible in any mirrors or cameras, I'm guessing. Maybe he's fixed it so that he can use it at will. He didn't even poke his head through, just stared at me through the crack when it was ajar and pointed toward the front door. I figured he'd find us if we went outside. He's clever and seems to be able to get where he wants to without being seen."

"A ghost," she said, backing out of the parking spot and driving away from the hospital.

"Why's he in here?"

"He slips in and out of reality and gets violent, I guess. No one really knows. His family has a lot of money. I think a wing of the hospital is named after his grandfather, but whatever happened to him, it had to have been really bad." She looked in her rearview mirror and caught a glimpse of the hospital, white bricks and pillared porch visible in the gloom of the dark day.

For a second she thought she saw someone standing off to the side of the porch, a dark figure half-hidden in the thick rhododendrons and staring down the drive, watching her leave.

She blinked and the figure was gone. Uneasy, she convinced herself she'd been mistaken, had only seen a shadow in the thick foliage flanking the hospital. There had been nothing sinister lurking in the wet umbra, just her mind playing tricks on her.

Even with Trent sitting close enough to touch, she couldn't wait to pass through the gates guarding the grounds and drive away from Mercy Hospital. Whether in her imagination or not, she believed evil lurked within its hallowed walls.

"Shane Carter wants to see me?" Nash asked into her cell phone as she threw her keys onto the desk in her den. She checked the time. Eight thirty-seven PM. The house was empty. Cold. More of a mausoleum than a home. And it was all hers. Every last slab of Carrera marble, every glossy plank of Brazilian hardwood, every glass tile in the pool and every one of five—count 'em, *five*—sports cars parked in the six bays of the garage. All hers. The final bay was proud home to the car she drove, her beloved Ford Focus. Everything else had, until recently, been owned by her stepmother, the ultimate collector of *things*. Now, thank you very much, Edwina Maria Phillips Rolland Nash, they all belonged to Rhonda.

And all of it, aside from some of the bottles in the wine cellar and the Ford of course, was for sale.

God, she hated this place.

"That's right," Double T was confirming. "Not only Carter, but Cassie Kramer and her husband want a sit-down."

"Why?"

"Don't know. Guess we'll find out."

"Guess we will. What time?"

"Tomorrow afternoon. Four."

"Works for me. It'll give me time to pull some things together." She hung up and felt better. Things were looking up. And the real estate agent had called saying she had an offer on this place. She went to the wine cellar, half a flight down to a climate-controlled room behind thick glass, and pulled out a bottle from Edwina's selection. A Pinot Gris. Good enough. She had no idea what the wine was worth, only that she was going to carry it upstairs to her bedroom, open the bottle, and sip the wine in the bathtub with its amazing view of Portland. That luxury, she would miss. The rest of it, not at all.

She stripped, put on a robe, and added bubble bath to the tub. Picked up in Paris by Edwina a decade earlier, the soap was mild and non-stinging as if for a child, yet exotic and smelling of lavender. To top off her ritual Nash poured herself a glass of wine and paused to light a candle, as she did every night.

"Mommy misses you," she whispered, but didn't cry as the tiny flame flickered.

She slipped into the warm water and closed her eyes. She thought briefly of her child. This was the one time of day when she allowed herself a few minutes to remember her baby's curly hair, blue, blue eyes, and soft giggle. If she thought hard enough, she could recall the smell of her, the oh so softness of skin. Tears pulled at the back of her eyes but she would no longer cry.

Five years had passed.

She allowed herself a few minutes of grieving still, but that was all. This was her life now. She cleared her throat. Took another sip of wine. Told herself that things were better, the pain lessening, maybe eventually it would even be tolerable. Finally she opened her eyes to the incredible windows with their spectacular view over trees and rooftops to the winking lights of the city below.

So this was how the other half lived. Or was it the other one percent these days? Didn't matter. She didn't like it. Some of the perks were nice, of course, like the in-home gym that was handy for daily workouts, and this soaking tub with its multiple jets to massage out her muscles, tense from a twelve-hour day, but really, who needed all the luxury?

Not Rhonda Nash.

At least not anymore.

Not with the road she'd traveled.

Absurdly, wealth seemed banal to her now; well, the trappings of the very rich at least. Money had failed her. There just wasn't enough to protect the innocent, to fight illness and death and expect to win. That, she knew now, was a fool's game.

She would live here for now, but only until she could sell the place and every shiny, expensive thing within its walls. Hopefully this new buyer would take the albatross from her neck. After everything she'd inherited was sold, she planned to move to somewhere a lot more cozy, a lot more homey with a lot less square footage and no amazing city view. Maybe she'd get a cat. Or a dog. Or chickens. More and more people in Portland were keeping chickens these days. Whatever. She smiled a little . . . maybe she should get the chickens now and let them roam over Edwina's five thousand square feet of opulence, scratching and clucking, pooping and shedding feathers all over the imported rugs.

Edwina's ultramodern home had been cut into the hillside, a wall of windows three stories high with a panorama of downtown Portland and several of the bridges that crossed the Willamette. She could also see much farther east to Mount Hood rising out of the Cascades. Now, she stared through the glass. The lights of the city winked in the rain and Hood was invisible in the darkness, but not far from the mountain's peak, in its shadow, was Falls Crossing, the town where Allie and Cassie Kramer had spent their teenage years, where their mother still lived.

And now ex-sheriff effin' Shane Carter himself wanted an audience. That should prove interesting. Did Cassie have a confession to make and needed dear old stepdad and her estranged hubby to accompany her? Were they her little entourage of bodyguards? The woman, after all, was a mental case.

Not fair, her mind taunted as she sipped from her glass. Ironically one of the neighboring properties, located just on the other side of the slope, was Mercy Hospital.

It was funny how tangled lives could become, how so many could brush against you only to disappear with the dawn. Again, she felt the pull on her heartstrings when she thought about loss, but she wouldn't allow her mind to dwell in the painful hole that had once been her life. Instead, as always, she turned her attention to her work, always her work.

When the Kramer case had first landed on her desk, Nash had wondered about Cassie Kramer admitting herself to the hospital to be placed in psychiatric care. What had forced her through the locked doors of Mercy Hospital on the heels of her sister's disappearance and Lucinda Rinaldi's near homicide? Nash had questioned if surrendering to psychiatric care had been a ploy, a slyly planned move that would ultimately be integral in her defense: insanity over guilt.

Something wasn't right with the Sisters Kramer; she knew it.

But she didn't know if Allie Kramer was dead or alive. That was a problem, a serious problem. Allie, and maybe Cassie, too, could be part of some intricate publicity stunt gone bad, or worse yet the victim of kidnapping or homicide.

So where's the body?

Where's the crime scene?

Why was Holly Dennison killed, her body left where it could be found, a bizarre mask placed over her face?

Where the hell is frickin' Allie Kramer?

Her ruminations brought more questions than answers, and her thoughts switched to the movie that was about to be released. Allie Kramer, Lucinda Rinaldi, and Holly Dennison were all a part of *Dead Heat,* which was to be released soon. A party to celebrate its opening was going to be held in the Hotel Danvers here in Portland. Everyone associated, at least those who could attend, would be in town, which might aid her in her investigation. She liked to talk to witnesses in person, face-to-face without relying on telephone calls or another cop's notes and instincts.

Warm water lapped over her, foamy bubbles hissing lightly as they disintegrated. The wine helped ease the day's tensions and frustrations from her muscles and bones. But her mind was spinning with half-baked theories and questions for Cassie Kramer.

There were more angles to consider as well.

Tomorrow, Nash thought, and finished her wine. Then she slid lower in the tub and stared upward through the surface of the water to look through the disappearing bubbles to the chandelier suspended overhead. The fixture dangled from the twenty-foot ceiling. She wondered, not for the first time, if the chandelier would ever fall and crash into the tub, maybe even kill her. Who, if anyone, would care? With no answer she held her breath as long as she could, silently counting off the seconds, trying to stay under as long as possible, fixating on the soft lights glowing overhead.

Her lungs began to ache.

Longer. Just a little longer.

She remained submerged.

How is Cassie Kramer involved in her sister's death?

Where was she when the bullets in the prop gun were exchanged?

She heard her heart beating in her ears under the water.

What was the fight with Allie about right before she disappeared?

Her lungs were starting to scream.

Why did Cassie just happen to be in LA when Holly Dennison was murdered?

Why would the killer leave the mask? Some sick joke? How did it tie in? What was that all about?

Pain burned through her chest. Serious pain.

Why kill Holly? What was the motive? Did she know something? Her murder wasn't a random act, couldn't be, not with the mask. So why her?

Her lungs were on fire.

What about Allie's interest in Cassie's husba—

She launched herself from the bottom of the tub and gulped in air. Huge lungfuls of air. She'd held her breath three seconds less than her best time.

Damn it all to fucking hell!

No—don't get angry. You'll do better next time. Take a few more breaths. Regain your equilibrium.

Slowly, she drew in air through her nose and expelled it through her mouth. Her heartbeat slowed and her anger melted away. It was still early enough that she could read a chapter or two of the paperback that had been sitting on her night table, or watch TV before turning in. She should probably catch the news. But she probably wouldn't. A much more likely scenario would be that she would spend the next few hours in bed, with her computer, perhaps a last glass of wine, while going over her notes in the Allie Kramer disappearance case.

Finally, as the bathwater cooled, she climbed out of the tub and didn't bother to towel off, just slipped on the plush robe and bent down to blow out the candle and whisper softly, "'Night, Love."

CHAPTER 23

"Do you know what time it is?" Dr. Sherling asked. Her voice was groggy with sleep.

Cassie had dialed the doctor's cell phone number on impulse. She really hadn't expected the psychiatrist to answer. She'd gotten lucky. She glanced at the readout on Trent's DVR player. It read nine forty-seven.

"I know it's late," she said. "I'm sorry."

Grumpily, Dr. Sherling said, "All right. I'm awake now. Sort of. But I have rounds tomorrow at six." She yawned. "I suppose you're calling about that television documentary, or docudrama, or whatever it's called these days, and my advice is to not watch it. If you want, you can schedule a session and we'll discuss it. Call my office. In the morning."

"What docudrama?"

"On one of those mystery channels. You know, unsolved cases or whatever. The woman . . . oh, what's her name, the nosy reporter, she's on it."

"Whitney Stone."

"Yes, yes, that's the one."

Cassie's insides tightened. "It's on tonight?"

"Yes, in a few minutes, I think, but it might be best if you don't watch it. I saw a preview for it, and the story isn't about your sister going missing, but about the near-death experience when you and your mother were kidnapped."

Cassie's pulse sped up. "I wasn't calling about the program," she said, and explained about her visit to the hospital during the day, how she'd wanted to see Steven Rinko and not being allowed, how she'd been thwarted and belittled by the receptionist.

"Constance can get a little territorial," the doctor admitted.

"Downright nasty. And judgmental."

"Really? I don't think so."

"For sure. Tre—my husband was with me. He can confirm."

"You're back with him?"

Cassie ignored the question. "The truth is I was so rattled I forgot to ask for the security tapes of my room."

"There are none."

"But there was a camera."

"Never operational. New laws. No tapes."

Cassie was flummoxed. She felt the air go out of her lungs. The tapes would have proven that the nurse out of the last century was inside her room.

"I think I was being watched."

"Nonsense." She said it as if it were fact, that anything untoward that Cassie may have felt or seen was paranoia and hallucinations. "The only ones watching you were the nurses who were assigned to you, and then not by camera. Only in person. We have hallway monitors and cameras, of course, but nothing in the patient rooms."

"So if a nurse or doctor or aide slipped something they shouldn't into my IV or food or whatever, there would be no record of it?"

"Not by camera. But we'd know from your monitors or lab results."

"It might be too late then."

"Too late?"

"If someone put something in my meds and I, you know, ended up dying."

Dr. Sherling sighed audibly. "But you didn't die."

"Of course not. That was just a hypothetical situation."

"All of our staff members, including Ms. Unger, go through rigorous background checks before they're hired. Is that the reason you called so late on my private number?"

Didn't she know that everything in Cassie's life was an emergency? "I know it's not life and death, but I need to know some things. Does anyone on the staff ever dress in uniforms from the past?"

"What?"

"Like the uniforms nurses used to wear," Cassie went on doggedly. "Not the scrubs they have on most of the time, but the outfits with heavy white shoes and white stockings and white dresses. Sometimes pointed caps and a blue cape."

There was a long hesitation, then finally, very seriously, "Why are you asking?"

The truth would not help her cause. "Just curious."

"There has to be a reason, and it has something more than curiosity behind it."

"I thought I saw someone wearing an outfit like that one night."

Another weighty pause. "I think we should talk about this in a session. In the office. If you're having hallucinations again, then—"

"I'm not hallucinating. She was there. In my room. In that uniform, and she even left an earring."

"An earring?"

"Yes! Red. In the shape of a cross."

"And you know it was hers?"

That stopped her. Was it possible that someone else could have dropped it?

"Most of the nurses wear earrings."

Had she seen the earrings on an actual caregiver at the hospital and then created them in her nightmarish dream? No, no, no. Steven Rinko had seen the nurse, too. He even knew the kind of car she drove and . . . but he suffered from delusions and hallucinations and boundary difficulties between what was real and what wasn't.

Cassie's throat went dry. She didn't know what to say. Had she really put all her faith in a genius of a boy who often lived in a fantasy world?

"Listen, Cassie." Dr. Sherling's voice was soft again. Kind and caring. Or so it sounded. "Call my office in the morning. I'll tell the staff I want to see you and they'll fit you in tomorrow after rounds. I really do think it would be a good thing if we talked again. About your treatment. If not in the hospital then outpatient."

All the spit dried in Cassie's mouth. The doubts that were always with her assailed her again and she heard herself saying, "I will."

"Good. I'll see you tomorrow. Good night." And then she clicked off. Cassie was left holding the phone and staring out the window. The fire was burning low in the wood stove, the dog curled into a ball and Trent . . . where was Trent? She heard a floorboard creak overhead and remembered he'd gone upstairs to sort out bills in the bedroom he used as an office.

She wanted to tell him about the phone call, but told herself she should deal with it herself; she couldn't always go running to her husband. Hell, what a mess!

A headache started to form behind her eyes. She found the remote for Trent's television, clicked on the flat screen, and scrolled through the stations until she found the cable channel that was hosting mystery shows. Sure enough, slated to be aired within a few minutes was *Justice: Stone Cold*. The subtitle read: *Terror in Ice*. The caption read like a horror story from her past: *Reporter Whitney Stone reviews the case that terrorized a small town in Oregon where celebrity actress Jenna Hughes was hunted and kidnapped by a serial killer who had targeted her and her daughters.*

Cassie's heart sank. Jenna's stalker was part of a month-long marathon of shows on serial killers. It seemed from the menu that the hour-long shows were running back-to-back, twenty-four hours a day, seven days a week. And as she checked the listings, she realized that this week, every twelve hours the show about the freak who had held her and her mother hostage ten years ago would run.

Over and over.

She shivered. Remembered the fear, the stark terror of waking up in his ice-cold lair, knowing that both she and her mother were doomed.

She dropped the remote and stared at the television as the program started. First there was Whitney Stone's face, perfect makeup, long, black hair, hazel eyes staring into the camera's lens. She was serious. Dressed in black. The screen behind her in shadows.

"We all know that Allie Kramer is missing, her whereabouts unknown, her condition undetermined. Police are investigating her disappearance as a missing person's case, but there is always the fear that she may already be dead, her body hidden, maybe never to be found."

Cassie's throat closed and she felt faint.

But Whitney Stone plowed on. "We at *Justice: Stone Cold* are currently investigating Ms. Kramer's disappearance and the bizarre events that happened in and around the set of her latest film, *Dead Heat*, which premieres soon. I promise you, we at *Justice: Stone Cold* will ferret out the truth, through exclusive interviews with Allie Kramer's sister, Cassie, an actress in her own right, but with far less star power than that of her sister. There are questions about her relationship with her estranged sister and rumors of a love triangle between Allie and Cassie Kramer and Cassie's husband, Trent Kittle."

To Cassie's horror, pictures of Allie, Trent, and herself flashed onto the screen while Whitney's voice continued. "Who is this man?" A close-up of Trent, unshaven, in jeans and an open shirt, lounging against a western facade, one booted foot propped against the weathered boards of what appeared to be a saloon. Cassie recognized the picture as one he'd used when he was briefly a stuntman looking for work in Hollywood while dating her. "If that isn't enough scandal in this bizarre tragedy," Whitney went on in a voice-over, "add in the fact that Allie had been involved in a white-hot affair with her costar, Brandon McNary." Trent's image faded to be replaced by a sexy head shot of McNary smiling slyly into the camera. "Could he have played a part? All these questions will be answered in the next installment of *Justice: Stone Cold.* But tonight's story is dedicated to another portion of Allie Kramer's life, when she was still an impressionable teen, a schoolgirl in a small Oregon town, her mother, Jenna Hughes, a famous actress who had escaped the pressures, stress, and yes, dangers, of Hollywood."

Cassie backed up until her calves hit the edge of the couch, where she dropped onto the cushions. Her eyes were trained on the screen and the debacle that was unfolding.

Turn it off.

Her common sense was silently screaming at her.

Don't watch this. Do not!

In a poorly acted sequence with commercial breaks cutting into the action, the story that had haunted Cassie since her teenage years was played out. She saw unknown actresses play the parts of her mother, her boyfriend, Allie, and, of course, herself. A man who resembled the murderer was also on-screen as he stalked the actress who played Jenna and re-created the terrible ordeal that she had lived through. Interspersed were actual clips from news reports of the horror that had claimed their lives.

In one sequence of footage of her family that had been shot just afterward, Jenna was ushering her children inside the house, waiflike Allie was clinging to her mother, while Cassie threw a dark, angry look at whoever was manning the camera. Quickly, Jenna eased her daughters through the door and away from the public's eye, but outside, even with the door firmly shut, the camera kept filming, sweeping across the wide front porch to focus on a window where Allie appeared and stared through the glass panes. Then the picture on the screen changed, morphing into Allie nearing adulthood. The same wide-eyed innocence was visible on the older Allie as she stared through another window. That now iconic image had become the poster for *Wait Until Christmas,* one of the films that had caught the attention of the American public and propelled Allie into stardom.

A cold shiver ran down Cassie's spine as the image faded back to the first shot again, of young Allie peering through the window of the family home. Even at her tender age, just after a life-shattering ordeal, Allie had been able to exude an ethereal quality. But in the next second, that image was destroyed as Jenna appeared and quickly yanked her daughter from the window. A second later the blinds snapped shut.

"Cass?" Trent's voice brought her back to the present. He took one look at the television. "What're you doing? What is this?" He found the remote on the floor and clicked the TV off. Then he gazed hard at Cassie.

"I wanted to see what Whitney had to say." She felt compelled to defend herself.

"And?"

"Probably not a good idea."

He tossed the remote onto the couch. "You okay?"

She nodded, not really sure.

He waited, the fire hissing, the dog snoring softly, the seconds ticking by. "Let's call it a night."

"I can sleep down here?" she asked, motioning to the couch.

"If you don't watch any more trash TV."

"Okay, Daddy," she mocked.

"Or you could come upstairs."

"With you?"

"Definitely with me." His smile was an invitation and she wondered what it would hurt. They were married, not that their marriage was the crux of her hesitation. They'd slept in the same bed last night. Nothing had happened between them, except for the fact she'd felt more secure and safe than she had in months.

But now there was a tiny gleam in his eye, the hint of sexuality that stirred a response in her. It wasn't the sex itself that scared her, it was the emotional devastation that was sure to follow any intimacy.

It had happened before.

"I think I'll stay down here."

His lopsided grin became more pronounced, as if he knew exactly what she was thinking. "Suit yourself." He found the sleeping bag and pillow in the front closet again and tossed them onto the leather couch. "Hud will keep you company. But if you change your mind, you know where to find me."

He pushed away from the doorjamb, walked to the front hallway and locked the door, then headed up the stairs, his boots ringing on each step and echoing in her heart. Should she just quit fighting it? Follow him up the stairs? Forget about all the pain of their short marriage? Actually start over as he'd suggested?

Biting her lip, she eyed the leather couch and the sleeping bag and pillow lying on the cold cushions. The rain was beating a soft tattoo against the windowpanes and she told herself she was just being stubborn. A night in Trent's bed did not a commitment make. Nor would it compromise any of her moral standards, whatever they may be. Sleeping with Trent's body curled next to hers wasn't some kind of sin or sign of weakness. It didn't mean that she'd decided to throw out all of her convictions or suspicions. It wasn't as if they were in a battle and he'd won.

It was just comfort.

Well, and sexual attraction.

She glanced over at the sleeping dog. Though Hud didn't appear to open his eyes, he thumped his tail. "Sorry, Buddy," she said, heading for the stairs where she intended to follow her husband. "You're on your own tonight."

She was on the third step when her cell phone beeped, indicating she had a text. Pausing, she saw that the text was from Brandon McNary and that her battery life was low. She couldn't remember when she'd charged it last or if she'd even packed her charger in her hurry to leave LA.

r u in PDX?

She considered not answering and didn't respond immediately. Another text came through.

need to see u. ASAP! info on AK

Cassie's pulse jumped. Information on Allie? Now? Bullshit. But she didn't want to just brush him off. He was the last man Allie was involved with, and maybe he knew something he hadn't imparted earlier.

She replied: coffee tomorrow am?

The response: now. Important.

She typed: I'm in Falls Crossing. Then she added: With Trent.

McNary replied quickly: come alone.

Cassie: What is this?

McNary: if you want the info meet me at Orson's at 11:30

Cassie: Sorry. No cloak and dagger cryptic crap for me.

McNary: You're the only 1 who can help.

Cassie: I'm not.

McNary: guess what she said about u was true all go no show.
She knew u didn't care about her

Cassie: Not true

McNary: prove it

Cassie: Don't have to.

She waited for the next text but it didn't come. Agitated, she
stood on the third step and contemplated heading upstairs. To Trent.
To safety. To . . . oh, hell, who was she kidding? She couldn't just go
to bed and pretend McNary hadn't tried to reach out to her.

But why?

Late at night, it didn't make any sense.

But then, what had in the disappearance of her sister? Nothing. At
least McNary was willing to talk to her. Unlike Little Bea or Dean Arnette or a lot of people associated with *Dead Heat* and Allie.

She looked up the remaining steps of the staircase and at the dark
floor above. Knowing she was giving in to emotions over judgment,
she started typing. What if he was on the up and up? What if Allie
needed her? What if, for some unknown reason, it was imperative
that Cassie go alone? I'll be there, but if this is some kind of sick joke,
Brandon, I swear, I'll kill you!

For a second she considered hurrying up the rest of the flight and
telling Trent about her plans, but she knew what his response would
be, what any sane person's responses would be.

Something along the lines of: "You're not going alone."

Or: "Why don't you just call the police?"

Or maybe: "This sounds like big trouble or a twisted prank. I don't
care what he said, I'm coming with you."

Her heart wrenched. Having Trent with her would be a helluva lot
more comforting and probably safer, though she wasn't really worried about her safety. She could handle a self-serving sleaze like Mc-
Nary and Orson's was a well-lit, popular bar in Portland; she'd be
okay.

After hitting the send button, she turned back, collected her
purse, keys, and jacket, then headed through the front door and into
the wet Oregon night. She hoped Trent was already asleep, that he
hadn't heard the dog's soft woof as she'd grabbed her things, nor
caught the noise of the latch clicking as she'd quietly pulled the front
door shut behind her.

What are you doing?

Are you crazy?

That nagging voice whispered to her as she clicked on the flash-light app on her cell phone, its bluish beam illuminating the wet grass, weeds, and puddles. Moving quickly, head ducked against the rain, she picked her way along the path to the gravel parking area near the garage. A security lamp mounted on a pole near the barn gave off an ethereal light, creating the illusion that the barn, silo, and garage's shadowed facades loomed larger around the graveled park-ing area.

"Don't be a fool," she whispered as she reached her car and slipped noiselessly behind the wheel. Before she had time to second-guess herself, she cranked on the ignition and looked up at the house to the second story and Trent's dark window. The shifting light of a tele-vision backlit a figure standing near the glass.

Cassie's heart lurched. Her head began to pound. She blinked, felt the blackness calling to her, beckoning, but she fought it. Her hands, despite the cold were suddenly sweaty against the wheel.

"No!" she said aloud. "Not now!"

She couldn't afford to lose time tonight, to have hours unac-counted for. As her headache began to thunder, she set her jaw and thought about Trent, how she'd deceived him.

She'd text him the second she was in Portland, but for now, she hit the gas and took off, turning on her headlights and wipers and telling herself that it didn't matter what Trent thought, she didn't have to answer to him, she could do anything she damned well pleased.

She gritted her teeth against the pain of the headache, possibly brought on by her deception. Of course she hadn't outwardly lied to him, but by not going upstairs and telling him what she was going to do, she'd kind of misled him. Omission rather than admission.

But this could be her best chance of ever finding her sister.

Then again it could be a big waste of time.

She'd find out soon enough.

CHAPTER 24

Trent swore under his breath as he watched the disappearing tail-lights of Cassie's Honda. He'd hoped she would come up to bed. He'd hoped they'd make love. He'd hoped she'd spend the rest of the night and maybe her life with him.

But, of course, that had been too much to expect.

Snagging his keys off his dresser, he charged down the stairs when he heard a beep from his cell phone indicating a text had come through. Cassie?

His jaw tight, he glanced at the phone's tiny screen and frowned. The message was a brief note from Carter:

Checked with L Sparks of the OSP. Larry Sparks was a lieutenant with the Oregon State Police. While at Jenna's house Trent had filled Carter in about the search for the 2007 Hyundai Santa Fe. Luckily, Carter hadn't balked at the source of the information, and had later confirmed that Sparks had promised to do some checking with the stipulation that Detective Nash of the Portland Police Department be kept in the loop. Neither Trent nor Carter had any problem with making certain the Portland PD was informed. Trent figured the more cops who were searching for Allie Kramer, the better.

Carter's text continued:

9 vehicles: 07 Hyundai Santa Fe, Arctic white, beige interior etc. in the tri-county area. No plates with bucking horses.

No surprise there. Nine vehicles was a start, though the tri-counties didn't include outlying counties in Southern Washington and out here, east of the Portland metropolitan area. Trent walked to the kitchen and found the dog on his heels. "Not this time, boy," he said as he snatched his hat and jacket from a peg near the back door. "You hold down the fort." After cramming his hat onto his head, he slipped his arms through the sleeves of his jacket and turned up his collar. Rain peppered the ground and the wind tore down the gorge as he jogged to his truck. Once inside, he switched on the ignition and dialed Cassie's cell.

"Pick up," he said, hearing the phone ring. Once, twice, three times. "Come on, damn it!" With the phone tucked to his ear, he turned the truck around, then hit the gas and started racing down the lane leading to the county road. He heard her phone click to voice mail. Damn! "Saw you take off. What's up? Call me." He hung up and tossed the phone onto the seat.

Why the hell hadn't she told him where she was going?

The simple answer was that she didn't want him to know.

"Screw that," he ground out as he reached the county highway and, with a quick look in either direction, cranked the wheel.

Fishtailing, the truck slid on the wet pavement before the tires caught. His cell phone jangled and he saw it was Carter. He picked up and wrestled with the idea of asking him if Jenna had heard from Cassie, but decided Carter would share that info if he had it and he didn't want to worry Cassie's parents . . . yet.

"Kittle."

Carter's voice was deep. Serious. "You saw my message about the tri-county area," he stated.

"Yeah, just got it."

"Sparks found about seven more scattered around the state, but the thing of it is, there are no Oregon license plates with an image of any kind of bucking bronco. Wyoming? Yes. Oregon? No."

Of course, that would have been far too easy, Trent thought, scowling through the windshield as the truck's tires sang against the wet pavement.

"So either your info is faulty, or you misunderstood."

"He said a bucking bronc. I was there." Frustrated, Trent snorted through his nose. He'd almost known this would turn out badly.

"Could he have been talking about the license plate holder? Not the plate itself, but some kind of decorative bracket fixing the plate to the SUV?"

"Maybe. But he seemed pretty sure of himself." Of course Rinko was a patient in a mental hospital so he lost some credibility there.

"There are plate holders with any kind of image you want, you know. Like the name of the dealership, or if you're a sports fan, you can get one for your favorite team, like the Trailblazers or the Oregon Ducks or Oregon State Beavers or whatever. Also, local dealerships offer to decorate plate holders."

To Trent, looking for a decorative license plate holder with a horse on it was a long shot, a stab in the dark.

But what else did they have to go on?

"Sounds good," he said, and clicked off, then turned the wipers onto the fastest speed offered. He tried his wife's mobile number again.

Of course, she didn't pick up.

His jaw slid to the side and he squinted into the darkness.

What the hell was she up to?

ACT III

Absently rubbing the scratches on her wrist, she stalked the perimeter of her room, barely eight by ten and dominated by her dressing table with its vanity mirror. A small window was cut into one wall. The other three were covered with large posters, mounted carefully. Each was from a movie starring either Jenna Hughes or Allie Kramer, one butting up to the next, a collage of pictures of the women in their most celebrated roles. There were other images on the posters, some with their costars' faces, but dominating each poster was a close-up of Jenna or her famous daughter.

Her stomach curled as she surveyed them, but she took in each individual poster, her eyes tracing the fine lines of the women's expressions, of their features, the sensual mouths, large eyes, and different noses. Always Allie appeared a pixieish, younger version of her mother, but the resemblance was evident, caught by the camera's eye.

Bile rose in her throat as she walked past the posters, circling the room, eyeing each print.

She felt edgy.

Fidgety.

Anxious.

It was time again, she knew. She couldn't fight the demons much longer, nor did she want to.

Which one? she wondered, retracing her footsteps as she slowly walked the perimeter of this, her safe place. Which one would be best?

It had to be of Jenna.

For tonight.

She made six circuits. Each time the poster with Jenna portraying Zoey Trammel called to her and seemed to follow her with her eyes.

"You," she said to the image of Jenna in a wide-brimmed hat, her head turned to look over her shoulder, her lips curved into the ghost of a smile. "Zoey."

Intent on not disturbing any of the other wall hangings, she bit her lip as she eased the mounted poster from its spot and carried it to a bench pushed against the wall with the window. After placing it in plain view of her makeup table she sat in the small chair at her vanity mirror and opened the drawer where she kept her cosmetics. Tubes and jars were lined in rows and she quickly picked those that would be perfect for her transformation: coral lipstick, smoky eye shadow, near-black eyeliner with a hint of green, a rusty-hued blush over lighter foundation.

Then she began her work, using the brushes, swabs, and cotton balls kept in jars on the table, leaning close to the mirror when she needed to while keeping the poster in her peripheral vision.

She was still young.

Age hadn't gotten to her.

Yet.

Growing older was inevitable of course, but at the thought her lips pursed, and she noticed the first signs of ugly, bothersome lines that would eventually require Botox injections.

She couldn't think about them now. She was losing time.

She could play Zoey. No, she could *be* Zoey. She had the heart-shaped face, though she would have to don a red wig, as Jenna had done.

Jenna!

Again her stomach roiled and her hatred ran a little faster in her blood.

With a slightly trembling hand she applied her makeup painstakingly, using the different brushes with their varying sizes and firmness, copying the shading beneath Jenna's cheekbones, the smudge of eyeliner/shadow at the corners of her eyes, the carefully outlined lips.

Jenna Hughes, who, at the top of her game, had walked away from Hollywood. What a coward. She'd thrown it all away. For what? To be a mother? What a joke! What a freaking joke!

Her hand trembled more violently and she closed her eyes and counted to ten.

This is not the time to unravel, for God's sake.

Slowly letting out her breath, she started in again. With forced precision she applied the colors, lines, and mascara, as careful as a painter with a masterpiece as she looked from the image on the poster to her own reflection and back again. The hues had to be exact. With the right play of shadow and light, she could make herself be Zoey . . . not Jenna so much really but . . . close enough to pass as Zoey Trammel . . . a final stroke of lipstick and . . . her hand wobbled wildly.

Her teeth clenched.

No! No! Don't lose it!

But it was too late, the shaking of her fingers had destroyed her look. The lipstick trailing from the corner of her mouth made her look like the Joker from a Batman movie.

"Shit!" She grabbed a tissue, tried to clean up. No, no, no! That wasn't what was supposed to happen!

Heart pounding, her pulse racing, she knew in an instant that if she didn't pull herself back, rein in her wildly raging emotions, all would be lost. "Get it together!" she screamed into the mirror, then gasped in horror. "Oh, Jesus!" The image staring back at her looked *nothing* like Zoey Trammel. The woman in the reflection was cartoonish, a caricature of the beautiful Zoey and the gorgeous woman who portrayed her, the colors bizarre.

"You sick, sick fake!" she snarled at the face staring at her, and noticed a bit of spit in the corner of her oversize orange lips. Her breathing was coming in short, sharp pants and her mind was suddenly disjointed. Fractured.

Gripping the edge of the table, she leaned closer to the hideous woman in the glass. "What the hell were you thinking, you miserable bitch?" Spittle flew from her garish lips to gob on the mirror, then run down the smooth glass, leaving a silvery trail over her reflection.

She gaped in horror.

This wasn't what was supposed to happen tonight.

Her blood was pumping through her veins, coursing hot, pounding in her temples. "For the love of God," she whispered to her image, despair entwining with her rage. "What's wrong with you? What the *hell* is wrong with you?" She swept the countertop of all her jars and tubes, sending them crashing to the floor, glass shattering.

Frustration boiled deep within and her hands went to her hair, her fingers digging deep into her scalp, as if she could physically drag the demons from her skull. "Why are you doing this?" The question was broken by a sob as a feeling of wretched hopelessness overtook her. "What're you doing?" She let the tears flow and buried her head in her hands. Shoulders heaving, sobbing quietly, she knew her

makeup was ruined and running down her face, but she would re-
pair it, change the look, come out of this. She could fix things. It was
just makeup, dye and powder and grease.

Drawing in a shaking breath, she lifted her head. Pointing a damning finger at the grotesque woman in the mirror, she said, "*You* can't
let this happen."

Sniffing, she swiped at the offensive tears and drew herself up.
Squaring her shoulders, she saw the ugly woman staring back at her
do the same. As if that obscene bitch with the sickening orange
mouth and mascara running in rivers down her face had an ounce of
backbone.

Ignore her. She's not the enemy!

She blinked.

Managed to retrieve some of the shreds of her sanity.

Felt her strength, her purpose returning. Sensed again her need
to become the characters that Jenna Hughes had portrayed.

Absolute despair and self-loathing gave way to a slow-burning
anger at her own ineptness to recapture the image, to prove to herself that she was as good as Jenna Hughes. Not just as good, but better. Younger. Stronger. More beautiful.

She glanced to the mirror and the hideous image glared back at
her, as if she knew a secret. Was the woman laughing at her? Did she
know that Jenna Hughes could never be bested?

Instinctively she yanked open the makeup drawer and rattled
through the jars, pencils, creams, and shadows until she found the
palette knife. Dull, but good enough.

Flinging one last look at the ugly woman in the mirror she kicked
back her chair and crossed the few steps to the bench and the poster
of Zoey Trammel.

Before her anger ebbed, she jabbed the dull knife into the poster,
gloried in the sound of paper tearing.

Then she pulled the knife back and stabbed again. And again. And
again. Faster and faster. In a frenzy, her gaze glued to the calm features of Zoey Trammel until Jenna's beauty was obliterated, her eyes
disappearing, her mouth stretched into a monstrous slash.

She was breathing hard, her heart a drum and in her furor, she
stumbled backward. Falling, she hit her arm on the edge of the dressing table aggravating the scratch on her wrist.

Pain sang up her arm.

She dropped the knife.

It clattered to the floor near to where she, herself, dropped. Wrapping her arms around her knees, her head tucked between her shoulders, she rocked slowly back and forth, trying to pull herself together.

Her rage spent, she drew in deep breaths and closed her eyes. "Oh, God," she whispered as slowly, bit by rational bit, sanity returned. The fire that fueled her madness eventually died, not to ashes, but to glowing embers that could ignite with just a little bit of stoking.

The pain remained. And the fear. That she was so different. A monster.

She knew she had to stop this. She had to stop accidentally maiming herself. She couldn't mar her skin. For the love of God, what was she thinking? That would be stupid and she was far from an idiot . . . right?

She managed to climb to her feet, then fall into her chair again. Now her reflection appeared clownish and sad, a pathetic creature. She told herself to calm down and think.

Go slow. Stick to the plan. Don't get distracted. Things will work out. You will make them work out.

Finally she breathed more easily.

Calmer, she picked up the knife and placed it back in her drawer. Once she'd swept the floor and thrown away the broken bottles and jars, and the tabletop was straightened to her satisfaction, she walked to the small window and peered through the clear glass.

A smile touched at the corners of her lips as she saw, through the fronds of palm trees, the Hollywood sign mounted high on the hills. Illuminated, its white letters stark against the night, the iconic sign was a silent reminder of her mission. And what she had to do next.

She was the one who should have been the star.

She was the one who should have taken Hollywood by storm, been adored by a million fans.

Fame was yet to be hers.

She turned and once more studied her wall where she'd remounted the disfigured poster of Jenna as Zoey Trammel. Wincing, she forced herself to stare at her handiwork. Maybe she'd learn to control herself. The torn print was a harsh reminder of her thin grip on reality.

Slowly, she turned and focused on another poster. This one of Allie.

In the poster for *Wait Until Christmas,* Allie was a vision, like a damned angel. With her face upturned as if she were actually glimpsing heaven and a divine light shining upon her, she was the picture of innocence and virtue.

Yeah, right.

Nothing could be further from the truth.

Worse yet, Allie had been horrible in the film. Horrible! Wooden. Like a damned marionette on a string. Hadn't anyone else been able to see Allie's lack of talent?

How had Allie Kramer's name ever been whispered for an Academy Award?

Fortunately, cooler, smarter heads had prevailed and Allie hadn't been nominated.

"Too bad."

CHAPTER 25

She was late. So late! Consumed by her whirling thoughts and a darkness she didn't want to consider, Cassie arrived at the bar over an hour later than she'd planned. Once she'd snapped to and seen the time on her car's clock, she'd texted Brandon.

He hadn't responded.

No surprise there.

The good news was that at this time of night Orson's was quiet.

Good.

The lighting was dim, soft jazz playing from hidden speakers, only a few customers sprinkled at the bar and even fewer at the surrounding tables. Cassie figured McNary had picked this spot specifically because the patrons were sparse so there was less of a chance of someone recognizing him. Maybe. With all of the publicity surrounding the release of *Dead Heat,* and the scandal surrounding the movie, anyone associated with the film was under the constant watch of the paparazzi. Didn't she have the phone calls, texts, and e-mails to prove it? Fortunately, there were fewer members of the press in Portland than LA, but that would change quickly with news of the premiere party that Dean Arnette had scheduled, here, in the City of Roses for this coming weekend. And these days, everyone had a cell phone, pocket camera, or iPad on them at all times. Any Tom, Dick, or Harriet could snap a shot and sell it to the tabloids, or post it on the Internet. No big deal.

The odd thing was that usually McNary didn't avoid publicity. He ate up all of the media attention and with *Dead Heat* about to be released, it seemed out of character for him to want privacy.

So something had to be up.

She glanced over her shoulder, but no one seemed to pay her any notice as she walked into the restaurant. Her hair was pulled away from her face and hidden beneath her hood. She'd wiped off all of her makeup to be less recognizable. A scarf, ostensibly to fight off the cold and damp of April in Oregon, hid her chin, but she didn't wear dark glasses. At night they would attract more attention than they would deflect.

As she picked a path through scattered tables, she sensed a couple of passing glances sent her way, but no one stopped to stare or interrupt their conversation as she made her way to a corner booth. She ordered a glass of wine, and still fighting a headache texted Trent while her cell flashed its irritating "low battery" warning. For now she ignored it, but she'd have to be careful. She needed the phone in case of an emergency.

In Portland. McNary said he had info on Allie. We'll see. Back soon.

Then she waited. Five minutes. Ten. Fifteen. Sipping her merlot she checked her watch. God, it was late. Her fault. Still, she was annoyed that McNary wasn't showing. Avoiding eye contact with the patrons and waiter, she did a slow burn as she told herself she'd been stood up. She was an idiot, a fool for trusting the likes of Brandon McNary. She should never have left Trent's house.

Suddenly McNary swung through the door and headed straight to her table.

Smelling of rainwater and cigarette smoke, wearing a hooded jacket not unlike her own, and with four or five days' beard stubble and tinted glasses, he was barely recognizable. He looked more like a strung-out junkie down on his luck than a Hollywood star who could command millions to be a part of a movie. "About time you showed," he said.

"Sorry."

"Don't be. Just pay for that," he said, motioning toward her drink, and when she was about to argue, he pulled out his wallet as if agitated, left a couple of bills on the table, then grabbed her hand. Before she could protest, he bent down and whispered, "Don't argue," then quietly led her down a short hallway and through a side entrance to the street, where beneath the awnings several men and women smoked cigarettes, the rain coming down in a steady drizzle.

"Where are we going?" Cassie demanded. She'd never trusted Mc-

Nary and she wasn't going to follow him blindly down the dark Port-land streets in the middle of the damned night, not when her sister was already missing.

"To my car."

With a shake of her head, she stopped short. "No."

"We need to be where no one can see us."

"No one recognized me in the restaurant."

He shot her a look that she read instantly. *Of* course *no one recognized you, Cassie. You're just Jenna Hughes's daughter and Allie's sister, but I'm famous, a household name, a big star.*

Her temper flared and she fought not to tell him off. "I told you I'm not into all this cloak and dagger. I just want to find my sister."

"Don't worry."

"Yeah, right. Like there's nothing to worry about."

"For the love of—Come on!" He tugged on her hand again and re-luctantly she started walking again, moving quickly down the rain-washed streets. They weren't alone. Traffic passed, a few late-night pedestrians walking along the streets.

"So where's Allie?"

"I don't know."

"Wait. You said—"

"I saw her. Okay?" he snapped, his breath fogging in the cold air.

"*Saw* her? Where?" Cassie demanded as they rounded a corner. He reached into a jacket pocket and withdrew a ring holding a single key and fob. With a touch of his finger an older SUV parked on the far side of the street beeped and flashed its lights. Still tugging on her hand, he started jaywalking to the vehicle.

"I thought you drove a Porsche."

"Lamborghini."

She shrugged. "Same difference."

"Hardly." He shot her a look of disbelief. "My car's in LA. Here I wanted to blend in."

She eyed the older Chevy Tahoe with more than a little suspicion.

"Come on now. Get in." He opened the passenger door for her, but she hesitated.

"What?"

"My sister's missing. You were involved with her. It's the middle of the night and someone killed Holly—"

"Oh, fuck! I know all that! Here!" He slapped the small ring with the key and fob into her palm. "You keep the damned key! Then maybe you won't be so paranoid!"

Not a chance. Her fingers curled over the cold bit of metal as he rounded the front of the SUV, then climbed inside. At least he couldn't drive off with her. Tentatively, she sat in her designated seat and pulled the door closed.

Now they were alone in the vehicle, rain pounding down, the windows starting to fog with their body heat.

"Tell me about Allie," Cassie said.

"Okay. But first, give the key back to me."

"No."

Sighing, he said, "The windows are electric. I just want to crack one. I need a smoke."

"Forget it."

"Seriously?"

"I've never heard of anyone dying from nicotine withdrawal, so quit stalling, okay? Where did you see Allie and when?"

"Two days ago. In Oregon City." His fingers drummed against his leg and he looked antsy.

"In Oregon City?" The historic town was situated on the east side of the Willamette River, just under the falls and south of Portland by nearly twenty miles. Cassie had never heard Allie mention the town. "Why would she be there?"

"Don't know."

"Why were you?"

"It's a place where I thought I was less likely to be recognized, I guess. Certainly I would be less likely to run into paparazzi. And I heard they have a great little microbrewery overlooking the falls. So I drove down there and went in for a brewski."

"And there she was?" Cassie didn't bother hiding her incredulity.

"Not in the brewhouse, no. But I was in a booth by the window and I looked out, it was just about dusk, and I saw her walking along the promenade that runs above the river, right over the falls."

"You're sure?"

"Fuckin' A!" He threw up a hand in disgust that she didn't blindly trust him. "You know where I'm talking about, right?"

"Yeah, yeah. I've been there," she said, still processing his words. "As a teenager." She remembered sneaking out with friends in the summer and taking the elevator that connected the lower part of the town to the upper, and then running down the stairs. The falls were a little farther upstream, past an old paper mill. They'd gone up there, too, balancing on the stone railing overlooking the falls. She could almost smell the spray, hear the thunder of water rushing over huge boulders and cliffs that made up the falls.

"So you talked to her?" She found that hard to believe.

"She was too far away and, as I said, I was inside. But I ran out of the place and took off after her."

"And?"

"She was gone. Disappeared."

"You didn't catch up to her? You didn't speak to her? You didn't even see her up close?"

He glowered into the night. "It was Allie."

Cassie felt cheated. "Everyone thinks they catch sight of her. Here, there, in Portland, or in LA, or wherever. People call in, I know. Mom told me. I even thought I saw her a couple of times, but she was never close enough to talk to or to catch up with." Disgusted and deflated, she added, "It's probably just what people want to see, or a trick of light. You really think Allie, who's been missing all this time, is going to just take a stroll along the riverfront in Oregon City? Does that make any sense?"

He leaned back against the seat. "I don't know. Does anything?"

She stared through the window and through the foggy glass, watched as a man and a woman linked arm in arm, both wearing jeans and bundled in thick jackets, crossed against the light. He suddenly grabbed her hand with the swiftness of a striking snake, opening her fingers and plucking the key from her before she could even cry out.

"Hey!" Heart thudding, she scrabbled for the door handle as he jammed the key into the ignition. He switched on the electrical system without engaging the engine and rolled his window down a crack just as she got her door open. Then he clicked open the glove box and reached inside. As he did a large plastic bag fell out of the crammed compartment. The clear sack tumbled onto the floor at Cassie's feet.

Cassie scooped it up and tried to make out the contents. "What's this?" she asked, shaking the bag and seeing small makeup bottles, false eyelashes, and small prosthetics often used by makeup people to change an actor's appearance.

He hesitated, then grinned sheepishly as he plucked the plastic bag from her fingers. "Sometimes I need a disguise."

"False eyelashes?"

"Whatever." Again the smile, one used to distract her. "I like to go incognito."

"As a woman?"

"Or a very pretty man." He shrugged, chuckling a bit, then stuffed the bag into the box, where he scrounged around and retrieved a pack of cigarettes. Then he slammed the box closed and locked it. "I told you. I just need a cigarette."

"Fine," she said, not really caring what his secrets were. It was late and she was getting more irritated by the second. "But I drove all the way down here to talk to you. In the middle of the damned night. And all you tell me is that you think you saw Allie from a distance. Be sure to tell Whitney Stone so she can blow it up, make a story out of nothing."

"I know. I know. Stone's been on my ass, too," he muttered. "Along with about a million other reporters." He blew out a stream of smoke. "But there's more."

"Okay," she said, her voice tight. She was starting to think he was completely full of shit.

A car rounded the corner and she yanked the door firmly shut. The sports car roared past, music blaring, bass throbbing.

"Check out this text," McNary said, pulling out his cell phone and tossing it to her.

"From Allie?" She didn't believe it, but glanced down at the phone.

"Yeah." He drew deeply on his filter tip. "Think so."

The screen message said: I'm okay.

Disbelieving, she said, "This isn't Allie's number."

"It's no one's number, I tried to call it back. It's a phone with a different SIM card or a prepaid burner phone or something. Untraceable."

"To you, maybe. But the police might have ways. But still . . . just a text that says 'I'm okay'? Anyone could have sent it."

"She wanted to let me know she's all right." He didn't believe it, though. His expression was of uncertainty and bewilderment, but then, he was an actor.

"Why text. Why not call? Or leave a decent message explaining where she is? Why not use her real phone, or better yet, if she can text, why doesn't she just show up so everyone who cares about her isn't worried sick!" Cassie was getting angry now, the smoldering rage that had been with her since before she'd admitted herself to Mercy Hospital beginning to catch fire again.

"I don't know!"

"Have you gone to the police?"

He shot her a look and blew a stream of smoke out the cracked window. "They'd laugh at me." His lips tightened. "Kind of like you're doing."

"I'm not laughing at you, McNary. I'm trying to figure out why you called me up so late at night."

"Check the time on that message. It's been a while. I'd just finished watching that miserable program with Whitney Stone and before the damned credits start rolling, I get this message. *Bam!* It freaked me the fuck out, okay? I knew you were looking for Allie and I called you." He gave her a pointed look. "What would you have done?"

"I'm not sure I would leap to the conclusion that Allie was on the other end of that damned text. Anyone could have sent it. It could be a mistake, sent to you in error, or a prank or—"

"Or it could be Allie. She might do this for fun."

"No way."

"You know how she was . . . is . . . she likes to play mind games and you're a liar. You *would* think it came from her, if you got it instead of me."

She was about to protest again, but bit her tongue. *Wouldn't you have thought exactly the same thing? Wouldn't you have leaped to that very conclusion? Especially after watching the episode of* Justice: Stone Cold? *After seeing images of Allie splashed all over the screen, and the text came through, wouldn't you immediately think of her?*

"So maybe I overreacted. Sue me," McNary grumbled as he took a final drag on his cigarette then tossed the butt out the window, the red tip arcing to die in the rain.

"You should take this to the police."

"I thought you didn't think it was Allie," he said with a bit of a sneer. Once again, she remembered why she didn't like him. There was something supercilious about him, something shifty. McNary, she reminded herself, was always looking out for McNary.

"I don't know who sent you the text, but still, you should let the cops know." She frowned, thought about telling him about the warped mask she'd found in her suitcase, then reconsidered. She and Brandon McNary weren't working together to find Allie, no matter how he acted. She owed him nothing.

"You could have just told me," she said.

"I thought it would have more impact if you saw it yourself."

She wrapped her fingers over the door handle, but before she could let herself out, he placed a hand on her shoulder. "I'll drive you to your car."

"It's just around the corner."

Did his fingers clench a little over her upper arm? Did his expression darken a bit?

"Only a couple of blocks. I need the air." She opened the door and half expected him to try to restrain her.

He dropped his hand. "Oh, and Cassie," he said before she slammed the door shut. "Give Cherise a break, would ya? I know you don't like it that she's working for me now, but it's not her fault that Allie . . ." He let the end of the sentence slide and started the engine.

"That Allie what?"

"Doesn't matter," he said under his breath as he rammed the Tahoe into gear. "I guess nothing does."

She barely got the door slammed and had stepped away from his SUV before he gunned the engine, narrowly missing the car parked in front of him as he took off with a roar and chirp of tires.

What a waste of time. All she'd learned was that *someone* had texted McNary, or he'd done it himself. It wasn't beneath him to use this as a ploy for publicity. The man ate up everything written about him, good or bad. He enjoyed being the Hollywood bad boy and it didn't bother him a bit that his face was plastered all over the tabloids, and he was fodder for the gossip mills. He loved it. Once, she'd overheard him say to Allie, "There's no such thing as bad publicity."

She started walking away, half surprised no reporter had been purposely tipped off about their private meeting. It would be just like McNary to set that up, another way to keep his name trending on social media. Her stomach turned at the headlines: *Star of* Dead Heat *Caught with Missing Costar's Sister*. No, make that Married *Sister*.

Yeah, she should never have come here.

As she hurried through the rain, she noticed the streets were now nearly deserted, the night thick, the glow from the streetlamps watery and weak. She pulled her cell from her purse and saw that Trent hadn't called again. Nor had he responded to her text. She figured she'd call him when she was driving east. For now, she didn't want to be too distracted, needed to be aware.

Her car was parked in a space she'd found near a hospital, only a few blocks from the restaurant. She half jogged along the sidewalk, not waiting for the pedestrian crossing lights to change, feeling suddenly anxious and alone. She considered calling Trent, just to hear his voice, but she didn't want to go into everything with McNary yet.

Her breath fogged. Her head still ached. The park was eerily empty as she passed it, a stray dog sniffing a trash can, the distant sound of the freeway a steady hum. The storefronts were lit only by security lamps, a few of the apartments rising above showing warm patches of light or the flickering blue illumination of a television, though most of the windows were dark, the world asleep.

Jabbing her hands deep in her pockets, she felt the rain drumming against her hood. She turned a final corner and heard a hint of footsteps behind her. Someone else out this late at night? Her pulse leaped. The footfalls worried her a bit and she turned, trying to see around the edge of her hood, but she could see no one.

Still, she definitely heard steps running behind her through these empty city streets.

The hospital, a red brick edifice, was only two blocks away. If someone were really following her, she could walk inside. Sure, there were security people who would be questioning her before allowing entrance, but that would be fine. More than fine.

The footfalls seemed to increase over the insistent pounding of the rain.

Cassie broke into a run. Rain slid down her face and she kicked up water, her shoes sodden. But she didn't care. The hospital was close. A behemoth of a structure that was, at its heart, over a hundred years old, though it had gone through several renovations to modernize and expand it over the past century. Now the hospital and surrounding clinics were connected by sky bridges and tunnels and sprawled over several city blocks.

Rounding a corner, she saw the red letters for the Emergency Room burning brightly through the curtain of rain. Thank God!

The footsteps behind her seemed to quicken.

From where?

Oh, God.

Breathing hard, Cassie craned her neck, this time looking behind her a little frantically.

Nothing!

Was she imagining the sounds?

Where the hell was the runner, the person following her?

Faster. Run, faster! You'll be safe—the hospital, just a few more feet and—

"Hey!" a deep voice shouted.

She stopped short, tripped, pitched forward.

Her heart flew to her throat.

Meaty hands grabbed hold of her shoulders, and she shrieked as she nearly stumbled into a huge bear of a man wearing a long, black coat, hat, and boots. "Watch where you're going!" he admonished as she fought back panic. His face too was wet from the rain, his eyes black as coal. "Hey, now, what's wrong?" he asked, and she realized his expression, at first startled, had turned to one of concern. Six foot two, if he were an inch, and African-American, he peered down at her. "You in some kind of trouble, miss?" And then she saw the white clerical collar peeking out from under his jacket.

"No . . . no . . ." She twisted her head around to the empty street behind her. No one was there. No one, not even a jogger out for a night workout. She swallowed back her fear and cleared her throat. "I'm fine," she insisted, though her voice sounded weak and high-pitched.

Slowly he released her. "You're sure? 'Cuz you look like you just saw a ghost."

"I—I'm sorry. Really. I'm okay." She was backing up, hoping she didn't run into someone else.

Dark eyes studied her hard. His eyebrows pulled together and beneath the brim of his hat his forehead creased. "Hey. Wait a minute. Aren't you that actress everyone's looking for? Allie . . . oh, man, what's her name?" He snapped his fingers as if to think.

She turned then and left him staring after her. She headed toward the bright lights of the hospital. He was probably putting two and two together, figuring out who she was, but, thankfully, he was harmless, a man of God.

She'd let herself get scared spitless over nothing. Slowly releasing the breath she hadn't known she was holding, she dashed through the rain and heard no more footsteps chasing after her. She went past the hospital in search of her car.

The night, aside from a few cars on the street, was still. She'd been foolish, letting her imagination get the better of her. Again. If she wasn't careful she'd end up back in Mercy Hospital trying to convince Dr. Sherling that she really was sane.

Still, she kept running until she spied her Honda, where she'd left it, parked on the other side of the hospital, closer to the main entrance. Unlocking it on the fly with her key fob, she heard the familiar sound of its beep and saw its lights flash as the locks released. Good. She was breathing hard by now. As she reached the driver's side, she took a sweeping glance of the back seat, saw it was empty, no bogeyman lying in wait, then slid inside.

Chiding herself for her case of nerves most likely from being a horror film fanatic, she started the car, locked its doors, and tore out of the parking space. She'd call Trent once she was out of the city and she could talk in her normal voice again, once the panic in her bloodstream had totally dissipated. She'd have to cop to the fact that McNary had lured her for God knew what reason on a wild goose chase. She wasn't looking forward to that.

As she wound her way to the freeway, she passed a coffee shop that was closed for the night. Her headlights reflected on the glass of the storefront and, for just a second, she thought she caught a glimpse of a woman who looked like Allie tucked into the alcove of the doorway. But the woman's face and upper body were in shadow, only her booted feet and bottom of her jeans really discernible. It was just an image, a thought, probably powered by the fact that she'd been talking about and thinking of her sister all night.

At the next red light, she slowed and while the Honda idled she stared into the rearview mirror. Had it been Allie?

"Stop it," she said aloud, but her mind kept circling back.

Had she even seen someone in the doorway?

If so, was it a woman?

And then the shadow moved, a figure slipped from the alcove and stood on the street in the pouring rain.

"Allie," Cassie mouthed, dumbstruck. She rolled down her window. "Allie!" she yelled.

The light turned green. Behind her, a car was approaching. Fast. The driver laid on his horn, then blinked his lights, nearly blinding her, as a bus heading in the opposite direction rolled through the intersection.

Cassie froze. The bus slowed, exhaust pluming, obscuring the face of the building as the van behind her zoomed past, the driver shaking his head. Once the rig was out of the way, Cassie hit the gas and did a quick and very illegal U-turn.

Overhead, a traffic cam flashed.

Crap!

Well, it was just too damned bad. So she got a ticket? So what? It didn't matter if she could just get to Allie!

The bus, not expecting her to be suddenly upon it, rolled into the lane in front of her. Cassie stood on her brakes.

Her car screeched to a halt, sliding on the wet pavement as the lumbering city bus rolled away, gathering steam and belching exhaust.

Her pulse on overdrive, her headache throbbing, Cassie glanced into the shadowy alcove of the doorway to the coffee shop.

It was empty.

The woman who'd been waiting there had vanished.

CHAPTER 26

Slap. Slap. Slap.

Brandi Potts's new running shoes pinched her toes a little and were getting wet as she ran through the city streets. It was later than she liked to run, as it was after midnight. If she weren't so fast and didn't always travel with her small canister of pepper spray, she might have been worried. But tonight, pounding through the Portland streets, music pulsing from her iPhone, she felt invincible, just as she always did when her endorphins kicked in. Right now, with the rainfall increasing and only a couple of miles left on her run, those little feel-goods were definitely horse-kicking in.

Around a corner, across a street against the light, faster and faster she tore along the sidewalks and paths, feeling the exhilaration of rain against her face, listening to an up-tempo song from Katy Perry as she cut through the park. The thought of a hot shower, good book, and tumbling into bed were her incentive. That, and needing to have a personal best in her next race.

Soon.

She had her eye on her next marathon. Okay, really if you wanted to get technical, a half marathon, but still. Thirteen-plus miles was nothing to sneeze at, even if her never-going-to-commit boyfriend, Jeff, thought the race was child's play. What a jerk. She called him a running snob to his face and something a little harsher behind his back. She should break up with him. But *after* she'd finished her full marathon. Only then. *Take that, Jeffrey-Boy!*

To train for the upcoming race she was into power walking, race-walking, and, of course, running, which was her workout for tonight though she would have rather avoided this section of town where that damned near-murder took place on the set of *Dead Heat*. Dodging a crazy-ass bicyclist who streaked past, tires zinging in the rain, caused her to veer, shorten her stride. She nearly stumbled, then caught herself and swore. "Bastard! Jerkwad idiot!" Seemingly oblivious, he sped off, gliding away, leaving her seething as she turned down the street where one of the key scenes in *Dead Heat* had been filmed, the very spot where the terrible accident had taken place. Her guts clenched as she thought of the day. She'd been there as an extra in the movie. She'd seen Lucinda Rinaldi stagger and fall, and had immediately sensed something was seriously wrong.

Now, as Brandi found her stride again, she thought about that accident. The police had quickly deduced that Sig Masters, the actor who had fired the gun, hadn't known the weapons had been switched. Brandi wondered. She'd never liked Masters, considered him a bit of a bully. And he was an actor, so he could probably fool the cops. The only problem was why would he do it?

Motive, motive, motive!

Dead Heat's last scene had been changed so many times, who could tell who the intended victim was? Maybe Lucinda Rinaldi, another A-one bitch, had just been caught in the crossfire, literally in the wrong place at the wrong time. At one point Cassie Kramer's character was supposed to be the second runner, then Allie's, in a reversal of the sequence during the reshoot. Maybe Sig hoped to kill Cassie or Allie. God knew the two sisters were insufferable in different ways. Cassie, not much of an actress and a mental case to boot, now fancied herself to be a scriptwriter. As if. Then there was Allie, an egomaniac's egomaniac. It was as if Allie had to prove to everyone else, or maybe herself, that she was a certifiable star.

Brandi turned her head and spit at the thought, never breaking stride. Thinking of the Kramer sisters made her grimace. She didn't like either one. Having both Allie and Cassie on the same film, in Brandi's estimation, had been a recipe for disaster. And she'd been right. What had Karen Stenowick been thinking? Casting the two siblings in the same film had been a colossal mistake. Brandi thought the idea of putting the two women in the same film had been a ploy for publicity, as Cassie couldn't act her way out of a paper bag. There had been rumors Dean Arnette had wanted to lure Jenna Hughes back to the screen by offering her the bit part of psycho aunt to the heroine. Jenna, another head case, had refused and the part had been written out.

All in all, *Dead Heat* might end up being a complete disaster and Lucinda Rinaldi almost paid the ultimate price.

Well, it was all water under the celluloid bridge now.

Brandi kept running.

Slap. Slap. Slap.

But thoughts of the accident kept coming to mind as she now was on the same flippin' street where it had all come down. During the filming she'd sensed the electricity of the set filmed in a real storm, though the lightning and thunder had been faked, of course. But the Portland drizzle, enhanced by sprinklers, had added to the dark mood.

Tonight no one, not one damned soul, was on the street, yet she suddenly had the eerie sensation that someone was watching her. She glanced around quickly. Saw no one. Nonetheless the hairs on the back of her neck stood on end. As much as she tried to convince herself that her fears where hyped because of the horrendous accident on the set, that her mind was playing tricks on her, she was still unnerved.

Something was wrong here.

Something evil lurked in the darkened facades of the stores and shops, she could feel it.

The skin on the back of her arms prickled.

Turning down the music, she listened hard. Nothing out of the ordinary. All she heard were raindrops splashing on the ground, water gurgling in gutters and downspouts, her own breathing and . . . were there other footsteps? Quick-paced? *Running?* She swept her gaze anxiously side to side.

The street was empty.

Just as it was supposed to have been when Lucinda Rinaldi was shot.

A cold stone settled in the pit of her stomach. She kept moving, kicking it up a notch, her shoes hitting hard against the wet concrete. Only about a mile and a half to go. Then she'd be home where she'd lock the door behind her, tear off her wet clothes, and hit the shower.

Maybe she'd indulge in one glass of wine. Maybe two. Just to calm her jangled nerves.

The night closed in around her, streetlamps glowing ethereally in the dampness, the air heavy in her lungs, but despite the cold, she was sweating, moving through the city. Gritting her teeth she started up the slight hill, felt the strain in her calves and thighs.

Work through it. Push yourself. Show stupid smart-ass Jeff what you can do!

Again she heard the sound of footsteps but she attempted to ignore the ridiculous feeling that someone was following her. Come on, who could keep up with her anyway? She chided herself for her case of nerves.

Even if someone else was running, big deal.

It was the damned city, right?

People were out at all hours doing all sorts of things, including getting their miles in. Unless the other runner had a machete or a gun, he had the right to tear up the streets just as she was doing.

Yet, she was edgy.

Something seemed off.

She looked over her shoulder.

Again, nothing.

No one.

She swiped the rain from her eyes and told herself she should have taken an alternate route. Unable to shake the sensation that whoever or *whatever* was following her was getting closer, she yanked the earbud from her ear.

Nothing but the steady drip of the rain.

You're crazy, she told herself, and fumbled to put the wet bud back into her ear.

As she poked the earpiece back in, she saw something out of place in the shadows a half block ahead. Movement.

Her heart clutched.

It's nothing.

Again, a quick flash of shadow and darkness . . . someone stepping from around the corner of a building, lurking? She squinted. Another jogger? A woman?

Brandi felt a moment's relief. Just another night owl, maybe out to walk her dog, or have a cigarette or whatever. Nothing to get worried about. Still, she decided it might be wise to cross the street. The woman could be a crackpot or—

Holy shit! Was it . . . ? *Wait a second . . .* She couldn't believe her eyes. Was the woman out here in the middle of the damned night really Cassie Kramer?

Rain collected on Brandi's eyelashes. The night was blurry and wet. But the person looked like . . . no, no, no. Wait! Not *Cassie.* The woman in the shadows was Allie effin' Kramer herself!

Brandi raised an arm. To convey that she recognized Allie, which was ridiculous. But now that she was getting closer . . .

No . . . she was just a woman who looked like one of the Kramer sisters. Her imagination, spurred by adrenaline and her own fears about this damned street, was running amok. She was mistaken. The darkness had confused her.

Nonetheless, the woman was closing the gap between them, coming nearer. As she passed under a streetlamp, she was more visible.

Brandi's heart nearly stopped.

Something was off with Allie's face. Or Cassie's face. Or whoever's damned face. Whoever this woman was, her visage seemed to be melting off her damned skull! Panic burned through Brandi's blood. She lunged to the side, intent on crossing the street. Frantically, she unzipped a pocket on her running jacket, reached inside for her can of pepper spray, felt the metal cylinder. Good. Still running, she pulled the can from her pocket and it slipped, rolling off her fingertips to clatter to the street.

"No! Shit!"

She kept running, didn't have time to try to find the canister or chase it down.

Your phone. Grab your phone. Dial Jeff or nine-one-one or someone!

But the woman was too close. Brandi couldn't slow down. Couldn't risk dropping her cell.

Spurred by her own fears, she increased her pace, shooting past the other woman and watching from the corner of her eyes, as if in slow motion, the disfigured monster spin, raising her arm, a long-barreled pistol in her hand.

Jesus, no!

What? NO!

Brandi was sprinting now, her lungs burning, her legs aching. She cut to the sidewalk between two parked cars. If she could just reach the corner—

Pop!

Her body jerked.

Her legs gave way.

She flew forward, twisting to land hard on the rough street. Her hands scraped, her skull hit the asphalt with a loud crack, the skin ripping off her cheek. Burning pain screamed through her face and everything on the darkened street seemed to turn upside down. Overhead the light was still shining, but there was darkness beyond, the thrum of traffic on the freeway somewhere in the far distance. She heard her own breathing and her heart pumping as she tried to fight the blackness overcoming her and climb to her feet.

Her legs wouldn't move.

Deep inside she was cold, so very cold, yet she felt a warmth oozing from her. In a distant part of her brain she realized it was blood and wondered vaguely if anyone would come to help her, if she would survive. Then she remembered Lucinda Rinaldi lying on this same street.

Help me, she thought desperately, and tried to yell, to scream over the sound of footsteps rapidly approaching.

The assassin!

No, oh, no!

With all her strength, she managed to get her feet beneath her and push, scooting backward on the asphalt, hoping to find some kind of cover or that, please God, someone would come to her rescue.

Bam!

Her shoulder rammed into a parking meter, jarring her. But she didn't give up. Wrapping her fingers around the cold metal pole she attempted to pull herself to her feet, over the curb and out of the gutter where water was gurgling in a rush.

She was wobbly, her hands slick and unable to do what her brain commanded.

"Oh, God," she gasped, tasting salty blood on her lips.

And then the would-be killer was there. Standing in front of her. The woman who had leaped from the shadows to attack her.

Allie Kramer with her weird face. No. Now that her stalker was close she realized the disfigured face with the black eyeholes wasn't Allie Kramer at all, but the twisted face of Jenna Hughes.

What the hell?

Brandi's eyes rolled back in her head and as she passed out, she felt her head being lifted, something slick and cool being placed over her face and then there was nothing but blessed, silent darkness.

ACT IV

She pocketed the gun and ran, afraid that someone had seen her. Adrenaline fueled her, spurred her on. She spied a woman looking out the window and turned quickly down an alley. Without the mask she could be recognized, identified. No way could she let that happen!

Not here. Not now.

The air was thick, rain pummeling down from the starless sky. Her legs ached and her lungs felt as if they were on fire, but she needed distance, more distance, so she pressed on.

Keep moving!

Just one more block.

Then another.

Breathing was damn near impossible.

She rounded a corner and finally, gratefully slowed. Taking in huge gulps of air, she felt sweat slide down her back and prickle in her hair, but she was far enough away from the killing ground to avoid suspicion.

She hoped. Prayed.

Still, a little more distance wouldn't hurt. As fast as her painful legs allowed, she walked, down two blocks, around another corner, getting ever closer to downtown Portland, where the city sprawled along the shores of the Willamette. There were more people out, the segment of the population who preferred night to day. She kept her head turned away and in the ghostly glow of streetlights in the rain, no one seemed to recognize her.

She was heading to her car when she spied the Vintner's House, a cozy little bar Allie Kramer had been known to haunt. Discreet lighting. Private booths. Even a gas fireplace. No televisions, just soft, eclectic music.

A slow smile twisted over her lips.

Oh, yes, she remembered the place, had spent many hours within its walls and knew its idiosyncrasies. First though, she checked her reflection in a storefront window and though she was pale, she didn't notice any dark spots staining her sweater, no blood spatter visible. Finger-combing her hair, she tossed it a bit, then slipped into her cool persona, the one most people who knew her would recognize. The other side of her personality, the hysterical, freaked-out portion, she managed to, once again, tuck deep inside. She only let it free when it suited her purpose.

Satisfied, she walked into the bar and reflected upon what she'd done, how, once again, she'd outwitted them all. She could almost taste the reaction and ummm, the taste was sweet.

She surveyed the small dining area. All good. Taking a seat at the bar, she inwardly smiled as she ordered a glass of Allie's favorite wine. From the corner of her eye, she thought the bartender did a subtle double take. That was fine.

Did she get a few quizzical stares?

Oh, yes. Of course she did, but that was expected. Even necessary. Vintner's House had a no cell phone policy, which was perfect, and, for the privacy of its customers, no security cameras, or so the management claimed. There was always a chance some yahoo who didn't play by anyone else's rules might sneak out his phone and risk taking a shot, if he thought he recognized her. But so what? It wasn't a crime to have a glass of wine. That's all it was. All anyone would know for now.

Besides, she thought, warming inside, she liked to flirt with danger. Always had.

CHAPTER 27

From beneath her thick duvet, Rhonda Nash heard the ringing of her cell phone and groaned. She threw back the soft covers and felt the chill of the night. The window near her bed was cracked a bit, allowing a cold breeze that brought the steady plop of rain and the distant scream of sirens into the room. A glance at the clock on the night table told her the ugly truth—that it wasn't quite four in the damned morning. Whoever was calling wasn't the bearer of good news. Half asleep, she tried to pick up her cell and only managed to knock it from the night table.

"Damn." Rolling to the side of the bed and hanging over its edge, she saw the bright display indicating that Double T was on the other end of the wireless connection. No surprise there. Scooping the phone from the floor, she clicked on and said, "Nash," around a yawn.

"We got another one."

"Another one what?" she asked, blinking herself awake.

"Another victim wearing a mask."

She sat bolt upright. "A mask of Allie Kramer?" Suddenly completely awake, she flew out of bed and hit the switch for the bedside lamp in one fluid motion. As her feet hit the floor she started stripping out of her nightshirt on her way to the closet.

"Nope. This one's of Jenna Hughes."

She stutter-stepped. "The mother?"

"Right."

Nash's brain clicked into gear, dozens of questions forming. "Is it disfigured? Laminated? Same as the others?"

"Oh, yeah."

"Got an ID on the vic?"

"Yes, ma'am. The killer was kind enough to leave the victim's license in her jacket pocket."

"Great." Shivering, she found the clothes she'd been wearing the day before, the pants and blouse she'd dropped on a bench when she'd been getting ready for her bath.

"Twenty-nine-year-old single woman. Brandi Potts. Lives in the Pearl. Got a couple of uniforms on their way over to the address now."

"Good." Already things were moving along. She poked the speaker button and set the phone on the counter in the built-in dresser within the closet. "Cause of death?"

"Won't know until the ME arrives and—"

"Yeah, yeah, I know that," she said, bothered as she stepped into her slacks. "But is there anything obvious . . . ?"

"Aside from the gunshot wound to her chest?"

"Funny guy." She wasn't laughing.

"Looks like she was hit from behind. Not a through and through. Bullet's got to be lodged in the body somewhere."

She snapped her pants over her waist. "Eyewitnesses?"

"Already got a couple. We're checking. Door to door."

"Who called it in?"

"Bouncer from a club a couple of blocks away, on his way to his car."

She zipped up, threw on a bra. "Give me an address."

"Get this. The shooting took place on the very same street where Lucinda Rinaldi was hit."

"What?" She went cold inside, her movements slow as she pulled on her sweater. "Where the movie was shot?"

"Not the exact location, but about a block and a half down the street."

Nash's mind was whirling. "Was the victim connected to *Dead Heat?*"

"Unknown. Yet. Workin' on it."

"Holy shit." She yanked her head through the sweater's neck and finger-tousled her hair.

"My sentiments exactly."

He gave her the exact address and she said, "I'll be there in fifteen, maybe sooner." Leaning over, she found her boots where she'd left them, pulled them on, and zipped them up.

"For once traffic shouldn't hold you up."

She located her service weapon, slid it into her shoulder harness, then slipped on her jacket. "I'm on my way." Another murder? The victim left with a mask of Jenna Hughes? This time in Portland? What the hell was this all about? She slipped her phone into a pocket and sped down the stairs, her boots clattering loudly on each of Edwina's marble steps. At the front closet, she snagged her raincoat, then took another half flight of stairs to the garage. Her mind was as clear as if she'd had a shot of caffeine administered by a syringe right into her veins. On the fly she slapped first the button to open the garage, then the second one, to do the same for the gates.

She was in her little Ford and starting down the hill before the garage door had locked back into place again.

Ignoring the speed limit, she sped down the winding streets of Portland's West Hills. Traffic was nearly nonexistent, the beams of her headlights cutting through the darkness to catch on the beady eyes of a raccoon that stopped to stare a second before waddling into the thick laurels that surrounded the neighboring estates. Soon the shrubbery and manicured grounds of the houses upon the hills gave way to the edges of the city where apartments rose, traffic lights glowed, and the energy of Portland pulsed around her. The rain was ever-present, her wipers working overtime. As she neared the water-front, more cars and a few pedestrians were out, braving the rain in the very early morning hours.

Her thoughts were on the victim, crime scene, and killer. Who had done this? Why? What possible motive was behind this newest homicide? It didn't take a great leap of intuition to know the crimes were linked. Lucinda Rinaldi had been shot on this very street, and there was the mask again. What point was the killer trying to make? She couldn't help but feel that the murderer was taunting them by leaving a clue, toying with the cops and playing that psychological I'm Smarter Than All of You game. Or maybe, he or she was just whacked out, acting out some kind of inner fantasy.

Like someone who might have been a patient in a mental ward? Like Cassie Kramer, who so recently waltzed out the door of Mercy Hospital?

"Keep an objective point of view. Look over the facts," she said, not realizing she'd actually voiced her inner thoughts out loud. *Now who's mental?* God, she needed to get a dog or cat or some other living thing to talk to. Her jaw slid to the side and she cranked the wipers up a notch.

Frustrated, she drove around a final corner and spied three cruisers, lights flashing, blocking a section of the street. Another two were parked at the far end where already a news van was pulling up to the curb. Good. Maybe the press would be able to help this time. She squeezed her car into a spot marked as a loading zone, ignored the sign, climbed out of her car, and flipped up her hood. At the barricade blocking off the street she met a cop who looked about twenty-two and who went by the book, page by page, letter for letter. She showed him her badge, then crossed a string of yellow tape.

In a rainproof jacket and baseball cap, Double T was crouched near the body of a woman sprawled upon the street. She lay half on the sidewalk near a parking meter, her shoulders raised slightly on the curb, her legs stretched onto the pavement.

"So this is our girl?" she asked, and Double T turned his head to look up at her.

"Brandi Potts. Hit from behind."

Leaning closer, Nash studied the victim. She appeared to be about five foot six or seven. Her face was serene in death, her long hair, clamped back in a ponytail, appeared a deep red, darker because of the rain. Her body was lean and fit, dressed in tight gray running gear with reflective piping. Rings decorated her hands, some of them diamonds, but the third finger on her left hand was bare. "Single?"

"Still checking."

"Out for a late-night run? Or is she one of those super-early risers?" Jesus, who would jog at this hour in a rainstorm? *An idiot. Or a very dedicated runner.*

"Looks like."

"Alone?"

"We're still sorting that out. Appears that way, but you'd think she wouldn't go alone at this time of night."

"You'd think."

"As I said, we've got a couple of uniforms checking out her apartment to see if anyone's home. Thought you and I might roll over there."

Nash stared down at the victim's face, a beautiful face, a young face, wet with the rain. As always, Nash felt an overwhelming sense of despair when she viewed a young life taken by another. The senselessness of it all. She wondered at the psyche of human beings. Who would shoot this woman? Her gaze traveled from Brandi Potts's face to her torso and the thick, dark stain beneath her, staining her tight running jacket.

As if reading her thoughts, Double T said, "Found this searching for shell casings." He held up a small canister that winked in the weak lamplight.

"Mace?"

"Pepper spray."

"It was hers?" She nodded toward the dead woman.

"Won't know until we fingerprint it. Maybe not then. Waiting for the crime scene guys." He glanced down the street. "Where the hell are they? Shoulda been here by now."

"What about the ME?"

"On his way, too." Double T looked down at the body again. "Looks like the shooting occurred less than half an hour ago. That's according to the witnesses, and the body's still warm."

So less than an hour ago, this woman was alive. Until someone decided to change all that. Nash's gut tightened. "I'll want to talk to any witnesses. Keep them here." She looked again at the corpse, lips blue, skin ashen. "Where's the mask?"

"In my car. The first responders had the presence of mind to take pictures before removing it. They had to take it off to try to save the vic, but she was gone already."

"Forensics isn't going to like it."

"Too bad." He walked her to his Jeep and she noticed a small crowd was gathering around the barricades, people milling as near to the scene as they could get, vultures wearing rain hats and hoods, sweatshirts and slickers, even a couple with umbrellas, all twisting their necks to catch a peek.

"We need a shot of the people who've come out in the rain to get a look."

"Already got an officer on it."

"It's amazing that many people are up."

"Big city. Night dwellers."

"Well, I want to know who they are, what they saw." The story was definitely breaking as a reporter and cameraman were already talking to the by-the-book cop, trying to get information. Looking up, Nash saw lights from the surrounding apartments coming to life, the occupants inside standing at the windows or on the decks. A second news van arrived and was trying to wedge into a parking spot. "Looks like we're having a damned party here."

"You know this is always how it is." Unruffled by the looky-loos who bugged the crap out of Nash, Double T unlocked his vehicle, then reached onto the front seat and withdrew a plastic envelope. He handed it to Nash.

Through the clear plastic, she viewed the image, which was, as Double T had said, a warped, laminated picture of Jenna Hughes cut into a mask, complete with an elastic band. Jenna's eyes were missing, the two jagged black holes that remained only making the bizarre image appear more evil. "Jesus," Nash whispered as she flipped the envelope over and saw that on the back of the mask, just as Double T had said, was a single word scrawled wildly in red letters: *Mother.*

The meaning was obvious.

"So Jenna Hughes is Cassie and Allie Kramer's mother. Allie's missing, but Cassie's back in the area."

Double T nodded. "Yep."

Her eyes narrowed on the back of the mask and the stark clue. "Makes you wonder."

"Uh-huh."

"Hopefully, the killer left prints."

"Yep. We'll look into it."

"Does Jenna Hughes have any other kids?"

"Not that I know of."

"What about any other family members who are on the outs with her or jealous of her and her daughters? Someone with a grudge. A major grudge."

"Again, unknown."

"We should double-check."

He nodded, rain dripping from the brim of his cap just as the ME's van arrived. A second later the forensic team's vehicle appeared. "Showtime," she said, handing the plastic case back to her partner.

"Let's talk to the witnesses."

He locked the mask in his Jeep again, then hitched his chin to a heavy-set woman of about fifty. Pale as death, she was bundled in a ski jacket, jeans, and boots. She held an oversize umbrella aloft even though she stood under the awning of a store whose window display was filled with baby clothes and toys.

"Not a native," Nash observed, and ignored a sharp little pang when she noticed a pink raincoat and matching boots in the window. Quickly, she moved her gaze, turning her attention to the witness.

"Peggy Gates. Just moved here from Phoenix."

"Big change."

"Yep. She's recently divorced and living temporarily with her sister. Unit 806-B at the Jamison," he said, indicating a building that rose at least fifteen stories. "Anyway, she says she couldn't sleep, walked out on the balcony to look upriver. They've got a view of the Marquam and Hawthorne bridges, I guess. But 'something' on the street below caught her eye. Probably movement. She didn't actually see the attack, but noticed a woman running toward the river, that direction."

"She's certain it was a woman?"

"No. She admitted it might be a small, thin man with long, dark hair, but the way the person moved, she's leaning toward a female."

Nash let her gaze follow along the path Gates had described.

"From her balcony, Gates could only see the victim's head, but she realized the person needed help, so she hurried downstairs to check it out and flipped out when she saw the mask."

"She didn't call nine-one-one immediately?"

"She had to run back upstairs for her phone. Then she called. But by then she heard sirens heading this way."

"The bouncer called it in."

"Right."

"The guy next to her, I'm guessing."

"Bingo."

Standing a few feet from Gates was a burly African-American man who stood over six feet tall. His head was shaved and earrings glittered in the lamplight. In the driving rain he was bareheaded and wearing only a thin jacket over jeans and a black T-shirt. With his muscular arms folded over his chest, he looked like a black version of Mr. Clean.

"Conrad Jones," Double T said. "Works down at The Ring, three blocks east."

"Guess I'd better talk to them."

As she walked to the small group beneath the awning, she thought again about the mask and the word *Mother* scrawled over its back. It seemed like a too-obvious clue pointing toward either Allie or Cassie Kramer.

An icy drop of rain slid down her neck and she shivered. It definitely felt like she was being played, and Detective Rhonda Nash didn't like it one bit.

"In here."

Trent's voice stopped Cassie cold.

She'd prayed he was asleep as she stepped through the front door of his house. She was late. Very late. He was obviously waiting up for her in the den.

Cassie had lost track of time. Again. Worse yet, she didn't know where she'd been. She remembered feeling as if she'd seen Allie and then following the bus and then . . . nothing. She couldn't remember leaving the city, merging onto I-84 to head east. Somehow, she'd maneuvered her way back to Falls Crossing and Trent's ranch, but she'd zoned out, driving by rote, her gas tank nearly as drained as the battery of her mobile phone.

She'd finally snapped out of her reverie or whatever it was and become aware of where she was when she'd turned onto the lane leading to this farmhouse and parked near the garage. Then, gathering her courage and hoping Trent was fast asleep, she'd dashed through the storm to the wide porch, getting soaked in the process.

She'd been careful of the door, winced when she heard it creak, and then had been greeted by Trent's low voice.

Now she closed the door behind her.

A low *woof* from the den followed by clicking toenails on hardwood told Cassie that she'd woken the dog as well. She'd hoped to sneak in quietly, not waking either man or beast. It looked like she failed on both counts.

Hud appeared in the doorway to the den, his tail wagging wildly and thudding against the jamb when he saw her. Wriggling, he sidled up to greet her with happy little yips. "Late, huh?" She bent down to pat his soft head. "Yeah. You're a good boy," she assured the dog, then straightened. Her hair was wet, her jeans damp, and the cold seemed to seep all the way to her bones.

She walked into the den. Trent was seated on the couch. No lamps had been lit and the television was dark. The only light came from the dying embers of the fire.

"You waited up?"

"Yeah." He was pissed.

"You didn't need to—"

"Didn't I?" he snapped, his face in shadow. "When all hell's been breaking out? If you haven't noticed, people all around you have been disappearing or assaulted or killed."

"Still."

"Still what? I shouldn't have worried? Is that what you're saying?" He climbed to his feet and for a second a bit of firelight reflected in his eyes. "Hell yes, I waited up. More than that, I tried to chase you down."

She felt her heart sink.

"What was I supposed to do? You wouldn't answer my calls. And when you finally texted that you were on your way home, I came back here." He rubbed the back of his neck and glanced pointedly at the digital display of the time on the television. "That was hours ago."

"I . . . I know."

"What have you been doing?"

"Driving around. Thinking," she hedged as he crossed the short distance between them. What could she say that didn't sound like a lie or whacked or both? How could she explain losing two hours?

"In the middle of the damned night? When people have been killed?"

"In LA. Lucinda was—"

"Lucky," he cut her off. He was towering over her, his face etched with concern. "If you can call it that. She could have died just as easily. What were you thinking?"

"My cell phone was nearly dead."

"Nearly."

"I thought I should save it for an emergency."

"You don't get it, do you?" he said, placing his hands on her shoulders. Warm, strong hands. Deeply worried eyes. "This is a fucking emergency. You're living it."

She wanted to argue, started, then thought better of it. "Okay. All right. I should have called."

She could see him struggle to rein in his own ragged emotions. He dropped his hands and took a step back. "So why the hell did you meet Brandon McNary? I thought you didn't like the son of a bitch."

"I didn't. I don't."

"Then why? What information did he have that was so all-fired important that you had to go racing off in the middle of the night?"

She crossed the room and put some space between them as she stood before the glass door of the wood stove and felt the heat radiating, warming the back of her legs. "He thought he'd seen Allie, in Oregon City, and of course he couldn't get near to her. When he tried to chase her down? *Poof!*" Cassie snapped her fingers. "She was gone."

"Big surprise," he said sarcastically.

"And then he got this text that he thought was from her. It came from an untraceable cell phone."

Trent's eyes seemed to bore into her and she shifted slightly.

"All it said was 'I'm okay.'"

He waited, then asked, "That's it?"

"Uh-huh."

"The text could have come from anyone."

"He's convinced it was from Allie."

"Someone's just messing with him," Trent said, taking a seat on the arm of the couch. He was close enough to touch her again, but didn't reach forward.

"That's what I told him."

"Or *he's* messing with you."

"I suppose."

"He could have sent the text to himself from a burner phone he bought. It wouldn't take a genius for him to leave his real cell at his place, drive ten miles away, to like, oh, I don't know, Oregon City? Then he could call himself so that if the police ever got involved, they could trace the ping from a tower there. They might think the message was legit. As long as no one saw him or his vehicle, he'd be home free."

Cassie thought about the older Chevy Tahoe Brandon had been driving. Definitely not his style.

Trent added, "Or he could have had someone else make the call, then toss the phone into the river near the falls. The fact that he got a text from someone doesn't mean it was Allie."

"I know. I essentially told him the same thing." She was finally starting to warm up.

"Don't you think it's weird that he lured you to leave, told you to not tell anyone, right? Why not go to the police? Why target you?"

"He knows I'm trying to find Allie."

"So are the cops." Trent's eyes narrowed. "I don't like it."

"I don't either. But Trent, I can't leave any stone unturned. And I can't go to the police. Detective Nash already thinks I somehow had something to do with Allie's vanishing act or . . . or whatever." She closed her eyes and was suddenly dead-tired and angry as hell. "None of this makes any sense." She just wanted to collapse and forget about everything. She felt as if she could sleep for hours, maybe even days.

"Hey," Trent said. "You okay?" He took her hand and made a sound of dismay. "You're freezing."

"I'm fine." She was still chilled but didn't want to admit it. "Just a little wet."

"A lot wet." He smiled faintly in that heartbreaking way that always got to her, touched her at a very private level. Though not exactly Hollywood handsome, Trent Kittle was rugged-looking, almost rangy, his face interesting, his eyes sometimes distant, other times focused sharply, his nose no longer straight, if it ever had been.

He found a blanket on the couch and wrapped it around her shoulders. The kind gesture nearly broke her heart. "You should go up and take a hot shower."

"Sounds like heaven."

"Just a sec." His fingers wrapped around her wrist, pressing warmly against the skin just above her palm, touching the spot where she'd been scratched.

"What?" She tried not to concentrate too hard on his skin touching hers, but her mind was fractured.

"You should know that your friend . . . Rinko?"

"Yes . . . Rinko." She silently cursed the breathless quality to her voice.

"You were right about him. He's like some kind of genius when it comes to cars. Carter took the information Rinko gave us about the Santa Fe to some guy he used to work with at the state police."

"Larry Sparks." She managed to draw her hand away from his, tried to quiet her hammering heart.

"Right. Anyway, Sparks did some legwork and started chasing down owners of all the 2007 Hyundai Santa Fes matching the description Rinko gave us."

"And?"

"And he got some hits. Rinko only failed with the whole bucking bronco imagery, but Carter's working on that, too. So," he finished, "it's still a long shot, but at least now it seems we may be able to track down whoever was in your room at the hospital. There's a chance she's not a ghost, but a real live person with a driver's license."

Relief was instantaneous. All her worries that the nurse had been conjured by her own frail mind dissipated. Cassie had almost come to believe she'd imagined the woman. "Thank God."

"We're not out of the woods yet," he said, and his gaze locked with hers.

He was right, of course. This bit of information about the Santa Fe didn't mean much, at least not yet. But, it was something. Maybe somehow this whole mess would be sorted out.

As if reading her mind, he said, "We'll figure this out, Cass."

"Is that before or after I end up back in the hospital or behind bars?"

"Pessimist."

"I guess."

"Don't worry."

She nearly laughed out loud. "Easier said than done."

"Trust me."

How long had it been since she'd been able to do just that?

"So you're in this with me?" she asked, remembering how he'd said he wanted to get back together with her, that he didn't want to divorce. "Despite me taking off and not telling you where I was going, you're still on board?"

"Yep. You can't get rid of me that easy. But I still think this is something that should be handled by the police."

"If only it were that simple."

"It is." When she didn't respond, he said, "I'm serious." His gaze held hers and she felt her pulse go wild at being this close to him. She swallowed with difficulty, her mind wandering down a dangerous, sexual path. She remembered the nights she'd spent with him, the way his skin rubbed against hers, his hot breath playing along her flesh, how he pressed urgent kisses at her hairline on her nape. Often she'd lain facedown in the pillow, the length of his body stretched over hers, his chest hairs scraping her back and lower as he'd slid against the curve of her spine and the rise of her buttocks.

Her throat went dry as erotic images played through her mind.

His hands covering hers, linking his fingers with hers, wet lips caressing her shoulders, his knees impatiently pushing her legs apart. She remembered all too clearly how it felt when he entered her body, how much she'd ached for him. She licked her lips, felt a familiar yearning deep within and realized how much she wanted him to touch her so intimately again.

Oh. Dear. God.

He was staring at her and sensed his own thoughts were following a similar path.

Heat swept up the back of her neck. Why was it that her emotions were always so raw whenever he was near?

Slowly he rubbed his chin, fingers scraping against his beard-shadowed jaw. As if he were struggling to stay on track, he said, "You know, Cass, this is dangerous business and I—"

"Just shut up and kiss me," she cut in, unable to stand the tension a second longer. Before he could react, she threw her arms around his neck and pulled his head to hers, kissing him hard. Her lips pressed to his, her heart pumping wildly with a storm of pent-up desire that she couldn't fight a second longer.

He kissed her back like a drowning man, his mouth open and hungry, his tongue seeking hers. Warm. Wet. Demanding. Strong arms surrounded her and he held her against him as they tumbled together off the arm of the couch and onto the cushions. He breathed her name against her ear and she melted inside. Though at some level she knew she was making a mistake of immense proportions, she just didn't care. Not in these dark, small hours of the morning, when his hands were rough and warm against her skin, when the taste of him brought back memories of making love for hours, when she could drown in the earthy male scent of him.

Yes, she might be falling over the brink of an emotional ravine, stepping into a calamity of untold personal pain, but right now, at this moment in time, thinking of the erotic images in the hours ahead, she didn't give one single damn.

CHAPTER 28

Cassie slept like a rock.

After making love with Trent until dawn, she'd burrowed deep into the covers, felt his arms surround her, then crashed for hours. When she finally awoke it was nearly eleven. He was no longer with her, the bed where he'd lain cold, reality hitting her like a freight train.

Today she had to face Detective Nash and whoever else in the Portland Police Department. Nash was gunning for her, she knew it, and then there was also Detective Hayes in LA. Surely he'd somehow be involved. Their conversations had been too short to satisfy him. He might even have flown up here to interview (translation: interrogate) her, or Skype in, or whatever.

She wasn't looking forward to any of it, and as she stared at the ceiling, she wondered if there was any way to avoid the inevitable.

Her stomach was in knots at the prospect.

Rolling to the side of the bed she found Hud, his snout resting on the mattress. "Geez, dog. You scared me!" His wet nose was only inches from hers, his brown eyes bright with excitement, his whole body wiggling.

"Yeah, I know. Time to get up and face the bad music."

She showered and put on the clothes she'd left strewn on the floor, then headed downstairs, the dog leading the way.

In the kitchen, coffee was warming in a carafe on a Mr. Coffee. She poured herself a cup, scrounged around in the near-empty refrigerator. No cream. Black would have to do, she decided as she spied a note tucked under the salt and pepper shakers on the table.

Didn't want to wake you.
Doing chores and running to town.
Breakfast in the oven.
Back soon.
T

So much for any sign of affection. No "Love you" or "So glad you stayed over" or even a little "xoxo."

"Come on, what did you expect?" she asked aloud, and walked to the window over Trent's ancient sink. Cradling her cup, she stared through the glass to survey the acres that made up this side of Trent's farm. The rain had finally let up though the day remained gray, dark clouds roiling overhead, the ground sodden, wet grass bent over. Near the pump house, rhododendrons and azaleas shivered in a bit of wind.

Her car was where she'd parked it, but Trent's truck was missing.

She felt a pang of disappointment and told herself she was being ridiculous. Just a few days ago she'd been set on divorcing him. Now, ending her marriage was the furthest thing from her mind.

She took a sip of coffee and considered. Was she signing herself up for another emotional roller-coaster ride?

A plate of bacon and toast was warming in the oven. Gingerly, she carried the hot plate to the table. Her stomach growled before she dug in. God, she was hungry!

She demolished the bacon, saving just one bite for the dog that snapped it up on the fly and looked eagerly for more. "Sorry, Bud. That's it." She plopped the last bite of toast into her mouth and heard the rumble of an engine and crunch of tires on gravel. "Maybe Daddy's home." As she dropped her plate into the sink where a frying pan was soaking, she peered through the window to see Trent jogging to the back door.

Her heart did a quick little flip as she heard his boots hit the first step of the back porch. Hud gave an excited yip, then raced to the back door and stared at it as if willing the thick panels to open. Then Trent rushed in, his face set and hard, his lips compressed.

"Hey, Cowboy," she started, then caught his mood. "What's wrong?"

"Do you know a woman by the name of Brandi Potts?"

The name rang distant bells, but she couldn't place it. Slowly shaking her head, she said, "Maybe I've heard the name . . ."

"Maybe as an extra on *Dead Heat*?"

"Possibly. Why?"

"You haven't seen the news?"

"No . . . I just got up. What happened?"

"She was murdered last night."

"What?" Cassie gasped. "*Murdered?*"

"Gunned down on the very street where *Dead Heat*'s final scene took place, about a block away from where Lucinda Rinaldi was shot. It's all over the news."

"My God." She couldn't believe it. Didn't want to.

"That's the second one with ties to the movie. Third, if you think Lucinda Rinaldi was an intended victim." He stared at her and didn't say the obvious, the unspoken thought: *Fourth, if Allie turns up dead.*

Shaken, her knees suddenly weak, Cassie leaned against the counter. "I don't get it. Why? This is horrible." She didn't know Brandi Potts, couldn't even dredge up a picture of the woman in her mind, but she felt a deep, overwhelming sadness. "How? What happened?" she asked as he took a seat at the table.

"Details are sketchy. I heard about it on the news this morning, called Carter and he checked, then called me back. Apparently she was out running late last night, early in the morning really, and her route took her on that same street, which is where she was attacked. Looks like a gunshot."

"Like the others." A coldness that started in her soul swept over her. She rubbed her arms, tried to think straight. Another murder? Why? She sat down opposite Trent.

"Yeah."

"What the hell's going on?"

The question was rhetorical, but he answered with, "I wish I knew. You think this has anything to do with McNary? Him being in town?"

"Because he was out last night? I don't know. The guy's a prick, yeah, but a murderer? That just doesn't seem right." Then she caught his drift and sucked in a breath. "*I* was out last night. Don't tell me that just because I was out, you think—"

"Of course not." His gaze held hers across the table. "But other people might. The cops."

Her stomach did a nosedive. He was right. She thought about asking him to lie for her, to say that they'd spent the entire night together, but she didn't. Couldn't. Instead she tried to concentrate on what had happened last night, the quicksilver moments in time that didn't hold together. Some events, though, were clear. "You know, I thought I was being followed last night. I mean I heard someone behind me on my way to the car after meeting with McNary."

She saw the muscles in his jaw tighten. "What happened?"

"Nothing, I ran into a big guy, a preacher, or maybe a priest, I think. He wore a clerical collar, but no one was following me and then . . . then, I know this sounds crazy, but I thought I saw Allie."

He froze. "You saw your sister?"

"I thought so at the time, for a minute anyway. She was standing in an alcove, a doorway to a coffee shop. Maybe waiting for a bus?"

"But you're not certain?"

"Of course not. It was dark and I was already freaked, thinking someone was behind me." She then explained where she'd been, how the woman she'd thought was her sister had disappeared when the bus rolled up. "I didn't know if 'Allie' got on, so I followed after the bus. I pulled up next to it at a traffic light and looked at the passengers inside, but I didn't see her. There were only four passengers and none of them remotely resembled my sister."

"Why didn't you tell me this last night?"

"Because I was exhausted and upset and you were already freaked out and then . . . and then, we . . . well, you know . . ."

"And then you kissed me and we ended up in bed." His unemotional voice worried her.

"Fast forward and I woke up, you were gone. So I didn't have much of a chance to explain." She couldn't help the bit of irritation in her words. Did he really think she was somehow complicit?

"You followed the bus to the end of the line? You talked to the driver?"

Uh-oh. Here's where it got murky. "I don't know."

His eyebrows slammed together. "You don't know?"

She bristled a bit. How could she explain? "That's right. It's . . . it's just that." Rather than let her anger get ahold of her again, she expelled a long breath. "It's just that I kind of blacked out, I guess."

"What do you mean, '*kind* of blacked out'? Either you're awake or you're unconscious."

"I know it's hard to understand, but it's happened before." He was staring at her so hard she pushed her chair back and stalked to the sink, looking out the window once more. "It's one of the reasons I checked into Mercy Hospital." Her insides churned as she admitted things she hated to acknowledge, even to herself. "You remember," she said, her voice softer with the memories, her fingers gripping the edge of the counter. "When we lived together, once in a while I was . . . a little fuzzy about things."

He nodded slowly.

"You thought I was being . . . what did you call it? 'Distant'? I think, or 'moody'?"

A muscle worked in his jaw and for a second he looked away. "I accused you of being out of it and avoiding the issues when we fought."

"Right." Sometimes she hadn't even really understood what they'd been arguing about. For years she'd hidden the secret that there were times when she couldn't account for hours of her life. "Well, it appears I really was mentally checked out. I don't know how else to explain it. I functioned, but I couldn't recall how I did what I did, how I got where I ended up, who I'd seen. It seems to occur when I'm stressed and last night it happened again. I know I drove here, but for the life of me I don't remember one thing about it. Not another car. Not merging onto the freeway. No town that I passed."

He was staring at her hard and she could almost see his mental gears meshing as pieces of the puzzle fell into place. She felt foolish for never confiding in him before, but she'd been scared that he would find her too bizarre, that he would leave her, when all along it had been she who had one foot out the door. She wouldn't allow herself to trust him, because she couldn't trust herself. "The truth is, Trent, I don't even remember leaving Portland, don't know what bridge I took, what area of town I cruised through. I just know that somehow I drove back here." She felt tears burn behind her eyes, but she refused to cry. As a distraction she found her cup of half-drunk coffee and topped it off from the glass carafe still warming in the Mr. Coffee. Her hands trembled.

"Does anyone else know about your blackouts?"

She shook her head. Took a sip. "Well, my doctor, of course."

"Not your mom?"

"I don't think so. I didn't have them as a child," she explained, remembering. "They started after the kidnapping, when she and I were nearly killed by that psycho ten years ago. Jenna didn't notice and I lied to cover up, and she was so upset herself, worried about me and Allie, trying to get her own head straight, deal with her own emotional damage. Carter was around, he helped, but I couldn't tell them about the blackouts. And they only occurred once in a while. Jenna and Carter chalked up the missing hours to me being rebellious, a secretive teenager who didn't want her privacy invaded, so I bluffed my way through."

"And then before anyone became suspicious or put two and two together, you took off for California."

"The first chance I got."

Rubbing his chin, his gaze still fastened on her, Trent said, "So when we were together, here in Falls Crossing, before you took off for California?"

"The blackouts were a big reason I had to leave. It scared the hell out of me to be so involved with you when I was barely over Josh and what happened to him. I was afraid that I was rebounding." Sighing, she looked straight at him. "You scared me. How hard I fell for you? I didn't trust it. Didn't trust myself and I didn't want you to find out. So I left."

"And when I followed you?"

She glanced out the window to the dark clouds scudding overhead, and decided the time for secrets was over. This was it, confession time. First with Trent, then later with Detective Nash. "When I saw you in LA I wanted to avoid you. I didn't think starting up with you again was smart, but well . . ." She smiled sadly into her cup. "I kind of find you irresistible."

He made a sound of disbelief. "You have a funny way of showing it."

"Maybe finding someone irresistible isn't such a good thing. It can be dangerous."

"I know," he admitted. "Boy, do I know."

Rather than stare at him and wonder if he really did feel as deeply for her, as emotionally strung out with her as she was with him, she ignored the implications, didn't want to consider the odds of their marriage surviving. "I thought that if I left this town, where all the trauma happened, the blackouts would go away. But they didn't. They happened in LA, too." She sent him a quick glance. "Looks like I was wrong. Again." A final gulp of coffee, then she tossed the dregs into the sink. "It's getting to be a habit with me."

He scraped back his chair to get to his feet. "This isn't good, Cass."

"Tell me something I don't know."

He slung an arm over her shoulder. "But it's worse that you blacked out last night, considering that you were in Portland when Brandi Potts was killed."

Horrified, she whispered, "You don't believe me!"

"I do," he said with conviction, "I do. But it's not me you have to worry about."

She shook her head and felt her anger ramping up again. "The police are going to think I had something to do with the poor woman's death, aren't they? I didn't know Brandi Potts. Why in heaven's name would I want to kill her or Holly or anyone!"

"Cass, I'm just telling you—"

"I get it, Trent. Truly," she cut in bitterly. "You're just trying to make sure I understand what's going on here, what the cops will think, what some of the supposed circumstantial evidence suggests. They probably think I've got Allie stashed away somewhere. Maybe I stuffed her body in a closet . . . maybe one of yours. We'd better check."

"You're forgetting I'm on your side."

"Are you?" she threw back at him. "Sometimes I wonder!" She tossed her hair over her shoulder, glared at him a second, then suddenly felt suffocated. Squeezed. Like she was in a room with no doors and the walls were slowly moving closer. "I need some air." Without further explanation she stormed out of the kitchen, out the back door, and down the steps.

Hud was right on her heels, sneaking through the open door before it banged shut. Even the shepherd's enthusiasm, as he bounded in front of her, did nothing to quell the storm of emotions raging inside. She stalked to the fence, her boots sinking into the soggy grass, and felt the cool air against her skin. The horses were scattered in the fields, mares with heavy bellies, tails and manes caught in the breeze as they grazed. Without a care in the world. The frigid air smelled fresh and if she closed her eyes maybe she could pretend that all this trauma would go away.

Fat chance.

She heard the door of the house open and close, then the sound of steady footsteps on the gravel.

She set her jaw. She didn't want to talk to Trent until she calmed down, until she could make some sense of what was going on. Deep down, she understood he was just trying to help, but damn it, she *knew* the cops had her at the top of their suspect list. She *knew* that oh-so-calm Detective Nash considered Cassie a prime suspect in her sister's disappearance and probably the murders. She *knew* things looked bad, and in the back of her mind she wondered again if she was being used, a pawn in some macabre chess game, easily sacrificed, but for what? Why would anyone do that? And who would know where she would be at any given minute? For the love of God, even she didn't have a clue sometimes when the blackouts happened.

When the blackouts happened.

The words rang in her brain and she blinked.

When they happened . . . the timing . . . *could someone know?*

Her mind started spinning. No. That was crazy, wasn't it? Or could someone know about the blackouts? Someone who could use them to his or her advantage? How? She bit her lip. Of course people did know of her condition. It was documented in the hospital. But that was the very hospital where she'd thought she'd seen the nurse in the cape, the nurse who'd told her Allie was alive.

Cassie shook her head. Was this too far-fetched? But it felt so right.

Her mental state wasn't exactly a secret. While she hadn't announced the fact that she'd checked herself into the psych ward at Mercy Hospital, the press had gotten wind of it and the story, along with the mystery of Allie's disappearance, had been tabloid fodder for weeks. How many times had she spied her own face squared off with Allie's, the two pictures photoshopped together and super-imposed over the shadowy image of a creepy old hospital in the background? Anyone who walked through a checkout line at most stores in America could learn about the time she'd spent under a psychiatrist's care in a Portland hospital.

But who?

And why?

If someone realized she could lose track of time, then ostensibly she could be made to appear culpable because of her own weakness. Really? Could that be done? It would have to be someone very close. Someone she knew or someone just a little further away, in the fringes of her acquaintances, someone hiding in the perimeter, watching her, someone who lurked nearer than she imagined?

A shiver ran down her spine.

Or was she just making excuses? Letting her paranoia run wild? She needed to pull herself together. Before her damned meeting with Detective Nash.

She heard Trent approach, felt his touch on her shoulder as he stood next to her. "Hey."

From the corner of her eye, she noticed the concern on his features, the shadows under his eyes. He, too, was suffering.

"I didn't mean to upset you, but you needed to be forearmed. I don't want you to be blindsided. Okay? You need to be ready."

She wanted to sink against him, but resisted. "This isn't just an interview, is it? The cops are going to arrest me."

"Nah." He shook his head, his eyes narrowing a bit, the first signs of crow's-feet gathering near the corners of his eyes. "Don't think so. Neither does Carter."

She stared. "You discussed it with him?" For years her husband

and stepfather couldn't stand to be in the same room with each other. Now they were allies? In cahoots? Talking behind her back?

"No, but I'm pretty sure he would have advised you not to talk without a lawyer present if he thought there was any threat of you being arrested."

"I don't know how many ways to say it, but I'm innocent. I don't need a damned lawyer."

He didn't reply. And the silence stretched between them, only the sigh of the wind and rustle of leaves in the trees audible. The hand on her shoulder gripped a little tighter as he finally said, "We'll get through this."

"Will we?" She sounded bitter and told herself he was only trying to help.

"Come on, Cass. You know it." He hugged her, rotating her so that he could brush a kiss across her forehead.

Her heart nearly broke.

"You ready to come into the house now or do you want to stand out here and freeze?"

"I'll be in. Just a sec, though. I need to grab a change of clothes— these are yesterday's—from the car. Oh, and my cell. And a damned charger if I brought one."

"If you didn't, I'm pretty sure I've got one you can borrow."

"Great."

Together they walked to her car. Her phone was where she'd left it on the passenger seat. "It's probably dead," she said, opening the door, "and filled with a kabillion messages from Whitney Stone. She still wants more information for upcoming episodes."

"It's hell to be popular," he said, and she shot him a look that could cut through granite. He held up his hands, palms out, as if surrendering. "Hey, just trying to lighten the mood."

"It didn't help." But she smiled and the icy wind blowing down the Columbia Gorge didn't seem quite so cold. Scooping up the phone, she noticed that the cell's battery life was hovering at two percent. She had four text messages. As predicted, three were from Whitney Stone. The fourth text had no name attached to it, but Cassie recognized the number, and she nearly dropped the damned phone. The number listed was composed of the same digits as the call on Brandon McNary's phone. The hairs on the back of her neck rose as she read the simple message:

Help me.

CHAPTER 29

Trent took Cassie's phone. "Don't buy into it," he warned, reading the text message and seeing the horror on his wife's face. "This isn't from Allie."

"How do you know?" Cassie's eyes were round, her face white, her hands shaking. She looked as if she might collapse against her Honda at any second.

She tried to grab the phone back, but he didn't release it. "Let me text back."

"To this number?"

"Yes!"

He hesitated. Felt a blast of wind against the back of his neck. What would sending a message back hurt? Or who would it hurt? Cassie? Even more than she was wounded now? Already she was embroiled eyeball deep in whatever this deadly mess was.

"I just want to ask who it is," she said.

He glanced at the screen. "'Help me'?" he read aloud. "Come on, Cass. Does that sound like her? You know better. When has Allie ever asked for help?"

"This is different."

"We don't know that."

She rubbed her arms as if chilled to the bone. "Why not?"

"I don't like you engaging with whoever sent it."

"I have to know."

"Oh, hell." He handed her the phone and while the battery life indicator glowed red, she typed: who is this?

"Okay," he said, "let's go charge it. And see what happens. But no matter what, when you go meet with Detective Nash today, you hand over this phone. Maybe the cops can trace the calls somehow. They've got all kinds of sophisticated equipment and techies and computer experts. Let them deal with it."

"After we get a response."

"No matter what. Or we can take it to Carter right now, if you like that option better. He's a damned PI with connections with the sheriff's department."

"But she contacted *me*."

"*Someone* contacted you. And I'd bet my best horse, the gray gelding over there"—he pointed to a small herd and the dappled horse kicking up his hooves and running, black tail aloft across the field—"that someone other than Allie sent that text, that someone's playing you."

"Why?"

"Good question. God, I don't know." He grabbed her hand and linked her smaller chilled fingers through his. "But let's find out." He shot her a look as he tugged on her hand. "I think we should start with Brandon McNary. He got a message, too, right? Something equally mysterious?"

"His said, 'I'm okay.' "

"What kind of message is that? Huh? Last night she was 'okay' and now she's not? She needs 'help'? From you? Does that even make sense?"

She didn't answer.

"Of course it doesn't. Come on." He started striding to the house, pulling Cassie along the path, the dog galloping ahead.

"So what does?"

"Good point." That was the problem. Nothing about Allie Kramer's disappearance and the murders of the other women and the damned text messages meant anything. At least not to him.

As they reached the porch, she said, "We're not giving Carter my phone."

"Why not?"

"It'll just upset Jenna. Let's . . . let's wait. I'll hand it over to the police when I go there this afternoon."

He sent her a disbelieving glance.

"Swear to God," she said, lifting a hand as if she were testifying on a Bible. At least for now she appeared less shaken. "Maybe before then, we'll get a response."

"Maybe," he hedged, opening the door and feeling as if by answering the text, engaging with whoever was on the other end of the wireless connection, they were walking into a trap.

*   *   *

Leaning back in her chair, Nash squeezed her eyes shut, then whipped her head around, cracking her neck. After eight or nine hours at her desk all of her muscles were tight, a headache beginning to pound at the base of her skull. She felt a second's relief before her muscles clenched again.

Her eyes burned from hours reading through files and notes, doing research on the computer, and just plain lack of sleep. In the early morning hours, once she and Double T were finished at the crime scene, she'd known she was too keyed up to go home and try to get a few more hours of shut-eye, so she'd driven directly to the office. The predawn hours had been quiet, the department nearly empty, so she'd taken the time to compare every detail of the murders of Holly Dennison in LA and Brandi Potts here, in Portland.

So many similarities.

So many loose ends.

With only the weakest of connections.

Her headache was starting to throb.

It didn't help that over the last few hours the office had become a madhouse with officers, suspects, and witnesses coming and going, the shuffle of footsteps and buzz of conversation accompanying them. Telephones jangled or blipped out messages, a printer or fax machine was endlessly chunking out pages near the reception area, and from every direction the frenetic click of keyboards could be heard. Despite the soundproofing of the movable walls, the department as a whole was a cacophony of sounds, all of which, today, permeated the insulation to reverberate in Nash's skull.

She found a bottle of ibuprofen and washed down two capsules with the dregs of her cold coffee. Her damned phone hadn't stopped ringing since seven this morning and as the day had worn on and news of the latest homicide had hit the Internet, the phone calls had only gotten more frequent.

For her part, she was pushing the lab for immediate results, asking for a priority on Brandi Potts's autopsy, wanting comparisons of the bullets found in each of the victims, needing to know if there were any fingerprints or DNA left on the masks. The ME had complied, the bullet that had buried deep in Brandi Potts already retrieved.

So far today Nash had been contacted by five different reporters, all of whom she'd referred to the Public Information Officer. A few tips were coming in as well, some about the shooting, and, of course, the usual Allie Kramer sightings.

If I had a dollar for every time someone thought they'd seen the missing actress, I'd be rich, she thought, and knew it would only get worse. As the release date of *Dead Heat* got closer, the number of calls from people who claimed to have caught a glimpse of the missing star had seemed to increase exponentially. The press had gotten wind of that little detail too, all of which had created some weird macabre buzz about the film.

Allie Kramer.

Her disappearance was at the heart of this, Nash was certain, she just didn't know how. But a prime opportunity to question witnesses was at hand. Tomorrow night. The all-star bash for the movie's premiere. People involved with the movie and the party had been flying up and down the coast. Los Angeles to Portland and back again. Nash had checked.

So it wasn't as if Cassie Kramer were the only suspect, just the most visible at this point in time.

Nash stood and stretched, loosening her muscles, but her mind was still on the case. She could believe that Cassie might have been involved in the disappearance of her sister, they had a documented volatile relationship, but why kill the other women? Was she really that far around the bend? Is that why they were decorated with distorted visages of the women closest to Cassie? Did she have to mock their relationships by scribbling them on the back of the mask? Did she need to kill Jenna and Allie over and over again and use other women even slightly associated with them as her victims? What kind of psychosis was that?

It just didn't quite fit. Not in Nash's mind.

At first Nash had thought Brandi Potts had no connection to the other women and the filming of *Dead Heat,* but that wasn't exactly true. As it turned out, when Potts's boyfriend, Jeffrey Conger, was interviewed and asked, he'd said that Brandi had been an extra in the movie, in fact she'd been on the set the day that Lucinda Rinaldi had been shot, but, no, he didn't think she knew either of the Kramer sisters. Of course he'd been broken up at the time, woken from a deep sleep, to find out that his live-in girlfriend wasn't just not in their shared condo, but that she was dead, killed by an unknown assassin.

He, who worked for a day-trading company, had been devastated by the news and had seemed genuinely shell-shocked. He'd even called Nash this morning, just after seven, wanting information and offering any help, but when Nash had asked him questions on the phone, he hadn't been able to come up with any new information to aid the investigation. According to Jeffrey, Brandi, who worked in a local bank in the trust department, didn't have an enemy in the world. Originally from Seattle, she was sweet and kind and made friends easily. They'd been college sweethearts and Brandi had followed him to Portland when he'd taken a job in a trading company downtown. They'd had plans to marry, though he hadn't yet gotten down on one knee and made it official. He had, though, put the ring she'd shown him in a local jewelry store on some kind of layaway plan and was making payments on it. He'd planned to propose at the first University of Washington home football game this fall, had hoped to get her sorority sisters on board, maybe pop the question while captured on the Jumbotron or whatever it was that filmed the game. He'd started choking up and had to end the conversation.

Jeffrey Albright Conger was a mess.

Or a very good actor.

As she dropped into her desk chair again, she made a note to meet him personally and check to see if anyone had a life insurance policy on Brandi Potts. Just in case. Though it seemed from outward signs that Brandi's murder was more likely related to the other women who were a part of *Dead Heat* than a kill-for-a-quick-payoff scheme, you never knew. Nash had already decided to look into Conger's finances and to check just in case girlfriend number two was stashed away somewhere.

Besides, Brandi Potts's connection was a thin thread as she was only an extra.

Nonetheless, Nash kept coming back to the film and the fact that *Dead Heat*'s female lead was still missing.

Where the hell was Allie Kramer?

Nash wrote the question down and circled it. The timing of the star of *Dead Heat*'s disappearance had to be significant. Had she been killed, an earlier victim of the same killer? Then why hadn't her body been left and displayed in plain view like the others? If the killer's MO was to leave the dead bodies at the killing ground and decorate them with a bizarre mask, then why hadn't he done the same to Allie? Or had she somehow escaped? Had she been warned of the attack that would happen on the set? If so, how? Who had tipped her off? Was she involved? If so, how had she vanished off the face of the damned earth?

Frustrated, Nash reminded herself to double- and triple-check the chain of command on the prop gun again. *Someone* had messed with the weapon. *Someone* who had access. It seemed a very unlikely coincidence that Allie Kramer's double had been gunned down on the last day of filming when Allie herself hadn't been on the set. The actual shooter, Sig Masters, was still on the list of suspects, but from all outward purposes he had no reason to try to kill either Lucinda Rinaldi or either one of the Kramer girls, each of whom, at one time in the script, Nash had learned, was to be the target of the killer in the movie.

She was missing something, she knew it.

The obvious link was Cassie Kramer, sister to Allie, daughter of Jenna, but that was just too easy, Nash thought.

One killing had occurred in LA.

The next happened in Portland.

Of course Cassie Kramer had been in the area of each homicide when it had been committed.

Convenient.

Others connected to *Dead Heat* had been up and down the coast.

It seemed unlikely that there were two killers, so whoever had shot Holly had come to Portland in the last few days and killed Brandi Potts.

Nash tapped her pencil on her notepad. Every damned lead was guiding her back to Cassie Kramer. She'd been on the set when Rinaldi had been shot, here in Portland on location, she'd been in LA and had drinks with Holly Dennison the night before the woman was murdered, and she was back in Oregon last night when Brandi Potts had been gunned down.

And, of course, there were the notes on the backs of the hideous masks: *Sister. Mother.*

Who else would refer to the women in the pictures as such?

Someone who wanted to set Cassie Kramer up as the fall guy while he or she had her own reasons for wanting the two women killed? What if the masks were a distraction? What if they were left with the sole purpose of keeping the police guessing and pointing them in the wrong direction? What if there were some other unknown links between the women? An ex-lover? The only witness, Peggy Gates, had said she'd seen a woman or small man running from the scene. Hell, that person, male or female, might not be the shooter. He or she could be a witness to the crime, who ran off or was running for some other reason.

Except there was another piece of damning evidence that had just come in via e-mail from the traffic department. Nash looked up at her computer monitor to study an image captured by a traffic cam late last night. A woman driving a Honda making an illegal U-turn within half a mile of where the murder took place. The traffic cam had time-stamped the picture at 1:14 AM and the woman behind the wheel of the car registered to her name? None other than Cassie Kramer.

Cassie was not only in the area, she'd been within blocks of the murder within the time frame that the crime had been committed.

Yeah, it was harder and harder to think Cassie effin' Kramer, certified mental case, wasn't involved with two homicides, one attempted homicide, and her sister's disappearance.

Still, it didn't sit right.

Disgusted, she threw her pencil onto the desk just as she heard someone outside the opening to her cubicle. As she looked up she found Double T entering her space.

Somewhere between the middle of the damned night and now, he'd managed to change into fresh jeans, an open-collared shirt, and jacket. In his right hand, he carried a bag with a sticker indicating that he'd stopped at her favorite local deli, located on the opposite side of the next block. In his left, he held a drink carrier with two oversize cups. "Figured you could use something besides bad coffee and ibuprofen."

"You're right." And to confirm, her stomach growled.

"I like the sound of that."

"Don't get used to it." Pointing at the bag she asked, "What've you got?"

"Vegetarian Delight or some such crap. And a Diet Coke. I know you're a purist these days and try to avoid soda and sweets and whatever, but go ahead, indulge. Live a little. A little caffeine and pseudo sugar could do you some good."

"Or more harm than good, but okay. I'm in." She needed a kick start and some days all the body cleansing, organic foods, and meatless Mondays got to her, so she broke training. Today just happened to be one of those days.

Double T set the drinks and white sack on the corner of her desk, then pulled up the visitor's chair and spread out the lunch. After a morning of bitter coffee, two power bars, and yes, the ibuprofen, the contents of the bag smelled like heaven.

From the first bite, the toasted sandwich of melted cheese, onions, tomatoes, and avocado topped with some kind of wasabi mayo hit the spot. Washing a bite down with the soda didn't hurt either. She could almost feel her energy level rise while Double T dug into meatballs, sauce, and melted cheese oozing over a thick slab of bread.

"Getting anywhere?" he asked, hitching his chin at her notes.

"Nowhere fast . . . or nowhere slow. Take your pick." She took another bite. "Forensics isn't back on the bullets from the victims, but I bet they match. And the lab is still working on trying to find any DNA on the laminated masks, also checking the paper and elastic bands so we can start tracking down anyone who might have bought the products used."

"A long shot."

"But a shot. Right now I'll take one from a BB gun fired two miles away." Another bite. Yeah, she was definitely feeling better. "What about you?"

"Got a call from Larry Sparks." At the raise of her eyebrows, he clarified, "Sparks is a lieutenant with the OSP. Get this, he's been tracking down registrations for a 2007 Hyundai. Santa Fe. An SUV."

"And you're telling me this now . . . why?"

"He's doing it as a favor to a friend."

She still didn't get it, but from the smug smile on Double T's face, this information meant something. "And I, or we, care?"

"Hmm." He took another bite followed by a long swallow from his cup. "His friend is Shane Carter."

"Jenna Hughes's husband." Now he had her attention.

"Yep. And they're looking for the vehicle because . . . well, here's where it gets a little off the grid." She waited impatiently while he chewed, then he said, "Some kid at the hospital where Cassie Kramer was a patient saw this car in the lot. An unusual car for the lot . . . well, the kid's unusual, too, knows all sorts of trivia shit and cars are one of his interests. Supposedly he can name any make and model since they were invented, or something like that." He waved his explanation away, as if it didn't matter. "Anyway, because Cassie thought someone came into her room and told her that her sister was alive, but you know, left without giving any information, she's trying to track the woman down."

"Whoa, whoa. Wait. Back up. Why is this the first time we've heard about a woman with information about Allie Kramer?"

"Well, that's the 'off the grid' part. Turns out the woman was wearing an old-time nurse's uniform, you know, with the stiff cap, white dress, and shoes? And there's no nurse at the hospital fitting that description."

"Of course," she said dryly, her sandwich temporarily forgotten. "So . . . what're you saying?"

"According to Carter—because I talked to him after I got the call from Sparks—Cassie Kramer didn't want to come off sounding like some kind of a nut."

"You mean more of a nut."

"Yeah. That's what I mean."

"So now she's got the OSP chasing ghosts?" she asked. She picked up her sandwich again.

"Maybe."

"Good use of the taxpayers' dollars," she observed.

"There's more."

"Of course there is. Hopefully not more detective work courtesy of a patient in a mental ward."

"Nope. According to Carter, they're bringing in another mask."

"What?" She was raising half the sandwich to her mouth, but stopped. "A mask? Like the ones found on the victims?"

"That's right. Of Allie Kramer again, and yeah, all messed up. Disfigured."

Nash leaned back in her chair, her gaze pinned on her partner, her interest spiked. She felt a little uptick in her pulse. The mask actually linked Cassie to the crimes, was concrete physical evidence. "Why does she have a mask? How did she get it?"

One side of his mouth lifted. "Get this: She claims it was left in her apartment in California, she found it in a suitcase after she thought her place was broken into."

"She file a report?"

"No. Nothing was taken, nothing disturbed. She's not really sure when the mask was left in her bag. It was a piece of luggage she hadn't used for a while, or so she claims. The only reason she thinks it was left when she was in California this last time was because not only did she find it when she started packing up, but somehow the neighbor's cat had gotten in and was trapped in her place and scared the hell out of her."

"Whoa, whoa. Wait a second. Start over. Tell me the chain of events, I want to get this straight." Nash pushed the remains of her sandwich aside and grabbed her pencil again before turning over a new page on her tablet. As Double T explained everything he'd heard about Cassie Kramer supposedly finding a mask in her luggage that sounded just like the ones left at the crime scenes, Nash took notes. It didn't make any sense. If Cassie were the killer, why would she come up with a mask herself? To throw the police off? As yet, information about the masks being left on the victims hadn't been leaked to the press. The few people who had seen the bodies, witnesses and cops, had so far held their tongues. So how the hell had Cassie Kramer come up with one?

"This really connects her," Nash thought aloud.

"Or makes her a victim?"

"You mean makes her *look* like a victim." Nash was playing devil's advocate, as Double T's doubts echoed her own, but she didn't want to ignore the obvious just on principle or gut feelings.

"You don't think she's a vic?"

"I don't know."

"So you're second-guessing yourself, too."

"Just looking at the big picture," she said, but still had the niggling feeling that something was off. She set her pencil down and rotated the computer monitor so that it was more visible to her partner. "Look who was out cruising late last night and got caught pulling a U-ey."

Double T let out a long, low whistle as he stared at the snapshot of Cassie Kramer behind the wheel of a Honda. "Nail-in-the-coffin time. All we need now is a murder weapon with her fingerprints on it."

"Or a confession." She started in on what was left of her sandwich again, but she barely tasted it as her mind was reeling ahead to the interview with Cassie Kramer, the questions she would ask. "This afternoon should be interesting."

"Hopefully she doesn't lawyer up." He wadded up the waxy paper in which his sandwich had been wrapped and tossed it toward the wastebasket near her desk. Banking off the wall of her file cabinet, he hit the shot. "Two points." He flashed her a smile. "See, the day's getting better already."

"Is it?"

"Just wait until we talk to Cassie Kramer," Double T said as his cell phone jangled and he answered, walking out of her cubicle.

"I can't," Nash said, and it was the truth. She couldn't wait. And she was a little worried that she'd made a major mistake in not driving out to Falls Crossing and interviewing Cassie immediately. Cassie did have a history of mental issues and probably didn't want to speak to the cops. Nash didn't blame her on that one; she was the prime suspect in their case. However, Shane Carter had promised she'd show, so Nash was staking her job on the fact that the ex-lawman would be as good as his word, even if his stepdaughter fought him.

She drained the rest of her drink and cleaned up the corner of her desk they'd used as a table, then turned back to work. For the moment, her headache was at bay and she was energized again.

Until Kowalski strolled by. "How's it goin'?" he asked, poking his head around the corner, the scent of a recent cigarette following him.

"Goin'."

"Heard you caught another one. Dead person linked to the movie, found wearing a fuckin' mask. Weird shit."

"Weird," she agreed.

"Forensics find anything?"

"No report yet."

"Prints on the mask?"

"None that mean anything."

"Weird shit," he said again, and made his way to his desk. He settled behind it and turned to his computer, but his wife's glamour shot was still staring at her from the corner of his desk. Oh, what she would have done for a door to shut off the sultry pout captured on Marcia Kowalski's face nearly thirty years earlier. Marcia's near-blond hair floated all around her face in permed curls, jewelry sparkled under the camera's lights, and her shoulders were bare as she cast a sultry look over her shoulder. The photograph was fading with the passage of time, Marcia Kowalski was twice the age she'd been in the shot, but still Kowalski kept it framed on his desk. Probably would until he retired. So Marcia would stare at Nash for at least five more years.

Her cell phone chirped. Whitney Stone's number appeared. For the fourth time today. Did the woman never rest?

Without a second thought Nash let the call go to voice mail.

CHAPTER 30

Another mask? Cassie stared in horror at the mask of her mother that lay faceup on the table in the interview room at the police department. She physically recoiled from the hideous image. "Oh, God," she whispered, hand to her mouth, eyes wide. Her stomach felt as if she might heave and yet she couldn't tear her gaze away from the mask. Jenna's beautiful face appeared to be melting, her mouth open as if in a silent, terror-riddled scream.

For a second Cassie couldn't focus, couldn't process. The room spun and she held onto the table for support. How could there be more than one of the gut-wrenching, horrid masks?

Despite the fact it was covered in plastic, the laminated visage of Jenna Hughes seemed to glare at her, those dark, empty eye sockets drilling into Cassie's soul as it lay on the table between Cassie and Detective Nash. It was all Cassie could do to stay in her seat in the small room furnished only with the scarred but functional table and two uncomfortable chairs. A camera was mounted high on the same colorless wall where a mirror was displayed. On the other side, she realized from all the cop shows she'd watched over the years, was a darkened viewing room where other detectives and maybe a DA were watching her and gauging her reaction.

"Where—where did you get this?" she managed to whisper.

"You've never seen it before?"

"No!"

"And yet you have another mask. The one you brought in."

"Yes." What was she getting at?

"Similar to this one," Nash said, pushing yet another piece of paper forward, across the table, closer to Cassie, who actually scooted her chair back an inch. The sheet of paper was a copy of another horrendous, twisted picture of Allie, her eyes missing, her mouth a red curling slash. "This is just a copy, of course. The original is in LA, with the detective who's investigating Holly Dennison's murder."

"Hayes," Cassie said, her voice a croak, her stomach threatening to heave. "Detective Hayes. He called. I talked to him."

"Briefly."

"Yes." She nodded, her gaze glued to the hideous masks. "Where . . . where did you get these?"

"You can't tell me?"

"No!" Cassie said.

"You're sure?" Nash was so damned calm. Cassie was suddenly claustrophobic, the walls seeming to shrink.

"Of course I'm sure. I've never seen those two before in my life. I thought . . . I mean I believed I had the only one. Where did you . . . where did you get these?" she asked, her voice strangled, her mind whirling. What the hell was going on here? What was with all the masks? Why would the police have them?

"These were found on the victims."

"What?" Cassie's mouth dropped open. "I don't understand." She didn't want to.

"On the bodies. Placed over their heads. Both here and in LA, when they were killed on nights you were in both cities."

"Oh, Jesus." She felt the blood drain from her face. "I don't understand." This was making no sense at all. Why in God's name would anyone go to the trouble to leave the masks on the dead women? And why was the detective staring at her so intently, as if she expected Cassie to tell her something new, offer up more information? Or . . . Jesus God, was she waiting for some kind of confession? No . . . that couldn't be it. Sweat broke out between her shoulder blades.

"How well did you know Brandi Potts?"

"I didn't."

"Did you ever see her?"

"I—I don't know. I don't think so."

"You don't think so?" Nash's gaze was hard. Scrutinizing.

"Well, maybe on the set? That last day? But I don't remember her."

Nash slid another piece of paper forward, the picture of a pretty woman with red hair and sharp features. "This is Brandi Potts."

Cassie stared down at the photo and shook her head. "I might have seen her. But really, I don't remember."

Another picture was pushed over the top of the first, the same woman, staring upward, her face ashen, her open eyes with a fixed gaze. She was obviously dead.

"Jesus," Cassie whispered and her stomach roiled. Spit collected in her mouth and she had to look away. "I don't remember her."

Nash hesitated a minute, then said gently, as if they were good friends,"Why don't you tell me how you found the mask that you brought in?"

"I thought I already did." Cassie wasn't going to be fooled by the sudden shift in attitude. Rhonda Nash was anything but her friend. She set her jaw and stared right back at the detective. She explained again about discovering the mask in her suitcase after being scared to death by the cat and feeling that someone had been in her apartment. After a few clarifying questions, Nash steered the conversation to the previous night.

Cassie wasn't quite as clear as she explained about her text and meeting with Brandon McNary, then the feeling that she was being followed on the way to her car. She held back, though, and didn't admit to the missing hours in her life. Confessing to losing track of time or even blacking out would only open a door she'd prefer to keep firmly shut.

"And that's it?"

"Yeah." Cassie nodded tightly and the muscles in the back of her neck stiffened.

"You're sure?"

Why did the simple question seem like a trap?

Without another word, Nash pushed the masks to one side then reached into her file and came up with a glossy picture. "Is this you?" she asked as Cassie, her heart turning stone cold, stared at a photograph of herself behind the wheel of her Honda. She saw the time-stamp, remembered the flash as she pulled a one-eighty in the middle of the street in order to follow the bus.

"Yes." Cold dread congealed in her blood.

"So how did this happen?"

"After I left Brandon, or rather, after he drove off, I got into my car—"

"After feeling that you were being followed?"

"Yes. Anyway, I was starting to leave Portland and . . . and I thought I saw Allie. She . . . she was waiting for a bus, which came." Cassie's heart was pounding, and it was all she could do to remain calm. "I think she got onto it, but the bus blocked my view of the stop, so I made a U turn to follow it and hopefully catch up with her."

"At one fourteen in the morning?"

"I don't know what time it was, but yeah, that's probably about the right time," she said and tried not to panic even though it was evident the detective thought she was lying, that she was somehow involved in Brandi Potts's murder. She should leave. Tell Nash she needed her lawyer with her, or just get up and walk out. But she didn't. Because, damn it, she wasn't guilty.

Upon questioning, Cassie managed to describe the bus, the advertising panel of a local real estate firm on the back end as it belched exhaust on the route.

Nash made a note. "So. Did you follow it? The bus?"

Didn't she just say so? *Be calm. Stay cool.* "Yes." *For as long as I can remember.*

"And was your sister on it?"

Cassie licked her lips. Had Allie been inside? "No. I don't think so, but I don't know. She wasn't in the alcove of the coffee shop when I drove past, but the bus was lit. I could see inside." She willed herself to remember driving and craning her neck, looking upward through the bus's windows. "There were only a few riders." Two twentysomethings in watch caps, wires from headphones running from their ears. An old man in a bulky coat . . . and . . . She didn't realize it, but she was slowly shaking her head.

"You didn't see Allie Kramer?"

Cassie knew how fantastic this all sounded, how unreal. "On the bus? No. Not unless she was lying down." But then where had she gone? If she hadn't boarded the bus, what had happened to her? Dear God, had she even existed? Cassie's head began a slow, low throb, from the base of her skull. *Not now!* She couldn't black out now!

"Do you remember where you saw her? Before she boarded?"

Cassie blinked. Stared down at the picture. "Right there!" She pointed to the photo of her, flashed by the traffic camera. "The coffee shop at that intersection and I already told you, she was there, standing in the doorway waiting for the damned bus!" Her voice had risen and she wanted to shake Nash to make her believe.

Making another note, Nash said, "And then what?"

"What do you mean?"

"After you followed the bus. What happened?"

There it was. The time gap. The black hole of her life where she had no idea what had happened. Had she chased Allie down? Driven aimlessly? She didn't know. "Nothing," she said quickly, her voice sounding strangled. *Don't let her get to you. Stay focused. Serene.*

You can do this. She said, "I drove home. I mean to my husband's ranch." It was all she could do not to squirm in her seat. But she did her best and wished to high heaven that Trent was with her. That, of course, hadn't been allowed. He'd driven her to the station and was waiting nearby, probably going to be asked to confirm what he could of her story, but for now, she was on her own.

Just like always, her mind teased as she'd always felt a little out of step within her small family. Allie, the baby, had always been Jenna's favorite, probably because she, during their growing up years, had complied while Cassie had rebelled. Their father, too, had been more interested in the younger of his two daughters with Jenna, but that, recently, was probably because of Allie's star power and how it had reflected upon him as her producer. With Cassie shifting her interests to screenwriting, Robert had lost a little interest in her.

And how would you write this scene? You wanted to use Allie's disappearance as inspiration for your next screenplay, so how do you think you'll do it from a prison cell?

Cassie gripped the edges of her chair and forced her mind to the interview.

"There is something else," Cassie said, and reached into her jacket pocket to withdraw her phone. "I left this in the car last night and this morning there was a text on it." She scrolled to the cryptic message and handed it to the detective.

"'Help me'?" Nash read.

"I don't know who it's from. The number means nothing to me but Brandon McNary got a text from a number he didn't recognize. It said, 'I'm okay.' Nothing more. He thought his text was from Allie and I thought mine was, too."

"You wrote back?" Nash said, staring at the screen. "But no response?"

"Right."

"Why do you think it's from Allie?"

"Who else?" Cassie asked.

"Someone pranking you?"

"It could be, but . . . I don't know. I thought you might want to see it."

Nash nodded. "Can I keep this?"

"Yes." Cassie hated handing over her phone, but knew the information on it could be accessed by the police through the phone company; all they needed was a search warrant, and though the detective would be searching through her phone's contacts, texts, call log, and apps, she didn't care. She didn't have anything to hide and she wanted to prove it.

Nevertheless, it made her nervous.

Nash asked more questions about the night before. Over and over again, as if she hoped to trip Cassie up, but Cassie held firm, never once straying from her actions, both in Portland and in LA, keeping her missing hours to herself.

Finally, exhausting all her inquiries, Nash said, "I think Detective Hayes will want to talk to you."

"Again," Cassie corrected, her heart sinking. She was already going out of her mind, wanted to leave this place ASAP. "Is he here?"

"No. The interview will be by phone. We're kind of changing it up a bit, if that's okay with you."

"Fine," Cassie lied, but wondered if she were making a big mistake, if the police would twist her words, if she really should have refused to talk to them without an attorney as Trent had advised.

"It wouldn't hurt to have counsel present," Trent had suggested. He'd been driving, Cassie in the passenger seat of his pickup as they'd left his place. She'd glanced in the side view and had caught sight of Hud waiting on the porch. Her heart had squeezed and she'd felt a premonition of doom, had almost insisted Trent turn the truck around. But it would have only put off the inevitable.

"I've got nothing to hide," she'd finally said, determined to get the damned interview over with.

"I know, but—"

"I can handle it," she'd snapped, just as his cell phone had beeped. He'd glanced at the display. "It's Carter," he'd said, and answered, driving one-handed on the county road leading to I-84 heading west. The conversation had been quick and one-sided. ". . . Well, at least that's something. Hopefully something will come of it . . . Yeah, we're on our way there now. Thanks . . . How long? You would know better than me, I think. A couple of hours? . . . Yeah, both of us . . . call when you know more. . . . Okay. Thanks."

He'd hung up and said, "Carter says 'Good luck.'"

"I'll probably need it."

"He's also said Sparks ran down a lead on the Santa Fe. He and Carter are on their way to Molalla. They matched one of the 2007 Hyundais to a dealership out there."

"And?"

"And this particular dealer sells all his cars with a license plate holder that not only has his name on it, but a little art."

"Let me guess," she said, astonished that Rinko's obtuse lead would go anywhere. "It's got a horse on it."

"Actually a cowboy riding a bucking bronco in honor of the Molalla Buckeroo, a rodeo event the town holds every year. Apparently Belva Nelson lives in some little farm outside the city limits with her niece and husband. The niece's name is Sonja Watkins. Ring any bells?"

"No." She'd been certain. She'd never heard of either woman. "Who are they? How are they connected?"

"Carter isn't sure, but here's the kicker: Belva Nelson is in her seventies and an RN. She worked in Portland, but she's retired now."

Cassie's heart had skipped a beat. "Did she work at Mercy? In the psych ward?" Was it possible? Had Carter and Sparks located someone who purported to know that Allie was alive?

"Unknown. They're working on it. This isn't really a job for the state police. It's Portland's case, but Sparks is intrigued and is doing this on his own time."

"Belva Nelson," she'd repeated, but the name still meant nothing to her. "How . . . I mean how did she get into the hospital?"

"*If* she did. Nothing's certain. Carter's gonna call back once they've visited the place."

"Hopefully he'll come up with some answers," she'd said, trying to figure out how a retired nurse from a town thirty-odd miles from Portland had anything to do with Allie seeming to vanish. Could this woman be the key to unlocking the entire mystery? Cassie had felt her pulse jump a little, then had refused to allow herself to feel the tiniest ray of hope. Belva Nelson could be just another dead end.

Now, in the interrogation room Cassie watched as Detective Nash gave a nod to the mirror and within seconds a phone was delivered by a uniformed officer who hooked it to a jack in the wall. The cord stretched to the table. Nash dialed. Less than a minute later she was connected to Detective Hayes in LA and the interview continued for another forty-five minutes, directed by Nash, with Hayes asking a few questions for clarification.

The whole experience was surreal. And unnerving.

The questions became pointed and went over the same information Nash had asked earlier: Did she see the victim, Brandi Potts, last night? Did she know Brandi? Was there a connection between Brandi and Holly Dennison or Lucinda Rinaldi? Did Allie ever talk about either woman? Did Cassie own a gun? Could she provide an alibi for the hours surrounding Brandi Potts's death? Did Cassie have any idea why the mask was left at her apartment in LA? Did she know about the other masks? Did she know of any reason either woman would have been killed? Any known enemies? Did she know if the two women were close? And just how close was she to either?

No, no, no!

How many times did she have to explain that she knew nothing? She answered each question as best as she could, but her knowledge of either victim was limited. Yes, she'd had drinks with Holly, but that was it. She'd driven her friend home the night before her death and hadn't seen her again. She wasn't even sure if she'd ever had a conversation with Brandi Potts.

The detectives' questions were getting them nowhere.

And still Nash kept firing them.

Why would someone place the masks on the victims or leave one at her apartment? Why scribble the words *Mother* or *Sister* on the back of each?

Cassie was losing her patience. "I don't know," she said for the dozenth time. "Look, if I knew anything, I'd tell you."

Nash's smile was icy. "Well, that's certainly reassuring."

"I mean it, I don't know." She'd almost pounded her fist on the table she was so frustrated, tired, and angry. But that wouldn't solve anything. She forced a calmness she didn't feel. "So I'm going to go now. I've told you everything I know, which is nothing, so there's no reason for us to waste any more of your time or mine, or his," she said, rolling a palm toward the phone from which the disembodied voice of Jonas Hayes had boomed. Standing, she headed to the door.

"I wouldn't advise you leaving just yet," Nash said, and Cassie whirled on her.

"Tough. I'm going." She only hesitated long enough to see if the detective would try to stop her. She didn't.

"I'm sure I'm going to have more questions for you," Nash stated, and was unable to hide her annoyance.

"I'm sure," Cassie said. "You have my number. Oh, wait. You also have my damned phone." Then she opened the door and nearly bolted from the room.

Sonja Watkins wasn't happy to find an officer of the law on her sagging front porch. Pushing forty and skinny as a rail, she stood behind a broken screen door and smoked a cigarette while a television blared from somewhere in the depths of the house. Two dogs of indeterminate breed lay on mats on the porch and chickens picked at bugs and grain or whatever in the sparse grass of the yard. The house, vintage 1940, sat on a plot that had to be five acres of fenced scrub brush. A boat and four older-model vehicles, two of which didn't appear to run, were parked in a wide gravel area in front of a weathered barn. No Hyundai SUV.

The surrounding small farms, visible from the front porch, were neatly kept, the yards trimmed, the houses and outbuildings painted and clean. Not so the Watkins property.

"What do the cops want with my aunt?" Sonja Watkins asked, eyeing Sparks's badge suspiciously through the screen.

Carter guessed this wasn't the first time the police had shown up at her door.

Sparks offered a thin smile. A tall man with curly black hair showing its first signs of gray, he was about six feet, his skin always appearing tanned, his eyes sharp and focused. Today, as usual, he appeared unruffled, as if he'd been through the drill a million times.

"Is Belva Nelson here? On the premises?" he asked, flipping his badge holder closed and stuffing it into his pocket.

"Why? She in some kind of trouble?" Sonja was little more than five feet, thin to the point of being skinny, her hair a dark auburn color, red streaks visible. A pair of readers were propped onto her head, and the cigarette burned between the manicured fingers of her right hand. She turned her head to yell over her shoulder, "Christ, Mick, could you turn the damned TV down?"

One of the dogs lifted his head and gave a soft *woof.* The volume from within didn't change. Pursing her lips in aggravation, she swung her head around again. "Wedded bliss."

Sparks was firm. "We just need to talk to Ms. Nelson."

"Well, *Ms. Nelson* ain't here."

"Where is she?"

"I don't know." A lift of the bony shoulders. A rounding of her eyes. "She don't tell me where she's goin' half the time. And I don't care. None of my business." She took a long drag, shot a stream of smoke out of the corner of her mouth.

"But she does own a 2007 Hyundai Santa Fe?"

"Yeah." Her look said, *What's it to ya?*

"Does she live here?"

"Why?" She drew hard on her cigarette and in the ensuing cloud said, "Don't you get it, she's not here. I haven't seen her in a couple of days."

"When do you expect her back?" Sparks asked pleasantly, though there was an edge of steel to his voice.

"Don't know. As I already told ya, she don't answer to me! Shit, half the time she just picks up and leaves, don't say a word about what she's doin' and shows up a few days later." She turned her lips down at the corners. "It's a real conundrum, now, ain't it? But once again, it's not my business. She pays her rent, I don't go pryin'."

"So this is where she resides?" Carter cut in.

She frowned. Shot him a look. Took a puff. Realized she'd given out more information than she'd intended. "You a cop, too?"

"Was."

"I thought I'd seen you before. You were that sheriff that was caught up in that mess with the damned serial killer a few years back. The . . ." She snapped her fingers as she thought. "I don't know his damned name, but he was the ice man guy."

"That's right."

"Sheeeit, that was one fuckin' mess! It was all over the news." She let down her guard for a minute and swung her gaze back to Sparks. "You were involved, too. I read all about it. Was kinda fascinated with the whole weird thing. So what the hell are you two doin' askin' about my damned aunt?" A dawning realization hit her. "This have somethin' to do with Jenna Hughes or her damned missing daughter? Yeah, yeah, I read all about it and you—" She pointed at Carter through the mesh, smoke from her filter tip curling from her hand. "You married Jenna Hughes. Now I remember! Holy shit, what the hell do you want with my aunt?"

Sparks asked, "Do you have a cell phone number for her, or some other number where she can be reached?"

Sonja hesitated; she obviously wasn't eager to help the cops. "She don't use it like regular people. I mean, she uses it when she wants to talk to someone but doesn't have it on all the time to take calls. She's a little old school, if ya know what I mean." She eyed them both and had another drag. "What's this all about?"

"She was a nurse," Carter said.

She gave a sharp nod. "A long time ago. Belva's been retired for years."

"Did she ever work at Mercy Hospital?"

She thought a second. "Don't know. But there were several different ones, I think."

"In Portland?" Sparks asked.

"Yeah." She was nodding. "Look, I don't remember the names. Mercy? Shit, could be."

Carter said again, "We'd like to talk to her."

"So you said."

"A phone number for her or the name and number of a good friend, someone who might know where she is."

"That would be me. We don't have much kin and Belva, she's not the kind to make good friends, if you know what I mean. I'll see if I can get you the cell number, but it won't do ya much good. Just a sec." She disappeared into the house and less than a minute later returned, the cigarette gone, replaced by a cell phone. After scrolling through a menu, she came up with a number and relayed it through the screen. "That's it, but I tell ya, she ain't answerin'. I've tried her for two days."

Sparks asked, "When was the last time you saw her?"

"Two days ago. She drove off around ten in the mornin', I think."

"Wednesday?" Sparks clarified.

Sonja stared at him as if he were an idiot. "Jeeezus Keerist! Didn't I just say so?"

Calm as ever, Sparks fished in his pocket for a card and withdrew it, offering it to Sonja. "Would you have her give us a call?"

"Sure," she said, opening the door a crack to snatch the card from his fingers. Not that he figured it would do any good. As they left, Carter had the distinct impression Sonja Watkins would toss the number into the trash and hope she never saw hide nor hair of them again.

ACT V

Everything was coming together.

She could feel it.

She slid on the long negligee worn in the boudoir scene of *Dead Heat.* How well it fit. Like the proverbial glove.

No surprise there, she thought as she surveyed her reflection in the long mirror she'd placed in the corner between the posters that still covered the walls of her dressing area. She frowned as her gaze moved from one of the elaborate pictures promoting various movies to the next.

Of course they were marred. Sliced by her own hand when she was in a rage which, it seemed, was happening more often these days. Was it because of the movie's premiere, or was it just a natural progression? She didn't know but felt more out of control than ever, the insecurities and fury more impossible to ignore. She wasn't always so volatile and now, gazing at the posters that had been taped painstakingly back together, she told herself she was sane; she'd always been sane, the doctors were wrong. As long as she kept herself in control and only gave way to the violent impulses according to her plan, she would be all right. In fact, everything would be as it should be. Once her nemesis was dealt with forever, then there would be calm and recognition and . . . a new life, a life, she deserved.

Again, she viewed the posters and in many, the heroine's face was a little off, distorted because of the jagged tears. Those, the disfigured images were what she used for the masks she created, the false images that always hid the real person beneath the cool facade.

Soon though, it would all be over.

But there was a new problem to deal with. All very irritating. Just when she'd thought she was home free. No worries, she told herself. She would handle it. Just as she'd handled everything all of her life.

Walking closer to the mirror, she examined herself with a trained eye, then scowled, noticing a tiny wrinkle between her eyes when she frowned. Though she'd told herself differently, age had started to show itself a bit. Her breasts, though full, weren't as perky as they once had been and, though she was loath to admit it, she was a tad thicker in the middle than nubile Annie Melrose had been in the movie. But still . . . not bad. That film had been shot nearly five years earlier, so a little extra flesh was to be expected. And there was always plastic surgery. Tummy tucks. Breast lifts. Whatever. When the time came.

She felt a new energy when she thought to the night ahead. The premiere party for *Dead Heat*. She'd have to hurry if she wanted to make her entrance.

She walked to the tiny window and looked outside to the Hollywood Hills and the sign visible through her window. This should have been her time. Her star should have risen, but, because of Jenna Hughes, it hadn't soared as high as she'd expected. "Thanks," she snarled under her breath at the woman in the poster. "You miserable self-serving bitch."

CHAPTER 31

"I'll be damned," Nash said under her breath as she stared at her computer screen on her desk. Lieutenant Sparks had called earlier and given her a short rundown on his trip to Molalla where he'd interviewed a woman by the name of Sonja Watkins. He and ex-sheriff Carter had been trying to locate Belva Nelson, Watkins's aunt and a retired nurse who had supposedly "visited" Cassie Kramer in the hospital, where, dressed in a costume straight out of the fifties, good old Aunt Belva had assured Cassie that her sister was just fine and dandy. Their tip had come from a mental patient who'd seen an SUV that didn't belong in the hospital lot. Nash had thought the story beyond far-fetched, but Sparks was a good cop, as Carter had been a good sheriff. Reluctantly Nash had done a little follow-up.

She'd asked Natalie Jenkins, a junior detective, to research the name Belva Nelson on the off-chance that not only was there such a person, but that she was a nurse and had some connection to Mercy Hospital, or Cassie Kramer, or both. Nash wanted anything Jenkins could find. And she wanted it now.

So far, lo and behold, Sparks's and Carter's information held up. Belva Mae Watkins Nelson, a widow, was indeed a retired nurse who lived in the small community of Molalla. Her work history included several clinics and hospitals in the Portland area, including a very short stint at Mercy Hospital over thirty years earlier. Nash had already called the hospital, talked to the records department, and requested a full history of Belva Nelson's employment. She'd been given some double-talk about the hospital being sold several times over the past years, its records archived, if said documents still existed at all. Nash accepted no excuses and told the records clerk to put her manager on the line, or if that didn't work, Nash wanted to talk to hospital administration. Upon realizing Detective Nash wasn't about to be sidetracked, the clerk had quickly lost her snippy it's-too-much-trouble attitude and promised to look into the request. Nash had told her she'd be by to pick up the information, if it weren't faxed over to the police department by eight the next morning. Just to keep the clerk on task.

Since Belva Nelson, in her seventies, was no longer working, what was she doing at the hospital in the middle of the night in Cassie Kramer's room? Initially Nash had thought Cassie Kramer was a liar, somehow trying to save her own skin, or else was certifiable, suffering from some mental health problem that caused her to be delusional and hallucinate. Now, Nash wasn't convinced. Could it be that Cassie Kramer was telling the truth? Then who was behind the bizarre murders? Who, Nash wondered, would have it in for Cassie Kramer so deeply that he or she would go to such lengths to make Cassie either go crazy or appear guilty?

The name that kept nagging at Nash's mind was Allie Kramer. Was it possible she was still alive, as the retired nurse had suggested? Was she sending random texts out just to mess with Cassie's head? Did she hate her sister so much as to set her up for murder? How off the rails was Allie and, above all else, was she capable of homicide? Nash hadn't yet talked to Brandon McNary. He'd been a ghost and hadn't returned her calls, but she was determined to track him down and find out about the text message he'd received, purportedly from the same number as Cassie.

First things first, though.

With a dozen questions running through her mind, she scooted her desk chair back and walked to Double T's cubicle. He was staring at his own computer monitor while talking on his desk phone. Though he never so much as glanced her way, he must've seen her in his peripheral vision as he held up a finger to silently tell her to "hold on."

". . . yeah, that's right. Tyronne with two *n*s. Thompson with a *p* . . . uh-huh. Okay . . . yeah, I'll be there."

He hung up and twirled his desk chair to face her. "Mix-up at the doctor's office. Seems there's actually two Tyronne Thompsons, but the other guy?" he said, flashing a wicked grin. "He spells his name wrong."

"He probably doesn't think so. Besides, I thought they used birth dates."

He shrugged. "Somehow this other dude got called for my appointment with the ENT. Guess we all have sinus issues. The climate."

"Right." She hitched her head toward the door. "Got time for a quick trip?"

"To?"

"Molalla. Thirty or forty miles southeast. Be there in less than an hour."

"Been there before. As a kid. Got themselves a hella rodeo."

"I've heard," she said dryly. "They also might have a witness." She filled in the blanks as Double T had already heard part of the information. "I know that Carter and Sparks already went out there, but I'd like to talk to Nelson, if she's there, and Sonja Watkins if she's not. Nelson lives with Watkins's family. Sonja's a hairdresser, her husband currently unemployed."

"Why go out there if Sparks already covered it?" He looked at the clock. It was long after five. "It's Friday. Traffic will be a bitch."

"I know, but it could be worth it. I just want to meet Sonja Watkins face-to-face since it seems that Belva Nelson is MIA. She's the one I really want to talk to."

"Maybe we'll get lucky."

"Since when?" She snorted a laugh. "Sparks thinks the woman's in hiding. He and Carter both are sure that Watkins was lying, probably about knowing where her missing aunt is holed up. Anyway, I'm already working on a warrant for the place and the phone records, but I need a little more reason for the judge to issue one; maybe Sonja or her ex-con husband Mick will give us what we need if we rattle their cage a bit."

"Okay. I'm in." He was already reaching for his jacket and his service weapon. "After all, who doesn't like a little drive in the country?"

"Trust in God, my child. He will help you make the right decision," the priest had said, his words comforting. For a few moments in the safety of the confessional, the dark cloud of guilt that she'd borne for over thirty years had been lifted from Belva Nelson's shoulders. And the priest on the other side of the partition had appeared young, but it didn't matter. His words had been a balm. For a few minutes she'd managed to convince herself that her faith was her strength. As she'd walked out of the hundred-year-old building with its stained-glass windows and spire that seemed to pierce the heavens, she'd held onto her faith, felt that God would guide her.

Save her.

Oh, that it were so.

But now, as she drove through the foothills of the Cascade Mountains, returning to the small cabin her father had built nearly a century earlier, her doubts assailed her again. The warmth and safety of the church in Mount Angel was far behind, and she was all alone in the world, driving on a narrow winding road far from civilization. Away from the danger into which she'd placed herself.

Her Hyundai was lugging down, the road getting steeper, the forest darker and more dense. She switched on her wipers, setting them to the slowest speed as the air was thick and damp, heavy with fog, moisture collecting on the glass.

She'd only seen one other car on the road, a vehicle that had sped from behind, its headlights nearly blinding before it had passed her on a straight stretch. For a second she'd thought the idiot behind the wheel was going to crash into her, but at the last minute he'd swerved into the oncoming lane and blown by until she saw only the red taillights of the car disappearing.

That was it.

No other car or truck behind her, none ahead and none going the opposite direction. Which was just as well. For now.

So what're you going to do? You can't hide out here forever. It's not safe! Why not go to the police? Expose what's happening, no longer be a part of it. There will be ramifications, of course, there always are, but you need to come clean. People are dying, Belva! Dying!

Her hands tightened over the wheel. She didn't really know that the recent murders had anything to do with this other matter, that seemed far-fetched. Yet the timing was too much of a coincidence to be ignored.

And she was scared.

So she'd gone to the church, seeking solace, searching for answers.

The forest seemed to close in on her, her headlights thin illumination against an obsidian darkness that surrounded the car and cut her off from civilization. Belva had never felt so alone. So isolated.

It will be short-lived. A temporary necessity. She swallowed hard, heard her own lie. She was only bolstering herself.

"Help me, Father," she whispered and sketched the sign of the cross over her chest with one hand while holding tight to the wheel with her other. She noticed the crucifix dangling on a rosary she'd hung over her rearview mirror. The tiny silver cross swung backward, to and fro, as she negotiated the sharp S curves.

Should she go to the police?

She bit her lip.

Had she broken any laws?

It could be dangerous. *No, Belva, it* will *be dangerous. Already people are paying the ultimate price. Deep in your soul, you know you're involved. Even if you don't acknowledge it, God knows. He sees.*

Oh, Lord, what to do? She had asked herself the same question over and over.

It had all started so long ago.

She'd been young and foolish at the time when she'd promised to keep her mouth shut and take the money she and her husband had so desperately needed. The economy had been lousy at the time and Jim had always had trouble holding down a job, even in good years. His affinity for whiskey had cost him a career and eventually his life.

But never should she have listened to him and accepted payment for her silence. It was as if the devil himself had been whispering into her all-too-willing ears. She'd been a licensed RN at the time, but because of Jim moving from job to job, she'd never settled into one clinic or hospital for more than a year or so.

And so she'd ended up at Mercy.

As a temporary employee, a nurse that "floated" from one area or floor to the next, to help out wherever she was needed most. Her job wasn't secure in the least, and her hours had been cut over and over again.

So she'd done the unthinkable.

She'd not only sold out; she'd sold her soul in the process.

God forgive me.

For a second she thought God was speaking to her, that the little crucifix seemed to glow in the darkness, almost as if it were reflecting light, but that, of course, was impossible in this Stygian night where the rain mixed with fog, and she felt more isolated than she ever had in her life.

She turned off at the lane that was barely visible, just twin ruts choked with weeds that cut through the ferns, berry vines, and fir trees. Branches scraped the sides of the SUV and mud splattered up from potholes as she veered into a clearing wherein her father's old fishing cabin still sat. The wood walls had grayed, the roof was covered in moss, and the lean-to carport had collapsed years before. The porch sagged and a few stones had fallen off the chimney, but the rest of the cabin was sturdy enough, just dirty and in the middle of no-damned-where.

This was definitely no way to live, she thought as the beams of her headlights washed against the windows.

For just a second, she thought she saw a shadow behind the glass, a movement of the tattered curtains her mother had sewn decades before. But as she stared more closely, she saw nothing and decided her nerves were just stretched tight.

Her cell phone beeped and she jumped, her heart nearly collapsing. The screen lit up and she saw the message was from Sonja.

Cops were here. Looking 4u.

Belva stared at the screen for a few minutes as she tried to calm down. The phone was a disposable that she'd bought a while back, supposedly untraceable, as was Sonja's, but who really knew? She should never have stepped into this mess, should have gone directly to the police. Maybe the fact that they were tracking her down was a good sign. She wrote back: **I will take care of it.**

How? You're making promises you can't keep.

K. Sonja had responded. Short for okay.

That was it. Sonja was making as little contact as possible, as they'd agreed. "Message received," Belva said and climbed out of the car. Once more she considered going to the police. Maybe they could protect her because once she broke her silence, she knew there would be hell to pay. In so many ways. She wasn't the only one involved. Innocent people would be hurt.

They already have, if your suspicions are correct.

Again she made the sign of the cross and sent up a prayer as she made her way up the creaky stairs. Dear Lord, the night was cold. Damp. Fog drifting in smoke-like tendrils through the trees. She unlocked the door and stepped inside.

Immediately she sensed something was different. Off. Not quite right. Or was it just her case of nerves? Shivering, she reached for the light switch and flipped it.

Nothing happened.

The room remained dark aside from a weak red glow emanating from beneath the ashes of the banked fire. "What in heaven's name?" she whispered, wondering if there was even an extra bulb or if she'd have to find a way to light the damned lantern on the mantel above the blackened firebox. Did it even have any oil in it or would she have to forget the lantern and use only the light from the nearly dead fire?

The hairs on the back of her neck stiffened. She squinted, her muscles tense. Slowly, eyes searching, telling herself nothing was amiss, she started toward the stone fireplace.

Sssssss!

Sweet Jesus!

A sibilant sound, so like the hiss of a snake swept through the room. Belva stopped dead in her tracks. Her heart leapt to her throat.

Her skin prickled as she strained to listen.

She heard nothing, no scratch of footprints. No slither of scales against floorboards. No movement or breathing.

Swallowing back her fear she took another step.

Sssssss!

This time she whipped around. *What? Dear God, what was that hissing noise?* "Who's there?" she called, then mentally corrected herself. Not who, but *what*? What creature lurked in the shadows? The skin on the back of her arms pimpled.

Did she see a pair of red eyes glowing in the corner, reflecting the fire's dim light? Was it Lucifer himself, come to call? She started to cross herself again when, from the very corner where she knew the beast was lurking an intense light flashed, burning her eyes.

Blinded, Belva took a step backward, her calves colliding with the sharp edge of an end table, the light so intense she couldn't see around its beam.

"You traitor," a low voice accused and then she heard the weird hissing sound again.

Sssssss!

"Who are you?" Belva cried and backed up further. The table with its useless lamp toppled. *Crash!* Glass shattered.

"Who do you think I am?" The voice was low and raspy as if from a demon on the prowl.

"I—I don't know—" But a dawning realization stole the words from her throat. Cold understanding crawled through her brain. "Oh . . . oh no . . ."

The spit dried in her mouth.

A horror as dark as midnight stole through her heart. The light nearly blinding her moved from Belva's face to illuminate the visitor's outstretched hand. Clutched in long fingers was a shiny piece of paper . . . no, that wasn't quite right. It wasn't a regular sheet of paper . . . no, something was wrong with it. As her eyes began to adjust Belva realized the paper was a cutout, a mask of a horridly disfigured woman. The subject's face seemed as if it were running off her bones, her mouth twisted open into what appeared to be a silent scream of sheer terror.

Then she recognized the subject: Jenna Hughes.

Her stomach dropped through the floor.

She nearly stumbled and saw the nurse's uniform stretched out on the couch. Her uniform. As if she were going to don that ancient dress and cape again. Oh, God.

All of her worst fears crystallized and she knew the monster hiding in the dark was, if not the prince of darkness, his wife. "No," she whispered as the woman hiding in the corner advanced. Belva backed up, the soles of her shoes crunching on the broken glass, her heart pounding an erratic rhythm. "Please . . . please. Have mercy."

"Mercy," the raw voice repeated.

She heard a soft *click*.

Is that what it sounded like when a safety was snapped off, or a gun was ready to fire? She didn't know, but didn't wait to find out. Frantic, she whirled, propelled herself to the front door.

Blam!

A gunshot blasted through the tiny cabin.

Her body jerked forward.

Pain exploded in her back.

She screamed, fear and agony twisted together as she slammed into the door.

Arms splayed, she slithered down the wood panels and heard her own heart pounding in her ears.

"Mercy?" the harsh disembodied voice hissed as if from a distance. "I don't think so."

As blackness pulled at the threads of her consciousness, Belva heard the distinctive *Sssss* of the plasticized mask being rattled once more. This time the mask was close enough that she felt a cool breeze as it fanned her face.

Finally, her struggle was over.

She was dying. No one could save her. Though she was aware of something being placed over her head, she felt her soul slipping away. She made one last plea to God, one last prayer as atonement, one final request of the Holy Mother.

Hail Mary, full of grace . . .

CHAPTER 32

Nash pushed the speed limit.

She was pissed.

The trip to Molalla had been a bust, Nash thought as she drove up the familiar road to Mercy Hospital.

Nash and Double T had been given the same warm welcome as Sparks and Carter had earlier. They, too, had been left to stand on the front porch of a small house, a broken-down screen door between them and Sonja Watkins while she avoided questions and smoked three cigarettes. She'd been nervous as hell and hadn't divulged where her aunt could be found, but Nash would bet her badge and a year's salary that the woman had been lying.

Nash couldn't help feeling she was spinning her wheels.

She had spent all day going over the autopsy reports on Holly Dennison and now, due to the rush that was put on it, Brandi Potts. She'd read the interviews of friends and family, witnesses and anyone close to the victims. She'd called with follow-up questions.

And she'd come up with a big, fat zero.

No big insurance payouts upon either woman's death.

In Potts's case, no other woman lay waiting in the wings for her boyfriend to become single, at least none that Nash, nor Jenkins had yet rooted out.

No enemies with deep grudges against the women had emerged. So far.

No gun-toting ex-lovers had been discovered lurking in the background.

Nothing about this case had been easy or normal.

At least so far. Sometimes the other women, monetary gain, ex-boyfriends, or psychotic enemies weren't initially noticed, but eventually floated to the surface like the scum they were. So far, nary a ripple.

Nash slowed for an S curve, then gunned her little car as she rounded the final corner. She felt the "usual suspects" didn't apply in this case. She kept coming back to the only connection she could find between the two victims which was, of course, *Dead Heat,* and therefore it seemed, Allie Kramer's disappearance.

What bothered her about it, was that it was almost too obvious. The masks. Really? It was as if the police were being given a road map.

To where?

Cassie Kramer.

Or maybe Allie?

With one hand, Nash drummed her fingers on the steering wheel. Who bore the Sisters Kramer and their mother such ill will? For a moment her mind sauntered down the jagged pathway leading to their father and his new family, but she did a quick U-turn. Robert Kramer was too self-serving. Yeah, out for himself, but not a killer.

So who was?

"That's the question," she said as she turned through the gates of the hospital and the white edifice flanked by lush gardens came into view. Despite the marble and brick facade and the huge columns, the hospital appeared austere and cold, almost foreboding, but then she'd had an aversion to any kind of medical buildings since losing her daughter. Refusing to let her mind wander down that painful path, she pulled into a parking space in the designated area, cut the engine, and with an eye to the gray skies, hurried toward the main entrance of Mercy Hospital. Her heels clicked loudly on the smooth floor of the grand reception area where she was met with all the warmth of an iceberg by the receptionist, who, after demanding to see Nash's badge, finally released the packet that was supposed to hold Belva Nelson's employment records. Nash opened the envelope in the reception area, just to make certain it was the information she needed and after confirming that copies of the records were enclosed, stuffed the packet into her case and left the hospital.

She swung by her house, grabbed a change of clothes and headed back to the office. A quick check on her dash told her it was after five.

Dean Arnette's party for the cast and crew was scheduled for seven and though, of course, she hadn't been sent an invitation, she thought she'd wander over to the Hotel Danvers, have a drink in the bar and see if she could find a way inside the ballroom where the event, a private party, was to be held. Of course the press had been invited.

Since the manager was a friend of a friend, the department had come to the hotel's aid on more than one occasion and Nash hoped to see some of the players in the drama that was her case. Especially the elusive and slippery Brandon McNary. For some reason *Dead Heat's* bad-boy star seemed to be steadfastly avoiding her.

That would have to end.

Tonight.

She tugged at her collar at a red light and tried to ignore the bothersome feeling that she was missing something important, something, she sensed, that had to do with the damned film. Staring through her windshield where the steady drizzle was being slapped away by her wipers, she decided she needed to change up her game to solve this case. Aside from going through the routine motions of the investigation of the homicides, she needed to think outside of the box. The masks and the movie were the connections between the murders of Holly Dennison in LA and Brandi Potts, here, in Portland. There was no doubt in Nash's mind that they were killed by the same person, but they were also part of a bigger plan that included Cassie Kramer, if she were to be believed about how she ended up with yet another similar bizarre mask.

Had Cassie gotten the mask as a warning? Did the killer leave them with the intended victims before actually murdering them? Had Cassie Kramer just gotten lucky and escaped California before the killer could strike? If that were the case, why not take her out up here in Portland? Why kill Brandi? And why hadn't either of the victims reported receiving them?

She glanced in her rearview mirror and saw a row of headlights. A delivery van idled beside her in the next lane, but she barely noticed she was so caught up in her own thoughts.

How did the masks and murders fit in with the disappearance of Allie Kramer? Was Allie, too, a victim, possibly already dead, maybe even wearing one of those obscene masks and left somewhere obscure, not yet found? Or was she behind the homicides?

Really? From a rising star in Hollywood to homicidal maniac?

That didn't pencil out.

And why put her own distorted image on her victims?

Again—it didn't make any sense.

The light changed.

Nash punched the accelerator, cut in front of the slow-moving van and drove through the rain to the office. She parked across the street, waited impatiently for the pedestrian light to change, then feeling as if she were running out of time, hurried through the crush of people. She jogged into the building and after catching an elevator car, tapped her foot impatiently as it slowly climbed to the floor for the Homicide Division.

Once in the office again, she hung up her wet coat, then, in her cubicle, settled into her desk chair where she opened the packet from Mercy Hospital again and studied the information. It wasn't much, but she did glean that Belva Nelson had been little more than a part-time employee over a span of five years. The hospital had been called St. Mary's at the time, some thirty years ago, and Belva had been hired to cover shifts in neurology, surgery, recovery, and maternity.

Nash felt a little sizzle in her blood as she stared at the list. There was the neurological link. Cassie had mental issues; perhaps they'd been inherited from someone in her family. Her father? Mother? And then there was the maternity listing.

She did quick mental calculations.

As far as she knew, Jenna Hughes did not grow up in Portland, but what if she had gotten pregnant, been a girl "in trouble"? The timing would be about right if Jenna had been a teen, and though it seemed a stretch, maybe not so much. Nash's eyes narrowed. Today's morals weren't the same as they had been thirty to forty years ago. Teen mothers weren't as likely to keep their babies. Oftentimes pregnancies were hidden, girls giving up their babies after leaving school.

Was it possible?

Did Jenna have another child?

One born before Cassie?

Nash's heartbeat ticked up. She sensed she might be onto something. Then again, she could be wrong in many ways. Even if Jenna had given a baby up for adoption, what would that child have to do with any of this? Could he or she be involved? A killer? An accomplice?

Whoa, whoa, whoa! Don't go jumping off the deep end here. You need facts. Cold, hard facts. Not some ill-founded concept straight out of one of Edwina's soap operas. Think, Rhonda, think.

She tapped her fingers on the edge of her desk and stared at the information a few more seconds before punching out the number for vital records. If Jenna Hughes had borne a child in Oregon, there would be some record of it. Nash just had to look.

"Seek and ye shall find," she whispered.

For the first time in a week, Nash actually smiled.

* * *

"What's this all about?" Trent asked as Cassie, behind the wheel of her Honda, turned into the lane leading to her mother's house. They were on their way to Portland to Dean Arnette's party, but Jenna had called and insisted that they stop by her house first.

"Don't know," Cassie said as she pulled up to the rambling house she'd called home for most of her teens, a home she'd once hated. She still had ambivalent feelings toward the rustic, now renovated, ranch house. "But it sounded urgent. Jenna wouldn't take 'no' for an answer. Believe me, I tried to beg off, but, uh-uh. No dice." Yanking her keys from the ignition, she felt more than a little trepidation. Jenna had been insistent. And there hadn't been an iota of levity in her request, no, make that demand.

"Please, Cassie, do this," she'd said.

"But we're already late."

"I don't care." Jenna had sighed, played the trump "Mom" card. "Look, I don't ask for much. Do me this one favor."

So Cassie had buckled and here she was, walking across the porch to the front door. Her breath caught as she spied her grim-faced mother peering out the window. An icy feeling of déjà vu crawled through her mind. Whitney Stone's footage had shown Allie at that very window, peeking out, then disappearing as she headed for the front door.

Oh, Jesus. Something happened. Allie!

Heart in her throat, Cassie was about to reach for the handle when the door flew open and Jenna, pale as death, sailed over the threshold to hug her daughter fiercely, as if she were afraid Cassie would disappear into thin air.

Like Allie.

"Hey. Mom. Are you okay? What happened?" she asked.

Jenna was actually shaking.

"Mom?" she asked, still in her mother's embrace. Looking over Jenna's shoulder, Cassie caught Trent's eye and cast him an I-don't-get-this glance, then saw movement on the other side of the door when Carter, unshaven, his jaw set, appeared in the hallway.

"Come on in," her stepfather said, his voice low, his face serious. As if someone had died.

Cassie's heart sank. All her fears congealed. "Oh, God, Mom, is it Allie? Is she all right?"

"Oh, honey, I don't know." Jenna's voice broke.

Cassie yanked herself free and held her mother at arm's length so she could stare into Jenna's tortured eyes. "What is it? What happened?"

"I . . . we haven't heard anything about Allie," Jenna said, tears forming as a gust of wind raced across the porch.

"Then what? Are you okay?"

Her mother and stepfather exchanged glances. "Come inside," Jenna said, blinking and managing a frail smile. "I need to talk to you."

Another time, Cassie would have protested. Jenna knew that they were late, they'd talked about it on the phone, so, the fact that Jenna was so insistent coupled with Jenna's emotional state warned Cassie that something major was up. Something not good. Apprehension propelled her into the house and she felt Trent's hand on her elbow as she followed Jenna and Shane into the kitchen with Trent one step behind. Like most of the other rooms in the house, the kitchen had been updated since she lived there—new tile floors, appliances, and countertops—but the layout much the same. She stood at the island and wondered what in the world was going on.

Her mother had always been theatrical, but this? It was over the top, even for Jenna Hughes.

"Can I . . ." Jenna started, seeming to have composed herself a bit. She swiped almost angrily at the unwanted tears. "Can I get you coffee or a drink or—?"

"No! Just tell me what's going on!" Cassie interrupted. "You look like someone died."

Jenna stiffened, then said to Shane, "Well, I need something. Strong."

"You got it." Her husband was already reaching into a cupboard for a bottle of some kind of whiskey. He poured two short glasses, added ice from the freezer, then raising his eyebrows in a silent question, looked at Trent.

Cassie's husband's face was as somber as Carter's, his jaw set in granite. He gave a quick shake of his head. "Another time."

"So what is it?" Cassie demanded. She'd rarely witnessed Jenna drink more than a glass of wine, maybe two, but tonight she took a long swallow, then cradled the small glass of amber liquid in both hands as if it were nectar from the gods. Leaning a hip against the counter, as if for support, she drew in a steadying breath. "There is something I never told you girls . . . well, anyone, for that matter. Not Shane, either, nor your father, no one."

"What?"

Jenna took a sip, pulled a face, then met all of the questions in Cassie's eyes. She took in a long breath, then admitted, "I had another daughter, one who's older than you by about four years."

"What?" Cassie thought she hadn't heard right. "*Another* daughter? Are you kidding me?" She couldn't believe it, but her mother's ashen face confirmed her words.

"Yes." She was nodding, staring into her glass as she struggled for the right words. "I gave her up for adoption." She cleared her throat. "I was only sixteen, still in high school when it happened."

Cassie stood stock-still, tried to process.

"I should have told you, well, everyone sooner."

"Wait a second. Who is she?"

"I don't know. I didn't want to know. My boyfriend, the father, it . . . it wasn't a good relationship." Her eyes glazed over in memory. "For God's sake, we were just kids ourselves and we . . . we'd only been dating a couple of months and yeah, I got pregnant. It wasn't quite the same then as it is now. Marriage was expected, at least in my family, but we were just too young and not in love and could never have made it. He took off when he found out, just moved out of town to live with an uncle, wanted nothing to do with the baby or me. My parents and I made the decision to go for a private adoption through a lawyer, here in Portland, and I promised never to . . . never to look her or them up." She squeezed her eyes shut and when she spoke again, her voice was higher. Strained. "I don't even know her name."

Cassie felt as if her world had just turned upside down. Everything she'd known, everything she'd believed was no longer sturdy and true. It was as if her past, that which had molded her, was no longer set in concrete but more like emotional quicksand. She had a half sister? An older half-sister she'd never met, never known existed? Dark thoughts swirled in her mind as she began to consider all the implications. "Why are you telling me this now?"

"Because I had the baby at St. Mary's Hospital." She cleared her throat. "That hospital, St. Mary's? It's now Mercy."

"What?" Cassie whispered, thinking of her own experience recently. Dear God, she'd been a patient in the same hospital where her mother had birthed a secret baby thirty-odd years earlier? What were the chances of that?

A tear had started to roll down Jenna's cheek and she sniffed. "When you checked yourself in there, all these old memories returned and I even thought about telling you then, but Allie was missing and you . . . you were struggling." Her back stiffened as she brushed the offensive tear away. "I didn't think it was the time to bring up that I had another child, one I didn't raise." She sniffed. Guilt wracked her features. "I . . . I guess there never was a good time. I . . . oh, dear

God. I made so many mistakes. First I was ashamed, but I finished school and drifted to California, where I met your father and got into films and . . . there just wasn't a time to come up with the truth. I was afraid of the press, of what it would do to *my* career and then, of course, to you and Allie. What it would do to you to know that I'd abandoned my first child."

"Shhh. You did the right thing," Carter said.

"Did I? Who knows?" Her eyes were wide. Guilt-riddled. "I should have at least put my name on some kind of registry so that she could have found me, could have gotten in touch, but"—Jenna was shaking her head—"of course I didn't. I thought it would be best and maybe someday I'd get in touch with her, but then I became this . . . this *thing* in Hollywood and I thought it would be best not to say anything." Her expression evolved to regret. "As I said, no one knew, and I felt that the child didn't need to be subjected to the spotlight of being Jenna Hughes's 'secret baby' or 'love child' or whatever name and stigma would be thrown her way. She needed to grow up in a normal family, with loving parents, a mother and a father who cared about her." Jenna's voice cracked and her drink wobbled in her hands.

Stern-faced, Shane took the glass and set it on the counter, then wrapped an arm over her shoulders. "Shhh," he whispered again, kissing the top of her head. "It's going to be okay."

"Okay?" Cassie repeated, disbelieving. "Are you nuts? How can you even suggest that everything's going to be okay? This . . . this is crazy. I mean, everything I thought I knew about you," she said to her mother, "—and Dad . . . all of it was built on a lie."

"Hey!" Carter said.

But Jenna's eyes reflected her own doubts.

In a chilling moment of realization, Cassie realized where this was going.

The masks!

A new fear strangled her as she saw, in her mind's eye, the hastily scribbled messages scrawled across the back of each: *sister. mother.* Her heart stilled and she dreaded what was to come. "You think it's her? The one who left the masks . . . who killed Holly and Brandi?" she whispered, the horror within her growing.

Jenna was nodding, the tears streaming now. "I can't be certain, of course, and I pray to God that I'm wrong, but . . ." Her voice faded and for a second Cassie was sure that her mother was going to collapse. ". . . it could be my daughter found out that she was mine and that she's mentally unstable and . . ."

"And a murderess?" Cassie whispered, her mind spinning to differing horrendous scenarios. "That she's leaving the masks to get back at you? At me? At Allie?" Her insides turned to ice as she considered the horrifying possibilities. "Oh, God, do you think she's held Allie somewhere or . . . or maybe even—"

"Oh, hey, whoa!" Trent cut in, holding up his hands, stopping the direction of the conversation. "We're all making some pretty big leaps here." He eyed Carter and Jenna. "We don't know anything. This is all just supposition."

"Yeah." Carter gave his wife a squeeze. "We know, but it's certainly a lead the police need to explore." His eyes narrowed as he said, "I've called the Portland PD. It seems Nash was already on the same wavelength, going at the idea from a different angle. Jenna supplied Nash with as much information as she has, date of birth, name of the lawyer who was involved, hospital, which they already knew. That seems to be the connection of Belva Nelson, the nurse you saw in the hospital room. She really did work there. At St. Mary's. She was in the delivery room."

Stunned, Cassie stared at her mother in disbelief. "But why would she come back to visit me?" She envisioned the nurse in the white uniform. "To tell me about Allie? How would she know that she was okay?"

"I don't know," Jenna said darkly.

"Have they tracked down this nurse, this Belva person?" Cassie asked, her mind spinning with dozens of questions. "Does she know where Allie is? What happened to her? Why hasn't she called or shown up?" For a fleeting second, Cassie's heart took flight with hope. Finally there would be answers. Allie would return! This whole mess and mystery would be behind them.

Jenna was shaking her head and Carter said, "No one knows what happened. And Belva Nelson is missing."

"Missing?" Trent cut in and Carter gave them a brief rundown of Belva Nelson's connection to Sonja Watson and the fact that the retired nurse was now MIA.

"What happened to her?" Cassie demanded.

"Don't know. But the police will find out. They're double-checking with her family."

So it wasn't over.

And Allie was still missing.

"I wanted you to know," Jenna said. "Before you heard it somewhere else."

"Like where?"

Jenna shrugged. "Who knows where it will pop up first. So many people have been digging into my life, it was bound to surface."

"Whitney Stone," Cassie guessed and Trent scowled.

"Or someone like her," Jenna whispered. "Once the police know—" She glanced at her husband. "Well, there are leaks in every department."

"Don't remind me," Carter muttered.

Seeing her mother so miserable broke Cassie's heart. She and Jenna had struggled over the years, and Cassie had often felt a distance between them, but maybe this explained it a bit, the secret her mother had harbored, the guilt she'd borne over her first child.

Cassie said, "They have to find the nurse. Maybe she could lead us to Allie, tell us why she told me Allie was okay."

"You're certain she was talking about Allie?" Jenna asked quietly. "That *Allie* was alive?"

"Yes, I told you that—" Cassie stopped short. Wasn't that what the nurse had said? What she'd meant? Or had Belva Nelson, who had been present at the birth of Jenna's first child, been talking about that other sister, the half-sibling Cassie hadn't known existed? Her gaze crashed with her mother's and she understood that Jenna's thoughts had traveled down that same unfamiliar road.

Cassie felt as if her world were shrinking into a deep, dark hole. Had the nurse actually said Allie's name? She thought hard to that ethereal night in the hospital when the woman had seemingly appeared, like a ghost from the past. The dreamlike conversation wasn't clear. "Oh . . . God . . . I think . . . I mean I'm pretty sure she was talking about Allie."

But she wasn't certain. Not a hundred percent.

"I don't remember," she said and her own voice sounded strangled. Had she held on to the old nurse's words, believing she was talking about Allie, when really, that was only because at the time, Allie was the only sister she knew, the only sibling in Cassie's world?

Jenna picked up her glass and took another drink.

"I think she was talking about Allie, Mom. Why would she tell me about someone I didn't even know existed?" She felt wounded and raw inside and Jenna recognized it.

"Oh, baby, I'm so sorry," Jenna said, setting down her drink and looking her daughter in the eye. "I hope to God I'm wrong about this. I hope my other daughter is somewhere safe, with a loving husband and kids and . . . and that she has nothing to do with any of what's happening." Stiffening her spine, she added, "Even considering that she may be a part of this seems like a betrayal. To her. To you. To all of us."

Carter's eyes turned dark. "You've got to quit beating yourself up about it." Again, he hugged her and she looked up at the ceiling in her fight to regain control of her emotions.

Cassie was fighting her own instinct of denial. Another sister? An *older* half-sister she'd never heard of? She wanted to think this was all wrong, but staring at her mother, witnessing Jenna's guilt and despair, she understood the worry, was infected with her mother's fears. She grabbed her husband's calloused hand. "Trent's right. We don't know anything, not yet."

Jenna offered the tiniest of smiles, one without any real warmth. "Look, you need to get going. I don't want to keep you, but I just wanted you to hear this from me. Not from someone else or a cheap tabloid or on . . . on stupid mystery week on a cable channel."

"So wait. Whitney Stone does know about this?" Cassie sensed her mother was holding back, probably protecting her again. "Shane?" she asked, eyeing her stepfather.

"You'd better let her know everything," he advised his wife, and Jenna sighed.

"Mom?"

"It's nothing. Just . . . well, Whitney Stone left me a pointed voice mail." Jenna found the chair where she'd tossed her purse and after sitting down plucked her cell from a side pocket. After scrolling through her messages she found the one she wanted and hit the speaker button. A second later the reporter's voice was audible.

"This is Whitney Stone *again.* I would appreciate a call back. Sooner rather than later. You know I'm working on the next episode for *Justice: Stone Cold,* and I would love to interview you. It really would be in your best interest. I've done a little digging into your life and I would love your input before the program airs. Some of the information I've found is private, I realize, but I still think the public, your fans, would love to learn about you, and your life before you became a star." A pause. As if she was constructing her thought. "To be clear, I'm not talking about the whitewashed version that your publicist spins, but the real truth. Your fans want to know who you are. The real Jenna Hughes." Another pause. Then, "So please, call me."

Click.

"Wow." Cassie stared at the phone. "You think this is about your first child?"

"Yeah, I do." Jenna nodded, then cleared her throat. "I don't know of anything else that would make her feel so empowered."

"It's a threat," Carter said, pissed. He walked to the window to stare into the night. "The woman's a vulture."

Cassie muttered, "Or worse."

"She'll be at the party tonight," Jenna predicted. "Members of the press have been invited, you know, to create a buzz about the film."

"As if there wasn't enough of one. Since Allie's been gone she and the movie have been in all the tabloids and on all the entertainment shows, the gossip columns. Everywhere." She didn't say it, but in some ways Allie's disappearance was the best publicity *Dead Heat* could get. Even the homicides of people associated with the film fascinated the populace and even appealed to the more macabre of film-goers, elevated the intrigue factor of the movie, created a buzz, trended on social websites. It was sick.

"I just wish . . . I wish Allie were here, too. I would tell her . . . everything." Jenna's tears began to fall again. "Oh, God, where is she? What happened to her?"

Carter was at her side in an instant, lifting her from the chair, holding her close.

Torn, hating witnessing her mother fall apart, Cassie said, "Mom, if you want me to stay—"

"No, no!" Jenna said emphatically as she pulled from Carter's embrace. "Go." She made a shooing motion. "Try and have a good time."

"Oh, yeah. Right," Cassie said dryly. "As if! Geez, Mom, I'm not going because I think it'll be fun, and Trent didn't want to go at all, but I might see someone there who knows something about Allie."

"Wouldn't they have said something by now?" Jenna said.

Cassie shook her head. "Not if they're hiding something."

Sighing, Jenna said, "I suppose anything's possible. Listen, I didn't mean to ruin the night. But I thought you'd want to know. About your half-sister."

"I did. Or do." A million questions about this mystery sibling skated through her head. Who was she? Where was she? Did she know about Jenna? What kind of family had adopted her? Were there other brothers and sisters? What had been her life?

Most importantly, what, if anything, did she have to do with the murders and Allie's disappearance?

CHAPTER 33

With Double T riding shotgun, Nash gunned her little car up the steep incline. Around narrow, hairpin corners that cut through the thick forest of the Cascade foothills. She drove as if the devil himself were on her tail, her fingers clamped around the steering wheel, her eyes focused on the twin beams of her headlights that knifed through the darkness and steady rain.

Even Double T, usually cool, was clutching the handhold and saying, "Sheeeit, Nash, this ain't the Indy 500!"

She didn't care. The sense of losing time, of sand slipping through the hourglass of this investigation caused her stomach to curl into a mother of a fist and her foot to tromp on the gas pedal. She couldn't drive fast enough to the cabin where she'd hoped to find Belva Nelson.

Through a search of city, county, and state records, Jenkins had located the property listed under Belva Nelson's father's name, which Nash had double checked with Nelson's niece, Sonja Watkins. At first Watkins had played dumb, but Nash had put the legal screws to her and when confronted with the fact that Watkins and her ex-con husband could be jailed for hampering an investigation, the woman folded. Reluctantly Watkins had admitted that her aunt had been holed up in the rustic property ever since learning of Holly Dennison's death. Beyond confirming the address, and the number of Belva Nelson's disposable cell, Watkins had offered up as little information as possible before clamming up.

There was more to the story, Nash was certain, but Sonja Watkins wasn't talking.

Nash negotiated another sharp curve. God, this mountain road twisted like a sidewinder.

Why had the nurse, who had held her silence for over thirty years, suddenly felt threatened and the need to sneak into the hospital in some weird, retro uniform no less? What was that all about? Why not just have a regular face-to-face, or call? What was with all the high drama? It was as if the nurse had been playing some part in a kitschy Jenna Hughes film.

How did she know that Allie Kramer was alive and okay?

Sonja Watkins wasn't saying. If Belva Nelson's niece had known any more, which Nash wholeheartedly believed, Ms. Watkins was keeping it to herself. Watkins had even mentioned she might not talk to the police any further except with an attorney present.

Which probably meant she was guilty of some bigger crime.

Nash intended to find out just what that was, after she talked to the retired nurse, the very nurse who, Nash had learned, had been in attendance at St. Mary's Hospital when Jenna Hughes had delivered her first baby.

"Hey! Take it easy. She's not goin' anywhere," Double T warned as her little Ford slid a bit and the forest grew more dense.

"You don't know that. She might already be running like a damned rabbit!"

"She picked a great place for it. This is like the ends of the earth."

Nash almost smiled. Almost. Instead she adjusted the defroster as the windows were starting to cloud. Outside, it was dark as pitch, a wind blowing harshly, tree branches swaying in a wild macabre dance as they were caught in the glare of the Focus's headlights. Not another car was on the skinny ribbon of asphalt that threatened to turn to gravel around each new bend.

"Jesus," Double T said. "When she decided to hide, she wasn't kidding around."

"She was scared."

"Don't blame her. But up here in the middle of nowhere? This is better than the city?" Snorting in disgust, he clung to the handhold. "Don't think so."

"We're almost there."

"Good."

What did the nurse know about Allie Kramer's disappearance? About the homicides?

Whoever was behind the murders hadn't killed people randomly, then placed weird masks over their faces. No way. The killer had picked people associated with the film. Nash didn't believe the choice of Holly Dennison and Brandi Potts as victims had been coincidental. Did Belva Nelson know why?

Nash frowned. The pieces of the puzzle were finally starting to fit together, but there were still huge holes that Nash didn't understand.

She hoped Belva Nelson could fill in the gaps.

In the meantime Nash had instructed Jenkins to cross-check any information on the birth of Jenna Nash's secret child with everyone associated with *Dead Heat,* on the off-chance that Jenna's first-born was somehow associated with the movie. It seemed far-fetched, as the connection to Jenna Hughes alone would explain the masks, at least to a deranged mind. So why bother using people connected to the movie as victims? And, in Potts's case, an obscure connection. Not many people knew that Brandi Potts was an extra on the film. Only those close to the production of *Dead Heat*, those in the inner circle, would even know Potts existed.

A rush of adrenaline shot through Nash. Someone connected with the movie had to have had a personal vendetta against Allie Kramer. Cassie Kramer? Brandon McNary? Some other person who had become Allie's enemy? Or the missing star of *Dead Heat* herself? Just how diabolical was Allie Kramer? Her beauty was only surpassed by her intelligence, which, according to IQ tests, was off the charts.

So many questions.

So few answers.

Yet.

But she had others working on the information. Detective Natalie Jenkins was determined to find out the identity of the family that had adopted Jenna Hughes's firstborn, and privacy codes or agreements be damned. *Someone* knew who had adopted the girl.

"Hey!" Double T said, interrupting her thoughts and pointing to an overgrown lane where the trees opened a bit. "I think we're here."

She might have sped right past except for the county deputy's car about fifty feet into the private road. With lights flashing, the cruiser blocked further access to the property. Nash pulled in behind the cruiser. She and Double T climbed out of her Ford and with heads bent against the rain, made their way through the muck and mud to the cruiser, where a deputy in rain gear stood guard. Rain was sliding from his weatherproof jacket and dripping from the bill of his cap. He was young, around twenty-five, and pale as death in the darkness, his mouth a thin line, his beady blue eyes nearly luminescent.

Quick introductions ensued as he inspected their badges, shining the beam of his flashlight over the IDs.

As he nodded curtly, Nash glanced into the back of the county vehicle. It was empty. "Where's Mrs. Nelson?"

"Don't know."

"Not inside?" Nash asked, her heart dropping like a stone.

"No. No one's here, but you'd better go in and take a look. My partner's there and we're waiting for the crime lab guys to show up."

"Because?"

"Looks like a homicide."

"But Mrs. Nelson is not inside?" Nash didn't wait for an answer, just headed to the ramshackle cabin in front of which a Hyundai Santa Fe was parked. The SUV's license was secured with a plate holder decorated with a cowboy upon a bucking rodeo horse and a couple of faded bumper stickers, one advising the reader to turn off his TV, the other professing love for the state of Oregon.

"This doesn't look good," Double T said, turning his collar against a rush of cold air that rustled the boughs of the trees surrounding the small clearing.

"You got that right." They climbed up two rickety steps and stepped through an open doorway.

"Hold it right there," a harsh female voice ordered and they both stopped to view the interior of the cabin, illuminated only by a flashlight held in the hand of a female deputy.

"Detective Rhonda Nash," Nash said, once again flipping open her wallet to display her badge while Double T introduced himself as he flashed his own ID.

The room, in the harsh white light from the flashlight, was a mess, turned-over furniture, a broken lamp, glass underfoot, and a huge dark stain that had spread from a river rock fireplace across the dusty floors.

"Looks like someone bled out here," the deputy said, running the beam of her flashlight over the wide stain. "I found no body inside. Could be on the grounds, or buried. We've got dogs on their way. Can't tell whose blood it is, but it's fresh, some not even dried." She hitched a finger behind her toward the back wall. "Found a shell casing back there. Figured that's where the shooter was when he fired."

Nash let her gaze rove over the small interior and she felt an angry disappointment. Belva Nelson had been the key to her investigation, the turning point. Nash had felt it, that sizzle of anticipation upon reaching the turning point in a case. Now, the retired nurse was missing, most probably dead, the lead withered away.

Using her own flashlight, she swept the interior and decided that someone, most possibly Belva Nelson, had died here last night. She spied an open purse on the floor beneath a table, the stain of blood beneath it. Within the leather bag Nash found a wallet. ID and credit cards issued to Belva Nelson were inside.

This could play out differently. Maybe Nelson wasn't the victim. Perhaps she was still alive. There was even a remote chance she had been the killer, but Nash's gut instinct told her differently.

Damn, damn, damn and double damn!

They were too late. Which wasn't really a surprise, considering that nothing in this case was ever easy, nothing fell into place. If only they'd had a chance to interview Belva Nelson. It was all so frustrating. "Son of a bitch," she said through clenched teeth.

"So now what?" Double T asked.

Nash stemmed her disappointment. Collected herself. She couldn't just wait here for forensics and the dogs. No, not with her feeling that time was running through her fingers. She checked her watch, then instructed the deputy to call her with information and left her card. They walked out of the cabin with not more information than they'd come with.

"You know," she said to Double T as they headed for her car again, picking their way through mud puddles that reflected the pulsing red and blue light from the cruiser's light bar. "If we wrap things up here and get back into town, we might not miss the end of the party for *Dead Heat*. You got a tux or extremely hip black suit you can change into?"

"You're serious?" Double T asked.

"Oh, yeah." She was nodding, sliding into the driver's seat, wondering about her own change of clothes. "Serious as hell."

Tonight the splendor of the Hotel Danvers, one of Portland's most famous and historic hotels, was lost on Cassie. As she and Trent entered through a side door to avoid the reporters camped out at the main entrance she barely noticed the gleaming woodwork, elegant chandeliers, massive staircases, stained-glass windows, or thick carpets. She was too keyed up, still trying to sort things out in her mind.

Jenna's revelation about another child, Cassie's half sister, had caught her off-guard, suggesting that the unknown sibling might be a killer was more than disturbing and it had haunted her on the drive into Portland from Jenna and Shane's ranch. Was it possible? Could it be that she'd even met the woman and not realized they were blood, that they shared the same DNA, the very same mother? The idea gave her goose bumps.

"Come on," Trent said, a hand in hers when they climbed the stairs to the cavernous second-story ballroom.

Through wide open doors, she surveyed the sunken room. Massive chandeliers, dripping with teardrops of crystal and lit by dozens of lights, were suspended from an intricately carved ceiling. On an exterior wall, windows stretched two stories and offered guests an unlimited view of the city. Across an expansive marble floor, French doors opened to a long balcony, that had been built over the main entrance a floor below. Guests gathered and moved through the center of the room.

"I wish Allie was here to see this."

"I think she is . . . kind of," Trent said just as Cassie saw the first of a group of sets, each decorated as individual rooms that had been butted up against the surrounding walls.

Cassie's heart dropped as she eyed the mini-rooms more closely and she realized each had been designed to be an exact replica of one of the sets for *Dead Heat*. "What?" she whispered, disbelieving because in each of the individual rooms, a life-sized mannequin of Allie dressed to look like Shondie Kent, the heroine of the film, had been staged. "Oh, no."

From the wide entrance of the sunken ballroom she was able to view each individual scenario:

Shondie in a business suit and glasses, leaning back in a desk chair, one high-heeled foot resting on the desktop.

Shondie without makeup, tears streaming from beneath oversized sunglasses as she walked through a park.

Shondie wrapped in a long negligee, posed provocatively on a bed with mussed covers, a fake mirror positioned over a fireplace. In the mirror's reflection a man's naked muscular back and neck were visible—Brandon McNary's character's backside.

This was so wrong.

There were other scenes as well, each with a mannequin of Allie.

The most heart-stopping set was of Shondie running down a dark alley, storefronts visible, as she glanced over her shoulder. She was wearing the very same outfit that Lucinda Rinaldi had been dressed in, an identical white jacket, when the fateful bullet had been fired and she'd been shot.

"Oh, Jesus." Cassie's throat turned to dust. Memories in short bursts flashed through her mind. Another place. Other mannequins. All dressed like Jenna Hughes in her starring roles. All macabre likenesses created by a crazed fan who nearly killed Cassie and her mother. She was suddenly chilled to the bone as she recalled that horrid time, ice water running through her veins.

Cassie wanted to run from the room.

"What the hell was Arnette thinking?" Trent's gaze wandered from one scene to the next, each one showcasing the film's missing star.

"He's thinking that if he can't have Allie, he'll come up with the next best thing," she guessed as she stared at a lifelike mannequin of Shondie in a hospital room. Lying on an old-fashioned hospital bed, Shondie appeared glassy-eyed, out of touch. Her dark hair was disheveled, her makeup nonexistent, her arms restrained by thick cuffs, almost as if she were handcuffed to the bed. On one of the partitions of the all-white room was a door with a small glass and mesh window. Peeking through the window was a blond nurse in a pointed white cap.

One identical to the one worn by Belva Nelson on her secretive nighttime visit to Cassie's hospital room.

The hairs on the back of Cassie's neck came to attention.

Apprehension collected in her heart.

Was this a coincidence?

Or part of some grand terrorizing scheme she didn't understand?

Cassie thought of her recent stay in a mental hospital. She'd never seen restraints used at Mercy, but, of course *Dead Heat* was a retro film, hence the white-uniformed nurse.

"Thank God Mom didn't come," she said, staring at the mannequins, her insides curdling.

Jenna had many reasons not to attend, and she'd decided to stay home. Thank God.

Cassie scanned the room with new eyes. Could one of the people within these walls, someone who had worked on the film, be her half-sister? It seemed impossible, but . . . Heart thudding, she swept her gaze across the room, landing for a split second on the possibilities. From Little Bea in her classic black dress and heels, to Cherise, elegant in red, or Ineesha, fit as ever in a backless gown, or Laura in ivory, or Sybil Jones in a man's black tux. All of these women were about the right age and, if Cassie let herself imagine it, could resemble her. Sure, Little Bea was tiny, but so was Jenna, and her chin was just pointed enough . . . and Laura's eyes. Didn't they look a little like Jenna's? And Cherise, she had Jenna's slim build, her heart-shaped face. Or was Cassie mistaken, just fantasizing? Seeing similarities when there were none?

Her head pounded a little as she spied Lucinda Rinaldi wearing a sequined blue strapless dress but seated in an electric wheelchair. Lucinda looked a lot like Allie, the resemblance close enough with the right lighting and camera angle to be her double.

"You okay?" Trent asked, sensing her hesitation.

She rolled her eyes. "Am I ever?"

He actually laughed. "Good point, Cass. Come on. Let's dive into the shark tank."

Following his lead, she took the two steps downward into the crowded, noisy room. She reminded herself that this was her chance to finally talk to some of the people who had avoided her. Little Bea. Dean Arnette. Sig Masters. And others. The problem was that Cassie was still a little unfocused, the life-sized mannequins of Allie, coupled with the recent news that she had a half sister and the murders of people associated with the film, crippled her slightly.

Pull yourself together.

Think!

Don't miss this opportunity.

But the individual sets and mannequins bothered her. Each positioned lifelike doll seemed to be watching her with those glassy eyes so like her sister's. Cassie had the unsettling feeling that Allie was here. Watching. If only in the form of the inanimate life-sized dolls.

Walking deeper into the room, Cassie felt swept into the sea of people. Actors, producers, grips, people who worked on the lighting and sound, the writers, and on and on. The press had been invited as well, of course, as this was an event to promote the movie. Posters from the movie abounded and an adjacent room nearby was showing clips of *Dead Heat* over and over. Champagne and cocktails flowed, and music from the score of the film had been piped in, barely audible over the hum of conversation. And then there were the staged scenes featuring Allie, as Shondie, in mannequin form.

Ugh.

Forcing her gaze from the sets, she walked through the throng, forcing a smile, murmuring a quiet, "Hi," to those who passed, avoiding reacting to the curious glances sent her way. Because of Allie? Because she was with the husband she'd vowed to divorce? Because she'd recently been a patient in a mental hospital? More likely, she thought sourly, all of the above.

"See . . . this isn't so bad," Trent said, leaning down to whisper in her ear. She caught his gaze and realized he was teasing. Parties had never been his thing and no doubt this over-the-top circus with the paparazzi in the wings and gossip flowing like water, was, for Trent, a form of pure torture.

At a table of canapés, she stopped and again surveyed the crowd. Along with those she didn't recognize were the people she'd worked with. Brandon McNary was holding court, his unshaven jaw fashionably scruffy, his dark hair mussed, a gray jacket, open-collared shirt, and jeans. Several women in their early twenties or late teens were hanging on his every word.

Oh, save me.

Cherise Gotwell stood nearby, sipping champagne and gauging the crowd, while Little Bea buzzed through the knots of people and Laura Merrick moved from one group to the next. Lucinda Rinaldi didn't even bother forcing a smile as she wheeled through the throng; and the rumors that she was still going to write a book and name names, all the while suing everyone she could who was associated with the film, hadn't died.

Cassie couldn't blame her. Allie's double's injuries were real and severe, so why wouldn't she make a few bucks because of it?

Like you, she thought, thinking of the screenplay of Allie's life she'd barely started, *taking advantage of the situation, the tragedy involving your sister and you don't even know how it ends.*

With an effort, she quieted the nagging voice in her head and spied Sig Masters. Despite the stigma of actually taking the shot that had wounded Lucinda, Sig had shown up and now was talking to one of the writers. Upon spying Lucinda rolling his way, he ended the conversation and headed straight for the open bar.

Cassie understood. Seeing Lucinda in the chair had to be tough for him. And yet he'd attended, knowing full well she might appear. Sig actually had more guts than Cassie had given him credit for. Or else he was a glutton for punishment.

She felt Trent's hand tighten over her arm.

"You okay with all of this?"

"No," she admitted, wondering if she should even have come. But the truth of the matter was that by not showing, she would have been making a bigger statement and here, at least, the people who had been avoiding her would have a tougher time ignoring her. She glanced up at her husband. "Let's get a drink."

"Great idea."

As they headed to the bar, Cassie caught Ineesha's eye. Wrapped in a conversation with Sybil Jones, the prop manager visibly started, her lips compressing, her eyes thinning. Obviously she wasn't over Cassie's intrusion at her gym workout in California. Quickly and pointedly, she ended her conversation and turned on her heel as Cassie approached.

"Wow. That wasn't obvious at all." Cherise watched Ineesha wend her way through the clusters of guests. "Don't let her get to you."

Cassie shook her head. "Never."

"She's just in a bad mood."

"When isn't she?"

Cherise giggled, then sipped from her glass of champagne, her green eyes dancing with mischief. "It doesn't look like she got in her million steps today."

Cassie actually smiled.

"I think her pedometer might blow up because she works out so much," Cherise said. "She's probably racewalking her way to the hotel gym right now."

"You're wicked."

"When I have to be."

Cassie had a sudden mental image of Ineesha in her long dress on some kind of weightlifting machine, her back muscles visibly straining as she moved a bar, her body sweating all over her designer gown. "Not a pretty image."

Trent bent closer to Cassie and said, "I'll get the drinks. Be right back." She nodded and he smiled slyly. "Don't go anywhere."

"Oh, wow, so you two are back together?" Cherise asked, her gaze following Trent as he slipped around a large group of guests and made his way to the bar.

"I guess."

"Looks like he's really into you." Cherise's eyes thinned before she sighed wistfully. "Must be nice."

"It is. Mostly." *Except when you act like a jealous idiot and accuse him of being in love with your sister.*

Dragging her gaze away from Trent's backside, Cherise rimmed the edge of her glass with a manicured finger. "I don't suppose there's any word on Allie?"

"No."

"That's too bad," she said without much empathy. "I'm sorry. But, you know she was kind of a pain to work for, but way better than Brandon. He's . . ."

"All about himself."

Cherise nodded, her eyebrows pulling together, her voice a barely audible whisper. "I think he's dating someone, but he's keeping it very hush-hush."

"Probably until after the movie's out for a while," Cassie said. "For the fans. They want to think that he's still in love with Allie." She made a sweeping gesture with one hand to the horrible stages of Allie lining the vast room. "For this. To keep up the fantasy. To sell more tickets."

"Maybe." Another swallow from her glass. Her lips pursed as if she'd just thought of something bothersome. "You know, I have this feeling . . . I mean he's never said it, of course, but . . . I think he never got over Allie." The words had a bit of bitterness to them and the corners of Cherise's mouth turned down. Cassie couldn't help but wonder if McNary's assistant had a secret crush on her boss. It wouldn't be the first time and, of course, McNary was considered a heartthrob.

Laura Merrick passed by and offered a quick, conspiratorial smile. "Not as fun as I'd hoped this would be," she said on her way to the bar. "Kind of a pall over the place. It's as if Allie is here and she's not here, y'know?" Hitching her chin toward the set of Shondie in the mental hospital, she shook her head. "Macabre, if you ask me. Arnette's idea of art." She looked past Cassie and added, "Uh-oh, here comes Picasso now. Talk later," and with Cherise in tow drifted toward the open bar where a crowd had gathered and two bartenders were busy mixing drinks.

"Cassie! There you are!" In a black suit and matching open-throated shirt, Dean Arnette approached. His smile, beneath his signature glasses, was wide. Friendly. He seemed pumped to be in the room.

"Hi," she said.

Tall, rail thin with a shaved head and hint of a beard, Arnette gave her one of those almost-hugs. As if he were actually glad to see her. As if he hadn't been ducking her calls.

As Arnette gave her a little space, Cassie caught a glimpse of Trent returning with their drinks. Walking carefully, agilely avoiding other guests while balancing the half-full glasses, Trent slid around the producer to hand Cassie her drink.

She held up the drink in shades of orange and yellow. "What is this?"

"Tequila sunrise. Signature for the party tonight, I guess. Kind of retro."

"Shondie drank it in a bar scene," Arnette clarified, "the character Allie played." He had the good sense to appear grave for a second, then said, "You're Cassie's husband." Quickly he stuck out his hand. "Dean Arnette. The director of *Dead Heat*." He flashed a quick smile as they shook. "I'm surprised we haven't met before." He acted as if Cassie were his long lost daughter rather than someone he'd deftly avoided.

"You know," Cassie said, "I've been trying to talk to you."

"Oh, right. Right. I know. Sorry. I'm just busy as hell right now." With a sweeping gesture, he motioned to the surroundings. "You know, putting this together was almost as difficult as filming the damned movie." As if he'd personally constructed the sets, hired the caterers, and overseen the publicity when he had assistants and minions doing the actual work. He flashed his grin then and it seemed practiced and false. "I'm so sorry your mother couldn't come. How is she holding up?"

Inwardly Cassie tightened. Suddenly she didn't want to divulge a word to Arnette. Her skin actually crawled as he studied her intently. As if he cared. "She's fine," she lied.

"Well, we all miss Allie. I had hoped she would, you know, show up before tonight. God, it's awful." He shook his head, the sweat on his bald pate visible in the light from the chandeliers.

"It is." Cassie nodded. "I was hoping to talk to you about her."

"Of course! Any time." Arnette was already looking around, searching for an escape route, someone more important so he could slither away.

"How about tonight?"

"Tonight?" He tossed her an exaggerated look of disbelief. "Seriously? Like after the party or something?" He swirled one finger as if to include everyone and everything in the ballroom. "Honey, I'd love to, but we'll both be exhausted. And I fly out tomorrow. At the crack. But I'll be in LA next week, I don't start shooting *Forever Silent* until next month."

"Dean?" a voice called from somewhere nearby.

He waved across the room to someone Cassie couldn't see.

"I could meet you in the morning—"

"My flight's at the crack. No, that won't work, but don't worry. We'll talk!" And then he was gone. Disappearing into the crowd.

"Cassie Kramer?" a woman's voice called from behind, and Cassie turned to find Whitney Stone not two feet away. Dressed in a long, black dress that sparkled under the lights, she was as beautiful as anyone in the room. Once more Cassie thought about her anonymous half-sibling and once more she saw a resemblance to Jenna in the slope of Whitney's cheekbones, the arch of her brows, her sleek, black hair with just the right amount of wave. Was it possible? Cassie felt her pulse elevate. Whitney Stone? Her half sister? Whitney had been in LA and Portland and . . .

Don't do this, Cassie. You're making yourself crazy.

Alongside Whitney was the goon who had been her cameraman in LA. She offered one of her dazzling but oh-so-cold smiles. "I've been trying to talk to you."

"I know."

"Do you have a minute?" she asked, as if they were best friends, two women in "the industry" out on the town.

"I really don't."

"So, I'm curious, what do you think of the decorations?" she plowed on. "A little macabre, don't you think? All these scenes with the mannequins dressed like Allie."

"Like Shondie," Cassie corrected.

Whitney tilted her hand. *Samey-same.* "It's a bit bizarre, don't you think? The life-sized dolls. They're really not all that different from the wax figures of your mother ten years ago, are they?"

Cassie felt her insides begin to shred. What was this?

"You were involved then, too. Right? You were in the killer's lair where he had all the images."

"Look, I think I made it clear before, in the park in LA. I don't want to talk to you." With a fragile hold on her patience Cassie added, "So, please, just leave me alone and give my family some privacy."

"Your family," Whitney repeated. A nasty little gleam appeared in her eyes. "It's a little bigger than you thought, isn't it?"

Oh, God, she knows. Crap!

"Did you know you had a half sister? An older sister?"

So there it was. If Whitney Stone knew, the whole world would soon enough. "No comment," Cassie said succinctly and saw the goon smile as if he were satisfied that she'd finally gotten a little of her own back.

"How's the toe?" she asked just as Trent placed an arm on her shoulder. Yeah, she hadn't actually run over it, but she had to make her points.

The cameraman's smile fell away and Whitney pulled a face reminiscent of the reaction of someone sucking on a lemon. Then she zeroed in on Trent and her cool facade fell easily into place again. "The husband," she said. To Cassie, "So the divorce is off? You're ignoring those rumors about Allie and him?"

"We're done here," Trent said, his fingers tightening over Cassie's arm and rotating her toward one of the sets from the movie, a scene where Shondie, terrorized, was cowering in a dark library, books scattered on the floor around her. "Haven't you learned your lesson? Avoid her."

Cassie tried to take a sip from her drink and felt someone bump her from behind. She jumped, though some of the cocktail splashed on her. "Ooh!"

"Sorry," Lucinda said as she backed up her wheelchair and looked up at Cassie without a drip of remorse. In fact, Cassie wondered if the "accident" had been intentional. Lucinda went on, "I just can't quite get the hang of this thing."

"I thought you were walking," Cassie said, remembering Lucinda struggling at the rehabilitation center.

"Oh, I am. But when I go out, I use this." She patted the arm of the wheelchair as a couple Cassie didn't recognize squeezed past.

They sloshed drinks and, giggling, muttered "sorry" several times as they tried to maneuver around Lucinda and her chair.

"Morons!" Lucinda said to Cassie. "So I hear you're writing a screenplay or a script or something. About the film and Allie's disappearance."

How did she know this?

"I'm thinking about it, but really, I'm more interested in finding my sister."

"Aren't we all?" Lucinda said, pointedly eyeing Trent. "I sure would like to talk to her and find out why she bailed on the very day that I end up getting shot. You ever consider that, huh?"

Cassie nodded, sipping the drink.

"It could have been any one of us. You. Allie. But I'm the one who got lucky." Her lips, painted a shiny peach, twisted bitterly. "Wonder how that happened? Your character was supposed to be the one running behind, then the scene was rewritten and on the day of the final take for the reshoot, Allie just vanishes and I end up with a bullet in my spine. What're the chances of that?"

"I don't know, but I'm really sorry."

"Sure, sure. Everyone's sorry." Lucinda waved in the air, as if she were shooing away an irritating mosquito, but her face changed slightly as she looked up at Cassie. For an instant, she almost appeared evil. Or was it, again, Cassie's mind playing tricks on her? She didn't think Lucinda could be her half-sister, but there was something about her, a familiarity she noted once more.

It's all in your head. Cassie's fingers clamped over her drink and the headache that had been threatening began to pulse behind her eyes.

"So," Lucinda was saying, "if you end up writing the script, will I be in it?"

"What?"

"I wouldn't want to be portrayed in a bad light, y'know. Be sure to run it by me. Or my lawyer." Her smile was intact but her eyes glittered. "The way I see it, this"—she swirled her hand to encompass the room, the guests, the scenes from the movie, and everything else in the room—"this is my story to tell. To write. I've been approached by a publisher, so I'll let you know if the book will be turned into a movie. My movie." Again she patted the arm of her chair. Her saccharine smile never faltered. "I figure I'm owed." She turned and hit a button, the wheelchair whirred into motion.

"Sweet gal," Trent observed as Lucinda, chair and all, was swallowed by the crowd.

"She has a reason to be pissed."

"I guess, but it seems like she's milking it."

Cassie glanced around the noisy room. Conversation was a hum punctuated by laughter, the score of *Dead Heat* playing in a loop, a musical undercurrent to the cacophony of voices rising from every corner of the expansive room. "Everyone here has an agenda, including me. I guess Lucinda has a right to hers, bitterness and all."

More and more people had arrived, the room was getting crowded, the temperature rising, a few people becoming tipsy and louder than the rest.

Cassie was well into her second drink. She and Trent had wandered out to the cool night air of the verandah. Her throat was a little raw, her nerves stretched thin, and she was certain she'd waded through enough small talk to last her a lifetime. Her headache was a low thrum and she thought if she had to answer one more question about Allie or fend off questioning looks aimed at her and the husband she'd accused of being unfaithful, or just keep a damned smile pinned on her face for another second she might explode. Worse yet was her clash with Brandon McNary. To her surprise, he'd accosted her as she'd left the ladies' room half an hour earlier.

"Thanks a lot," he'd said, pulling her into a pillared alcove.

"For what?" She'd yanked her arm away from him.

"For the cops, and what you told them about the text message. From Allie."

"I told them about *a* message you received, that you thought was from Allie. Who knows who it's really from, but don't blame me." She'd been furious, already sick of the party. "I had to tell them. God, where have you been? Brandi Potts was murdered that night. Not far from where we'd met."

"And I had nothing to do with it. Didn't even know the woman. Was she involved with the movie? I don't know." He'd shrugged. "The extras? Come *on*. I had no reason to kill her and I don't even think I should have to explain it." He'd shoved stiff fingers of both hands through his hair in frustration. "The deal is that I don't need some detective crawling up my ass. I'm on a publicity tour, for fuck's sake."

"Whoa. Wait! Aren't you the guy who said, 'There is no such thing as bad publicity'?"

"I wasn't talking about murder. Jesus Christ, Cassie, use your brain, would ya? I'm already a major suspect in her disappearance." When she'd looked at him as if she didn't know what he was talking about, he'd added, "Oh, fuck! You didn't know that? Come on! The on-again, off-again boyfriend who had public blowups with the missing woman? Of course I'm a suspect. That's basic. Homicide 101."

"But I thought—"

"I know what you thought. That you were suspect *numero uno*, and maybe you are, I don't know, but what I do know is that I've been up on Detective Nash's popularity list, too. In fact, she's been calling me day and night." Furtively, he'd looked around the pillar to the heart of the party. "You know, I'm surprised she isn't here right now, trying to interrogate me. You've met her, right?" he'd asked, his gaze holding hers. "The ice-queen cop?"

"You know I have."

"It was a rhetorical question, but, listen, just so we're on the same page? Where the cops are concerned, keep your damned mouth shut about me." His eyes had burned with a quiet fury. "Got it?" he'd asked through clenched teeth, but he hadn't waited for a response, just turned on his heel and made a beeline to the bar. As he'd leaned into the bartender to give his order, two blondes in miniskirts had descended out of thin air to hang on his every word.

Pathetic.

She took another sip of her drink.

"Let's go," she said finally. Trent was leaning over the balcony, staring down to the street. Cool air ruffled his hair and the scent of the Willamette River was discernable in the dampness in the air. Below, on the sidewalks, pedestrians in coats with hoods or tucked under umbrellas moved quickly, while cars and trucks rumbled along the streets.

She was tired and the party had been a struggle. She hadn't learned anything that would help her find her sister. Her *younger* sister, she reminded herself, still adjusting to her new reality. She'd just have to walk through the giant room with its ridiculous sets featuring Allie as Shondie one more time, then she and Trent could drive home, which is what she was beginning to think of his ranch.

Home. The word had a nice ring to it.

She was turning to step inside the ballroom when, from the corner of her eye, she saw a movement on a balcony a few floors overhead. Pausing, she saw that a woman was standing, almost posed, looking into the night.

Cassie's heart clenched.

She squinted and her throat closed.

Was it? Could it be? Dear God, the woman looked like Allie!

No way! It's the drinks. The imagery of the sets! The lifelike mannequins. All of the talk about the missing star of Dead Heat. She looked again and the woman had disappeared into the night.

"Stupid," she whispered.

"What?" Trent asked. "Ready?"

"Yeah, just remind me the next time I want a tequila sunrise, that it's a bad idea. Make that a *very* bad idea."

"You got it." Trent's thin lips curved into that bad-boy smile that still got to her.

As she headed for the door, she glanced up one more time and the woman reappeared on the balcony. She was wearing a gray dress and raincoat that billowed away from her, a coat similar to one that Cassie had seen Allie wear several times last year.

It couldn't be!

The woman looked down; smiled that Allie signature smile.

Cassie stared. Disbelieving. Her brain screaming at her that what she was seeing was a fake, a distortion, her mind playing tricks on her. "Holy shit," she whispered, her mouth suddenly devoid of spit. "Allie," she whispered.

And the woman stepped out of sight again.

No!

"What?" Trent said.

"I saw Allie." Her voice sounded odd, even to her own ears.

"Allie? No. Wait a second."

"Up there! On that balcony." A jumble of emotions tore at her and she was jabbing her finger in the air, pointing wildly at the seventh-floor balcony. "The corner room! Five floors up."

Trent tilted his head, his gaze scouring the side of the building. "I don't see anything."

"That balcony right there, with the . . . the damned door is open, the curtains billowing. I'm telling you it was Allie!" she said, nearly hysterical. Frantic, she headed for the doors. "We have to go. I have to find her."

"Cass—" His voice was reproachful. "There have been tons of sightings and none of them panned out, you know that. I think your mind is playing tricks on you."

"Then let's find out!" she said angrily, knowing he was right, rational thought arguing with what she was certain she'd seen. "I know it sounds crazy, Trent, but I'm telling you it was Allie!"

He grabbed her shoulders, concern in his gaze. "I think you've had a drink or two and all this talk about Allie, seeing her on the screen or—"

"She's here!" Cassie peeled out of his grip. "And I'm going to find her." She didn't wait, just flung herself through the doorway and tore through the ballroom.

"Cassie?" someone called after her as she jostled first one group of people, then another. She felt as if she were swimming upstream, fighting the current, trying to pass rocks and logjams. "Cassie Kramer!"

She didn't stop to see who it was, just plowed through the throng, her heart pounding, her head screaming that she was hallucinating. Again. The weird scenes of Shondie Kent, no, Allie Kramer, closed in on her, the eyes staring as if to find her soul. She had to get out. Gasping, the world spinning out of control, she somehow made her way up the steps, through the open doors and out of the ballroom. Somewhere behind her, Trent was following, but she couldn't wait, had to know if she'd really seen her sister! As she rounded a corner, she cast a look over her shoulder to the ballroom to see that Whitney Stone and her cameraman had stymied Trent. Obviously the reporter was trying to engage him, blocking his path.

Cassie didn't wait.

She had to find her sister.

Allie! Dear God, where have you been?

Why are you here?

Why would you hide, in this hotel?

Why not come down to the party, make a splash?

Oh, God, is it really you?

Faster, faster, faster!

Her headache was nearly blinding.

People were collecting at the elevators, all oblivious to her situation, that she was in a panic to locate her sister. Frantically she searched the signs and found the staircase. She was through the door in a second.

Up, up, up!

She took the steps two at a time in the narrow stairwell, the steps metal, the shaft dark. Ignoring the feeling of the walls closing in on her, she continued upward, flying past the third floor, then the fourth. On the fifth, she was gasping for breath and clinging onto the railing. Far below she heard a door click open, then slam shut. Boots began to ring on the stairs below.

"Cassie?" Trent called, his voice echoing up the shaft.

"Up here!" she yelled and kept climbing, feeling claustrophobic but mounting each step, not wanting him to catch her. She knew what he'd say, that everything she was doing was the actions of a person who had lost touch with all reality. Doubts assailed her as she reached each floor.

What if she were wrong?

What if this was a wild-goose chase?

What if, oh, God, she were hallucinating again, seeing things that didn't exist?

She passed the sixth floor and her legs were starting to cramp.

"Cass!" he yelled again. "Wait!"

She kept hurrying, her feet flying up the steps.

Breathing hard, her legs aching, she finally saw a red number 7 painted on the fire door of a landing. Finally!

"Cass!" Trent yelled after her again, but she didn't stop, heard him closing in on her. "Hey! You can't just go busting into a person's room."

Using all her weight she shouldered the fire door open and nearly fell into the hallway with its shabby carpet, half-painted walls and skeletal scaffolding. Electrical wires were exposed, holes in the wall were visible, and she realized that this was an older part of the hotel, an area that hadn't yet been renovated and obviously wasn't currently used for guests.

So why would Allie or anyone, for that matter, be up here?

She skirted ladders and paint cloths and equipment littering the dim, long hallway that was eerie, but wasn't about to turn back. This was the floor where she'd seen Allie or her damned lookalike and Cassie wasn't leaving until she'd checked out every corner.

The stairwell door opened again.

"What the hell is this?" Trent asked, his voice reverberating through the deserted hallway.

"Renovations." She was already moving toward the corner room. Trent was right on her heels. "Cass. Stop this! Look around. There's no one here."

He sounded frantic.

Worried.

She was having none of it and reached the door.

Trent caught her arm. Spun her around. Stared down at her with eyes filled with concern. "This is crazy. You know that, don't you?"

She blinked. He was right. She was acting like a lunatic. Seeing things that didn't exist. Willing her missing sister to appear. Believing above all else that Allie was alive and here in this hotel, five floors above a party thrown for her latest movie. Why in the world would she be holed up here? Hiding out?

She saw the pain in his eyes, knew that he didn't want to believe that she'd lost all connection with sanity, that she was creating images that weren't there, that she was hallucinating again and was easing her way back to a psychiatric ward. "I saw her, Trent, I did!" she said, nearly spitting out the words. Desperate to believe them herself.

"Cassie. This is . . ."

"Nuts?" she supplied. "A half-baked fantasy?"

He didn't answer. For half a heartbeat Cassie hesitated and then she said, "Well, you're right. It is. But it's my fantasy and I'm going to see it through and find my damned sister!" Spinning out of his arms, she grabbed the handle of the door and pushed hard.

To her surprise it gave way.

Easily.

Without a key.

Creaking inward to a dark void.

"Allie?" she whispered, her voice cracking as she fumbled for the light switch.

Click!

The overhead fixture snapped on. Bright light washed over a room that housed no one, just like the other rooms on this floor. The tattered carpet was dust-covered. A queen-sized bed with a bare mattress and a forgotten bubble-faced TV were the only furnishings.

But the balcony door was cracked, curtains billowing through the opening, and carelessly tossed over the battered headboard was a raincoat that appeared identical to one Cassie was sure belonged to her sister.

CHAPTER 34

Allie Kramer stood on the dark corner. The wig she was wearing was sodden, the baggy sweatshirt and jeans wet as well, the rain coming down in buckets, and yet she was rooted to the ground, looking back at the hotel where the party for the release of *Dead Heat* was in full swing. She'd snuck into the hotel and done her part, pulled off her "appearance," and before that, she'd managed to gain a peek at the setup for the party, where she should have been in the limelight.

But the staging in the ballroom had soured her stomach—all those sets featuring her as Shondie Kent were disturbing. The worst had been seeing herself strapped down in a mental hospital. That image, though she'd played it, had chilled her to the bone. Even though she knew that these days patients weren't physically re-strained, being locked away like that was Allie's worst nightmare and she couldn't imagine how her sister had actually committed herself into a psych ward for a few weeks.

Then again, that was Cassie.

Forever the drama queen.

Like you?

Like your bitch of a mother?

She didn't want to acknowledge what was so patently obvious. At least not while she was standing here in the frigid Oregon drizzle.

She wondered, not for the first time, if she'd made a huge mistake agreeing to this sham. Things had escalated. Gotten ugly. Scary.

She was scared.

But determined.

Her thoughts skittered to her mother and she felt a pang of regret for the pain she was causing Jenna, but that jab of guilt quickly disintegrated, as it always did. Jenna didn't deserve it. She'd lied to her children. To her husbands. Two-faced bitch.

And then there was Cassie.

At the thought of her older sister Allie's blood boiled and she gritted her teeth. There had been a time when she'd looked up to Cassie, when she'd admired Cassie's rebellious I-don't-give-a-damn attitude, but everything had changed ten years ago in the aftermath of the maniac who had nearly killed Cassie and Jenna that cold, cold winter.

They had both survived and clung to each other. Jenna had felt guilt that Cassie had nearly lost her life because of her mother. And Cassie, that thick-skinned rebel? She'd been reduced to a whimpering, frightened shell of her former self. Neither had time for the baby of the family. Neither seemed to notice that she, too, was hurting.

Glaring down the street now, watching cars drive past the Hotel Danvers, seeing pedestrians hurrying along the sidewalk, observing the huge windows and veranda of the second story where Dean Arnette's party was still going on, Allie tried and failed to tamp down her anger, the blinding rage that had stemmed from being ignored, from being the forgotten one, the girl who had faded into the background.

Jenna, that lying bitch, had taken up with Shane Carter, even going so far as to marry the bastard. Her hero. So Allie had been ignored, but then Jenna had a history of that. Allie knew. She, while doing her duty and cleaning her room for one of Jenna's marathon remodels, had spent a little time in the attic, where she'd found her mother's old diary.

"Tsk. Tsk," she whispered, remembering reading the pages, mostly boring until she'd come to the part where Jenna had fallen in love and gotten pregnant. A stupid teen, she'd written about it in the small leather-bound book that girls used to keep like a million years ago. So Allie had set about trying to find the kid her mother had abandoned. It had taken years, but Allie Kramer was nothing if not patient. Now, she knew, she had the dirt on Jenna.

She thought of her half-sister.

Who woulda thunk? She was beautiful and smart . . . but there was something off about her, something Allie didn't want to dwell on.

As for Cassie, what a nutcase. Soon after the horror of the madman, when Cassie had first started going around the bend, Cassie had found Trent, who was, even then, a cut above. A man. Allie had been fascinated with him then, but he hadn't paid her the least bit of attention. Which had been par for the course. Every boy Allie had dated in high school had been half in love with her mother, asking for memorabilia and probably jerking off with something swiped from the house that reminded him of Allie's mother. What was the phrase? MILF? Mother I'd Like to Fuck? Yeah, that was Jenna.

Cassie, too. She'd gotten a lot of press and looked like Jenna, so the boys had been all over her, but Allie, in high school, had gotten the leftovers and few of them. She'd been a real nerd, into books and grades and avoiding the limelight until Cassie had invited her to LA.

And then, she'd gotten her own back. And then some. Become the star Cassie could never even dream of being. Proven to her sister that she was better. Not just smarter, but she could outdo anything she put her mind to.

She smiled, though her success was paper thin, a shell. No one really cared for her. No man had sworn his undying love for her, at least none she'd believed. Even Brandon. He ran hot and cold and she'd seen him giving Cassie, yes, and even Jenna the eye.

Men!

She hated them.

Wanted them.

Needed their adoration.

Or did she?

The truth was, she only wanted real love. The kind both Jenna and Cassie seemed to so effortlessly inspire.

"Bitches," she muttered, feeling the cold of the night, the dampness worming its way into her bones, the streetlights giving off an ethereal, almost eerie glow. How could one feel so alone in a city filled with thousands of people?

And she only wanted one. One lousy man.

Cassie had one and Allie, to get back at her, had set her sights on Trent Kittle. Not that she'd ever cared for him. God, he was such a . . . cowboy. Sexy, yeah, but not in the least urbane. Allie had gone after him just to mess with Cassie, who'd never even known that every boy Allie had ever liked had been more enthralled with wild, hot Cassie; that is, if they weren't drooling over Jenna. Christ, she'd even found one would-be boyfriend riffling through Jenna's bureau, looking for a pair of underwear when he'd claimed he was just going to use the bathroom.

Her stomach curdled at the thought.

But, at that time, Ryan Dansworth wasn't even interested in getting into her pants. Oh, no, but give him a shot at Jenna or Cassie and he was practically creaming his damned jeans. Cheap jeans at that.

She wondered how much old Ryan boy would pay for a chance to fuck her now. He probably went to all of her movies and beat himself up for missing his chance. Too bad. Eat your heart out, Ryan. You, and the rest of the men in America could stand in line.

She felt a moment's triumph before the old doubts assailed her.

Yeah, if so, then why the hell are you out here in the rain, looking in. Again. The damned party is all about you. You're the star. Remember that.

A car rolled up, loud music audible, the passenger window rolled down, the smell of weed filtering from the windows. "Hey," a male voice called from within the smoky interior. "Hey, babe? You need a ride?"

If they only knew.

She ignored them.

But the car inched closer.

"Wanna hit?"

"Fuck off!" She didn't need some pimply teenager trying to jump her bones.

"Ouch. Hey!" another, higher-pitched voice said. "Anyone ever tell you that you look like Allie Kramer?"

"She's hot!" the first voice said.

"No, man, I'm serious," the second boy said, but she was already gone, slipping away through a back alley, melding in with pedestrians so busy with their own lives they didn't notice the waiflike girl in the oversized sweatshirt. She'd gotten to be a pro at disappearing.

Good.

She had work to do.

Sliding her phone from her pocket, she punched out a familiar number. "Go time," she whispered and jogged the two blocks to the parking garage, where, avoiding cameras, she found Brandon McNary's beat-up SUV and unlocked it. She climbed behind the wheel, then opened the glove box, where she located the plastic bag filled with paraphernalia for a quick disguise. She popped a fake, more bulbous nose over her small one, added some wadding to her mouth to fatten up her jawline, slipped on a pair of oversized glasses, then tugged at the strands of her wig so her real hair wouldn't show in any cameras. There might be questions asked. But she didn't think so. Just how smart were the cops?

Had they found her?

Or figured out that Jenna had a baby before she was married, one she gave up for adoption?

Allie smiled as she drove out of the lot without the sleepy-eyed attendant giving her a second glance. She'd figured it all out. The diary had been the start and from there it was just a matter of digging.

And she'd met her half-sister. Worked with her. Shared laughs with her. Before she realized how really messed up the woman was. Their shared hatred of Jenna and Cassie had been a bond. At first. But later, Allie had discovered just how sick her half-sister was.

But murder?

Really?

Allie hadn't believed she'd go through with it, but Lucinda Rinaldi had nearly died and now two others had. Now, Allie was caught in the middle.

If only she could go to the police.

If only she could unburden herself.

If only she'd never met the woman!

Knowing her half-sister was at the party, that she had no idea of Allie's intentions, Allie drove to the apartment she'd never seen. How ironic that she'd used the very same method of gaining a key as had her sibling, but lifting it from an open purse, making a copy and using it to gain entrance.

She parked two blocks from the apartment building and kept her head ducked as she walked inside, and used the stairs. On the third floor she stepped into the hallway and was surprised at her case of nerves, how anxious she was.

Then again, the woman was a murderess.

Looking over her shoulder, certain the woman would leap out at her from any doorway, Allie hurried to the right apartment. Her hands trembled slightly as she inserted her quickly made key into the lock and with a *click*, it snapped open.

"Awesome." Nerves twisted, she stepped inside and flipped on the light switch only to be stopped dead in her tracks. Any relief she'd felt upon entering had instantly evaporated. Her hand flew to her mouth as she viewed the room, a dressing room of sorts, and on every wall were posters, large mounted pictures of Allie herself and her mother, even Cassie, from the movies they'd made.

But they weren't pristine, oh, no. They were cut and slashed, horrid, jagged pieces torn from them only to be taped and retaped until they were nearly unrecognizable.

Sick.

Mental.

Crazy as a loon.

Homicidal.

Allie's lungs constricted.

She could barely breathe.

What had she gotten herself into?

Again she looked over her shoulder then scanned the ceiling, search-ing for a deceptively concealed camera. Thankfully she saw none, but she didn't doubt her newfound sibling was paranoid enough to have one installed.

The makeup mirror was still lit, bulbs burning bright, brushes and bottles and jars neatly arranged, in stark juxtaposition to the dam-aged posters that looked as if they'd been nearly destroyed in a fit of rage, then lovingly repaired . . . sort of.

"God in heaven," she whispered and walked to an odd-looking window, pulling the cord for the blinds and seeing that the glass had been covered, and backlit with a thin bulb. The artwork stretched over the glass was a view of the Hollywood Hills, complete with the iconic white letters spelling out HOLLYWOOD.

As if the woman who called this her "Portland pad" believed that she had an authentic view of Hollywood. God, there were even fake palm fronds positioned perfectly.

How nuts was she?

"Off the charts," Allie whispered, creeping and tiptoeing, as if she really did think the crazed woman was somehow observing her. Allie's skin pimpled at the thought and she felt the lingering presence of pure evil, like a bad smell that seeped into the walls and carpet.

Don't go there. Don't get all freaky. Just check this place out.

From the fake window she spied a portable copy machine on a table in one corner. It looked to be connected to a laptop computer positioned near a laminator, a machine that melted plastic onto paper. Beside the laminating machine was a short stack of pictures. Curious, she picked up the glossy head shots. Seeing the images, she nearly screamed. Each page was different, a picture that had been photoshopped and distorted to make the subject appear to be in in-tense agony, as if her face were dripping off her skull. Horrid, chilling images, the creation of a sick mind. Every head shot was of Allie Kramer.

"Oh shit," she whispered, terror building. Her eyes rounded and her body shook as she stared at the horrifying photos. She felt the hatred that had created them, the evil that spent hours in malicious glee making such hideous pieces of art.

She dropped the pictures as if they burned her fingers.

Her stomach heaved and she sensed that she was losing it; that, like her sister, she might lose touch with what was real, what was fantasy. Hadn't it happened before, when Lucinda had been shot, when she'd first realized what she'd gotten into? And then, dear God, she'd played along with it, listening to Brandon, who had cared for her, letting him tell her that her disappearance was a good thing, that there was a new buzz around the movie, that she would be more popular, more mysterious, than ever.

"What have I done?" she thought, her grip on reality slipping.

She was turning to leave, to get out of this horrible place when she spied the mask lying on a counter. Obviously one of the sick pictures had been cut, carved around Allie's hairline, her eyes hacked out, the paper laminated and a thin strip of elastic glued to the back. "What the fuck?" Allie whispered and turned the mask over. A single word had been scribbled across the back in uneven red letters.

"Sister," Allie read aloud.

For the first time she understood the depths of her half-sibling's depravity, the lengths she would go to, how far she'd step over the line of sanity to get what she wanted, to prove that she was as good as the others, as talented, and even though she had been discarded and forgotten.

Allie had been fooling herself if she believed she was safe.

Her throat closed with an ice-cold, newfound fear.

No one was safe while the monster was on the prowl. Not Cassie. Not Jenna. Not even Allie, who had been her "partner in crime," who had actually, at one time, thought the world would be a better place if Cassie dropped off its face, if Cassie actually died.

How sick was that?

Maybe, Allie thought, mental weakness ran in the family.

The oldest was a homicidal maniac, the middle child had already spent time in a psych ward for hallucinations and blackouts and the youngest, the Hollywood star, was jealous and depraved enough to have agreed to be a partner in her sister's murder, and then let horrendous things happen.

Again, she flashed on the set of the mental hospital at the party, a mannequin in her own likeness confined to a solitary room, strapped to the bed and obviously deranged. The woman who used this apartment, who slashed movie posters and made horrible, distorted masks of Allie's family, who had already killed two people that Allie knew of, wouldn't stop. She wouldn't be satisfied until she'd murdered them all. Cassie. Jenna. Even Allie herself.

Allie's insides turned to mush. She thought she might throw up. She'd been a part of this madness, had aided it, had fed her own insecurities and rage by wishing members of her family dead, and this woman, this maniac who was her half sister, had not only fed her fury, but implemented a plan to satisfy it. Now, unleashed, the monster would never stop! She couldn't be called off.

She glanced once more at the posters of Jenna, the mother who had given up her career to move her daughters to safety, to a more "normal" life, which of course, it had never been. But Jenna had tried. Even if she'd lied about her firstborn, even if she'd lavished attention on Cassie after the madman had nearly killed her ten years earlier, even if she'd ignored her introverted, bookish child while tending to the one who had nearly been killed. And Cassie—God, she was a mess—the hatred and jealously she'd harbored for her sister still burned in Allie's gut, but, really, did Cassie deserve this terror? To lose her life?

Maybe.

Then again, maybe not.

Allie had seen enough. She left the apartment in a hurry and didn't care who'd seen her. Somehow, some way, she had to end what she'd so blindly started.

Before she, too, was a victim.

She knew what she had to do; she only hoped she wasn't too late.

Nash wanted to throttle Cassie Kramer. In an administrative office of the Hotel Danvers, Cassie was huddled in a chair, her husband standing at a window and Nash sitting on the opposite side of a wide desk that was so clean Nash couldn't believe someone actually worked at it. Kittle had called 9-1-1 and Nash, already having arrived at the hotel, took over. She'd listened to Cassie Kramer's fantastic tale and visited the room on the seventh floor where Cassie swore her sister had been.

The party, of course, had been interrupted, the buzz of another Allie Kramer sighting having created a life of its own and now was trending on the Internet. All good news for Dean Arnette and the premier of *Dead Heat*.

Once again, Nash wondered if this recent sighting, by Allie Kramer's sister no less, was just another publicity stunt. Why not? For the love of God, the whole party had been a publicity stunt, and those elaborate sets constructed for the event, how bizarre had they been, almost macabre since the star was missing and many presumed her to be dead.

How far would these people go to promote the film, she wondered.

Certainly not far enough to place their star in hiding or murder innocent people. Right? Nash wasn't certain she had been born suspicious and her job had only enhanced that trait.

"I saw Allie," Cassie stated for the third or fourth time. "And that coat was hers. I've seen her in it before."

"I don't know about that. I talked to one of the producers, Sybil Jones, who said it was a costume from the film."

"Maybe she wore it off the set."

"Maybe. I don't know. Yet. What I do know is that no one's registered in that room, or any room on the seventh floor as it's being renovated. So we'll check into it." The coat was clean. Everything else in 706 was covered in a thick layer of dust. "But it's unlikely that—"

"So why was the coat there?" Cassie blurted, her eyes snapping. "Why did I see her on the balcony, huh? If Allie . . . or someone wasn't on that balcony, how did I know where to go and find the damned coat?"

"Anyone could have put it there."

"But I knew which room . . . oh . . . no, wait." Her skin stretched tighter over her cheekbones. "You don't think I left it up there and went up to check just to cause a big stir, do you? Because I didn't."

"I'm not making any assumptions."

"I was with Trent all night!" She glanced at her husband, but he didn't move. "I didn't leave that room except to step on the balcony!"

Nash wondered. In a crowd of that size it would be easy to slip away for ten minutes and no one would notice.

"There's something else I need to discuss with you."

"Great." And before she could say the words, Cassie said, "You don't have to mince words with me, Detective. I assume you found out that my mother had another child, born before me at St. Mary's Hospital. You know, the one that's now called Mercy, where I was just a patient? Ironic, huh? Anyway, I know all about it. Just not the name of my sister, or if she's involved in any of this." Some of the starch seemed to drain from her. "God, I hope not. I mean, that's unlikely, right?"

"We don't know anything more." That was a lie. Nash had spoken to her associate. Jenkins thought she might have identified the family who had adopted Jenna Hughes's firstborn, a family by the name of Beauchamp. Gene and Beverly Beauchamp of Seattle, who had adopted two girls, one soon after the birth of Jenna Hughes's baby. Jenkins had contacted the couple and was gathering information. As soon as the morning, they would have answers. Then, Nash would share them. And hopefully either arrest someone or at least bring them in for questioning. The name Beauchamp rang bells with her and she thought she'd seen it somewhere. When she got home, she'd double-check her notes.

"What about the nurse?" Cassie asked. "Belva Nelson?"

Nash hedged. "We're still looking for her." So far they'd found nothing.

"Have you come up with the name of the family who adopted the baby . . . my sister?"

"No." Another dead end. So far.

Cassie let out a long breath. "I'd like to meet her," she said, "but it might not be so good."

"How so?"

"How would you like to wake up one morning and find out that you were the daughter of Jenna Hughes, the woman who was nearly killed after giving up on Hollywood? And then you find out your siblings are Allie and Cassie Kramer." She snorted a little laugh. "We're not exactly the poster children for stability, now, are we?" Suddenly serious, she asked, "Do you think she's involved?"

Good question. "I don't know, but I'll find out."

"So, do you think I could have my phone back?"

Nash had anticipated that question. She fished in her purse, retrieved Cassie's cell and handed it to her.

"Did you find out who sent me the text?"

"Not yet, but—"

"I know. You're working on it."

The husband moved from the window. "I think we're done here," he said. "It's been a long night. We've told you everything we know."

And it's not enough, Nash thought, but kept her observations to herself.

For now.

CHAPTER 35

Sleep had proved impossible.

After making love to Trent, Cassie had stared at the ceiling while the wind and rain lashed at the house, rattling the windows and rushing through the trees. The smell of smoke from a recent fire in the wood stove drifted through the air and Trent, lying next to her, was dead to the world.

While he snored she thought about the party with its weird stage sets and mannequins of Allie. Had her sister, the one she'd never met, been in the crowd? Had Allie? Where the hell was her sister?

Tossing and turning, throwing off the covers only to shiver and pull them to her chin, she wondered about Belva Nelson and Whitney Stone and all the peripheral players. And the masks? Who had sent the horrid masks? Who?

She forced her eyes closed and tried to clear her mind. No more thoughts of the evil that she sensed surrounding the movie, no more worries about siblings, real or imagined, no more—

From the foot of the bed, the dog growled. Low. A warning.

"Shh," Trent mumbled, rolling over and wrapping an arm around her waist. Snuggling up against him, her naked body cupped by his, she felt the warmth of his breath tickle her nape. She relaxed and hoped to keep the demons at bay.

Another growl.

This time the dog was on his feet; she heard his claws clicking against the floor. Cassie opened a bleary eye, and swearing under his breath, Trent released her and rolled to the side of the bed.

"What's wrong?"

"Don't know." He walked to the window to stare into the night, his silhouette visible against the watery light from an outside security lamp. Long legs, slim hips, broad shoulders, all sinew and muscle. He waited a few seconds, staring outside.

The dog was at the door, whining.

"He usually doesn't spook easy," Trent said and reached for the pair of jeans he'd tossed over a side chair.

"You're going outside."

"Got to check the stock." He glanced at the bed where she had scooted to the headboard, the blankets pulled to her chin. "Maybe just a coyote."

"Maybe."

He pulled on the jeans, zipping them quickly and hooking the button. "Shorty said he saw one the other morning. Got to make sure the calves are all right."

"In the middle of the night?"

"Looks like. Damned varmints. They just don't seem to care that I need my shut-eye." He leaned over and kissed her forehead.

"Don't go."

"Got to."

"No. No, you don't."

"I'll be fine."

The dog was whining and growling, claws clicking against the hardwood as he paced in front of the door.

Cassie threw off the covers. "I'm coming with you."

"Nope. You stay here. I'll be right back."

"Trent. Hold on. People have been murdered."

"Lucky for me I didn't have a bit part in *Dead Heat*," he teased, then more seriously, "This is my place, Cass, I know it like the back of my hand. No worries."

"Many worries."

"I'll be right back. It's probably nothing."

The rumble in Hud's throat was growing louder, the hairs on the back of his neck raised.

"I don't like this."

"I'll be fine." His grin flashed white. "I'll take my old Winchester. Should do the trick."

"And the dog?"

"Right." He pulled on his boots and threw a shirt over his shoulders. "Don't think he'd have it any other way."

She started to climb from the bed and he said, "Look, Cass. I'm serious. Stay in. With your phone."

"I'm getting dressed. Just in case."

"In case what?"

"I don't know. In case you need help."

"If I need help, call nine-one-one." He paused, walked to a desk pushed against the window, withdrew a ring of keys, then dropped the entire set into her hand. "The small ones open two boxes in my closet. One holds a pistol. The second ammo."

"What? For the love of God, Trent, that's not going to help. I don't even know how to load a gun."

He stopped and in the darkness stared at her.

"Never even held one," she said.

"I guess you'd better learn. Fast." Another quick smile, an irreverent slash of white in the semidark room. Then he whistled to the dog. Hud bolted out of the door with Trent right behind, his footsteps fading down the hallway and stairs. "Lock the door behind me."

"So the coyote doesn't get in?" she yelled.

"You got it."

"Yeah, right," she said under her breath. Sometimes he could be so bullheaded, so damned frustrating.

She heard the front door open and close.

Great.

His keys still clutched in the fingers of one hand, she held the blankets to her chest with the other, then walked, dragging the coverlet on the floor as she made her way to the window. The night was cast in a thin blue light from the fixture mounted near the silo that was attached to the barn. She watched him cross the gravel lot, passing in front of the shed, the dog galloping ahead, beelining to the door of the barn.

A frisson of fear spiderwebbed at the back of her neck and she nervously licked her lips as he stepped inside.

For God's sake, the outbuildings were only twenty yards or so from the house, not attached, but not far.

So why did she feel so alone? So fearful? Why did she think that whatever was in the barn was far more deadly than a coyote?

The old house creaked, settling, and her case of nerves increased. Staring at the barn door, she said, "Come on. Come on." While the wind whistled and the rain drizzled down the panes, she waited, glanced at the clock. He'd been inside two minutes.

Then five.

She fidgeted and told herself she was being foolish, jumping at shadows, but was she? Was this all in her mind? After all they'd been through? No, damn it, there was a maniac out there somewhere, a killer who possibly had Cassie and those around her in his sights. The fact that she'd received one of the frightening masks was warning enough. So why would she think Trent, the man she loved, would be safe?

The man she loved.

There it was; the God's honest truth.

She loved him and she wasn't going to lose him.

Not again.

Eight minutes. Damn it.

She tried to stay rational, reminding herself that just because the dog had heard something didn't necessarily mean anything serious was happening. Maybe Trent was right. A coyote or cougar or even a racoon would get the shepherd going. Maybe he and Hud would scare whatever it was that was slinking around in the shadows.

Or maybe not.

Whatever the case, no way was she going back to bed alone. For what? To toss and turn, worry and stare at the ceiling? No thanks. Since she was now fully awake, she decided to stay up.

Without turning on a light, she started getting dressed in jeans and a sweater from earlier in the day, before the gawd-awful fiasco of a party.

As she hooked her bra, then pulled a sweater over her head, she thought about the long day, the revelations from her mother, the way her entire world had been turned upside down. She had an older sister? She had enough of a hard time wrapping her brain around that, let alone that the sister was somehow behind Allie's disappearance and the murders. No—she couldn't buy into that at all.

She picked up the keys.

What the hell would she do with a gun if she had one?

What good is it in a locked box?

"Fine." She snapped on a bedside lamp, then walked to the closet. Checked the clock.

Ten minutes.

Too long.

Standing on her tiptoes, she retrieved both boxes, then with a little effort opened each to withdraw the gun and bullets. "It's not rocket science," she told herself and managed to load the gun, even figuring out the safety. "Piece of cake."

Carrying the pistol, she took another look from the bedroom window and saw no lights go on in the barn. Why? If there were an animal prowling around, wouldn't a bright light scare it off?

Something wasn't right. She snapped off the light near the bed, letting the room fall into shadow, so that she could stand at the window and view the parking area and barn lot without the reflection of the room distracting her. She saw the trees swaying in the breeze, but no other shadows moved, observed no dark figure crouching in the deeper umbra, no four-legged beast slinking away from the outbuildings, all of which loomed darker.

"Come on," she said, wishing Trent to return, her gaze pinned on the barn door. She considered texting him, but if he were in some kind of trouble, if some unseen enemy were out there with him, she didn't want any noise or light from the phone to give him away.

You've seen too many horror films.

She hesitated. Fifteen minutes. She couldn't stand it a second longer. She typed a quick text to him.

r u ok?

She waited. Stared at the phone. Counted the seconds. Expected a quick response.

Nothing.

"Come on."

Again she texted.

What's going on?

Again, no response.

If you really think he's in trouble, you should call the police.

Biting her lip, she let her hand hover over the keypad of her phone, then, deciding not to freak out, to give it a few more minutes, she made her way downstairs. She'd make some coffee or hot chocolate or—

"Aaaayeeeeooow!"

Outside, a bone-chilling scream splintered the night.

What the hell was that?

Oh, God. Trent!

Startled, she flinched on the final three stairs and missed a step, her ankle twisting as she spun, pain so sharp she stumbled, throwing out her hands to catch herself. The gun and phone flew from her fingers. She scrabbled for the railing but everything happened so fast and she fell, her shoulder glancing off the newel post before she landed hard on the floor, cheek slamming against the hardwood.

Stunned, pain throbbing from several points on her body, she silently cursed her clumsiness. But the scream? Had it been Trent? Something else? An animal, possibly wounded?

Heart thundering, she gingerly pulled herself to her feet. She winced as she tried the ankle, but despite a jab of pain, it supported her. Her shoulder ached and her face smarted. She'd have a few bruises come morning, but she'd live. "Klutz," she muttered, grateful she hadn't shot herself. She listened and heard nothing over the rush of the wind, but that was it. She wasn't going to sit in the house while God knew what was going on.

Snapping on a light, she found her phone near the den and snapped it up. The screen was shattered but it still seemed to work. The pistol had slid across the hardwood to the front door and she gathered it as well, then she turned off the light and headed to the back door. She'd text Trent and—

Blam!

The crack of a rifle.

Instinctively, she hit the floor, every muscle tense, fear shooting through her blood.

Was it Trent's weapon?

Or someone else's?

Didn't matter.

This was no good. *No good.* Whether he was shooting or being shot at, he was in trouble. Big trouble.

Over the rush of the wind she heard the frightened neighing of the horses.

Fingers trembling, heart drumming, a thousand questions darting through her mind, she dialed 9-1-1 and slid to the back door where she sat with her back against the wall.

Horrid thoughts gripped her.

Was Trent shot?

Even now bleeding out in the barn somewhere?

Oh, God, please, let him be all right! Please, please, please—

"9-1-1," a female operator said over the wireless connection. "What is the nature of your emergency—"

"Help! Send help!" Cassie nearly screamed. "I heard gunshots and screams and . . . and my husband is in the barn, I think." She was starting to panic and had to force herself to be coherent. "We were in bed, the dog got all weird and started barking and Trent went out to investigate and then I heard the scream and oh, God, just send someone. My husband's outside!"

"Ma'am, if you'll slow down," the operator said calmly. "Is anyone injured?"

"I—I don't know. But I heard a scream. First some kind of animal, horrible scream and then . . . a little bit later, a minute maybe, a gunshot." She was frantic, her pulse ticking wildly. "I texted him, but he's not responding! For the love of Christ, just send help!"

"What is your name and your address?"

"It's Cassie, Cassie Kramer, and the address? Oh . . . crap, I don't know . . . it's on Benning Road . . . about, about a mile from . . . the Cougar Mountain turnoff. Trent Kittle's farm. Please just send someone." She was shaking all over, her fears congealed.

"Are you injured?"

"No! No! I'm fine, but my husband. He could be hurt! I don't know!" She was panicking, but thought of Trent and how much she loved him and how, oh, God, he couldn't be injured or worse. No, no, no! She wouldn't go there. "The address . . . Oh, Jesus. Wait. Hold on." She scrambled to her feet and ran through the dark hallway, phone to her ear, ankle twinging. Hadn't she seen a stack of mail on the table, a bill with an address on the kitchen counter? She flipped a switch. Light flooded the kitchen and she picked up the top envelope. "Okay, okay. . . . Here it is." She read the damn address to the operator and repeated it, all the while hearing the *click* of computer keys as the woman typed. "Please send someone now."

"I've already dispatched officers," the officer said calmly, as if the situation weren't life and death. "They're on their way. If you'll just stay on the line."

"No . . . no, I have to go. I have to find Trent." Images of him, bleeding, in pain, battling for his life, flared behind her eyes. Didn't this calm woman on the other end of the line realize that time was running out, that even now . . . She squeezed her eyes shut to fight the fear.

"No, ma'am," the operator was saying. "Stay on the line. Officers will be there soon."

"Soon's not good enough. They need to be here now!" Cassie was having none of it. This operator didn't understand. "This is an ongoing case. Call Detective Rhonda Nash of the Portland PD, her and her partner, whatever his name is. Detective Thomas, no, that's not right." She was starting to lose it. "Thompson. That's it! Detective Thompson. Tell them to get out here now!" Before the operator could break in, Cassie added, "Just tell them Cassie Kramer called and it's urgent, that there's gunfire at the ranch." She didn't wait for a response, just clicked off, then flipped the light switch so that the kitchen was again blanketed in darkness.

Quickly she made her way to the back door. She only paused long enough to call her stepfather's cell phone. She should have called Shane first. One ring. Two. "Hurry up," she said, and then as the phone rang a third time, his groggy voice came over the connection.

"Cassie?"

"Yes! I need help. Trent's in the barn and there's been gunshots. Well, just one. But there was a scream and—"

"A scream?"

"Yeah. Maybe an animal. Maybe human, I don't know. It was awful. Trent was already outside and then I heard a gunshot. I texted him and he hasn't gotten back to me. Oh, God, I'm so worried. I called nine-one-one, but you're closer."

"On my way," he replied. "I'll be there in five."

That could be too long.

Shane said, "Stay put."

She clicked off, slid the phone in her pocket, held the pistol firmly. Her stepfather's advice rang in her ears as she opened the door and stepped into the rainy night.

Stay put.

"Like hell."

CHAPTER 36

Lying on the barn floor, breathing the scents of dust and horses and urine, Trent sucked in his breath and cursed himself a dozen times over. Pain screamed up his leg and he dragged himself to one of the empty stalls while the horses in boxes all around him neighed in terror. Blood stained his jeans and he hoped to God his femoral artery hadn't been hit by the damned shot.

He'd entered the barn carefully and seen nothing. Still, cautious, he hadn't snapped on a light.

Hud, however, had been agitated and the minute they'd stepped into the barn, had taken off like a streak, running down the corridor, toenails clicking, racing past the stalls where horses were shifting nervously in their stalls.

That was odd. The hackles on the back of Trent's neck had raised and he'd lifted his rifle, though he'd been loath to fire it in the tight confines of the barn. He'd reached for the light switch.

"*Aaaayeeeeooow!*"

A shrill, blood-curdling scream rose to the rafters.

What the hell?

He'd started jogging. Toward the sound. Toward the silo. Ignoring the pain. Heading to the area the damned dog had disappeared. The interior was dark, what little light there was coming through the tiny windows, the security lamp providing the barest of illumination, but he knew every timber and rafter inside, had repaired all the walls and feed bins and stalls, remembered where each tool was hung.

Still he'd moved cautiously, squinting into the darkness, listening hard for any sounds over the rapid beating of his pulse drumming in his ears, and the nervous whinnies of the horses pacing and pawing in their boxes.

Nothing.

Not even a noise from the dog, or none that he could hear.

He'd had a flashlight on his phone, but turning it on would only draw attention to him, and someone or some*thing* was inside this barn. Whoever or whatever it was didn't seem friendly.

He'd been about to duck into the tack room and text Cassie to call the police when he'd heard something . . . the soft tread of footsteps? And he'd felt a rustle in the air, movement behind him. He'd spun and lifted his rifle to his shoulder in one motion, but it had been too late. The would-be assassin had gotten the drop on him, somehow silently dispensing with the dog, and fired the instant Trent had been in his sights.

Son of a bitch, Trent thought now. He'd been foolish, too comfortable in his own ranch, believing that some animal was causing the dog to go nuts.

He should have been more careful.

Christ, he'd been in the damned military. He knew better.

Shit.

Now, he was waiting in the dark, his back against the wall of the stall, his rifle ready, though firing in the building would be a disaster with bullets ricocheting against the walls and posts.

But here, he was a sitting duck. If the killer had night goggles, Trent was as good as dead.

Without making a sound, he fumbled in his jacket pocket for his phone and realized he was weakening, his brain not as clear.

Damn!

Did he hear the sound of footsteps outside the stall? Was the killer taking aim? Or were the noises just the sound of restless, nervous hooves in the straw or his own imagination running wild? Tensing, he focused on the open stall door. Waiting. Expecting to hear another blast from a gun.

Get a grip, Kittle.

You can't lose it now. Think of Cassie. She has to get to safety. Somehow.

He blinked. Concentrated. Heard a banging and realized he'd left the damned door open and it was catching in the wind to pound against the siding.

Making sure the phone was still on silent, he saw that he already had two texts. Both from Cassie.

r u ok?

Hell, no.

And shortly thereafter:

What's going on?

I wish I knew.

He typed his response quickly:

Leave now!

Call 911

Then he added:

I'm ok

That was a lie, but if she had any inkling that he was wounded, she might do something stupid and put herself in danger. God, he felt weak. Lightheaded. It took all of his effort to send the text, but he managed to click off and send another to Carter:

Under attack.

In the barn.

Cassie is in the house.

Save her.

Sweat ran down his face despite the fact that he was cold to the bone.

God, how could he have been so stupid? He clicked off his phone, couldn't risk the attacker seeing its light.

Where are you, you fucker? He had to start moving, find the assailant before he went after Cassie, because that's what this was all about. Trent knew it. Deep in his gut. Whoever was skulking in this barn was after his wife.

Not on my watch.

He knew this barn like the back of his hand, but with the blood he was losing, he was also fighting to stay awake. Shit, the artery probably had been nicked.

If only he could fashion a tourniquet . . . Oh, Jesus. He sagged against the back of the stall and realized he hadn't heard a car's engine starting, no crunch of tires on gravel. Either Cassie hadn't gotten the message.

Or she chose to ignore it.

His jaw clenched and he swiped the sweat from his face. Not looking at the growing stain on his jeans, he aimed his rifle at the stall door.

Then he waited.

The phone rang.

At two-fifteen in the damned morning.

Nash recognized the number as belonging to Jenkins, the rookie gung-ho junior detective who was young and therefore never slept. Especially on a Saturday night. Make that Sunday morning.

"Nash," she said automatically and hated the sound of sleep in her voice.

"Hey, sorry to wake you." Jenkins sounded as chipper as if she'd had a triple-shot espresso. "But I thought you'd like to know."

"What?" she asked, instantly awake.

"The name of Jenna Hughes's love child."

"You found it."

"That I did. She was adopted by Gene and Beverly Beauchamp, as we knew. She has a sister, or had a sister as well, but the girl died. Single car crash. This one, Jenna's daughter, was with her but survived. I'm still checking on that."

"So who is she?" Nash demanded. She was annoyed at being played with.

"Well, the reason we couldn't figure it out is that she's been married a couple of times, so the names didn't quite match up." There was a smile in her voice. The little twit loved dragging out the suspense.

"And?"

"And that girl is someone we know," Jenkins finally said, before reeling off a name that was all too familiar.

ACT VI

A *nd now the moment leading up to the climax.*
Odd that it should end here, in a rustic claptrap of a barn, she thought as she hid in the shadows of the musty building where horses shifted and neighed, their warmth and smell a little disturbing. So rural!

She'd imagined something more glorious, more glittery and far more Hollywood than this immense edifice in the middle of No-Damned-Where. No spotlight. No cameras. No stage.

Still, she had used the barn to her advantage, even if she'd blown it by screaming when the damned horse had snaked its head over the half-door of its enclosure and bitten her as she'd slunk by. The nerve of the animal. She probably should have shot it right then and there, but she hadn't wanted to make any noise.

It hadn't worked and of course Trent, hero rancher that he was, had shown up.

She passed by a pillar supporting the hay mow overhead and stiffled a sneeze. Squeezing the trigger and seeing Trent go down in a heap had been satisfying and long overdue. He really was a bastard.

On silent footsteps she passed by the tack room.

It was so cliché of Cassie to end up here, at the ranch of her lover, her hero. But it had worked, for it was easy enough to follow them, to deduce where she was hiding out, where she'd sought shelter.

After all the years of waiting, of the frustration, of being so close to stardom to taste it, after rubbing shoulders with the rich and famous and being a part of their bloodline, though they, of course, didn't know it.

Fools.

Spoiled brats!

How she'd waited for this!

The original plan had been interrupted, of course. Cassie was supposed to die on the set of *Dead Heat,* but the bitch had changed the script. Almost as if she'd suspected that an "accident" was going to happen. The ironic part of it was that she'd twisted the script and Allie was to be the second runner, the woman shot.

Not perfect.

But good enough.

But then Allie had bailed and disappeared.

How frustrating.

But the movie wasn't over.

There was still the final act.

And in it there would be blood and death and mournful, guilt-riddled cries from those who were lucky enough to survive.

If only for a few tortured seconds . . .

CHAPTER 37

*B*e *calm.*
You can do this.

Cassie held the pistol in a death grip. With the wind slapping her face in icy gusts and her ankle shooting pain with each step, she skirted the pooling light from the security lamps and kept to the darker shadows as she headed to the barn. She replayed the horrid sound of the gunshot over and over in her head, then sent up a prayer that Trent was alive. Not injured.

The barn door banged against the exterior wall, the doorway a gaping black maw. For a second she thought of running into it, but stopped herself. Yes, she wanted to get to Trent, the sooner the better, but the open doorway could be a mistake. Whoever was on the other side might be watching.

She clicked off the safety of the pistol and prayed to God she wouldn't have to use it. But she had to find Trent. Was he alive? Injured? Or . . . *Stop! Don't even go there. He's alive. Maybe hurt, but alive. So help him, Cassie. But be smart about it.*

Fear chasing through her bloodstream, she slipped through a gate near one side of the barn. She edged around to the back of the massive building, where she hugged the exterior wall. The wind wasn't as sharp here, as she was protected by the barn but the ground was a sodden, trampled mess with deep pockets of mud, rainwater, and manure created by hundreds of hooves. Picking her way as carefully as possible, all the while worrying about the seconds ticking by, she passed through the wide doorway used by the cattle as they entered and her boots slid and caught in the uneven glop. Inside the enormous, cavernous room that, thankfully tonight, was empty of ani-

mals, she moved more easily through the darkness. Straw and saw-
dust had been spread over a concrete slab and the muck wasn't as
deep. Here, where the smell of animals lingered, the footing was a little firmer, thank God.

Hurry, hurry, hurry!

Where would he be within this massive, creaking building?

*Focus, Cassie. Find Trent. That's all you need to do. And try not
to get shot while you're doing it.*

Rather than risk exposure by darting across the open space, she
started easing around the edge of the wide enclosure. Her ankle was
beginning to throb now, but she ignored it, couldn't be bothered.

Where was he?

Where was whoever or whatever he'd encountered? She expected
the attack had been human, she didn't think Trent had fired his rifle,
but she didn't know.

God help me.

Her phone vibrated and she pulled it from her pocket.

She saw Trent's text and nearly collapsed in relief.

He was alive! That was the good news. The bad? He was warning
her, telling her to get to safety and he wasn't calling or leaving the
barn. He'd said he was okay, but she doubted it as he was still in the
dark barn. Somewhere. Hiding? Hoping to get the jump on whatever
enemy he faced? Or injured?

She looked at his message a last time and decided to ignore it,
only typing in **Where are you?** before pocketing her phone and
moving again. She ran the fingers of her left hand along the rough
boards of the wall as she stepped steadily toward the main area of
the barn, the space accessed by the door Trent had used on the opposite side of the building. At the inside corner of the room, she felt
the edge of a manger butt up against the wall. Carefully, she followed
the feed trough's length, stopping at a spot where she could see a
dim light filtering through one of the windows high overhead, just
enough illumination that she could quietly find her way into the heart
of the barn.

*Hurry, hurry, hurry! Time's running out. What if Trent is even
now dying somewhere in the barn? God, where the hell are the police? Where's Carter?*

Her mouth arid, her muscles tense, her damned ankle throbbing,
she crawled up onto the trough and then through the supports to a
spot where she finally swung her body over the half wall separating the

area for the animals from the interior of the structure. She landed lightly, felt another splintering shot of pain, then froze to get her bearings.

Move it! Keep going! Find Trent!

The horses were boxed in a line of stalls that ran down a long corridor. On the far end was the silo, on the opposite wall another wide door on rollers to allow equipment to be driven inside. In between, opposite from the stalls, were a series of small rooms that housed grain, tack, and barnyard equipment. She'd seen tools hung on the bare walls, and in the very center a ladder that led up to the hayloft and down lower, to the same level as the area where the cattle entered and fed, the space she'd just passed through.

So where was her husband?

She checked her phone.

Nothing.

Damn.

She couldn't risk calling out, and didn't want to take a chance at being shot, either by Trent or whoever else was within the building. Fortunately there was a bit of light filtering in through the windows. As her eyes adjusted, she could make out shapes and shadows caught in the feeble illumination. Because there were few interior walls, Cassie was able to see. A little.

And so can anyone else.

If she could just find Trent! Holding her breath, she listened hard and hoped she might hear the sound of a boot on the floorboards or a soft moan, but heard nothing but the sough of the wind and the shuffle of nervous hooves in straw.

She wished she had the nerve to turn on a light, the guts to whisper to Trent, but she knew instinctively to stay as quiet as she could and hope that the noise from the animals would cover her own footsteps and breathing.

Did she hear the distant wail of sirens?

Oh, please!

She prayed the police were on their way.

She moved a little closer to the equipment area.

In the edge of her peripheral vision, she thought she saw movement. Her heart leapt to her throat. She spun, her gun leveled. *Don't shoot. It could be Trent. Or some other innocent.*

But the area was empty.

Maybe it was the dog? Or a barn cat?

Or perhaps nothing. Your effin' imagination.

Yet, her senses were on alert, her ears cocked and listening, her eyes scanning the shadowy interior, her nerves strung tight as bow-strings as she inched along the hallway. Horses snorted as she passed. One, startled, whinnied and the air snapped with an electricity.

Damn it, Trent, where are you? Give me a sign.

And Hud? Where's the damned dog?

Wouldn't Hud be with Trent?

Crouching low, she inched along the wall, nearly called out Trent's name in a whisper when she saw another movement from the corner of her eye.

Whirling, she expected the image to have disappeared, the phantom to have vanished, a figment of her wild imagination.

But she was wrong.

Dead wrong.

Crouching in the corner, glaring at her with hateful eyes that caught the weakest light was a woman.

What?

Cassie nearly screamed.

Oh. Jesus.

"Who are you?" she whispered, her heart in her throat as the features, in the dark, came into view. Dark hair, wide eyes, arched cheeks, but all distorted in the gloom. Dear God, it was a shadowy image of herself, a twin.

She bit back a scream.

Realized the woman had a gun trained on her.

In a second she would pull the trigger and take off the mask and—no! Her eyes widened as she stared at the woman staring back at her. Her own gun was raised and shaking in her hands. And . . . and the assailant's pistol was raised and shivering and . . . She blinked. And fired, just as she noticed the clothes and the expression on the terrified woman's features were identical to her own before the woman shattered into a million pieces.

The roar of gunfire sent the horses screaming and kicking. Cassie's own heart nearly stopped as she was sprayed with bits of glass, the mirror that had been propped into the corner decimated.

She hadn't come upon a murderous assailant. No! She'd shot at her own damned, shuddering, gun-toting reflection. Oh, God, she was losing it! And not by inches, but miles. Her headache pounded, threatening to consume her, and her ankle wasn't getting any better. She needed to find Trent, get the hell out of the barn and make tracks. Let the police sort out whatever it was that had gone on here. She let out a breath slowly. She had to find Trent and get the hell out of here. Now she was jumping at shadows and . . . and . . .

Scraaape.

Over the sound of the horses, wind, and her own frantically thumping heart, she thought she heard a footstep.

Crrrunnch.

Another one, this time on the shattered glass! And to her horror, in the jagged pieces of glass still clinging to the mirror's frame, she saw that she, indeed, wasn't alone. Behind her, caught in the reflection, was a partial image of a woman.

And she, too, was armed, a bit of a gun visible in one shard.

Their eyes met.

The gun was leveled.

From his position in the stall, Trent, woozy from the loss of blood, thought he heard footsteps . . . not one set, but two. Each pair coming from a different direction.

What did that mean?

Did the assassin have an accomplice?

Or did the second set of soft footprints belong to Cassie?

Oh, Jesus. Would she have come out here after she heard the report of the gun? Would she have been that stupid? Dear God, he hoped not. He silently prayed that she had the presence of mind to call the police and then get the hell out. Drive away.

But then he knew better.

Fuck!

Damn that woman! Why couldn't she ever do what she was told?

Because she's Cassie Kramer, that's why.

With an effort he drew himself to his feet, steadied himself for a second, tried to get his bearings and nearly passed out. He waited until the wave of blackness receded and took several deep breaths. Dragging his bad leg, he made his way to the edge of his stall, the one farthest from the silo. He was dizzy as hell and used a post for support. He'd lost his phone when he'd been shot, it had skittered across the floor and was hidden somewhere, probably inoperable. Geez, he'd bungled this. All because he'd been ridiculously stupid thinking an animal and not a prowler had been on the farm. He'd thought the rifle and dog would be enough protection.

So where the hell was the dog?

Craaaack!

A gun blasted, the roar echoing to the damned rafters, and the sound of glass shattering and spraying reached his ears.

Cassie! Oh, Jesus!

Fear grabbed his throat and held on tight.

Horses neighed in terror, kicking at their stalls, and footsteps rang on the concrete floor, running footsteps, heading the opposite direction, toward the silo. And another sound, the loud rumble of a truck's engine, came through the open door.

A second later light washed over the windows, headlights burning in the night. Thank God! He started for the door and heard the distant wail of sirens, never sounding sweeter as they shrieked through the night.

Help was on its way.

He only hoped it wasn't too late.

Dragging his useless leg, propping his rifle on his shoulder, he pulled himself along the stalls with his free hand and nearly passed out. He leaned over the top rail and cleared his head, told himself to press on.

The police might be coming, but they were too far away.

He couldn't wait.

Cassie didn't look over her shoulder, just took off on her injured ankle, pain shooting up her calf.

Bam!

A gun fired again, a bullet miraculously missing her as it zinged past her head.

Fueled by adrenaline, ignoring the throb in her leg, she took off. She ran headlong into a post, her injured shoulder ramming into the rough timber, her feet slipping, the gun nearly falling from her hand.

Don't drop it. Hang onto the damned pistol.

Forcing her legs to work, she spun around the post, her arm throbbing, her heart in her throat.

"Cassie!" She thought she heard Trent call to her over the cacophony of sounds, the whistling neighs of horses, the rush of the wind battering the siding, the thudding of her heart, and the deadly tramp of footsteps following her, taking their time, knowing that she was running blind. She listened, didn't hear his voice again, thought she probably imagined it. But the sound of approaching footsteps was unmistakable. And closer.

Onward she raced, her boots ringing as she stumbled through the maze that was this part of the barn. Where the open area for the animals had been easy to work through, the interior of this area was cut with rooms and bins.

Without hesitation, determined footsteps followed her. Getting closer. Echoing through her skull.

Desperate, she rounded a corner and came up short.

Ahead was a blank wall.

One side was a tack room, she thought, the other an empty area to store tools.

There was nowhere to run.

No exit.

No escape.

She had to face whoever it was, this woman who wanted to kill her.

Steadily the footsteps came.

Who was it?

Allie? Or Cherise? The sister she didn't know? Ineesha? Laura? Little Bea . . . or someone she didn't even know?

Rotating, she fumbled with the gun in her hands. Freaked out of her mind, she raised the pistol, ready to take aim on her attacker. Her headache thudded, her body ached.

Could she use it against another human?

A person who's firing at you? Who wants to kill you? Who probably already killed Trent?

No problem!

ACT VII

Through the umbra, she walked slowly, patiently, knowing her prey had nowhere to run, nowhere to hide, nowhere to escape. Finally, after all the years of pretending, of sucking up, of acting as if she weren't as important as the Sisters Kramer and their has-been of a mother, it was time to set things right.

The wind whistled around the old barn, a tree branch banged against the wall, and the tingle of excitement was in the air. Like one of the suspense movies in which Jenna Hughes had played the heroine, a woman in jeopardy, or, more recently, Allie Kramer's role in *Dead Heat*.

At the thought of the star, her lips curled. Allie should have been dead by now, lying in a coffin, her legion of fans distraught, her mother destroyed and feeling alone. That part of the plan had backfired, but she'd set it right. Allie had been in on the original plot, the one in which Cassie was to die on the set of *Dead Heat*, but then Cassie had come up with a new twist to the end of the movie and changed things up, so Allie, as Shondie Kent, would have been the one to take the real bullet from Sig Masters's gun. She'd freaked and pulled an effective disappearing act, and poor Lucinda Rinaldi was nearly killed.

Boy, that pissed her off. She'd made so many plans, and then with a stroke of Cassie's pen, everything went sideways and Allie, the sister who had figured out their connection, had realized she might be shot and quickly double-crossed her, never reappeared. *Pfft!* Just vanished.

She wasn't about to be played for a fool. It had been easy enough to come up with a way to terrorize Allie. The DIY masks had been the perfect touch. Since she had connections to *Dead Heat,* knew the cast and crew, she could pluck her victims at random. Truth to tell, she loved the thrill of the killings, the supreme sense of power she felt when she'd pulled the trigger on that twit of a set designer, Holly Dennison. Even now she experienced a little thrum in her blood when she thought of it, an adrenaline rush. With Brandi, not as big of a thrill, of course, as she'd only met the extra once. But she'd been easy to track, her stupid midnight runs had made her an easy target, one more dead body to decorate with a mask she'd created especially for the event.

And how convenient that Cassie had all those mental problems, the hallucinations and blackouts. They'd come in handy, hadn't they? So nice of Allie to spill her guts. And so interesting how deep Allie's hatred of Cassie had been. All things considered, Allie was the successful one, the rising star who appeared on top of the world, but inside she was little more than a gelatinous glob of insecurities.

All because of men.

Go figure.

She heard Cassie breathing hard, from somewhere near the end of the building. Trapped and fearful.

Good.

Dealing with that nut-job had been a pain; pretending to befriend her made her gag and now it was over. "Little Sister," she called out, thinking she was funny, her voice high-pitched and sing-song. But it was true. She herself was the "Big Sister," Cassie the "Little Sister," and that stupid, missing, double-crossing celluloid princess, Allie, the youngest, thereby "Baby Sister."

"Baby" had yet to be found. She'd gone dark.

What the fuck was that all about?

The bitch had double-crossed her.

Oh, Baby Sister, that's dangerous.

Ah, well, that's what happens when you mix business and pleasure and family. Someone always gets burned.

"Little Sister," she called again, more loudly to be heard over the wind and the animals. "Come out, come out, wherever you are."

It was a game. Like one she'd never gotten to play with her half-sisters, never had been given the chance. Instead she'd been tossed away, handed over to the stuffy Beauchamp family where she'd never fit in. Oh, she'd had another sister, one that had been hand-picked for her, barely six months younger, but now, of course, she was dead, like these others would soon be.

She felt her eyes shimmer at the thought of the sister she'd grown up with. So beautiful and self-assured, so happy and bright, as if Gene and Beverly had picked the perfect child.

Her stomach turned.

They'd never really done anything wrong to her; the Beauchamps were decent enough people, but they'd been boring and common and she . . . she was born to Jenna Hughes. Her child. She should have been rich and famous and grown up in Southern California and been offered movie roles instead of being forced to go to a trade school and encouraged to marry young.

She'd been born to be a star.

And she'd been robbed.

Not only by the mother who had tossed her aside but by the biological half-sisters who'd grown up as Hollywood princesses. Just thinking about it caused the back of her neck to burn and the demons in her head to start to scratch and claw. Cassie needed to die tonight.

It was time to be done with this.

She had a history of destroying anyone or anything that got in her way; that's why she'd made a success of herself despite being left with the moronic Beauchamps. It had been fine until she'd learned the truth, though. When her "mother" had slipped up, leaving the adoption papers on the desk before quickly locking them away again. That's when it had all clicked.

She'd been sixteen at the time, the same age Bitch-Mama Jenna had been when she'd decided she didn't want to be burdened with a baby girl, when her dreams of becoming a movie star and celebrity overshadowed any thoughts of motherhood.

Well, until Cassie had come along.

Her blood boiled at the unfairness of it all, and the anger that she'd had to tamp down for all of these years burned hot. Now, finally, vengeance was hers. Her pulse began to pound in her ears and she remembered every poster she'd ever collected, every time she'd tried to apply her makeup, the instances when she'd stared into the mirror and searched for the telltale resemblance. Hers, she admitted to herself, was slight, not as strong as her half-sisters.

She obviously took after the loser who had impregnated Jenna, though, so far, she hadn't come up with his name. It hadn't been on the birth certificate. But she'd find him, and when she did? Bye-bye, Daddy.

The cockles of her heart warmed at the thought. She'd let Jenna know about that, too. She wanted the woman who had given her away so blithely to crumple to her oft-photographed knees.

And it all started in a few seconds.

The demons were anxious now, bloodthirsty. Their talons scraped against the inside of her braincase and she actually winced. But it was nearly over.

Just a couple more steps and then she'd look her sister in the eye before blowing her to Kingdom Come!

CHAPTER 38

The roar of a gun blast still ringing in his ears, Trent took off, trying to run. Pain shot up his leg, but he kept moving, limping as he strode, all the while trying to stay clear-headed, though the loss of blood had definitely dulled him as well as slowing him down.

Damn.

He wasn't about to stop now. Not when Cassie's life was threatened.

This was his fault.

He should have taken her advice and called the police, shouldn't have come out here like some damned cowboy thinking he could solve the problem. Who was the nutcase chasing his wife? What the hell was she doing here?

He passed the frantic horses and wondered where the hell were the damned cops? His boots crunched on something on the floor.

Broken glass!

But he heard the women at the far end of the barn, near the silo.

"Little Sister," a voice called out, and he felt a new, debilitating terror. *Little Sister?* What the hell did that mean? Cassie was the oldest . . . except for the daughter Jenna gave up.

Was it possible?

Had her firstborn turned out to be a monster? A homicidal maniac?

While the horses paced and snorted in their stalls and a high-pitched scream of a siren reached his ears, he shouldered his rifle and shoved the Winchester 30-30's bolt into place. It snapped with a loud, distinctive *click* and he was ready.

Again a wave of blackness threatened to pull him under and he set his jaw. A light was pouring into the barn from the open doorway. He moved toward it.

Little Sister? Cassie's heart was beating frantically, her breath ragged, adrenaline pumping through her system as the truth became crystal clear: The woman chasing her was her older half sister. The sibling she found out about earlier tonight. The baby Jenna had given up for adoption years ago. Just as she'd feared.

What were the chances?

"Come out, come out, wherever you are." The familiar voice sang through the barn where the air was cold, but Cassie's hands sweated over the grip of the pistol. Teeth chattering, she clenched her jaw and, using both hands, leveled the gun as she prayed she could blow the bitch away.

"Come on, Cassie," the voice called out from the darkness, and there was something familiar about it, a quality she recognized.

Who? Think, damn it, who is it?

"Don't you want to meet me?"

No!

Cassie stared at the hallway, into the darkness. Did she see a bit of movement? Was it the woman stalking her? Or something else? Trent? The dog? A horse? *Damn it.* Throat dry, she squinted and moved the muzzle of the pistol toward the shifting light. That voice, disembodied and muffled, kept getting nearer.

"Come on, Little Sister," she coaxed. "We could have some fun."

Fat chance.

Cassie drew in a shaking breath and thought she heard sirens. Oh, God, were they wailing ever closer?

Please, please, please . . .

The gun wobbled in her hands.

At that second her attacker stepped from around the corner.

Cassie screamed, her finger frozen on the trigger.

In the half light she saw a woman's slim figure and above it a gruesome face. *What?* In the shadowy light she realized it was her own face, like the reflection in a mirror from a house of horrors, the image distorted and melting off its skull. A mask. "Oh, God," she whispered, then noticed the long-barreled gun pointed directly at her chest.

Cassie squeezed the trigger, but the shot went wild, ricocheting through the rafters, blasting loudly as Cassie tried to scramble away. With the killer blocking her escape, Cassie tried to get off another shot.

Too late.

The killer fired.

Craaack!

The noise was deafening.

Pain erupted in Cassie's shoulder and the blast propelled her hard against the back wall. Hot, searing agony shot through her as her body slammed into the wood and the killer took aim again.

She's going to kill me, Cassie thought wildly as the wall behind her suddenly gave way and she was falling backward, tumbling into a Stygian vortex.

I'm dying, she thought frantically, as she sommersaulted through the darkness.

Bam! She landed.

"Oof!"

Her skeleton jarred, but whatever she'd fallen on gave way. Sank a bit. Was even squishy in some places. Dust filled the air and there was a noise like tiny pebbles shifting in a jar.

What?

Where the devil was she, and in God's name, what was she lying on?

"Did Little Sister fall down and go boom?" her half-sister taunted and Cassie, her mind unclear from the fall, looked upward to see a bit of light falling through the opening from which she'd fallen. The woman in the awful mask was leaning through the small door, her arm extended, the pistol aimed into the darkness.

Cassie was a sitting duck.

All the killer had to do was start firing and the ricocheting bullets would probably riddle Cassie's body.

Bracing herself, dread filling her heart, she stared upward and thought of Trent. Was he already dead? Had this maniac killed him? Why? Oh, God, why?

"Say your prayers, Little Sister," the woman said, aiming, then suddenly the arm moved sharply, as if wrenched, fingers opening. The gun fell, tumbling down the well and glancing off Cassie's shoulder.

"What the fuck?" the killer cried in her so-familiar voice, but she wasn't leaning into the opening any longer, not speaking to Cassie, but someone else. Someone who had startled her. "Where the hell did you come from? Ouch! Jesus!" The words were muted, but there were other noises as well. Scuffling footsteps. A struggle? Could the police have arrived, or was it her savior Trent?

He had to be alive. Relief washed over her, but she couldn't just lie here. She had to help.

Groaning, her shoulder on fire, she twisted, rolling to the side, off whatever had broken her fall and suddenly felt the entire floor shift and rattle. More dust. The silage or feed or fodder was giving way. She hadn't fallen from the very top of the structure, but closer to the bottom, the main floor of the barn to the lower level where the cattle were fed, less than a story. Rattled, still trying to get her bearings in the darkness, she reached out a hand. Touched the object that had broken her fall and felt the cool clamminess of bare skin beneath her fingers.

Human skin?

An arm?

Her stomach turned in on itself.

Screaming, her voice reverberating up the shaft of the silo, she flung herself away, tried to swim in the shifting sea of grain. But the *thing* moved, too, and the arm stretched out, a clawlike hand scraping against her, fingernails scraping her face.

Get out, Cassie. Get the hell away from that thing!

Frantic, she pressed against the wall, circling away, the kernels swirling and swishing, almost laughing at her impotent attempts to get free.

Think, Cassie, think. Find a way to escape!

She was in a full-blown panic now, her headache thundering, her fear so real she could taste it. She moved along the edge of the cylindrical structure. The body swayed closer.

There had to be a way out. A chute to pour the grain from the silo, but where the hell was it. *Where?*

The ocean of grain rolled again and this time, not just the arm, but the entire torso of the unknown person fell against her. Cold. Clammy. *Dead!* The body hadn't moved on its own. No. It had only shifted on the waves of grain that moved because of Cassie's attempts to get away, and had fallen against her, nearly pinning her, the head rolling to one side.

Springy hair brushed against Cassie's neck.

Oh. Dear. God.

She pushed it away, felt her thumb touch an eyeball that gave way under the pressure.

Cassie shriveled at the thought as she tried to put some distance between her and God, who? Who was this dead person trapped here with her? Again the body rolled closer and this time she felt a leg slide across her. She touched it long enough to fling it away and realized her fingers had brushed nylon.

In her mind's eye she thought of the nurse who had visited her late at night. The curled hair under the cap, the white stockings.

Oh. Ick! This was Belva Nelson and she was dead?

Stomach roiling, her brain pulsing with the need to get free, she pressed harder to the sides of the silo, and her shoulder, already screaming in pain, hit something hard and metal.

A door latch?

Oh, please! A way to get out!

With an effort, she turned and fumbled at the metal.

Not a door, but the bottom rung of a ladder that stretched ever upward and back to the floor above.

Using all her strength she started climbing.

Trent's bad leg gave way and he grabbed the edge of a post for balance near the yawning open doorway.

Silhouetted by the headlights shining through the doorway, Shane Carter, weapon drawn, made his way into the barn.

Relief swept over Trent. "Don't shoot! It's Kittle," he said.

Carter looked in his direction but didn't drop his weapon.

"They're down there, toward the silo," Trent said, pointing, trying to stay clear-headed as he swayed and clung to the post for support. "Someone tried to kill me and I think Cassie's here." But his mind was swimming; he wasn't certain of anything.

Craaack!

A gun went off and the horses went nuts, shrieking and kicking in terror. Hud, who'd been cowering somewhere in the shadows, let out a mournful howl and belly-crawled to Trent.

"Stay!" Trent said to the dog as Carter took off running in the direction of the gunshot and Trent, moving slowly, followed.

A woman's scream tore through the barn.

Cassie!

His heart turned black with a dread as dark as all of hell, but he kept moving and ignored the pain ripping through his body. Holding onto poles, bracing himself on sawhorses, propelling himself forward and dragging his useless leg, he wasn't about to wait and cower in the shadows.

If something had happened to his wife, damn it, if the assassin had wounded her or killed her, he'd take the son of a bitch out himself.

* * *

Adrenaline firing her blood, Cassie started climbing the ladder, the sounds of a struggle above.

"You murdering bitch!" a woman yelled, a new voice, one that rang deep in Cassie's soul.

Allie? Allie was here? Alive? In cahoots with this other sick sibling?

Gritting her teeth, her hands sweating from the exertion, her fingers slipping on the rungs, Cassie hauled herself up by one hand.

"Like you weren't in on it." The other woman. "Come on, Baby Sister, admit it, you liked to see your mother squirm and your sister"—she hissed the word—"freak out and end up in a mental hospital."

"But no one was supposed to die!" Allie yelled.

"Oh, get real. You set it up. You were the one who planned the shooting on the set. You just needed me to do the dirty work."

"I *talked* about it," Allie said. "I didn't mean for it to actually happen."

"Then why did you disappear?"

Good question, Cassie thought, pulling herself up, wanting to strangle both of her siblings, the murderer and Allie, freaking Allie who had let everyone believe she was dead.

Upward she climbed through the darkness, dragging herself, the dust from the silo suffocating, her own breathing and pounding heart making listening to the conversation impossible. Only a few more rungs.

"Fuck!" one of the women said, the other one, not Allie, the familiar but unnamed voice. "Do you hear that? Sirens! What the fuck did you do?"

"Nothing."

Cassie was close to the top now, the half-light spilling into the silo's shaft just over her head.

"But the cops! Oh, shit!"

Blam!

A gunshot fired, rocking the building. Cassie nearly lost her grip, but she clung on, her lower body swinging off the ladder for a heart-stopping instant. She had to clench her jaw to keep from crying out. Agony ripped through her shoulder and she squeezed her eyes shut, willed her body back and forced her toes to find a rung.

A long, low moan ripped through the building.

She thought of Trent. No, it couldn't be.

But her fear drove her upward.

Fighting the pain in her shoulder, dragging herself upward, rung by rung she climbed. She had to make it! She had to get to him! At the opening, she peered through and, saw a body on the floor. Her heart collapsed. Was it Trent? Allie?

Standing over the wounded person her back to the opening was a woman, while holding a gun pointed at the already wounded victim. Jesus God, the shooter was Allie, her victim Laura Merrick! With the hideous mask half-on, half-off her face, Laura writhed on the floor and groaned in agony. Allie aimed her gun at Laura's ever moving forehead, as if she were planning to shoot her literally right between her eyes.

No!

Cassie coiled, then sprang, propelling herself through the opening and rolling, knocking Allie off her feet. The gun went flying, skittering across the floor.

Lithe as a cat, she pounced on the gun, then rolled over and agilely hopped to her feet. The girl who had once been a nerdy bookworm, then a famous Hollywood star and then a ghost, vanishing without a trace was now a cold-blooded killer?

"Allie?" Cassie whispered as her sister pointed the gun at her. "Allie!"

Allie's hands wobbled. Her eyes were wide, her expression cold.

"Don't shoot!" Cassie yelled. "Allie!"

Ashen faced, thin as a rail, her eyes hollow, as if she didn't recognize Cassie, Allie hesitated.

"Allie, it's me. Cassie. Your sister."

Heavy footsteps thundered toward them, but Allie didn't seem to hear, just stood over Cassie.

"Drop it!" Shane's voice boomed through the room. "Allie Kramer! Drop your weapon." Then his voice softened. "For the love of God, what happened?" His jaw clenched, a muscle jumping, and for a second Cassie witnessed his pain. He'd thought of Jenna's daughters as his own. As quickly as his bewilderment appeared, it disappeared and he slipped back into his lawman persona once more.

In a daze, Allie looked away and in that instant, Cassie sprang. She ripped the gun from her sister's fingers. Without thinking she threw the damned weapon through the opening to the silo. "What the hell are you doing?" she thundered raging at her sister. "You idiot! We all thought you were dead!"

"I am," Allie said, as if she really were a zombie.

"What? Don't give me that!" Cassie roared, incited.

"Cass, it's okay." Shane tried to step in.

But Cassie wasn't finished. "Where have you been? Huh? Where the hell have you been? We've been looking for you forever. People have died! What were you thinking? Damn it, Allie, were you really going to kill me?"

"Little Sister," Laura whispered. Blood drizzled from the corner of her mouth, the mask still halfway on and she was pale as death. Sirens screamed. They were so close they sounded as if they were inside the damned barn.

Cassie turned on the wounded woman. Laura Merrick. Seriously? The makeup person and hairdresser to the stars was Cassie's half sister and probably a psychotic killer? Or was the murderess Allie?

"Why?" Cassie demanded, but Laura only groaned.

"Why?" she asked again, this time focusing on her younger sister, the little girl who had turned into a monster.

Allie just stared, and Cassie couldn't help but wonder if she was indeed almost catatonic or this, like so many scenes in her life, was just an act.

"It's not my fault," Allie whispered.

Cassie lost it.

Before thinking, she whirled and she slapped the wretch that her little sister had become. Allie's head snapped back and her lost, forlorn expression instantly morphed into an ugly rage.

Barely aware that the barn was suddenly alive, blue and red light pulsing through the windows, policemen and women converging on the barn, Cassie plowed on. Shaking, she said, "It is your fault. You could have let us know you were alive! You didn't need to put Mom and me and everyone else through this hell!" She was shaking. "Quit faking it and acting like you didn't know what you were doing, Allie! You're not a frightened little girl anymore."

"And you hate me for it," Allie said, her facade slipping a little, her lips curling in disgust.

"You effin' thought I was going to die on that set!" Cassie said and lunged at her sister as Laura moaned at their feet.

Shane stepped in. Grabbed Cassie. Held her back. "It's over," he whispered into her ear and she heard the sound of other footsteps thundering through the barn, echoing on the floors. She struggled, wanting to beat the living tar out of the woman Laura had dubbed "Baby Sister." It was fitting, really. Allie had always played the part of the wounded little girl, at least in their family.

"Police! Drop your weapons!" a man shouted.

From the floor, Laura, one eye exposed glared up at them. With an effort, she said, "This isn't the way it's supposed to be. Don't you get it? I should be the star. Not you, Baby Sister!" She spat and coughed. "*I'm* the firstborn. Me!" She was gurgling now, spittle and blood frothing red on her lips. "I'm the Big Sister and you two are the interlopers." She glared at Cassie and snarled. "You're a freak, Little Sister, that's what you are. You could never make it in the business even though you had the chance!" Her words garbled then, and Cassie, looking over her stepfather's shoulder, met Trent's eyes.

Leaning against a wall, his face chalky white, blood staining his jeans, he looked as if he might pass out at any second. "Oh, Jesus," she said, her anger evaporating, her heart wrenching. "Trent!" Hurtling out of Shane's arms, she ran to him. "Oh, God. We need an ambulance."

He forced a bit of a smile. " . . . or two." He hugged her fiercely and buried his face in her hair. She collapsed against him, drinking in the smell of him, feeling the strength, his incredible strength waning. The thought of losing him was too much to bear. "Hang in there," she whispered over the rush of other officers arriving and the bleating of a rescue vehicle piercing the night.

"Cuff her," Shane said to the first deputy on the scene. He was motioning to Allie. "And get this one," he indicated Laura, "to a hospital. Keep her under guard. She's dangerous. But first," he hitched his thumb toward Trent, "get this one to a hospital STAT. After you see to Kittle here."

Cassie said, "And there's . . . there's a dead body in the silo. I think maybe Belva Nelson, but I'm not sure." Involuntarily, she shuddered remembering the brush of cold flesh against hers.

"Check it out," Shane ordered another deputy and the man responded, despite the fact that Carter had no jurisdiction, was no longer an officer. Still no one questioned his authority. Not tonight.

Carter bent down on a knee and tried to revive Laura.

"Come on. Stay with me," he ordered, but the woman was still. "Come on, Laura! Hang in there." But it was obvious to Cassie the woman she'd known as Laura Merrick was gone.

Allie watched it all. As her hands were forced behind her back, cuffs snapped into place, she seemed to suddenly become aware of what was happening.

"It . . . this . . . it's not my fault. And my disappearance, that was staged, too. It was Brandon's idea to hide. I mean, after I realized that she"—Allie hitched her chin to the still body of Laura Merrick— "was serious about killing people, that she actually exchanged the prop gun for a real one." With big eyes, she looked at Cassie. "You have to believe me, I wouldn't have let you go to jail and I was going to come out . . . to show up. You know, before the premier and pass it off as being odd or eccentric, but then I got scared . . . people started dying." She looked pleadingly at Shane.

His jaw tightened and he said to the nearest deputy, "Read her her rights."

"No! Shane," Allie cried. "Please. Daddy!"

He physically jerked and looked about to point out that he wasn't her father, but didn't.

Footsteps rang and two cops, weapons drawn, appeared. "What the hell's going on here?" one asked.

Carter said, "We need an ambulance."

One of the cops nodded. "On its way."

"There's a body," Cassie said, pointing behind her to the opening into the silo. "In there."

"What?" One of the deputies pulled a flashlight from his belt and peered inside. "Jesus H. Christ. It's a nurse . . . like from the fifties or something!"

"She's dead." No doubt the nurse was Belva Nelson and Laura had hoped to terrorize Cassie one last time. Cassie might have fallen down the shaft by mistake or it might have been all part of Laura's sick plot, but she'd dressed Belva in her old uniform and dumped her body into the silo.

"Call Detective Nash," Shane said to the remaining deputy as the first descended the shaft. "Portland PD. She's been looking for this one."

The distinctive bleat of an ambulance's siren drew near, more cops and paramedics arriving. Too late for Laura Merrick.

At that moment, Hud appeared limping slightly. "Hey, Buddy," Trent said. "We'll get you fixed up."

"But you're okay," she asked and felt Trent's hand tangle in her hair. She was so thankful he was alive, so happy to be his wife.

"I am now, baby," he whispered, kissing her forehead and holding her tight against him. "I am now."

CHAPTER 39

Detective Nash walked through the three rooms Laura Merrick had rented in a little dive in Portland, one last time. They were odd. Merrick had decorated them to appear as if she were actually living in LA, even going so far as to put in a fake window, actually a back-lit poster with a view of the Hollywood sign.

The room was filled with costumes and wigs she'd collected over the years, those from Jenna and Allie in their various movie roles, and the walls were covered with movie posters of her mother and half-sister, many of which had been torn or ripped to shreds and then taped back together. A makeup mirror was front and center. And a printer sat in a corner along with some kind of laminating machine. Nash had even found a box of elastic bands to be used for the making of even more masks, the fronts of which littered the floor.

Handy.

There were a lot of questions left about Laura Merrick, whose adoptive sister had died when she was in her teens, the result of a tragic car accident. The Beauchamps, too, were deceased, both killed in a house fire. For now, the questions would remain unanswered as Laura had been pronounced DOA at the hospital, three nights earlier.

Since that night, the police had identified Belva Nelson's body, stuffed into the empty grain silo at Trent Kittle's farm. Kittle himself had been shot by Merrick, but was surviving, the bullet tearing through his thigh, but not hitting his femur or femoral artery. He was lucky.

Jenna Hughes was rumored to be a wreck with guilt over her children, but Cassie, who had been a rebel in her youth and at odds with her mother, was stepping up. A good thing.

Nash picked up a makeup brush and held it, then looked in the mirror. Laura had been obsessed with Jenna and her daughters. Had tried to get into films herself, but when that didn't pan out had turned to making Hollywood stars more beautiful and glamorous than they were naturally. Though successful, she'd always felt abandoned.

Had her parents lived, maybe her story would have turned out differently.

As for Sonja Watkins, her link was beauty school, where she'd met Laura and kept in touch. Sonja now wondered if she'd been used, if Laura had kept up the relationship because she knew that Belva was the nurse in attendance when she'd been born. She'd paid Belva to gaslight Cassie, but the plan had backfired. Seeing the old nurse hadn't escalated Cassie's mental illness; if anything it had caused Cassie to want to get better, to find Allie. Maybe Belva Nelson had left the earring on purpose, so that Cassie would know she wasn't hallucinating. Nash had learned from talking to her niece that Belva had serious guilt over her complicity in the sham and also for having taken some kind of hush money way back when during the private adoption, though that was still, and might always be, unclear.

Laura had been in cahoots with Allie, though Allie insisted she had no part in the murders, that she was only trying to kill Laura that night, to end it all. And she had. She'd killed her half-sister. Nash would like nothing better to see the Hollywood princess wearing a prison jumpsuit for the rest of her life.

Nash put the brush back in its holder.

Allie Kramer herself had admitted that her disappearance was all a publicity stunt. Allie was now in custody, the death of Laura Merrick being investigated, reporters besieging the department. Somehow Allie had hidden in plain sight, with Brandon's help. They'd set up sightings, and created the fake text messages, and had milked it for all it was worth.

Nash wasn't really buying Allie's innocent act.

She could have come forward at any time.

Despite the murders.

Of course, Laura Merrick had been behind Holly Dennison and Brandi Potts's deaths. Airline records proved she was in each city at the time. The only crime she hadn't committed was the abduction of Allie Kramer. As for the original shooting on the set of *Dead Heat*? The working theory was that Laura had lifted the key from the prop manager Ineesha Salinger's purse, when she'd come in for a touch-up on her hair. Laura had slipped out and made a copy while Ineesha had waited for her color to process. The timing had been right. According to the prop manager, Laura had been gone "twenty minutes or so" and come back with a box lunch. There were two hardware stores between Laura's shop and the café where Laura had ordered the croissants and brie. The LAPD was checking with the stores.

It was all coming together.

Rumor had it that Allie had agreed to an exclusive interview with Whitney Stone for an undisclosed sum of money. Another rumor had it that she was planning an insanity plea.

Typical.

By her own admission, Allie Kramer had disappeared to create a buzz surrounding herself before *Dead Heat* opened.

Looked like she got her wish.

Even if she did end up in jail.

Nash walked out of the little apartment and headed to her car. The sun was peeking out from behind the clouds, weak beams playing against the rain-washed streets. She glanced around the neighborhood and considered it briefly as a place where she might move since the sale on Edwina's mansion was going through, but no, this area was too close to the case. She'd be forever thinking about Allie Kramer if she lived here and God, no, she didn't want that.

Cassie drove up to the house she'd lived in as a teen, the home she'd so despised and wondered if she'd ever feel anything but hatred of the place. Though the rambling house with the broad porch had been her mother's sanctuary, Cassie thought of it as nothing but evil.

Ten years ago a madman had terrorized them all when they'd lived here and now, again, the unthinkable had happened. She parked and climbed out of the car, the May sun weak, the grass green, crocus and azaleas in bloom. The door opened before she reached the top step and she saw her mother, ten pounds lighter than she had been a few months before, a few more strands of silver hair marring her once glossy black tresses.

"She's inside?" Cassie asked, and Jenna nodded.

Allie Kramer had made bail. Of course she would have to go to trial for her part in the deaths of Holly Dennison, Brandi Potts, and Belva Nelson, though it was generally believed that she was not the shooter, had only been on the periphery of the homicides.

Detective Nash was pushing for harsher charges, but Allie's team of lawyers, bought and paid for by the money she'd made off her films, were fighting the charges tooth and nail. Of course Lucinda Rinaldi was suing and really, Cassie thought, unzipping her sweater and walking into the kitchen, who would blame her. Lucinda's recovery was iffy at best and she'd already talked to Cassie, warning her that any story surrounding Allie Kramer and her duplicity in the shooting was Lucinda's property.

Well, maybe.

Allie was seated at the kitchen table, a cup of tea growing cold in front of her, shafts of sunlight filtering through the French doors to bathe her in an almost angelic glow.

Cassie knew better.

She wouldn't be fooled.

"Hi," Allie said, looking up, not smiling. Without makeup she looked so much younger than she had in any of her films.

"Hi."

Allie's gaze slid around Cassie. "No Trent."

"No." She sat in the chair across from her sister while Jenna, ever the peacemaker, hovered on the other side of the kitchen island. "I hear that you might plead insanity."

Allie's jaw tightened and her eyes slid to the side. "Maybe. It's not been decided."

"You know, I think you owe me some explanations." Cassie rubbed her shoulder. It was healing, but still twinged now and again. She'd been lucky. Trent, too. Other than losing a lot of blood and, as he'd said, "needing a refill," he'd been relatively unhurt, the bullet going through his leg to lodge in the barn, his femur, artery, and his life spared. Thank God.

"Me, too," Jenna said. "I've never asked you, but I know you read my diary. Is that how you found Laura?"

Allie nodded, picked up her cup. "That was the start."

"You contacted her?" Cassie asked.

"No way. It was Laura. She figured it out on her end."

"So she approached you."

Allie rolled her eyes. "Yeah. Since I knew it was true, I'd found the diary as you said, done a little digging around, found the Beauchamp family, I knew she was the real deal."

"So you decided to murder me?"

"No, no, it wasn't like that. It was a fantasy, that's all, but Laura took it to another level. I figured it out and disappeared. Brandon liked the idea of all the buzz it caused, and so there you go."

Jenna cleared her throat. "If you read my diary, you know how hard it was for me to give her up . . ." Tears welled in her eyes and she cleared her throat. "Well, what's done is done. Right?"

Cassie thought about what she was going to say. "Maybe not," she admitted. "I'm writing this story, despite what Lucinda Rinaldi thinks, and so I've been doing a lot of research, you know, while Trent was recovering and even though both of Laura's parents are dead, there's all kinds of information about them and her adoptive sister. She was almost the same age, only six months difference."

Jenna was staring at Cassie so hard she squirmed.

"What?" her mother asked.

"Well, here's the thing. I had Laura's DNA tested. From her hair."

The temperature in the room seemed to drop ten degrees.

"And?" Jenna asked.

"She's not your daughter, the DNA wasn't a match to mine at all."

"But . . . What . . . I mean . . ." Jenna gripped the counter for support. "What're you saying?"

"That Laura Rae Beachamp Wells Merrick was not your biological daughter. Most likely her sister, Elana, was." Cassie reached in to her pocket and withdrew a photo of a teenaged girl, a girl who despite her coloring had the same shaped face and nose and large green eyes as Jenna. She laid the picture on the table and Jenna came close to look at it.

"No."

"I think so, yes."

"What?" Allie whispered. "No. No." She was shaking her head wildly. "I . . . I wouldn't have gotten involved with her. I mean . . . no, this can't be right."

Cassie leveled her younger sister with a deadly stare. "Do you think I would have brought this up if I didn't believe it? I already sent these photos to Detective Nash."

"No! Why?" Allie was on her feet, her tea spilling. "You can't do this, Cassie. Just butt the hell out. I—I'm in enough trouble as it is."

"And whose fault is that?" Cassie threw back as Jenna, holding the snapshot in quaking fingers, stared at the image.

"Is it possible?" she whispered.

"Possible and probable. Laura was nuts. I think she killed her sister. She miraculously survived when Elana didn't. And her parents, they died in a house fire. How about that. Careless smoking, though they'd both given up the habit years before."

In her mind's eye Cassie saw Laura as she had been in her shop, desperate for a cigarette and desperate to tell Cassie the news about

Holly. She'd played a part, yes, she could act, but deep down, no doubt, she'd loved telling the story, reveled in the taking of a life.

Jenna was shattered and Cassie couldn't help but wonder, was it worse to know that your child was the victim of murder, or a killer herself? Did it matter? Both were now dead. And Jenna, no doubt, would feel forever guilty for giving up her firstborn.

There really was no good news.

"I don't know why you came here," Allie said, her eyes dark.

Cassie sighed. "Because we're a family. Like it or not, 'Baby Sister,' we're what each other's got."

With that she left, gave her mother a kiss on the head, promised she'd be back, noticed the still simmering hatred in her sister's eyes, and drove home. To Trent's ranch, where both he and Hud, who had somehow been injured, were recuperating.

As she drove past the lush fields and noticed the new foals next to the mares in one pasture, calves and cows in another, she realized how much at home she felt. It was ironic, she thought, that Allie had been right about one thing. She had found happiness. With Trent. Who would have thought it would be in Sticksville, Oregon? Certainly not she. But as she parked and picked her way around puddles, stopping to pat a wiggling Hud on his head, she understood why, so long ago, Jenna had packed up her daughters and moved away from the glitz, glamor, fame, and stress of Hollywood. This really wasn't such a bad place.

She walked into the kitchen, the dog limping slightly as he raced down the hallway in front of her, and she heard Trent's voice. "Hey, there, Hud," he said, loud enough for her to hear. "Did you find my wife?"

Hud yipped loudly.

"Oh, you did? Well, do you think you could convince her to bring me a beer?"

She walked into the den and saw him stretched out on the couch, the TV on low, one heel propped on the pillows.

"Not a chance in hell," she said to him and grinned wickedly. She walked to the couch and trailed a finger from his waistband to his neck before winking. "Get your own damned beer."

Epilogue

She didn't belong here, Allie thought as she stared through the window to the manicured grounds of Mercy Hospital.

No matter what the doctors or the lawyers or the judge thought, Allie Kramer did *not* belong in a psych ward, and especially not the same one where Cassie had so recently stayed.

It was outrageous.

And she'd told them all so.

No one had listened.

Her doctors insisted she needed help.

Her mother was relieved she was "safe."

Her damned sister seemed to think it was ironic.

Her lawyers told her to stay put; they were pleased that she was in the hospital rather than jail and promised to spring her soon.

But she really was going out of her mind. As she walked through the connecting rooms of the psych wing she itched to get outside, to be free again. The other patients, well, they should probably be here, especially that freaky Rinko kid who studied her so intently. He'd been Cassie's friend and he was weird as hell.

She made her way into a common area where a couple of patients were playing checkers, another one knitting, and still another reading a book. Rinko was there, too, going through a magazine about cars.

Ugh.

She flopped onto the couch and wanted to scream and rail at the heavens at the unfairness of it all, that she was a star, damn it, that she was Allie Kramer. But she didn't and forced her gaze to a television in the corner, one of those old bubble-faced ones. On the screen an advertisement for some antacid gave way to a promo for another show, and there, bold as brass, was Whitney Stone's intense face.

Allie couldn't stand it. She snapped off the television and walked out of the room and onto the sunporch where she stared outside to the lawn. And there on the porch, too near to her for comfort, was Rinko. Had he followed her here? God, the kid was weird.

"Hey!" a female voice called, and she turned to spy an attractive woman of about twenty standing under the archway. She walked into the room and offered a smile. "You're Allie Kramer, aren't you?"

"Yes," Allie said, relieved that someone recognized her. From the corner of her eye she saw Rinko moving stealthily, trying to get out of the room. She ignored him. "And you're?" she asked the girl with the sad eyes.

"I'm new. A transfer," she explained. "And my name's Shay."

Rinko, standing behind the newbie paused and looked over his shoulder. He gave his head a slight shake, a warning, as he stared at Allie. She felt as if a ghost had crawled up her spine. What was *that* all about?

"So," Shay said, commanding Allie's attention again, "I hope we can be friends."

"Sure," Allie agreed and slid her gaze to the spot where Rinko had been standing.

But he was gone.